WONDER W...
The ... of
GOLDEN ANGEL

WONDER WOMAN LEGACY
The Rise of
GOLDEN ANGEL

Wonder Woman: Legacy, The Rise of Golden Angel is dedicated to all of those who are fighting the battle against breast cancer, all of those who will face it in their lifetime, those who have triumphed over it and all who lost their battle against it. Some names used in the story are those who did not survive their battle against breast cancer and Wonder Woman Legacy, The Rise of Golden Angel is a memorial to them and the countless thousands still unnamed. Please help support **The Breast Cancer Research Foundation, Susan G. Komen for the Cure,** or any of the other organizations who make it their mission to stop breast cancer.

Proceeds from *Wonder Woman: Legacy, The Rise of Golden Angel* go directly to the fight against breast cancer!

DC Entertainment has not sanctioned this story.

Story by J. R. Knoll, Vultross@aol.com

Artwork by K.R.C., Jasric.DeviantART.com

Cover Design by Zach Jordon, HeroforPain.DeviantART.com

WONDER WOMAN AGAINST BREAST CANCER image created by Sandi Johnson, goldenSalamander.DeviantART.com

CHAPTER 1

Themyscira, seventeen years ago…

So much to do. So much to consider.

Darkness had settled hours ago and the house was finally quiet.
Though weary from a long day, Diana knew that sleep would be a
difficult prize to claim, especially with everything in her mind that
vied for her attention. She lay on her back, right in the middle of her
spacious bed as she stared at the ceiling with troubled blue eyes.
With one hand laying on her belly and the other arm curled around
her head, she did her best to relax her body, hoping that her mind
would soon follow. Her long black hair was pulled to one side and
was flailed out on her pillow and bed. Her spacious bedroom was
dimly lit in the warm blue glow offered by the full moon. There
were not many furnishings, only the bed, desk across the room under
the window and a wardrobe that was made of some dark wood. Two
other pieces had joined them in recent weeks, though, and one was
beside her bed, between it and the wall, and from here a sound came
that had not been heard on this island for more than a thousand
years, and the Princess of the Amazons sprang up from her bed in
quick response to it.

"Shh," she soothed as she gently took the fussy baby girl from her
white and red bassinette. Cradling the baby gently in her arms, she
backed up and sat on the edge of her bed, her full attention on the
squirming little girl she held. With a big smile, Diana wrapped the
baby in her pink blanket and said in a low, slight voice, "I thought
you were asleep, Little One. Are you hungry yet again?"

The baby did not cry, but she stared back at the Amazon Princess
with trusting blue eyes. Not quite two months old, she knew her
mother well on sight and by the sound of her voice, and being in her
mother's arms always calmed her.

Raising her brow as she stared down at the baby, Diana insisted,

"We need to sleep. That means both of us." When the baby smiled at her, she could not help but smile back. "You are going to be a horrible little scamp, aren't you?"

"Much like her mother," another woman said softly as she approached.

Diana looked over her shoulder to see her own mother, Queen Hippolyta, striding silently around the bed, but her attention did not remain there long as it was reclaimed quickly by the child she held.

The Queen was wearing white sleeping attire much like her daughter's and her long black hair was pulled over one shoulder and bound with three white ribbons. She sat gingerly beside Diana, slipping an arm around her shoulders as she asked in a low voice, "Is she fussy again tonight?"

"Afraid so," Diana confirmed. "Sometimes she sleeps well; sometimes she wants to be up all night."

Hippolyta smiled as she stared down at the baby in her daughter's arms. "I'll bet she is just anxious for a name."

The Princess looked away and grumbled, "I know."

"You've had almost a year to think about it," Hippolyta pointed out. "Is it so hard a decision?"

Looking back to the baby, Diana declared, "I want her name to be perfect, one that will suit her well and have meaning for who she will be when she grows up."

"And who will she be? Another great hero like her mother?"

Diana loosed a deep breath and shook her head. "I hope not. I pray that her life will be full and rewarding but not fraught with conflict as mine has been."

Gently stroking her daughter's hair, the Queen pointed out, "That may be a matter of destiny. Both of her parents are heroes, after all, and both stubbornly defend what is just and good."

Closing her eyes, Diana grimly said, "I know, and I don't want that life for her." Looking back to the little girl she held, despair was in her eyes as she clenched teeth, and with a shake of her head she continued, "She should only know about the best of this world. She should know how loved she is, how... Mother, I just could not bear the thought of what would happen if my enemies ever found out about her."

"Or her father's enemies?" Hippolyta added.

"Or his," Diana confirmed just over a whisper.

"So you will never tell him about his daughter," the Queen concluded.

Her mouth tightening to a thin slit, the Amazon Princess hesitantly shook her head, tears welling up in her eyes. "I want to. Hera knows how I want to, but… Mother, I am just so afraid of what could happen, what our enemies would do to her if they ever found out about her." She ran her fingers through the baby's soft, black hair. "She is so innocent, so… so sweet and perfect. It must be my vow to protect her first and always, my vow to her, to our people and to the Gods to keep her safe."

"Your vow to the Gods," Hippolyta said softly, absently. A sparkle lit her eyes as they cut to Diana, and she simply said, "Elissa."

Diana's eyes snapped to her.

"It is from the old language," the Queen explained, "Greek, from the land we came from."

"Elissa?" Diana breathed.

"It is an ancient name, one that means a commitment to the Gods. If that is your vow to her and to the Gods…" She raised her brow.

A little smile found Diana's mouth and she looked back down to the girl, to her daughter. "Elissa. Mother, it is beautiful, and it suits her so well!"

Hippolyta pulled the Princess to her, hugging her tightly. "Then my granddaughter is finally named?"

With a nod, Diana confirmed, "Yes. That shall be her name. It is perfect. She shall be my commitment to the Gods, to the world, to peace, and she shall have my absolute commitment. I will protect her with all I am, teach her all I know, and I shall give her as wonderful a life as you gave me."

Something solemn took the Queen's face as she stared at the innocent baby her daughter held. "And her father can never know about her? You will never tell him of his daughter?"

"I want to," Diana assured, "but I don't dare. She can never be like him, or like me. No, she will see beauty in the world, not its ugliness. She shall be warrior trained but she shall know compassion and mercy." She kissed the baby's forehead, then stroked her hair and smiled. "Warrior trained, yes, but when the time comes the world will see her as the beautiful and sweet angel she is now."

Patriarch's World, present day

Golden Angel slammed into the double doors back-first and exploded through them, not stopping until she hit the bookcase on the other side of the lavish meeting room. Crumpling to the floor, the small heroine was pummeled by books and decorations from the shattered shelf, and she took a few seconds to collect her wits before raising her dark, crystal blue eyes to the enemy who strode toward her, her brow low over them. With a little snarl on her mouth, she stood, her red gloved hands clenching her bare fingers into tight fists. Golden gauntlets encased her forearms and sparkled under the fluorescent lights of the meeting room. Her right shoulder was bare and a single strap held her red top in place, a top that left her midriff bare as well. Right across her chest was a symbol of the two worlds she came from, the golden image of a falcon but with the lower wings of a bat. Her long blue trousers were adorned with white stars down the outsides of the legs and met gold trimmed red boots that were nearly as high as her knees, and a pouch laden belt was buckled around her waist. Though her hair was worn in a pony tail that dropped to her lower back, many locks had stubbornly spilled over her gold tiara, one with a blue star right in the center, and she angrily combed them out of her line of vision. She was not a tall girl, slightly less than five foot six, and while generously built for a girl of only seventeen years and well muscled in arms, legs, shoulders and back, she was very lean and not heavy looking at all. At a look, one would never guess that this small, almost fragile looking heroine was endowed by her Amazon heritage with strength many times that of any mortal.

But her opponent was not just any mortal.

The nine men at the long, heavy conference table all sprang to their feet and looked to her as she squared off against her big opponent again. These were mostly fellows in their thirties and forties, but for the white haired man, the best dressed of them, who was at the far end of the table. They got but a glance from the beautiful little Amazon who had disrupted their meeting, but she had their full attention.

Raising a hand to the businessmen, she glared at the big woman who stormed into the room and ordered in a voice befitting a girl in her teen years, "Stay back. I've got this."

They all retreated, and all turned their eyes to the door as Golden Angel's opponent strode in with heavy steps. This was a huge woman, about six foot six and very broad shouldered. She had a thick jaw for a woman but attractive features otherwise with lovely dark amber eyes that had her brow held low over them. She wore ancient Roman style armor that was gold in color, Roman infantry sandals that had straps winding around her legs all the way to the knees and a short red skirt. Her arms were immensely thick, much thicker than most men and her legs were even thicker. This was a woman who had more a man's muscle tone and size, but her gender was given away by her generous bosom, her small waist and broad hips. Long red hair was restrained behind her by a big metal barrette that was gold and in the shape of a human skull, and nearly the size.

Stopping halfway to her tiny opponent, she pointed a thick finger at her and shouted, "Now you've made Herculeeta mad, little girl!"

Golden Angel's eyes narrowed and she growled back, "Do not call me that!" She charged with amazing speed and as her much larger opponent threw a crushing punch she ducked under her arm and delivered a solid blow to the big woman's solid belly, caving in the armor plate that she hit.

The big woman's elbow came back hard and slammed into Golden Angel right between the shoulders, sending her down to the floor.

Slow to push herself up, the little Amazon found her neck seized by her bigger foe and she was hoisted from the floor and slammed into that book case again. She rose quicker this time, but clumsily, clearly trying to get her wits about her.

The big woman tore the damaged armor plate from her belly and tossed it aside, then she held her fists before her, cracked her knuckles as she stood a few feet away, her eyes locked on those of her young opponent. "Oh, yeah. It's time for Herculeeta to bring some serious pain."

"Come and get it," the little Amazon challenged as she assumed her battle stance.

With a mighty yell, Herculeeta charged and swung her fist hard, intending to crush her little opponent once and for all.

Golden Angel darted aside and the big woman's big fist narrowly missed her, and when that fist slammed through the bookcase and into the concrete wall behind it, Angel kicked as hard as she could, slamming the top of her boot into the now unarmored belly of the big woman and doubling her over. Wasting no time, she followed up with a hard punch to the side of the woman's head, finally felling her with a loud, floor shaking thump. She backed away, her eyes on her downed foe as she drew in deep breaths.

"Okay," she said as if to herself. "One down." Her eyes widened as her big opponent pushed herself up and turned an infuriated glare on her. She backed away, into the conference table, and there she saw a large silver tray that had a pot of coffee, five white cups and a box of doughnuts on it. She picked up a cup and turned it upright, set it down on the tray, and then picked up the coffeepot. With a quick check to see Herculeeta clumsily getting to her feet, she looked over her shoulder to the men who were huddled on the other end and asked, "Is this decaff?"

They all shook their heads.

"Good," she said as she poured a cup. Setting the pot down, she picked up the cup of steaming hot coffee and smelled it, smiling slightly as she observed, "Mmm... Rich Columbian." She looked up to her big opponent, who approached with apprehensive steps.

With her hands curled into tight fists, Herculeeta stopped about two feet away, towering over her small foe as she suggested, "Grab you one of those doughnuts too, and enjoy it. It's gonna be your last meal."

Raising her brow, Golden Angel asked, "Want some coffee?" Without waiting for a response, she splashed the hot coffee into the big woman's face.

Covering her eyes with both hands, Herculeeta screamed as she stumbled backward.

And Golden Angel wasted no time in charging and ramming her shoulder into the big woman's belly, driving her back a few steps. She picked her up, then lunged forward and down, driving her opponent's shoulders and head as hard as she could into the tile floor and the room shook as she hit. Leaping on top of her, she raised her

9

fists and pummeled the big woman in the head and face, striking as hard as she could.

Herculeeta struck back, her big fist slamming into her smaller opponent's side, her ribs, and Golden Angel cried out and lurched over. The brawl on the floor continued under the fearful, watchful eyes of the men across the room.

It ended suddenly after a hard uppercut to the big woman's chin, one that knocked her unconscious.

Staggering to her feet with her tiara dangling from the middle of her ponytail, Golden Angel stared down at her defeated foe, struggling to catch her breath for a second before she spat, "Hair pulling? Really?" When she turned toward the men who had witnessed her battle, her tiara fell from her hair and she looked down as it hit the floor. Retrieving it from the floor, she combed her hair back before putting it back in its place. "Everyone okay?" she asked.

They all nodded, and the white haired man stepped forward, striding slowly around the table. He never took his eyes from her as he slowly approached.

With four steps, Golden Angel had approached the table, looking to the box of doughnuts before turning her attention to the man who neared her, and innocently she asked, "Can I have one?" When he nodded, she offered, "Thank you," as she picked through and selected one.

A young blond woman wearing a red top with Wonder Woman's symbol across the front and blue jeans ran into the room and stopped halfway there as her eyes found the unconscious Herculeeta. This was a very attractive woman, a little older than Golden Angel and about the same height, though better muscled and slightly thicker in the body. She had silver colored gauntlets clamped around her forearms and a gold tiara on her brow that bore a red star in the center.

Golden Angel turned to her, chewing on a bite of the doughnut she had selected as she greeted with a full mouth, "What up, Wonder Girl?"

Setting her hands on her hips, Wonder Girl stared down at the big woman who slumbered on the floor and asked, "So, you got her, huh?"

"Yup," the little Amazon confirmed.

"What happened to observing and gathering information?" the blond woman asked.

Golden Angel finished her doughnut and shrugged. "I had a decision to make and..." When the blond woman raised her brow and shifted her eyes to her, she heaved a heavy breath and confessed, "Okay, she saw me—right after I blindsided her."

"Red Robin's not going to like this," Wonder Girl warned.

Turning her eyes to the floor, Golden Angel nodded.

WW

Titans headquarters, located inside a mountain that towered over a beach at the coastline, was not designed for comfort, but its inhabitants had made it so. A large, well lit sitting area with two big, comfortable couches flanked by three recliners with a third between the couches was as colorful and homey as any house would be. A big screen TV hung over a console that was both a remote computer station and gaming center. This day it was off as the young heroes who lived there were just getting settled in after a long day.

Wearing blue jeans and a dark red tee shirt, Red Robin was dressed for comfort, but still wore his mask as he stormed into the common area. Behind him were Superboy and Kid Flash, neither of whom seemed to be in a good mood. Superboy's attire never seemed to stray from his black tee shirt with the red 'S' symbol of Superman in the middle and his blue jeans. Kid Flash was appropriately dressed in shorts, sandals and a yellow button up shirt with a variety of floral patterns.

Behind them was Wonder Girl, still in her blue jeans and red top. She had abandoned her boots, leaving them in her quarters. Walking with her was Golden Angel, whose foul mood could easily be read on her expression. She had abandoned her crime-fighting attire altogether and only wore blue running shorts and a red tee shirt that read *Chicks Rule!* in big white letters. She was also barefoot and this only exaggerated her lack of stature among her colleagues.

Red Robin stopped behind one of the couches and laid his hands on the back, leaning on it as he angrily stared at the table in the middle of the room. When everyone caught up to him, he simply barked, "I don't care anymore. This is the third operation in less than a month you've screwed up!"

Golden Angel folded her arms and informed, "We got

Herculeeta."

"We've got nothing on her," he snapped.

"She was attacking two people!" Golden Angel cried. "Did you want me to just let that go?"

"What happened to her not seeing you?" he demanded.

"She only saw me after I came in and flattened her," Elissa spat. "What did you want me to do, Tim, allow her to hurt or kill someone?"

He pushed off of the couch and wheeled around, storming right up to her as he shouted, "We only got one of them, and now the rest know we're on to them and that's going to complicate things. This was the last time, Angel. I don't need someone on my team who can't follow the plan!"

About five inches shorter than him, she set her hands on her hips and glared up at him. "We also have to think on our feet out there! That and I was kind of under the impression we were supposed to protect people!"

"How about protecting them a little more quietly," he suggested with venom in his words. "If you couldn't take her then you should have called for back-up."

"I did take her!" she pointed out, taking a half step toward him. "You want me to show you how?"

Superboy stepped between them from one side, Wonder Girl from the other.

"Look, guys," Superboy cut in as he nudged Golden Angel back a step, "we don't need to come to blows here. It's over with, okay?"

As Wonder Girl nudged him back a step as well, Red Robin growled, "We didn't have any problems like this before she showed up. In fact, everything was running smoothly."

"Well," Kid Flash corrected, "as smoothly as can be expected with this bunch. Look guys, let's just go to our corners and cool off for a while."

Robin and Angel glared at each other for long seconds, and finally she wheeled around and stormed toward her quarters.

WW

Golden Angel's quarters were in disarray. Clothing littered the floor, her desk was a mess, the bed was unmade and a bath towel hung over the back of the chair that was pushed into the desk. The closet door was open and inside the closet was littered with items that did not quite make the laundry basket. Shelves on the wall by the desk and door were also cluttered and disorganized.

This was just how she kept things.

As the door slid shut behind her, she threw herself onto her bed and rolled over on her back, staring angrily at the ceiling for a time as she tried to allow herself to calm down. She vented a few deep breaths to relieve her anger, but she was a little too agitated for this to work. Here she lay for about a half an hour. Things just were not going well and she felt like the new kid who was just too easy to blame.

When someone knocked on the door, she knew that it was Wonder Girl, and she heaved a heavy sigh. Really wanting to be alone, she did not want to answer, but a second knock prompted her to call out, "It's unlocked, Cassie."

The door slid open and Wonder Girl padded in, her eyes on her little Amazon friend as she neared.

Golden Angel turned her head away, feeling that she was near tears.

Ever so gently, Wonder Girl sat on the bed beside her. She was unable to speak, even though they both knew there was much to say.

Drawing a deep breath, Golden Angel guessed, "So I've been voted off the island, huh?"

Wonder Girl turned her eyes down and nodded, confirming, "Yeah." There was a pause, and finally she looked back to her friend and suggested, "Take some time off. Go home for a while and..."

"Get my head on straight?" Angel grumbled.

"Nobody wanted it to be this way," Cassandra informed. "The team has to come first. I mean, everyone likes you—"

"Except Tim," Golden Angel interrupted.

"Elissa, Tim's just that way. He can be really abrasive sometimes, especially when we're on a mission. I guess Batman really rubbed off on him."

Golden Angel finally turned her head and looked to the blonde Amazon girl. "He's resentful because Batman's my father. That's it. He thinks I'm trying to push him aside or something."

Looking away, Wonder Girl softly admitted, "I don't know."

Elissa sat up, anger in her words as she said, "Yes you do. He hasn't liked me since I came here and he's looked for any excuse to get rid of me."

"It isn't that, Elissa," Wonder Girl informed. She finally looked to the smaller Amazon and continued with harsher words, "You seem to think the rules here don't apply to you. You jump in and start a brawl when we're supposed to be quietly observing, and then it's never your fault when the mission fails. It's happened three times in less than a month and I've tried—"

"So now it's all *my* fault?" Golden Angel barked. "I guess it hasn't occurred to anybody that I don't need some stuck-up little butthead telling me my job! I did just fine before!"

"You weren't part of a team before!" Cassandra loudly countered.

Elissa stared back quietly, then looked away from her.

"Everything must be coordinated," Wonder Girl said with an authoritative tone. Standing from the bed, she set her hands on her hips and continued, "That means we have a leader, someone who coordinates the mission, and like it or not Red Robin was that leader on those three missions you botched up for us." Her hair flailed as she wheeled around to leave. "When you go crying to Batman and Wonder Woman, see if you can tell them what really happened here."

Golden Angel watched her leave, and watched the door for a moment even after it closed. Slowly, she turned her eyes down, then just as slowly she raised a hand to her eyes as the cruel truth began to finally sink in.

Later, in the subterranean garage of the Titan's lair, Elissa strapped her packed duffel bag onto the back of her big red and white motorcycle. She had changed into black boots, tight fitting blue jeans with holes worn into the thighs and the same red tee shirt beneath a leather jacket that was unzipped and open. She turned to take one last look at the vehicles they would use in their missions, the other motorcycle that belonged to Tim, and her eyes found Red Robin standing a few feet away.

He was watching her with blank eyes and his arms folded.

She stared back at him, then turned back to her labors and pulled the strap hard one more time. "Well, it looks like you're finally getting what you want. I'm out of here."

"What makes you think I want this?" he countered.

Elissa wheeled back around to face him. "Oh, come on, Tim. You've wanted me out of here since we first met." She turned back to her motorcycle and slipped the key into the ignition. "You're getting what you want so just leave me alone."

He grabbed her arm and spun her back toward him. "Maybe if you'd take just a minute to quit feeling sorry for yourself you'd see the big picture. This is a team and if just one member doesn't pull her weight then the whole thing falls apart, missions fail and someone can get hurt or killed. We're out there doing what we need to and you go charging in like some glory seeking newbie and wreck everything we've worked for."

She jerked her arm from his grip and spat back, "Situations change and plans become useless!"

"You changed those situations," he pointed out, "just like you did today."

"She was going to hurt those guys!" Elissa cried. "What did you expect me to do?"

"I expect you to do your job. You can protect people without jeopardizing the rest of us!" He looked away and vented a hard breath. "Look, Angel, you're good at what you do. Really good. You just need to get your head in the game and work on being part of a team."

Folding her arms, she narrowed her eyes as she pointed out, "I guess I'm just too much like my father."

"Batman knows how to be part of a team," Tim countered. "He also knows how to make a plan work and how to look out for his team mates." He turned around and walked away from her, saying as he did, "Call me when you grow up and can do that."

She watched him leave the garage and kept her eyes on the door for a moment even after it slid shut. His stinging words would not leave her. He was right, and that was painful.

Turning back to her bike, she picked up the helmet and just stared at it for long seconds before gingerly sliding it over her head.

WW

She stopped at a gas station just outside of Gotham City to refuel her thirsty bike, and while she filled the tank, her cell phone rang and she reached behind her with her free hand to retrieve it.

Opening it with her thumb, she looked down at the caller ID and a little smile found her lips as she put it to her ear and greeted, "Hey, girlfriend! What's up?"

"I am so tired," Stacy's voice complained from the other end.

"Oh, come on. Terrance working you that hard?"

"Um, yeah! When we're not working we have these all night parties to go to, then it's wardrobe checks, dealing with twiggy little supermodels and then runway rehearsals... Oh my God!"

Elissa laughed. "Yeah, sounds like fun."

"He never sleeps!" Stacy cried.

"I know somebody like that," Elissa assured. "So how's Paris?"

"Oh, it's great! Walter flew in to spend some time with me and Terrance is going to give me some time tomorrow to spend with him. We're going to do the whole tourist thing."

"Sweet." The pump shut off and Elissa put the nozzle back. "So when are you coming home?"

"First of next month if everything goes as planned. I can't wait to see you and have some girl time, but I guess you're going to be pretty busy with the Titans, huh?"

She turned her eyes down and admitted, "No, not really. I'll be free when you come home."

Stacy shouted with her hand over her phone, "Okay, I'm coming!" She said in a regular tone, "Hey, roomie, I got to go."

Elissa nodded and said, "Yeah, okay. Find some time to enjoy Paris and I'll see you next month."

"Sooner if I can talk you into coming out here. It's great!"

With a little smile, Elissa assured, "I'll try, okay? Catch you later, BFF."

"Take care, BFF. And be careful with your job!"

Slowly closing the phone, Elissa finally started to realize how much she missed her little roommate. She slipped the phone back into its pouch and climbed aboard her motorcycle, and she felt the weight of a very heavy heart as she started it.

Not even an hour later she found herself in the city, cruising along as she had on the highway and passing car after car on her way toward the coast. The chirp of a siren behind her prompted her to check her mirror and she found a police cruiser in close pursuit. Checking her speedometer, she mumbled, "Oh, crud," as she realized why.

Pulling over at the next opportunity, which turned out to be on the side of the road at a busy sidewalk, she cut off the bike and pulled her helmet off, combing a hand through her hair as she laid it on the fuel tank. She looked to her left as the officer, who was a big man in a black uniform, strode up beside her and opened his ticket book, looking down at it through his dark sunglasses.

With an arched brow and a pitiful look, Elissa timidly greeted, "Hi."

"Ma'am," he said with a dry voice, "may I see your license and registration?"

Her brow shot up and she asked, "My what?"

An hour later she found herself in Gotham City's police station, huddled in a chair beside a cluttered desk. Her many infractions did not warrant sitting in a jail cell, but they did warrant her motorcycle being impounded and her being detained. Granted a phone call, she only knew of one person to call, and she prayed her mother would not find out.

Some time ago the officer who had been processing her had taken her information, what little she had to offer, and walked off, assuring that he would be back for her. He had not returned for a while.

That nervous crawl in her stomach only seemed to get worse and worse as she was made to wait.

He finally returned and sat down, his eyes on the paperwork he had brought with him. This was a big man with thinning hair and a bushy mustache. His shirt was dingy and he wore brown trousers that were held up by suspenders, and a shoulder holster for his gun. His old brown jacket was laid on the back of his chair and he leaned back against it as he put on his reading glasses to look over the papers in front of him.

"Okay, he finally said, "Miss Prince. No driver's license, no ID, no registration, no inspection on the bike, no Social Security number..." He pulled his glasses off and looked to her. "You want to tell me your real name?"

"Elissa," she replied. "Elissa Prince. I already told you."

"Yeah," he drawled. "Well, Elissa Prince, you were clocked going twenty over the speed limit and driving without a license on a bike that's not registered in this state, or at all. So where did you get the bike?"

"It's my mom's," she answered timidly.

He raised his brow. "Your mom's."

She nodded.

"Elissa!" a man called in an English accent.

They both looked to see a very well groomed and very proper looking white haired man in a black suit approaching them. He was wearing an English driving hat and had driver's gloves in his hand. A thin salt and pepper mustache was on his lip and he held his eyebrows high as he approached them with long and dignified steps.

As he reached them, he held a small black purse to her and informed in that same English accent, "I noticed that you left the house without this again and somehow I knew it would get you into trouble this time." Shaking his head, he looked to the officer and declared, "Sometimes this younger generation needs to be watched so closely."

Elissa hesitantly took the purse, her eyes on the strapping, thin gentleman who stood before her.

The officer looked to her and asked, "Your ID in there, Miss?"

She glanced at him, then looked to the purse and opened it. Finding a pink leather wallet inside, she retrieved it and was about to fearfully open it and look, but the gentleman took it from her and offered it to the officer.

"I say," the English gentleman said as he shook his head, "you would forget to dress yourself in the morning if not reminded."

The officer took a driver's license from the wallet and looked it over, then he cut his eyes to her and handed the license and wallet back to her. "Okay, Miss. That takes care of that problem. Now we just have to clear up the issue of your mother's bike."

The gentleman sighed and turned his eyes to the ceiling. "You took your mother's motorcycle? Elissa, don't you remember our talk?"

"I guess not," she mumbled.

He shook his head again and looked to the officer. "I trust it has been impounded."

"Afraid so."

"Very well," the gentleman sighed. "I'll send for it in the morning and take care of all of the necessary fines." He looked to Elissa and shook his finger at her. "You have a good scolding coming, young lady. Now come along. We should retrieve your belongings and get you home."

"She says she's seventeen," the officer informed. "I'm afraid I can only release her to a family member."

"Oh," the gentleman said, "not to worry. My name is Alfred Pennyworth and I am the girl's uncle."

Raising his chin, the officer declared, "Oh! You work for Bruce Wayne, don't you?"

Elissa's eyes widened.

Alfred confirmed, "Why, yes, I do. I've been employed by the Wayne family for quite some time."

Nodding, the officer assured, "No problem then. I'll process the bike and have it ready to pick up by morning."

"You have my thanks, my good man," Alfred offered. "Come along, Elissa. Let's get you home. I have to be back in time to prepare Master Wayne's lunch."

As she stood, the officer, barked, "Hey, kid!"

She looked to him with frightened eyes.

Pointing a finger at her, he ordered, "You stay out of trouble."

Nodding, Elissa assured, "Yes, sir. I'll do my best."

Down on the street, a long black car awaited them right outside of the police station. Elissa carried her duffel bag over her shoulder and Alfred led the way to the car. Arriving there, he pushed a button on the key, the trunk lid swung up, and he turned and took the duffel bag from her.

As he laid the bag in the trunk and closed the lid, he looked to her with a little smile and asked, "Are you hungry, Miss Elissa?"

She turned her eyes down and nodded.

As he walked by her, he patted her shoulder and assured, "I'll have lunch ready shortly after we arrive at the mansion."

"Thank you," she offered timidly as he opened the back door for her.

She removed her jacket and folded it over her arm, and as she slid in, she froze as her eyes met the blue eyes of Bruce Wayne, and he did not look happy. When the door closed, she suddenly felt trapped.

Settling herself gingerly on the bench seat as far away from him as possible and pressed up against the door, she turned her eyes to the floorboard and laid her jacket across her lap.

The engine started and the car lurched forward. It was a very smooth ride and the inside of the car smelled like fine tooled leather. In fact, the seats were leather, a dark tan in color marbled in a light brown. The deep carpet on the floorboard was red, as was much of the trim in the car. Ahead of them and beneath the window that looked into the front seat was a glossy wood console with a few hatches in it, speakers mounted on the ends and in the middle, and what appeared to be drawers underneath with gold colored round handles.

The quiet in the car was unnerving and she timidly cut her eyes to him.

He was still staring at her. Dressed in a silk business suit that was a navy blue, he had his legs crossed and his hands clasping that knee. Black shoes were perfectly polished. His hair was perfectly groomed.

Forcing a little smile, she waggled her fingers at him and greeted in a meek voice, "Hi."

His eyes narrowed slightly.

She cringed and drew her shoulders up. "I, uh... I guess you talked to Tim already."

"Yes," his deep, authoritative voice confirmed. "You mind telling me what happened?"

Turning her eyes down to her lap, she shrugged and confessed, "I guess I don't work and play well with others."

"That sounds about right," he agreed. "Three missions in less than a month, Angel. That team had a perfect operating record until about three weeks ago."

Her mouth slowly tightened to a thin slit.

"Why did you come to Gotham?" he asked.

She took a while to answer, then shrugged and replied in a whisper, "I don't know."

"I don't accept that answer," he informed coldly. "Now tell me why you came to Gotham."

Reaching down for the deepest truth, she finally, slowly turned her attention to him and confessed, "I... I want..." She drew a deep breath. "I want to know my father."

Bruce's expression did not change, but he raised his chin slightly.

"I want to know you," she repeated. "I'm... I'm part of you and..." She looked out the window. "I know, it sounds childish and corny but I just want to know my father."

Silence consumed the inside of the car and only the drone of the engine could be heard.

He shattered that silence with, "It doesn't sound childish or corny."

She slowly turned her attention back to him. His expression was no longer so hard and she swore she saw the hint of a smile there.

"I really thought you wanted to join up with the Titans and continue working," he told her.

"That was Mom's idea," she corrected. "I want to join the Justice League, but all I hear is I'm not ready."

"Judging from the last month, you aren't."

That stung and she turned her eyes down again.

"Do you want to be?" he asked.

With a little nod, she softly confirmed, "Yes sir."

Bruce shifted in his seat, turning slightly toward her. "What kind of a commitment are you willing to make?"

"I don't know," she replied.

"I don't accept that answer," he barked with a harsh tone. "What kind of commitment are you willing to make?"

She slowly turned her gaze on him again and answered, "Whatever commitment I need to, I guess. Do you intend to teach me some stuff?"

"Do you want to learn?" he countered. When she nodded, he nodded back and said, "Then I'll teach you. But first, I want to know you." He finished with a wink.

A little smile curled her mouth. "I want to know you, too."

A half hour later they arrived at Wayne Manor and Elissa's attention was fixed on the huge house as they drew closer. Once in a while her gaze would drift to the scenery, the statuary, the groves of tall trees, but for the most part she was mesmerized by that house.

As the car slowed to a stop in front of the huge mansion, she had her hands pressed against the window and her gaze fixed upward, and a little smile on her face. "Wow," she breathed. "That has got to be the biggest house ever!"

Bruce opened the door and began to step out, pausing to say, "It's got a pretty impressive basement, too."

Elissa had her duffel bag slung over her shoulder when they entered and she froze in the cavernous foyer, turning her eyes up to the grand ceiling and the elaborate woodwork and carvings and chandeliers above her, the huge arched window and the two gargoyles perched on its ledge.

Alfred walked past her and her father, who had stopped a few steps beyond and looked back at her, informin as he strode into the house, "I'll have lunch prepared within the hour, Master Bruce."

"Thank you, Alfred," Bruce offered, his eyes still on his daughter.

Striding forward with slow steps, Elissa turned circles as she looked around her at the amazing antiques, the woodwork and paintings, the huge staircase that swept up toward the open second level... She followed him up the staircase where more antiques and paintings and suits of armor waited. Even the ceiling was ornate and finely crafted.

When she paused at the top of the stairs, he cleared his throat and asked, "You coming?"

"This place is totally awesome!" she declared dreamily. She finally looked to him with wide eyes. "You live here? Seriously?"

Bruce nodded. "Yes, seriously. Come on. I'm going to give you the southeast room with a great view of the ocean. There are also some wonderful sunrises from there."

All of the doors appeared to be nine or ten feet tall and made of some kind of dark hardwood, and he opened one and strode in.

The room he led her into had a huge canopied bed on one wall, two matching antique dressers that looked like they were crafted of oak, an antique wardrobe on the opposite wall from the bed, a door on that wall that appeared to go to a private bath and a door on the other side that opened into a huge walk-in closet. Right between the two tall windows, each at least six feet high and about three wide, was an old oak roll top desk with a high back and very comfortable looking leather chair pushed into position. Light was offered not only by the windows, but by two crystal chandeliers that hung from the ceiling. About forty feet wide and almost twenty deep, this room was huge! Two ornate rugs were on the floor, one in the middle of the room and one under the bed. The nightstand had an old looking, very pretty lamp on it, and on the other side of the bed there was an identical nightstand with an identical lamp. An old chest was at the foot of the bed, one that was ornately carved with brass that trimmed it and heavy brass locks that kept it closed.

Elissa dropped her duffel bag as her eyes swept the room once more.

Bruce stood beside her, and after a moment he asked, "Is this okay?"

"This is *my* room?" she breathed.

"If you want it," he replied, "and for however long you decide to stay. The bathroom is right over there. I've had it modernized and it has a whirlpool bathtub and separate shower, a vanity and everything you should—"

She wheeled around and threw her arms around him, burying her face in his chest as she cried, "Thank you!"

Hesitantly, he slipped his arms around her and hugged her back. "It's no problem. Alfred will make sure you have fresh towels and he'll turn your bed back when you're ready to go to sleep."

She nodded, still holding onto him.

"Go on and freshen up," he suggested. "Alfred will have lunch ready in about an hour."

"Okay," she whispered, still holding on to him. "Thank you, Daddy."

The words touched him as none ever had and he hugged her a little tighter. With a little kiss on the top of her head, he whispered back, "You're welcome, Angel."

WW

Lunch was all she expected and more, and Bruce was amazed at how much his petite but muscular little girl could eat!

The dining table was more than twenty feet long and crafted of darkly stained oak. The ten chairs that surrounded it were crafted of the same oak and ornately carved on the high backs. They had leather seats and leather backrests, deep cushions and were very solidly built.

Bruce sat on one end of the table, closest to the door where the kitchen was. He had changed from his suit and now wore khaki slacks and a black tee shirt. Elissa, seated cross legged in the chair to his right, wore black shorts and a red tee shirt that had Batman's symbol across her chest. The shirt fit her very tightly and her bosom stretched the bat symbol quite a bit out of form.

Resting his cheek in his palm, Bruce asked, "So let me get this straight."

She pushed her now empty plate away from her and took a drink from her crystal glass, her eyes fixed on his.

He continued, "You got taken in for speeding, no registration and no driver's license."

Elissa nodded and set her glass back down. "Yeah. The speeding part is something I just got careless on. The driver's license thing… Who knew you needed a license just to drive one of those? I mean, come on! They should let the public know about these things!"

He shook his head.

"So what do you want to do today?" she asked.

"I have a watch with the League this evening," he replied.

Her eyes lit up and she asked, "Oh, can I come?"

"I'm afraid not, Angel," was his answer, "not this time. Getting you to the watchtower is going to take more than just a trip there. The senior members of the Justice League all have to agree that you're ready."

The sides of her mouth drooped and she slammed her chin into her palm, looking down to her empty plate as she grumbled, "Oh."

"Want to see the Bat Cave instead?" he asked.

Her eyes snapped to him, and her lips curled up into a big grin.

WW

"This is totally awesome!" she declared as they stepped from the elevator and into the cavern below the mansion.

Lights had come on as they entered the cave and everything in there was illuminated. There was a workbench of some kind to the left, glass display cases to the right, beyond them were racks of equipment and tools. To the far right, and across a wide stone and concrete bridge that spanned a small subterranean pond was a huge computer console that had one big screen right in the center and above the main work station with two smaller screens on each side that were controlled by four more work stations. It also had other ports for all kinds of input devices, lights all over it and three black leather chairs waiting in front of it, the tallest of which was at the center console. The whole apparatus was about nine feet tall and was black and covered with a variety of lights, some of which blinked on and off as hard drives activated and rested and data was processed.

Looking beyond it, Elissa saw something she recognized, a huge, fast looking car with a jet exhaust at the back and the form of a jet fighter. With a long nose, it was black and dark gray in color and had a fighter's canopy over the cockpit, and she smiled as she saw it. Parked in the center of a huge turntable, it was facing a tunnel that looked like it headed to the outside. There was so much to see, and yet she knew there was no way to see it all at once. Bruce stopped beside her and folded his arms. "This is where I do most of my work. I also conduct quite a bit of League business and research down here. There are more rooms and I have a training center back on the other side of the elevator."

"How big is this place?" she asked almost dreamily as she scanned the cavern.

"It winds under most of the estate," he answered. "I'll give you the fifty cent tour, then I want to do some sparring with you."

She cut her eyes to him. "Sparring? With me? Daddy, I'm little but I'm still an Amazon."

He patted her shoulder. "I'll try not to hurt you."

With a big smile, she folded her arms and said, "Yeah, right."

"I have to report to the Watchtower about midnight and I'm likely to be up there until tomorrow evening. Do you think you can occupy yourself while I'm gone?"

She looked up to him again. "I'll figure out something to do. Can we spend some time together until then?"

He slipped his arm around her shoulders and pulled her to him. "I'm going to spend every minute with you until I have to leave."

She wrapped her arms around him and smiled as she laid her head on his chest. "Cool. Can we go out and fight bad guys tomorrow night?"

Bruce took long seconds to answer, but finally he squeezed her to him and replied, "I'd like that, Angel."

CHAPTER 2

The lights were low in the central control room of the Watchtower and when the doors slid shut behind Wonder Woman she did not stray more than a step or two from them as her eyes found that one lonely figure sitting at the main console. A familiar creeping began in her stomach and she drew a calming breath. She feared almost nothing, but this was a conversation she had hidden from for almost two decades. Finally striding forward, her steps were as confident as she could manage and she was able to control the shaking of her knees very well. It was not a long walk, but it sure seemed to take forever.

Finally reaching the occupied chair, she grasped it with one hand, the console with the other as she looked to the large view screen that was right in front of the man who worked the controls. Silence thickened the air around them and the tension mounted.

"Quiet night?" she finally forced herself to ask.

Batman's eyes did not stray from the monitor as he simply replied, "M-hmm."

She nodded. "We could use one once in a while."

He nodded.

Diana still would not look at him, but she smiled ever so slightly. "Remember that quiet night we had in here some time ago?"

"I remember," he answered dryly.

Loosing a hard breath, she finally took the chair beside his, finally looked to him. "Bruce, we should talk."

He entered coordinates to scan a different location, changing what came up on the monitor.

Frustration began to boil up in her and she suppressed it as best she could, venting yet another hard breath. "Would you at least look at me? Bruce!"

Batman turned his eyes down to the keyboard as he entered new coordinates. "This talk you want to have should have taken place about seventeen years ago."

Turning her eyes down, she softly admitted, "I know. I was afraid. I... I thought it would..."

"Change things?" he finished for her. Anger was seeping into his voice and he continued, "You disappeared for more than a year without even a word. When you came back, you were so distant from me it was like you had never returned at all. Then you introduce me to my sixteen year old daughter for the first time and *now* you want to talk."

"I did what had to be done at the time," she informed. "Only a few people knew about her."

His eyes finally slid to her. "And one of those few couldn't have been her own father?"

Diana closed her eyes. "I wanted to tell you hundreds of times."

"But you didn't," he countered.

"If you didn't know," she pointed out, "then your enemies wouldn't, either."

"And one of *your* enemies nearly killed her," he pointed out with cold words.

Pivoting her chair away from him, she folded her arms and hissed, "That isn't fair."

Looking back to the monitor, Batman studied what was there for long seconds before replying, "I suppose that's not fair. But then, keeping my daughter a secret from me for that long—"

"Bruce!" she shouted. Heaving another deep breath, she shook her head and grumbled, "I'd hoped you would understand. I never wanted her to come here and take up crime fighting."

"And yet here she is," he pointed out. "She even has her own identity as a crime fighter now. How long were you going to keep her isolated on that island, anyway?"

Springing to her feet, she stormed away, only to stop and yell, "I don't know! I didn't expect any of this to happen!" Spinning around, she shook her head when her eyes found him. "Bruce, I was afraid. I didn't know what to do. Do you want me to apologize? Is that it? Do I owe you an apology for trying to protect my..."

Slowly, he turned his head to look at her.

Her eyes darted away and tight lipped, she finished in a whisper, "Our daughter."

He stared at her for a moment, then looked back to the monitor. "You wanted to protect her. To that end, you did not want her to know about me or me about her."

Crossing her arms over her belly, Diana softly admitted, "No, I didn't."

Batman nodded. "And you really thought that it would be better that way. Run home, have our daughter, and then come back here and continue like nothing ever happened. Oh, except the part where we don't see each other anymore." He glanced at her. "We'll just go our separate ways as if those three years between us never happened."

A snarl took her lip and she hissed, "You clearly don't understand. Do you know what your enemies would do to her if they got her?"

"I know what Red Panzer did to her when he got her," Batman countered.

That stung and Diana ground her teeth and turned her eyes away from him.

"I missed sixteen years of her life," he informed coldly. "You wanted to protect her from all of the evils of the world, but I don't think it was for her benefit as much as it was for yours."

Spinning around, Diana stormed toward the door again, her hands clenched into tight fists at her sides as she shouted, "You just let yourself think that. Raising her alone was not all the fun and games you seem to want to think it was!"

"She came to the mansion today," he said right before she reached the door.

Diana froze where she was, her wide eyes locked on the door before her.

Punching in a few new numbers as she watched the monitor, Batman went on, "She didn't quite make it with the Titans after all. Too many personality conflicts. She came and asked to work with me for a while. We had lunch, did some training..." He raised his chin. "There seems to be quite a bit about combat and hand to hand training that you didn't think to teach her. She learned quite a lot from me and we really enjoyed the day."

Diana turned her eyes down, her fists clenching tighter. "You weren't seen with her, were you?"

"Probably not," he sighed.

Spinning around, Wonder Woman stormed back to him, barking, "Who did she spend that time with, Bruce Wayne or Batman?"

"She spent time with her father," he answered.

Reaching past him, Diana turned the monitor off and glared down at him.

His eyes slowly, calmly turned up to meet hers. "She asked me if she could stay with me for a while so that we could get acquainted. She also asked me to invite you to the mansion. It turns out that she likes the idea of having a whole family all together." Pushing away from the console, he stood and faced her. "Elissa, her mother *and* her father." He turned and strode toward the door, calling back, "So you're invited. Dinner's at seven if you care to actually show up this time."

She watched him leave and watched the door for a moment after it closed behind him. She had dreaded this talk, knowing how badly it could go. If only she knew that it could have gone this badly.

WW

Bruce did not watch the old clock as it rotated back into its place to conceal the entrance to the Bat Cave. He really did not have to. Back in his charcoal gray business suit, he was simply a wealthy tycoon again, one who had the burden of a world defender behind his eyes. Lost in his thoughts, he strode directly to his study, to his huge desk, and sat down. Wayne Enterprises always generated a lot of work for him to get himself lost in for a few hours, but even this could not distract him. He felt hurt and betrayed and this was evident on his face as he stared down at folders and charts left on his desk the night before. One thing was certain: He could never allow his daughter to know about this, even though she was a very perceptive girl and was likely to figure it all out on her own.

Evening had set in and the sun was down. Somewhere outside, beyond the high windows of very old glass was the crashing of the surf at the bottom of the cliff below the mansion. One window was partially open to allow the evening air and the sound of the ocean to drift in.

For some time he just sat in his chair and stared down at the unfinished work before him. There was nothing urgent awaiting him on the desk and nothing that would draw his mind away from the new turmoil within him. He needed distraction, but this simply was not doing it. What finally did was an aging butler who peered into the study.

His eyes shifting that way, Bruce greeted, "Good evening, Alfred."

The old butler finally entered carrying a tray with a teapot, a cup and a newspaper. Setting it down on one of the few clear spots on the desk, he picked up the teapot and poured the cup full, his eyes intent on what he was doing.

As Alfred handed him the cup, Bruce leaned over the desk to take it with one hand, then he leaned back and stared into it for a while.

"You seem preoccupied," Alfred observed.

Venting a hard breath through his nose, Bruce simply nodded.

"Should I leave you with your thoughts, Sir?" the butler asked.

"It won't matter," Bruce finally replied. "There may be one more for dinner, by the way."

"Anyone I might know?"

Bruce nodded.

Raising his brow, Alfred observed, "Hence you are preoccupied. Dinner will be a little late tonight. I'll prepare something to tide everyone over until it is ready."

Bruce's eyes shifted to his butler. "A little late?"

Alfred turned toward the door with the tray and teapot and replied, "Miss Elissa was helping."

Rubbing his eyes, Bruce mumbled, "Oh, God."

Moments later he rose from his desk and strode out of the study himself. Heading to his private sitting room, he found his head throbbing at the prospect of the impending visit as well as what awaited him in his own home.

He paused in the doorway and folded his arms. This was a comfortable and well furnished room with four high backed chairs covered in leather, a love seat of the same leather and a long sofa along the far wall. All of the seating faced the same spot in the center of the room; it was clearly meant to entertain small parties as the chairs and love seat were spaced far enough apart to allow guests to be served cocktails or whatever the occasion called for. Expensive paintings hung on the walls, very high windows were along one side, a door out on the far end, a fireplace on the other end and a huge rug covered the floor beneath the sitting area.

There, lying belly down on the couch, was what he sought.

Elissa did not notice him standing there and was reading some magazine which had her full attention. Her long black hair in a pony tail that rested on her back, she was dressed in short red running shorts and a white tee shirt. She was barefoot and her muscular legs were bent at the knees and crossed at the ankles, slowly kicking back and forth as she read, her eyes panning back and forth on the pages. Wires coming out of her ears led to a tiny, flat box that lay on the arm of the couch and her head slowly bobbed from side to side to some unheard music.

Bruce leaned on the door jamb and folded his arms, and a little smile found his lips. But for the gold colored gauntlets that were snugly around each of her forearms, one would never guess that she had been raised on the island nation of the Amazons, that she was a warrior trained, immortal fighter and a miniature version of the Princess of the Amazons herself. No, this was a vision of a quintessential teenager, a lovely young lady who lingered somewhere between girlhood and womanhood and did not seem to realize the destiny ahead of her. Listening to her music with her eyes sweeping along the pages of the magazine she studied, she looked like any other girl, but this one had a connection to him that he could no longer deny.

A moment later Elissa's big blue eyes slid toward him, then she quickly raised her head and looked fully to him, and a big smile overpowered her lips. Pulling the wires from her ears, she sprang from the couch and darted to him, squealing "Daddy!"

He stood from the doorway and only took a single step toward her before she reached him.

Elissa wrapped her arms around his chest and hugged him as tightly as she dared, burying her face in his neck as she did so.

His arms slowly wrapped around her back and that rare smile he wore broadened. He was unaccustomed to being greeted in his home with such enthusiasm but he was sure that he could easily get used to it.

Pulling away from him, Elissa took his hands and backed toward the sitting area, her eyes locked on his as she asked with a girlish eagerness, "So how was your day? Kick the crap out of any bad guys today?"

He followed her easily and shook his head. "No, Angel, it was a quiet day."

"What about tonight?" she pressed as they reached two of the chairs. "We're still going out tonight, aren't we? Oh! And is Mom coming? You said you'd ask her."

He sat down in one of the high backed chairs and nodded as he watched her sit cross legged on the couch across from him. "I asked her," he replied, "but I don't know if she'll be able to get away tonight."

Elissa's mouth tightened and she nodded. She was trying to hide her disappointment but was unable to keep it completely at bay.

"I'm sure she'll make it if she can," he added quickly, "but this is an unpredictable business we're in."

"Yeah," she said, nodding again. "The bad guys can be really inconsiderate, can't they?"

"So what happened with dinner?" he asked suddenly.

Her eyes shifted away and she informed, "Well, I tried to help." Looking back to him, she smiled again and went on, "Alfred was making something wonderful with duck and..." She shrugged. "Who knew brandy was *that* flammable?"

Bruce smiled again. "I can see where a little detail like that would take you off guard."

"It sure did," she mumbled. "Anyway, we ordered pizza after that and I helped clean up the kitchen... Your fire extinguisher makes an awful mess, by the way!"

Listening to her with all his attention, Bruce found himself consumed by the ramblings of this girl who talked to him about her day, what she had seen and done and how much she was enjoying her time at the mansion. Everything else seemed to just melt away. There was no Wayne Enterprises, no Justice League, no Batman or Wonder Woman... There was only Elissa, his daughter, the sweet, bubbly teenage girl who wanted nothing more in this moment than his attention. Many people clamored for his attention every day, but always because of who he was. In this most precious moment he was not Bruce Wayne, not Batman. He was Daddy.

Elissa raised her brow and lowered her feet to the floor as she sat on the edge of her couch, holding her palms toward him as she warned, "Now don't be mad, but I found your garage and your motorcycle collection..." She trailed off as his brow tensed. "I didn't take anything off of the property!" she assured, "but I might have ridden one or two around the estate." She clenched her teeth and stared back at him for long, horrifying seconds.

"Which ones did you take out?" he asked in a calm voice.

She swallowed hard and looked away from him. "Well, there was the blue one, um, the red touring, the, uh..."

"The Harley?" he prodded.

Her gaze returned to him and she declared, "Daddy, I had to!"

Unexpectedly, he smiled. "What did you think?"

She was long seconds in answering, but finally she smiled and cried, "It was so awesome! My bike at home isn't anything close to that thing!"

"Your bike?"

"Yeah, when they thought I was Wonder Woman the police chief at the time and a few other people had a special bike made for me that I could use for patrols and to respond to calls and stuff. Wait, you know all of that. Anyway, it's supercharged and has everything, but that Harley! Dad!"

"Biggest engine they make," he informed. "I should also point out that it's Tim's."

She grimaced. "Oh. You don't think he'll mind, do you?"

Bruce assured, "I don't think he'll mind."

"I would so love to take it out on the highway or something!"

With a little smile, he assured, "I think we can see to it."

She responded with a tight lipped smile of her own as she declared, "Best Dad ever!"

Alfred strode in and announced, "Miss Diana has arrived, Master Bruce."

He looked over his shoulder and offered, "Thank you, Alfred. Please, show her in."

Elissa saw right away that his body language changed, that there was a shift in his whole demeanor. Strain came across his features as if he had been kicked in the gut, but he maintained his bearing as he had hundreds of times and drew a deep breath. Her perceptions saw through it, though, and she felt a nervous crawl in the pit of her stomach.

Still, it was not the time for a lot of tension and she intended to do whatever it took to alleviate it, and that meant calling upon the little girl in her to defuse anything that might arise. She beamed a big smile at the tall woman who strode into the room and stopped there.

Diana was not dressed as Wonder Woman. Instead, she entered wearing a knee length light blue skirt and a white button-up blouse with full sleeves. She wore her hair up in a bun with long locks that dangled from her temples. Long earrings dangled from her ears and a gold and diamond necklace was around her neck. She was an image of stunning beauty, and yet there was strain behind her eyes as well. Elissa got but a glance before Diana's gaze shifted to Bruce and remained there.

He was not looking back at her, but he did greet, "Good evening, Princess."

"Thank you for inviting me," she offered softly.

Bruce just nodded, then stood and turned toward the door. "Dinner should be ready shortly."

Alfred met him at the door and reported, "Master Bruce, the signal is up."

"Sweet!" Elissa declared as she sprang to her feet. "Let's go kick some bad guy butt!"

Half turning his head, Bruce corrected in the voice of Batman, "No, Angel. You and your mother stay here and enjoy dinner. I'll be back as soon as I can."

Disappointment dominated Elissa's features as she watched him leave. "Aw, come on, Daddy!"

"Let it go, Little One," Diana ordered softly, her eyes turning to the floor.

"But Mom! That's totally not fair! We're supposed to go out tonight anyway! Why can't we just..." She trailed off as her mother raised her hand to her. Still, she looked away and tightly folded her arms, grumbling, "It isn't fair. Why can't we go, too?"

Diana's eyes slid to her daughter and a slight smile curled one side of her mouth. "I didn't say we aren't going, Junior." She finished with a wink.

Elissa's eyebrows shot up, and when her mother raised a finger to her mouth, she smiled and did the same.

Reaching to a concealed pocket in her skirt, Diana removed her Justice League communicator and ordered, "Get changed. We'll just meet him there." Raising the communicator to her mouth, she called, "Wonder Woman to Watchtower."

WW

Commissioner Gordon stood on the roof, his hands in the pockets of his overcoat as he stared up at the bat signal that shined brightly on the clouds above. With him were two uniformed police officers, both of whom watched the signal on the clouds as well. The spotlight that sent it there illuminated much of the roof surrounding it, but behind it and in the distance, all was shrouded in shadows, and everyone present knew that Batman would emerge from those shadows. The sounds of the blowing wind would mask the approach of the Dark Knight and tensions were high as the three awaited him.

A loud, mechanical click sounded from behind them and the spotlight went out, plunging much of the rooftop back into darkness. Only the two lights that flanked the one door that accessed the roof illuminated the roof to any degree. Even as the two policemen spun around, Gordon turned almost casually, looking to the shadowy figure who stood beside the big spotlight.

"Thanks for coming," the Commissioner greeted. "I have that information you asked for." He produced a yellow envelope and handed it to the Dark Knight.

Batman took the envelope and removed the contents, examining the papers for a moment before he spoke. "How did you get these?"

Gordon smiled and folded his arms. "You have your sources, I have mine. Suffice to say, the how is also part of the problem. We can't get a warrant for any of those places but we know what's going on at all three locations and who's involved. I can't even use anything based on that information to arrest or prosecute."

"I see your problem," Batman assured. "Good thing I don't need warrants."

"It sure is," Wonder Woman confirmed as she emerged from the shadows across the rooftop.

Batman looked to his right and the police officers and Commissioner looked to their left as the Amazon Princess strode toward them. Behind and a little beside her was Golden Angel.

Gordon's eyes narrowed. He recognized the girl. He had seen her two other times, once on this very rooftop months ago, though she was not dressed as Golden Angel at that time. She had been dressed

35

as Wonder Woman, was posing as Wonder Woman, but he knew even at the time she was not.

Wonder Woman stopped and looked to the Commissioner, setting her hands on her hips as she asked, "Mind if we help out?" Her eyes strayed to Batman and the disapproving look he had for her was apparent even behind the mask he wore. Her posture explained that she did not care if he approved.

Commissioner Gordon tore his eyes from Golden Angel and looked to Wonder Woman, replying, "I don't mind at all. We'll just leave you three to hash all that out. Batman, I'll have three teams near those locations who can respond in a couple of minutes if you need them."

"Don't bother," he advised. "We'll handle it, and I'm sure at least one of them is a decoy."

"Whatever you say," Gordon said as he strode toward the door, the two officers following. "I'll still have some patrols close by, just in case."

Batman watched the Commissioner and the officers disappear behind the door, and when it closed he turned to Wonder Woman with narrow eyes and folded his arms.

With her hands still set on her hips, she raised her brow and informed, "I thought you might need some backup, or at least some company."

Golden Angel took her mother's side, looking up at the Dark Knight as she pled, "Please, Daddy. Just let us—"

"Not in costume," he snapped. Looking to the girl, he said with stern words, "Remember our talk about safeguarding our true identities?"

She turned her eyes down and nodded, confirming, "Yes sir. Sorry."

Batman looked back to Wonder Woman.

"There are three locations," she said straightly, "and there are three of us. We can check out all three, deal with what needs to be dealt with and be home for dinner in no time."

"I have it under control," he growled.

"But we can control it faster together," Elissa assured. "You already said Nightwing is going to be out of town for a few days, I heard you put Batgirl on a stake-out tonight and Robin is on the other side of the country. Please can we help out?"

His gaze shifted to her again.

She frowned and stuck her lower lip out, and she gave him the saddest eyes she could muster.

He heaved a deep breath and looked away, then to Wonder Woman. Pulling one of the pages from his hand, he offered it to her and said, "The address is at the top. It's about six blocks north of here." When she took the paper from him, he looked to Elissa and offered her the next. "That one is four blocks south, some kind of abandoned store with three loading docks out back. Check the docks first."

She took the paper from him and nodded, confirming, "Yes sir."

"And check in as soon as you find something," he ordered.

Setting her hands on her hips, she complained, "I'm not a little kid anymore."

"That's how it is done," Wonder Woman snapped. "All team members stay in contact with each other, especially when on a mission. Report to one of us immediately as soon as you find something, understand?"

Nodding again, she assured, "Yes, Mother." Elissa glanced aside. "Um, I don't have a Justice League communicator."

Diana vented a patient breath. "Do you have your cell phone on you?"

Reaching behind her, Golden Angel produced it from a pouch and assured, "Right here."

"Just make sure the ringer is off. You'll need to be swift and silent. I'll check in with you in a half an hour to see how things are going."

Slipping it back into its pouch, the girl said, "No problem. They won't know I'm there until I'm all over them and I'll call as soon as I know something."

WW

A bright light was over each dock and two of the rusty blue doors were down and secured. The third, furthest to the right, was open and had a white van backed up to it and it seemed to be about two feet away from the dock. The building was sizeable and the docks were recessed into the back wall about fifty feet, no doubt to give large trucks enough maneuvering room to turn off of the street and turn to back into them without obstructing traffic. The brick structure was in disrepair and appeared to have been abandoned for some time, though lights were on inside and shining out of a back window about forty feet to the left of the docks.

Elissa had hoped for more cover so that she could approach the docks unseen, but the only cover would be that van, and she peered around the corner of the back wall and toward the docks. The van was only twenty feet away and nobody was outside, so it seemed like a good time to cross open ground.

Sprinting as fast and quietly as she could, she reached the van in seconds and pressed her back to the front of it, looking to one side, then the other. Her heart thundered as she expected someone to emerge any second and find her.

Long seconds passed.

With everything still quiet, she slid along the front of the van, toward the driver's side and between it and the side wall which was about ten feet away and led to a rusty steel door that was closed. Her eyes were on this door as she slid her back along the van to try not to be noticed. She reached the rear of the van and paused, turning her attention to the open dock the van was backed up to, and she crouched down as she heard voices approaching from within.

The first voice she heard was a little gravely and spoke with an accent that one would expect from a mob boss from long ago, and this one was doing most of the talking.

"Just make sure nobody comes around asking a lot of questions, and don't let nobody in here."

"Sure thing, Mister Scarface," a deeper voice with a similar accent replied.

Footsteps stopped near the edge of the dock and Elissa ducked down, turning her head that way.

"I mean it, Rhino. I don't want no problems this time. Day got de Bat clear across town and duh cops are about to get real busy and we don't want 'em coming around here until we're done, got it?"

Elissa's eyes narrowed.

"I got it, Mister Scarface."

"See that ya do."

Footsteps clopped away until the sounds faded to a distant echo.

Half turning, she placed her hand on the van, the other on the ground as she prepared to slip into the building. Something big hit the ground, then she heard heavy footsteps slowly stride the other direction. Daring to peer around the van, she watched the huge man in the blue-gray suit walk toward the other side of the van. He was very tall, very broad shouldered and very thick in the body and arms, and he looked immensely strong. She stood and noiselessly crept around the corner of the van, her wide eyes on the big man as he turned slightly toward the building and strolled toward the other side. He was not very vigilant and slipping inside should be easy.

Still watching him, she gently placed her hand on the edge of the dock and prepared to roll quickly and quietly inside as Batman had shown her only the day before. Everything was going perfectly until her cell phone rang, and a cold breath washed into her as her eyes widened.

The big man spun around and he was not wearing a pleasant expression as his gaze fixed on her.

As he approached, Elissa held a finger to him and reached behind her to remove the phone, holding it to her ear as she greeted, "Hello? Oh, hey."

Rhino stopped right in front of her, folding his arms as he loomed over her with an ominous expression.

She stared back up at him. "Yeah, everything's going about like you'd expect. Hey, can I call you back? Okay, talk to you in a little bit." She closed the phone and reached behind her to slide it back into its pouch. "Sorry about that. My Mom." Leaning an elbow on the edge of the dock, she asked, "So how's it going?"

"You ain't supposed to be here," he informed coldly.

"Yeah," she confirmed, "probably not." Extending her hand to him, she guessed, "You must be Rhino." When he took her hand to shake it, she introduced, "My name's Golden Angel and I'm the girl who will be kicking your butt tonight." She clamped onto his hand and jerked him toward her with all her strength as she spun around and delivered a brutal kick to his gut. The air exploded from him and he doubled over, and she took the opportunity to spin the other way and throw him over her shoulder. She was less than a third his size and weight, but her Amazon strength was something he clearly did not anticipate.

As he slammed into the ground, she watched for a few seconds after to be sure he was out, then she turned her attention to the dock again. With one hop she was inside and standing on the edge, looking around the inside of the old store to make certain it was clear.

Before she made it that first step, someone grabbed her ankle from behind and she did not have time to even turn to see her attacker before she was thrown out of the dock, barking a scream as she was.

She twisted around in the air and controlled her fall well, rolling quickly back to her feet. Assuming her battle stance, she was not that surprised to see the big man stomping toward her with his hands clenched into tight fists.

"Okay," she conceded, "it looks like you're going to be tougher to deal with than I thought."

Reaching her, he threw a punch she quickly dodged away. Another and the results were the same. She was much quicker and far more agile and every time he struck she simply moved out of the way.

"Hold still!" he ordered.

"Nuh uh!" she countered, spinning away from his fist yet again.

The more he attacked, the more she dodged and backed away, reasoning that someone that big would eventually tire, and then she would make her move. However, before that happened, she felt the brick wall on the far side against her back and her eyes widened as she realized she had run out of room.

He punched hard at her and she slipped quickly aside, looking back to see him slam his fist into the bricks. When he turned toward her again, she saw that hitting the wall like that did not hurt him at all!

"Hold still you little brat!" he shouted.

She backed away from him along the wall and toward the building. "No, I'm not quite as dumb as you."

When he drew his fist back to throw yet another powerful but sluggish punch, she crouched down and sprang into him, ramming her shoulder into his gut. Yelling in Amazon battle fashion, she drove him backward, picked him up and lunged forward and down, slamming him back-first onto the concrete of the driveway with chilling force and hard enough to make the ground around them tremble. He seemed stunned again and she acted quickly, pouncing on him and ramming her knee into the middle of his chest as she grabbed his coat and raised her own fist to strike back. She hit him in the face three times as hard as she could, but before she realized, he had a handful of her ponytail and she was yanked from him and slammed back-first into the wall.

They were both a little slow to stand.

Holding her head low, Golden Angel glared at this big man from beneath a low, angry brow. Most likely the people inside the building knew they had been discovered and all of her element of surprise was gone.

Rhino snarled at her as he clenched his hands into tight fists and squared off with the little Amazon again.

This time she did not wait for him to come at her. She charged and ducked under his hands as she had before. He did not seem to know to expect this, did not react to it again and she rammed her shoulder lower into his solid gut, picking him up as she had before, but this time she wheeled around and slammed him into the wall where she had hit, and this time many of the bricks shattered and broke away.

Backing away as he fell to the ground, she barked through bared teeth, "Yeah, how do *you* like it?"

Clearly infuriated, he scrambled to his feet much quicker this time, lowered his head and charged.

Golden Angel charged to meet him head-on and seconds later slammed back-first into the side of the van that was some distance away from where they collided, causing it to rock over to one side. As it recovered, she crumpled to the ground, leaving the impression of her back and upper arms in the steel as she fell away from it. Her long black pony tail had fallen over her left shoulder to the front of her and she whipped her head around to get it back behind her, but many locks stubbornly hung over her tiara and fell back into her face. Combing the hair out of her face with one hand, she took a couple of steps forward and snarled in a voice befitting her seventeen years, "That the best you got?"

As he charged her yet again, she ran toward him, but this time sidestepping and wheeling around to kick him as hard as she could in the gut, and when he doubled over she brought her other boot around to slam into his backside.

He stumbled into the van he had thrown her into and caved in the side door with his head, and it lurched over much further. Unlike his much smaller foe, he did not go down, rather he turned on her to resume the fight.

Setting her hands on her hips, Golden Angel shook her head and commended, "I have to hand it to you. You're as strong as a rhino, but you're not quite as smart as one."

He yelled and charged at her again, and again she met him head-on. Grappling with him had proven useless, but she wanted to try something different.

Ducking under his arms, she brought her head up into his chin, then grabbed his coat and lunged backward to throw him over her, badly underestimating his strength. Her head-butt did nothing and he grabbed her around the waist and easily hurled her away from him. This time she controlled her fall and rolled on one shoulder to end up on her feet again, spinning around to meet him as he charged her yet again. Her Amazon strength *had* to count for something! Lowering her shoulder, she went at him low again, ramming her shoulder into his gut and this time getting him off the ground. Wrapping her arms as far around him as she could, she yelled as she arched her back under his massive weight, then she lunged forward and down, driving him back-first into the ground with all of her might.

He was not even stunned this time and grabbed her pony tail, then hurled her toward the van and got to his feet.

Golden Angel rolled expertly to her feet again and quickly faced him, drawing a wide eyed gasp as she found him upon her already.

His shoulder rammed into her and he drove her easily backward, slamming her into the white van, and this time it turned over with them. As the van landed on its side, he rolled off of it and scrambled quickly to his feet. Stunned, Golden Angel fell limply off of it and crashed awkwardly to the ground. She moaned weakly as she struggled to get her wits about her and had just barely pushed herself back up when he grabbed her by the hair again and picked her up, slamming her into the roof of the van with her feet dangling a foot off of the ground. Grimacing as she reached for her hair, she finally turned fearful eyes to his.

Baring his teeth, he raised his fist.

Golden angel held her palms to him and bade, "Wait!"

He hesitated.

Her brow arching, she whimpered, "Come on. You wouldn't really hit a girl, would you?"

Eying her suspiciously, he raised his chin, trying to process what she had told him.

She looked behind him and barked, "About time you got here, Superman!"

With a deep gasp and fearful look, he dropped her and spun around, readying himself as his eyes darted about for the Man of Steel.

Acting quickly, she grabbed his collar from behind and with a mighty Amazon yell she pulled him backward and down as hard as she could, slamming the back of his head into the van and caving in the metal where the side met the top. This time he went limp and fell to the ground, and in a moment was unconscious with his back resting against the van, his legs sprawled out in front of him, and his head hanging down.

Golden Angel sat down beside him and patted his thigh, smiling as she observed, "Yeah. The back of your head's not quite as hard as the front, is it?"

She reached to her belt and into a pouch there to retrieve her cell phone. Looking down at it, she punched in some numbers and then raised it to her ear, waiting for a few seconds before she heard it answered on the other end. "Hey, Mom. Yeah, I have it under control here. There was only the one guy guarding the dock and I took him down." She shook her head. "No, I don't think there are more than three or four more in there." She looked to the big man said, "Yeah, one of the others called him Rhino. He's really strong! No, sleeping like a baby." With a little smile, she pushed herself up and assured, "No, it's cool. I'll just take out the rest and call the police in to pick them up. No biggie." She turned around and slowly turned her eyes up. "Ah, crud," she mumbled as she slowly lowered her hand to her side.

On the other side of the van was a man of massive proportions, almost twice the overall bulk of the man she had just taken down. He wore a mask over his entire head, one that was white with the black outline of what appeared to be his face and covered everything but his mouth and chin. Something was over his eyes and they appeared to be a ghostly white. He wore no shirt, only black commando trousers and black boots.

Golden Angel's eyes were locked on the huge man as he just stood there with his fists set on his hips. Unaware that her mouth was hanging open, she raised the phone to her lips again and nervously cleared her throat before speaking. "Hey, Mom? Yeah. Um, never mind that last part and get your butt here as soon as you can, okay?" With that she closed the phone and slipped it back into the pouch on her belt, never taking her eyes from the huge man before her. Mustering her courage, she raised her chin slightly and narrowed her eyes, asking defiantly, "So, you want to mix it up with me, too?"

He casually reached across his chest, twisting around slightly to grab onto one corner of the overturned van.

Though a little wide eyed, she watched with no other expression as he easily slid it out of his way. Rhino slumped to the ground as the van was moved. Slowly, she looked back up at him, lifting her brow slightly as she warned, "You know, I'm an Amazon warrior. I've trained for combat my whole life and I've never run from a fight."

He raised his hands before him and cracked his knuckles.

Slowly sliding one foot back, she assumed her battle stance and offered, "I'll give you this one chance to give up peacefully, just this one chance."

He folded his arms.

A tense few seconds passed quietly between them.

Without warning, she spun around and slammed her foot into his belly, stumbling away right after she did. Quick to turn back, she found him just standing there and staring back at her with his arms still folded. He was solid, very solid and built like a tank! Swallowing hard, she resumed her battle stance and raised her fists before her.

This time he advanced and she was quick to back away.

Clenching his hands into tight fists as he strode toward her, he finally asked, in a deep voice and thick Spanish accent, "So you have never run from a fight?"

"No," she nervously replied, "but I think this might be a good time to start." A breath shrieked into her as she ran back-first into the cold, brick wall of the building behind her and her eyes locked wide on his. She had managed to get herself cornered and fear surged up through her and left a lump in her throat.

He stopped well within arm's reach, his arms at his sides and ready as he asked, "What do they call you, little girl?"

"Golden Angel," she replied, then she set her hands on her hips and barked, "And I really don't like to be called *little girl*! What if I called you big... stupid... mask guy?"

"You may call me Bane," he growled back. He leaned his head and gently took her chin between his huge thumb and finger. "It would be such a shame to crush a pretty little flower like yourself. Come with me quietly and I promise you will not be harmed."

She smiled back and sweetly informed, "Thanks, but it's really time for me to kick your butt now." She brutally knocked his hand away with her left and drove her right as hard as she could up into his chin.

His head snapped back, but that was all.

When Bane growled and cocked his arm back, Golden Angel knew what was coming and leapt away from him, narrowly avoiding his fist. She rolled over one shoulder and back to her feet, looking back to see him removing his hand from a hole he had just punched through the brick wall, and he was turning to face her. "Oh, this is some major serious wicked doo-doo," she mumbled as he advanced on her again. The time looked right for a retreat and she spun around to do so, greatly underestimating his speed and she barked a scream as he grabbed her hair.

She slammed hard into the brick wall and crumpled to the ground, lying there trying to collect her wits for long seconds as he loomed over her. As she tried to push herself back up, he reached down and took her upper arm, lifting her easily from the ground and to his eye level to leave her feet dangling as he held her with no effort at arm's length. With a few locks of hair hanging into her face over her tiara, she turned horrified eyes to him, her lips parted in fear as she stared back.

"Now," he said with a patient tone, "are you a little more receptive to my offer, little girl?"

She snarled, "I told you not to call me that!" With a defiant yell, she kicked as hard as she could, her boot connecting with his chin with brutal force, and she followed this kick with the other across the side of his head. He was not even stunned, and growled something in Spanish as he turned and threw her again, this time into the roof of the overturned van which thankfully caved in about half way and cushioned her impact. Still, she was barely conscious as she rolled to the ground again. Before she regained her wits, his hand closed around her neck and she was lifted from the ground, and this time she was slammed back into the van and held there by the throat.

Baring his teeth, he growled, "I offered you a chance to live, you little brat, and now—"

"Now you'll let go of her," Wonder Woman ordered.

Bane raised his chin, looking to the other side of the van where the Amazon Princess stood with her hands set on her hips.

Grasping his thick wrist with both her hands, Golden Angel rasped, "You're about to get your butt seriously kicked, Pal!" He threw her away from him and she rolled to the ground some distance away, springing back to her feet as quickly as possible to turn back on him, flailing her arms to keep her balance.

Wonder Woman watched Golden Angel as she collected her bearings, then her eyes shifted back to Bane and narrowed. Raising an eyebrow slightly, she observed, "Someone has to teach you how to treat a lady."

He snarled back, "Perhaps it is time for you to learn who you should not challenge." He reached down and slid his hand under the van, and with a mighty yell he lifted it over his head.

Golden Angel's eyes widened as she watched him hurl the heavy van at Wonder Woman, and she smiled slightly as the Amazon Princess leisurely moved aside to allow the van to pass by her and loudly crash to the ground behind her.

Bane sounded another battle cry as he charged Wonder Woman, swinging his fist. This time she did not dodge aside and met him head on, easily blocking his fist and slamming her own brutally into his face, and this time he stumbled backward.

"Yeah!" Golden Angel shouted. "Take that!"

Powerful arms were suddenly wrapped around her and she was crushed to a huge, solid body and picked up off of the ground. With her arms pinned to her sides, she found she had little hope of breaking free, but struggled with everything she had anyway.

"I ain't done with you yet," Rhino growled as he proceeded to squeeze the little Amazon as hard as he could.

Elissa yelled as he tried to crush the life from her, struggling with everything she had, but she could not break his grip on her.

"I'm gonna squash you like a little bug!" he said through bared teeth.

Batman swung in from the darkness above and delivered a hard kick to Rhino's face.

Dropping Golden Angel, the big man staggered backward and reached for his face, then he wheeled around as the Dark Knight slammed onto the ground between him and the docks and crouched down.

Slowly standing, Batman's narrow eyes were fixed on the huge man as he advanced.

Elissa scrambled to her feet and turned her attention from Batman to the other fight to see Bane deliver a solid punch to her mother's belly.

Wonder Woman doubled over and staggered backward. When Bane pursued, she spun around and slammed the heel of her boot solidly into his gut. He struck back expertly and connected with her head and she blocked his follow-up strike and brought her fist hard up into his jaw. This looked like a pitched battle, but Wonder Woman had things well in hand. In fact, she almost seemed to be toying with him.

Looking back to her father, she raised her brow as she watched the big man charge and Batman simply move out of the way. Rhino turned and charged again, swinging his fist hard, but Batman simply diverted the strike with a sweep of his arm and spun around, redirecting his big foe into the brick wall to his side.

As Rhino staggered away from the wall and turned back on the now advancing Dark Knight, Elissa rushed in from behind the big man, and as her father leapt up and delivered a hard kick to his chin, she grabbed the collar of his jacket and pulled him downward, then planted her other palm in the small of his back, picked him up and threw him the other way.

Rhino crashed hard to the ground flat on his back, raising a ring of dust around him as he did.

Looking to her right, Golden Angel saw Batman take her side, and she smiled at him as she met his eyes.

Even behind that mask he wore he had a proud look about him and he gave her a little wink.

Elissa sensed something and wheeled around, looking to the open dock as two men who were dressed in dark gray business suits and white ties jumped out of it and hit the ground. One crouched down while the other remained standing and they both aimed semi-automatic pistols at her and Batman.

Barking, "Look out!" she stepped between them and the Dark Knight, and when they opened fire her arms were a blur as she deflected bullet after bullet from her gauntlets.

In seconds they were empty and both men reached to their belts to find fresh magazines.

Batman took Golden Angel's side again and the two of them simultaneously reached to their belts and each removed a bat-arang. Glancing at each other for only a split second, they turned their attention fully to the two gunmen as they finished reloading their weapons, and they let the little metal bats fly at the same time. Each bat-arang found its mark and both gunmen were disarmed. Together, Golden Angel and Batman charged; the two men barely had time to retreat a single step. Elissa reached hers barely ahead of Batman, spinning around as she delivered a solid kick to his head that dropped him immediately. Batman hit his target with a right cross that knocked him back into the wall behind him, then a left uppercut that finished him off.

Looking to each other, Batman and Golden Angel bumped fists then turned on the stirring Rhino.

"I've got him," Batman assured.

With a nod, Elissa spun back around and leapt into the open dock.

She trotted into the dark building, past stacks of steel racking and pallets, papers that lay randomly about, and a couple of ladders that leaned against one wall. Crouching down as she reached the cavernous sales floor, she squinted slightly as her night vision scanned the darkness within. There was no movement, and nobody about, but along the wall to her left she heard something, a faint shuffle, and she stood and made her way silently along the wall and toward a doorway about fifty feet away.

As she neared, she saw that it was a steel door with paper taped over the one window, and right at the edge of this paper and tape she could see a little glint of light from within the room.

Stopping as she heard that shuffle again, she realized that the sound was about halfway up the wall, as if someone was pressing their shoulder against it and moving ever so slightly, anxiously.

Her eyes narrowed and she crept forward, holding her right arm ready while she allowed the fingers of her left hand to gently glide along the wall. As she reached the door she stopped, tensing up as she thought out what to do. The door would open away from her and she would have little time to react once whoever was inside emerged, but she was confident that it would not be a problem since they would also have little time to react to her. Reaching to her belt with her left hand, she slowly withdrew another bat-arang, took it in her right hand and flung it out into the store, and it flew with a rapid spin.

Reaching nearly to the ceiling, the bat-arang stopped and hovered for just a second, then it traveled back down at the same angle, veering slightly away from Golden angel and finally hitting the wall just on the other side of the door.

It burst open and another man in a light gray suit this time followed it and crouched down, wheeling around to face the source of the sound and aiming his gun in that direction.

Elissa dispatched him with a single kick to the head, and as he fell another stormed out, this time turning his gun toward her! Her arm whipped up as he fired and the single bullet ricocheted upward. Lurching back slightly, she kicked him hard in the chin, knocking him out cold and she watched as he fell over the other man.

With a little smile, she stared down at them for a few seconds to make certain they were out, then she turned her eyes back to the doorway, stepping over the two unconscious men as she slipped inside.

Inside was what appeared to be a dilapidated office. About ten feet by ten feet, it was painted a light blue, or had been years ago, and had an old metal desk off to one side, facing the door with a new looking chair behind it. A door on the right side was closed and did not look like it was often used. Her eyes were on it for long seconds before returning to the desk. None of the items on the desk interested her. They were merely clipboards, pencils, papers and a briefcase, one that looked expensive and new. All had been recently put there and this escaped her notice, but the doll laying on the edge of the desk near the briefcase had her full attention.

She approached slowly, her gaze locked on the doll and her lips parted inquisitively. Leaning her head as she reached the desk, she hesitantly picked the doll up, slowly raising it to eye level.

No. It was not a doll. It was a ventriloquist's dummy. It was dressed in the pinstripe suit and the hat of an old gangster and in its hand was a small Thompson machine gun. Its face was rough looking, mean looking and had a scratch or scar down one side from above the eye all the way down the cheek. There was even what appeared to be a cigarette in its mouth, mounted to the lower jaw.

Seeing it gave her a cold chill. There was just something about it...

"Rhino responds very well to little Scarface," a familiar voice informed from one side.

Elissa drew a quick gasp and dropped the dummy as she spun around, backing away a step. Her wide eyes found someone she knew, someone she did not expect to encounter this night, but someone she had hoped to find again.

Doctor Shipley looked a little different. There was no longer gray in his hair and the beard had been shaved from his thin face. His thin rimmed glasses were also different and his piercing eyes no longer looked so friendly. There was a menace about him, and his thin frame was covered in a very expensive looking silk suit with a black jacket and trousers, a light gray vest and white shirt beneath and a solid black, silk tie. He wore a smile, clearly just for her, but this smile was not as she remembered. There was something wicked about it, something horrifying.

"In fact," he went on as he slowly closed the door behind him, "he would rather take orders from him than from a real person. I've thought about writing a paper on it, how he thinks a dummy more real than the man controlling it." He raised his brow. "So how have you been, Wonder?"

Finding herself a little afraid, she dismissed the feeling easily and ground her teeth, setting a hand on her hip as her eyes narrowed, and she leaned her head slightly. She fired a disapproving, angry look his way, making no secret of her feelings for him now.

"Sorry," he offered. "I guess you aren't Wonder Woman anymore, are you? But then, you never really were." He strode forward with slow steps, angling toward the desk.

Elissa circled toward the door, ready for anything.

Reaching the desk, he looked down at the briefcase and worked the wheels of the combination locks. "I'm guessing you have some questions, perhaps some unresolved anger toward me." He raised his brow as he pushed the buttons to release the locks. "So how have you been?"

Grinding her teeth, Elissa snarled, "I'm guessing you already know, Shipley. I'm guessing that you also know your butt's getting kicked tonight for what you did to me!"

He slowly turned his head, meeting her eyes with the deep pools that were his own. "Unresolved anger. I think we're making progress."

Her eyes narrowed again. "Are you just trying to provoke me?"

"We both need to just face reality, Wonder," he interrupted. "I'm unarmed and I don't see you beating someone who won't or can't fight back." He turned fully toward her and folded his arms. "We both know I don't stand a chance against Wonder Woman, or even some child who thinks she is."

"I don't think I'm Wonder Woman," she growled, glaring back at him.

"When we first met you did," he pointed out. "So what do you call yourself now?"

"Golden Angel," she replied with hard words.

"Thank you for your honesty," he said softly.

"So," she started loudly and with authority to her words, "are you coming along quietly, Doctor Shipley?"

"I suppose I should be honest with you," he suggested. "My name isn't Gordon Shipley."

Watching him turn his attention to his brief case, she raised her chin. She watched his motions as he slowly opened it, suspicious and a little nervous, and more so as he looked back to her and removed his glasses.

"Then tell me who you really are," she demanded.

A slight smile took his mouth. "My name is Crane, Doctor Jonathan Crane." He tossed his glasses down and removed something made of burlap from his briefcase, and he slipped it over his head, looking back at her through the eyeholes of the horrible mask he now wore. "But your colleagues call me Scarecrow."

Elissa's eyes widened. Wearing the mask, he had become a most horrible apparition. It had an oversized mouth sewn in and an almost skull-like nose. Straw stuck out of it in places, much thicker around where the neck was. She tensed up, raising her chin slightly. He was just trying to frighten her, to intimidate her, and she would not allow him to. Setting that hand back on her hip, she leaned her head slightly and replied with a disbelieving and annoyed look, and her other hand clenched into a tight fist.

"Huh," he said in a huff. "I thought for sure you would scream like a little girl and bolt out of here when you saw this."

She reached behind her and retrieved her handcuffs. "You coming along quietly or what?"

Scarecrow sighed. "Oh, I suppose I have no other choice." He held his arms straight out with his hands to her, ready to be cuffed. "Just don't hurt me, Golden Angel."

Elissa strode toward him and grabbed his wrist, grumbling, "No promises."

Before she could get the first cuff on him, something sprayed from his sleeves, an aerosol with a noxious stink to it that burned her eyes as it hit her face. Stunned, she backed away, turning her face away from him and tightly closing her eyes. She coughed and dropped the handcuffs, raising a hand to cover her mouth. Tears streamed from her eyes as she continued to back away and she was finally stopped by the wall behind her.

The immediate effects were only temporary and the burning in her nose and mouth subsided in seconds. Blinking her eyes back open, she found a strange anxiety washing through her and she looked back to Scarecrow, suddenly seeing him very differently. Her anxiety began to worsen. Her heart thundered and she could not catch her breath, could not focus right.

Scarecrow slowly approached her and his voice was different, deeper and more menacing as he asked, "What's wrong, little girl? You suddenly don't look so confident."

Pressing her back to the wall behind her, she mustered her draining courage and ordered, "Back up."

He did not stop and closed on her inch by dreadful inch. His mask distorted and he looked like he was speaking through the mouth in his mask. His eyes were glowing red and he appeared bigger, though she knew he could not be.

"Don't you want me to come along quietly?" he mocked.

Her eyes widened as she watched him remove a syringe from his jacket pocket, and when he pulled the cap from the needle, it looked huge!

"I have something to calm your nerves," he informed, holding the syringe and the huge needle in front of her and ready to deliver. "You look like you could use a sedative. This is going to hurt, so be very still and take your medicine like a good girl."

Frantically shaking her head, she whimpered, "I don't want a shot!"

He leaned his head and the mask seemed to snarl, showing very long, very sharp teeth that were clear like glass and appeared to be filled with some horrible liquid. "Now now, little girl. Your mommy will be here shortly and you want her to know that you were brave and took your medicine like a good girl. Hold your arm out."

Pressing her arms to the wall behind her, she shook her head again and screamed, "Stay away from me!" Charging him crossed her mind but she was terrified of being stabbed by that needle, terrified more of what was in the syringe.

He slowly aimed at her with the needle, making sure she could see what he was doing with it. "Your mother says you need this," he informed coldly. "Don't run away or your parents will have to bring you right back here, they'll be very angry about having to do that, and then it will hurt much worse."

Wide eyed, Elissa began to slide along the wall to elude him, and she shook her head and begged, "Please don't. Please."

His voice became more demonic as he shouted, "Be still you little brat!"

Finally close enough, he thrust the syringe and the needle jabbed into her upper arm, and panic exploded from her!

Elissa screamed and knocked his hand away and she charged past him, running for the first door she found. Pulling it open, she darted out, only to find herself cornered in another small office. A breath shrieked into her. Shallow breaths did the same as she frantically looked around her. She did not see an abandoned room that was littered with papers and packing material and an old desk that was broken and covered with boxes and old papers. What she saw was something from months ago. She found herself standing in Red Panzer's office in that warehouse. She saw his big oak desk, the old phone on it, the papers and the elaborate wooden box. The portrait of Adolf Hitler was behind it, the comfortable chairs to her right and the vending machine beyond it.

"It can't be," she breathed. Wheeling around, she screamed as she saw Red Panzer standing in the doorway and blocking the only way out. She backed away and found herself crying as he advanced. There was nowhere to go. He was going to kill her!

That metal, skull with those blacked out lenses seemed dark and so horrifying. The old helmet was black and dull in the dim light. His long red coat simply added to his size and she knew the armor beneath it was impenetrable. She knew his strength far surpassed hers, that his skill in combat surpassed hers, that his weapons could fire bullets right through her gauntlets…

Slowly he raised that left arm and the barrels of the machine guns slowly emerged from that flap in his sleeve.

Breathing in quick, shrieking gasps, she tried to raise her hands to defend herself, but could not lift them. Looking down, she cried out as she saw them snared by vines that had grown out of the floor. She tried to rip them free, looking back up at Red Panzer as he stood in front of her, aiming at her.

A red glow overtook his eyes and the jaws of that skeleton mask he wore parted, revealing that it was not a mask, it was his head! Straightening his arm, he simply said in that deep, synthesized voice, "Die."

Panic took complete control of her and she dropped to the floor, balling herself up as she screamed and cried hysterically. "Please!" she begged in a scream. "Please, don't! Please!" All she could do after was cry, and her hysterics only grew worse as she did. Shaking and sweating, she was no longer a formidable Amazon warrior. She was just a terrified girl.

Someone grabbed her and she twisted and struggled away, not

wanting to look at her attacker as she scrambled to the corner of the room. She heard her name, but could not see through the cloud of fear that she was lost in.

"Elissa!" Wonder Woman shouted this time, grabbing her shoulders.

This made the girl panic further and she cried, "Leave me alone!" as she tried again to struggle free.

"Elissa, calm down!" Wonder Woman ordered. "Calm down, Little One! Elissa, look at me!"

Her struggles ceased, but Elissa kept her eyes shut tightly and her face turned away as she whimpered, "No."

"It's all right," Diana assured, raising a hand to the girl's cheek. "Elissa, it's all right. Just relax. Nobody is going to hurt you."

Her eyes flashing open, Elissa shrank away and shook her head, her wide eyes locked on her mother as she shouted, "You sent them! He said you told them to do this to me! Why, Mommy, why?"

"Little One, I didn't tell anyone to hurt you. There isn't anyone else here."

"Liar!" the girl accused. Looking behind her mother, she began to cry again, to shake her head again, and she shrank away, pushing herself against the wall as she cried, "Please leave me alone! Go away!"

Batman crouched down beside Wonder Woman and ordered, "Hold her still."

Elissa sprang to her feet and yelled, "No more!" As she tried to dart around them and escape, her mother grabbed her arm and stopped her. Panic surged forth again and she fought to free herself as Wonder Woman grappled to restrain her, and finally Elissa lashed out, striking Diana as hard as she could in the face.

Stunned by the attack, Wonder Woman did not allow surprise to keep her entranced and she seized the girl's other arm, and somewhat brutally she pulled the girl to her and wrapped her powerful arms around her. Crushing Elissa's little body to her own, she held her as tightly as she could.

With her arms pinned between her and her mother, Elissa screamed in terror and fought with all her strength and vigor to escape, twisting and pushing back against her mother as best she could. Something cold was put against her neck, there was a pop and a brief shot of pain and she cried out against it, then strength drained from her. Her eyelids grew very heavy very quickly and a deep sleep washed through her. She fought it as best she could and with every part of her, but soon her head rolled back, her eyes closed, and in seconds her body was limp and held up only by her mother's powerful arms.

Wonder Woman turned wide eyes to Batman.

He put the hypo gun away and explained, "It's a fast acting sedative. She'll be out for a few hours. In the meantime, get her back to the Batcave and onto the examination table before she wakes up. I'll finish up here."

Diana reached down and took the girl behind the knees, gently cradling her limp form as she looked down at her sleeping face with fear in her eyes. "What happened to her?"

"I have my suspicions," he reported, "but I'll need to draw some blood to be sure."

"How long until you know?" she demanded.

"It shouldn't be too long once I have a sample." He turned and strode out of the office, saying as he left, "I'll see you there."

CHAPTER 3

Elissa moaned softly and rocked her head to the left, then the right, and her eyes opened to thin slits. She blinked and struggled to bring the world around her into focus. Drawing a deep breath, she tried to make sense of where she was, how she got there...

Anxiety surged up again and quickly she felt herself near panic as she looked around her. When she tried to sit up, a strap around her chest stopped her. Trying to raise her hands to remove it revealed that she was cuffed to the bed she lay on. Looking down at herself, she saw that she was only covered with a white sheet and white wool blanket, and over these were leather restraints over her legs and hips and she could feel her ankles cuffed and strapped down beneath the sheet. Her eyes darted about. This looked like the Batcave, and yet it did not. Drawing a deep breath, she tried to calm herself and reason out what had happen, where she was.

With another deep breath forced into her, she scanned where she was, and finally, desperately called, "Mom?"

What answered was only a faint echo.

Her eyes swept the cave around her. There was the huge computer complex across the cavern, glass display cases filled with various items... They were familiar, and yet they looked so different.

"Mom!" she called again with a fearful voice.

The clop of boots approached from the other side and she turned her head to see. No one was approaching and the clopping stopped. Looking quickly to the other side, she gasped as she saw Batman standing right at her bedside. Looking the other way, she saw her mother standing across from him. Both of them were staring down at her and she looked back and forth at them. These few seconds should have given her some comfort, but they were horrifying.

Glancing at each other, Batman and Wonder Woman turned and walked away, and as Elissa looked on with wide, horrified eyes, they both disappeared into the darkness.

She breathed in shallow gasps, looking one way and then the

other. "Mom!" she called. Looking the other way, she shouted, "Daddy! Where did you go?" Looking back toward where her mother had disappeared, her breath froze inside her as her eyes were filled with Red Panzer.

He stared down at her from behind those blacked out lenses, said nothing, did not move.

Again she could not catch her breath as she stared back at him, and slowly she shook her head.

Red Panzer raised his head slightly and ordered in that thick German accent, "Begin the procedure."

Looking to the other side, she whimpered as she saw three people on that side, all in surgical garb, and one holding some kind of horrifying, metal tool that was covered by a long plastic cap. Images were becoming blurry and she was sure she was going to spill fearful tears from her eyes, though none came out.

One of the people in the surgical garb reached to the bound girl, grasping the sheet and pulling a flap back to expose the bare skin of her belly.

"What are you going to do to me?" the girl whimpered desperately. When she saw the plastic cap removed from the instrument to reveal a huge needle that was as big as a drinking straw, she shrieked, then looked to Red Panzer and begged, "Please don't do this to me. Please!"

He seemed to ignore her and ordered, "Proceed. Insert the instrument."

"No!" Elissa gasped as she watched the huge, chrome colored needle as it was placed against her skin, and once more she begged, "Please don't! Please!"

The man behind the mask would not even look at her and kept his eyes on what he was doing as he changed the angle of the huge needle.

Another quick breath shrieked into her, and as the needle was brutally shoved into her, she sat up and screamed, doubling over as she grasped her belly. She could not feel the needle in her, but she had seen it pushed into her, knew it was still there. Horror was in control of her as she drew another breath and it screamed all the way out of her, then another.

The door to her bedroom burst open and Diana charged in, right to the bed, and she sat down beside the girl and enveloped her in her arms. She was wearing a soft white button-up blouse with full sleeves and a long red skirt. She wore no shoes nor was Wonder Woman's tiara in place.

As she tightly pulled the girl to her, she rocked her back and forth and laid her cheek on top of the girl's head as she soothed, "Shh. It's okay now."

"Get it out of me!" Elissa screamed as she clawed at her belly. "Get it out!"

Pulling back slightly, Diana grabbed the girl's wrists and pulled them away from her, assuring, "There is nothing in you, Little One. It was a bad dream. You are okay. Just calm yourself."

Elissa followed her mother's voice through the fog of panic and terror and finally opened her eyes, looking first down at her belly to see that she was wearing the long tee shirt she always slept in. Slowly, she turned her gaze to her mother, her own eyes still wide with fear, but her breathing slowed from quick gasps to deep, calming breaths. Seeing Diana, she relaxed, and finally looked around her to see that she was in her bedroom in the mansion.

Diana stroked her hair and asked, "You okay now?"

Staring blankly ahead, Elissa absently nodded.

"I think the worst of it is over," Diana assured. "Come on. Let's get up and get dressed. Are you hungry?"

Finally looking to her mother, Elissa nodded again.

Diana gave her daughter a reassuring smile. "I thought you might be, Little One." She stood and took the girl's hands, pulling her gently from the bed. "You've been asleep for almost two days. That's a long nap even for you."

Elissa swung her feet to the floor and found her whole body a little stiff as she stood. "Two days? Seriously?"

Reaching to the nightstand, Diana turned the lamp on and looked back to her daughter. "I'm afraid so. We were awfully worried about you that first day. You slept very restlessly and I could tell you were having bad dreams, but it's over now. In fact, Alfred's been waiting for you to wake up. He's made something special for you."

Her eyes widening, Elissa winced as she saw the swelling around her mother's eye. Broken memories flashed back into her, and one overshadowed them all, the memory that she had struck her mother in a blind, terrified panic. Slowly reaching to her mother's face, tears filled her eyes as she breathed, "Oh, Mother. I'm so sorry. Oh, Hera, what did I do?"

Diana responded with another smile and pinched her daughter's nose. "Don't flatter yourself, Junior. I got that fighting Bane."

"But I..." Elissa stammered. "I hit you. Mommy, I'm so sorry." She threw her arms around the Amazon Princess, burying her face in her mother's neck. "I'm sorry. I'm so sorry. I didn't mean to."

Diana slipped her arms around the girl and soothed, "Shh, it's okay. I know you didn't. I'm not angry with you, Elissa."

Still, Elissa wept and sobbed, "I promise I'll never hit you again. I promise! I'm sorry."

Stroking the girl's long hair, Diana assured, "It's okay, Little One. It's okay. I know it was not you acting with a clear mind. Just settle down. It's okay."

A moment passed before Elissa finally pulled away, keeping her eyes down as she tried to collect herself.

Diana kissed the girl's forehead and ordered, "Get yourself dressed and come downstairs."

Elissa nodded, then raised her eyes as her mother turned to leave, asking as Diana reached the door, "He got away, didn't he?"

Pausing at the door, Diana looked over her shoulder and nodded. "He did this time, Junior. We'll get him the next."

Hearing this broke the girl's heart a little more.

The one small table in the kitchen already had a chair pulled out and Elissa seemed to know it was for her. She had put on a white tee shirt with the words *Girl Power* and a folded pink ribbon beneath them. She also wore black running shorts with pink stripes. Her hair was not worn in the long ponytail she had come to wear it in most of the time, but it was down and unrestrained, and some of it was unruly at the sides and a few locks hung in her face. She sat cross legged in the chair and folded her arms on the table in front of her, laying her chin on her arms as she stared forward at nothing.

Alfred had gone unnoticed as he turned from the stove, watching as the girl had perched herself on the chair and laid her head down. He had a bowl in his hand and a little smile on his mouth and he slowly strode to her, gently laying the bowl beside her.

Her eyes shifted to it and she noticed that it had the handle of a spoon already sticking out of it and it smelled of cream and oranges. Lifting her brow, she looked up at him.

"It is something I concocted myself," he told her, "something I thought you might enjoy."

"I guess you know then, huh?" she asked grimly.

He reluctantly nodded. "I do, Miss Elissa, I do."

She turned her eyes down, feeling even more ashamed and embarrassed.

"Not to worry, Miss," he assured. "It happens to the best of heroes." He turned back to the counter and picked up a towel. "It has happened to your father a time or two. He always managed to bounce back quickly." Looking over his shoulder, he smiled. "I see that quality in you."

She forced a smile back and looked back to the bowl. Finally raising her head, she picked up the spoon and stirred the orange cream stuff in the bowl for a moment before slipping some between her lips. "This is really good," she observed.

"Thank you," he said as he turned toward the refrigerator. "I was hoping you would enjoy it."

Taking another bite, she nodded. "It's really good. Wow, it even changes flavors!" Looking down into her bowl, she saw it begin to slowly swirl on its own and she mumbled, "Ah, crud," as she slowly turned her eyes to Alfred.

He spun around, wearing Scarecrow's mask and he still had that syringe in his hand as he batted the table aside and informed, "You never got your injection, little girl!"

She lowered her feet to the floor and tried to spring up, and found herself strapped to her chair, and her chair secured to the floor. With all of her strength, she tried to break the straps, but they would not yield and she felt more wind around her ankles and bind them securely to the legs of the chair.

Scarecrow moved in on her with slow and terrifyingly fluid motions, leaning his head as he told her, "Not in the arm this time. We go right for the neck!"

She shrieked as he grabbed her hair and wrenched her head over, positioning the needle right on the side of her neck, and she watched him with wide eyes as he laughed and prepared to push it into her.

Batman slammed into him from the right, knocking him to the floor of the kitchen and making his stand between him and the girl. Looking back at her, he asked, "Are you all right?"

She nodded, then looked across the kitchen as the door opened and she screamed, "Watch out!" as Bane burst through the door.

Elissa screamed as her wide eyes were filled with a bright light that hung above her. She tried to sit up and quickly discovered that she had been restrained by a black leather strap across her chest, another around her midriff that held her wrists down and two more holding her legs down. In a panic, she struggled against them and tried to rise up off of the table again.

Grasping her shoulder, Batman pushed her back down to the examination table and ordered, "Lie still, Angel."

She found herself catching her breath much easier this time as she stared back at him. Looking to the other side, she saw her mother approaching and drew a long breath as she realized she was under the mansion, in the Batcave.

Finding her mother's eyes, she grasped her hand and asked, "Was I really out for two days?"

Diana exchanged looks with Batman, then shook her head and looked back down to the girl and shook her head as she began to unbuckle the restraints. "No, it's only been about six hours."

Elissa nodded and looked back to Batman. When her wrists were freed, she reached to her head, feeling for her tiara and not finding it there, then she looked down at herself to see she was still dressed as Golden Angel and her mother was removing the last of the restraints. Slowly laying her head back down, she closed her eyes and drew one more, deep, calming breath, keeping them closed as she asked, "Please tell me we got that guy."

"What guy?" Batman demanded.

She looked to him with eyes that reflected defeat and shame. "It was Doctor Shipley, but that's not his real name. He admitted that his real name is Jonathan Crane."

Batman's eyes narrowed and he growled, "Scarecrow."

She nodded. "That's what he said people call him." She looked away from him. "He sprayed some kind of smelly gas at me. It burned my eyes and stuff and I guess it made me freak out a little."

Squeezing her hand, Diana corrected, "You freaked out a lot,

Junior. You were thrashing about so badly we feared you would injure yourself."

Golden Angel vented a long breath through her mouth and nodded. "Then strapping me down was actually a good idea."

"Yes it was, Little One. I'm sorry to frighten you."

"It's okay, Mom." Her apologetic eyes slid to the Amazon Princess and she offered, "Sorry I hit you."

Diana smiled. "We're good, Junior. I know you weren't lashing out with all of your wits about you."

"I've given you an antidote for the gas," Batman informed. "It should all be out of your system now." He shot an unpleasant look at Diana, then turned and walked away. "I'm going to get some rest. You two had better do the same. I'll debrief you later, Angel."

Elissa looked up at her mother and grimly observed, "He seems upset."

Watching after the Dark Knight as he disappeared behind the sliding door to the elevator back up to the mansion, Diana's lips tightened and she nodded.

WW

Elissa bounded down the stairs wearing a red tee shirt with the words *Girl Power* in big pink letters across the front and a folded pink ribbon beneath them. The shirt fit her very tightly and showed off her shape almost like a second skin. Her shorts were black with pink stripes. With her long black hair restrained in its usual pony tail, she was barefoot and was always happy to be so, especially when going to the beach as she and her mother planned.

Diana met her at the bottom of the stairs, wearing a red tank top and solid black shorts beneath. She was also barefoot and waited at the bottom of the stairs with her arms folded and her piercing blue eyes following her daughter down to the bottom. Her hair was in a long pony tail, much like Elissa's, and she appeared ready for the day ahead of them.

Their gauntlets were concealed, disguised as cuff bracelets, silver around Diana's wrists and gold around Elissa's. They wore no other jewelry, knowing that they would not need it.

Finally reaching the bottom, Elissa stopped in front of her mother and looked up at her with a little smile as she offered, "Sorry. Couldn't decide on a shirt."

Diana raised her brow and asked, "Bra?"

The girl smiled a little broader and nodded. "Remembered this time. Everybody's supported and happy."

"Good," Diana commended. "Let's go while the sun's still high."

A half hour later found them running side by side along the beach south of the manor. Diana's strides were much longer and Elissa could never match them as she took three steps for every two that Diana took. They would run for miles like this and barely become winded by it.

"Public beach ahead," Elissa informed, then she smiled. "And there are always cute boys out there."

Diana's eyes slid to the girl and narrowed. "Remember our talk?"

Elissa's smile broadened. "I remember. No boys until I'm fifty years old."

With a little smile of her own, Diana confirmed, "That's right."

They did not keep track of how far they ran nor how long they were gone. They got long stares and wide eyed looks from every man and boy they passed, and some of the women. They talked back and forth about trivial matters, reminisced about Elissa's childhood, her experiences posing as Wonder Woman the year before, what they would like to have for dinner and little things like that. Ignoring the world around them, they simply enjoyed some time together, and despite the stresses of the past few days as well as everything else on her mind, Diana found her smile, managed to laugh with her daughter, and somehow forgot she was much more than the mother of an amazing teenage girl.

Near the outskirts of Gotham City, the pop of gunfire drew their attention and they stopped, looking up toward the street that was on the other side of tall hotels and restaurants. Both women had Amazon hearing that could pinpoint very distant sounds and they could both make out an approaching car chase and gunfire. Looking to each other, they smiled. Elissa backed away and both women extended their arms and spun around. Both were enveloped in a bright flash of light and in seconds they stopped, setting their hands on their hips as Wonder Woman and Golden Angel.

Wonder Woman gave the girl a confident look and raised an eyebrow. "Let's go to work, Golden Angel."

With a big smile, Golden Angel assured, "I got your back,

Wonder Woman."

The chase involved a stolen armored truck and three police cars pursuing it through narrow, winding streets that catered to beachside condos, tourist shops, restaurants and the occasional towering hotel. Cars and pedestrians darted out of the way as the rampaging armored truck sped toward them. One of the back doors was open and two men shot at the police cars chasing them, holding no regard for the safety of the people all around. They all wore ski masks and thin green sweat shirts, long black trousers and black boots. Five of them were in the van, including the driver and one who fired out of the passenger side window, and all were armed with semi-automatic pistols.

The truck had to slow down to take a hard turn to the left, and here is where Wonder Woman was waiting for it. Seeing her, the driver instinctively hit the brakes, and as tires slid on the road, the man in the passenger's seat barked, "What are you doing? Run her over!"

Diana's eyes narrowed as the engine roared and the truck began to accelerate toward her again, but she did not yield. When it was only about twenty feet away, she lowered her shoulder and met it head-on, grasping the bumper with one hand and pushing back against the hood with the other. She slid backward, her boots smoking, and with a mighty yell she picked up the front of the heavy armored truck and twisted hard, flipping it over.

It rolled onto its roof and slid sideways for twenty more feet before it stopped.

One of the men fell out of the open back door and staggered to his feet, his gun still in his hand as he shook his head and tried to get his bearings. Looking ahead of him, he froze as he saw Golden Angel standing only about ten feet away, her hands on her hips and a confident little smile on her mouth. He raised his gun and fired with a straight aim.

Almost casually, Golden Angel swept her arms and knocked away bullet after bullet, and as she heard the gun make an empty click, she reached behind her and withdrew a bat-arang, hurling it at him with one fluid motion.

It hit his gun hard enough to knock it from his grip and he grasped his hand and backed away a step, looking up to see her already upon him.

She grabbed his shirt with both hands, pulling him brutally toward her and head butting him as hard as she could, knocking him out cold, then she tossed him aside and set herself to receive the next. Predictably, the next man shot at her as well and she deflected each round with ease, just waiting for his gun to go silent. When it did, she charged, this time kicking him in the chest and knocking him backward into the third man who had just emerged from the back of the overturned truck. As they fell back inside, she darted in after them.

Wonder Woman strode around to the back and folded her arms as she heard the sounds of the struggle within. The one closed door burst open as one of the men hit it hard back-first. She watched him fall unconscious to the ground, then turned her eyes back to the truck and raised her brow as the second flew out head first, screaming until he hit the ground flat on his belly. He moaned and pulled his arms to him, struggling to get his wits about him and push himself back up, but Golden Angel emerged from the back of the truck and strode to him, reaching to her belt to retrieve her handcuffs. She dropped down and straddled his lower back, pulling his arms behind him as she cuffed them one by one, then she turned a look to her mother that Diana did not expect.

Motioning back to the truck with her head, she reported, "It's empty."

Wonder Woman's eyes narrowed and she looked to the overturned truck, striding that way. Looking inside, she found it just as Golden Angel had said: empty.

Golden Angel took her side and folded her arms. "This doesn't make sense. Why go to so much trouble to steal an empty truck?"

Walking around to the side of the truck, Wonder Woman shook her head and countered, "Not all things are as they appear, Junior. This is probably just one phase of a much bigger plan they have." As the police swarmed to them, she ordered, "Keep everyone clear of the other side of this thing. I'm going to turn it back over." She started to reach down to the roof of the overturned truck, then she hesitated and turned her eyes to her daughter. A smile found her lips as she backed away and extended her hand to the truck, offering, "Think you can?"

Elissa found a little smile of her own as she waved her mother aside and said, "Step aside, Wonder. I got this one." She reached down and wedged her fingers under the roof of the truck, took several deep, quick breaths, then strained with all her might to lift it. Grudgingly, the truck creaked and that side of it began to rise from the ground, and as it rose higher, the girl yelled and poured everything she had into the task.

As onlookers watched in amazement, a small, five foot six Amazon girl lifted the heavy armored truck from its roof, and everyone applauded as it crashed onto its side.

Glancing around, Golden Angel smiled and waved to the gathering people and police who watched.

Wonder Woman folded her arms and said, "Okay, halfway there."

A little out of breath, Golden Angel scoffed, "No problem," as she reached down to grasp the truck again.

Getting it to its wheels was far more of a challenge than rolling it to its side had been, but with everything she had, Golden Angel righted the heavy truck and backed away as it bounced a little on its tires and suspension, and the crowd around them applauded and cheered anew.

With deep breaths, Elissa bent over and grasped her legs just above the knees. The strain had nearly exhausted her, but she smiled nonetheless, and when she looked to her mother, she saw her applauding, too, and smiling a proud smile.

After talking to the police, they found a private area to change back into their street clothes, then they made their way back to the beach to finish their run. Many people had seen them change before and waved to them, and they graciously waved back.

"How can you ever get tired of this?" Elissa asked with a certain girlish enthusiasm. "This is great!"

"Believe me," Diana warned, "when it comes time to have a normal life or a day of shopping, a date or anything like that, you'll wish nobody recognized you."

"I guess," the girl sighed. "So, when can I join the Justice League? I think I'm ready."

Diana simply glanced at her and did not answer.

"Come on, Mom!" Elissa complained. "There are people there with absolutely no Amazon abilities or strength or anything—"

"They all bring a wealth of drive and experience with them," Diana interrupted. "I'm sorry, but you just aren't ready."

Elissa stopped and dropped her arms to her sides as she watched her mother stop a few steps beyond her and turn around. "I am to ready! Look what we did back there!"

Approaching the girl, Diana grasped the sides of Elissa's neck and lowered her forehead to her daughter's reminding, "Look what Scarecrow did to you."

Tight lipped, Elissa turned her eyes down.

"I don't want to see you run blindly into anything unprepared and…" Diana vented a deep breath. "Little One, you simply aren't ready for all that you would have to face in the League. I am not saying that you can't become a member of the Justice League, just not now. You have to be patient, you have to learn more and you have to work really, really hard to prepare yourself."

"I am working hard," Elissa pouted, staring down as she folded her arms.

"I know you are," Diana assured. "I've seen more drive and focus in you in recent months than I've ever seen in you, but you still have much to learn and much training ahead of you before you are ready. Allow yourself that before you dive in unprepared again. All of us will always be here to teach you whatever you need to know."

Huffing a breath, Elissa grumbled, "So now I'm just your sidekick?"

Diana smiled and kissed the girl's forehead. "I don't have a sidekick, Junior."

Watching her mother turn and walk down the beach, Elissa followed, dropping her arms to her sides as she barked, "Then what am I? I'm not a sidekick, I'm not a hero…"

"You are a remarkable young woman who is doing an amazing job at helping people. You are making a huge difference to everyone you meet. And yes, Junior, you are very much a hero."

Catching up and taking her mother's side, the girl looked up to her with lost eyes.

Diana smiled at her. "Look at the lives you've touched. Look at everyone who has had their lives changed just by meeting you."

"I was Wonder Woman then," Elissa pointed out, turning her eyes down. "Of course everyone looked up to me. I was you. Now I'm just Golden Angel, and Golden Angel's a nobody."

This time it was Diana who stopped, and she folded her arms as she watched her daughter stop a few strides beyond.

For a moment, only the sound of the crashing surf and the seagulls surrounded them. Elissa stared at the sand before her, feeling her mother's eyes on her, but unable to turn and look at her.

"A nobody?" Diana questioned.

"I'm just your sidekick, Mom," Elissa complained, "and I'm Daddy's sidekick, and Superman's sidekick. I went from being a hero to just a sidekick. Do you know what that feels like? It's like I was demoted or something. Do you really think anyone's ever going to take me seriously now? A lot of people figured out that I wasn't really Wonder Woman and now... Now I'm just a fake to everyone, just some poser who pretended to be you and... and failed. I'm a nobody."

"Are you really doing this for fame and glory?" Diana asked, her harsh words sounding more like those of Wonder Woman than Elissa's mother. "Is that all you've become, someone who seeks the spotlight and the attention of the masses you want to love you?"

Closing her eyes, Elissa bowed her head and drew another really deep breath, venting it slowly from her nose. The words hurt. More than that, they rang true, and that made them hurt even more. Slowly, she turned and forced herself to look to her mother, who stood a few feet away with her hands resting on her hips. Her mother was a real hero, someone who did not seek accolades. She did not seek the admiration and attention of the public and for the most part she avoided it.

As Diana strode to her, Elissa's brow arched and she admitted, "I kind of sound like a little brat, don't I?"

Diana raised her brow and nodded.

"I'm sorry, Mom," Elissa offered as the wind blew a lock of hair across her face. "I know you raised me better than that."

With an unexpected smile, Diana combed the hair from her daughter's face with her fingers and ordered, "Quit taking my lines, Junior."

Elissa responded with a strained smile of her own. "So, could you use a sidekick?"

Taking the girl under her arm, Diana strode with her down the beach and admitted, "I realize I'm your mother, but I'm afraid there's a long line of heroes looking to have Golden Angel as their sidekick."

"Really? Who the heck would want me as a sidekick?"

"You made a name for yourself, Junior, and everyone knows it. Everyone knows that you're a girl who can be counted on. Almost everyone I know wants to work with you, but to be honest, I don't think you even need to be a sidekick. I think you stand on your own very well."

Elissa wrapped her arms around her mother and hugged her tightly, declaring with a big smile, "Best mom ever."

WW

They returned to the mansion in high spirits and Elissa seemed to have forgotten about her failure with Scarecrow. Clinging to her mother's arm as they entered, she laughed and declared, "You have got to be kidding! And she knew nothing about it?"

"I didn't keep many secrets from your grandmother," Diana admitted, "but some things are much better left unsaid."

"That is just totally wicked," the girl said with a laugh.

"Just don't get any ideas," Diana warned. "I'm way ahead of you on that."

"I believe you, Mom. Hey! Maybe we can, like, go and do a Justice League mission or something. It would be all kinds of fun!"

With a little smile, Diana confirmed, "Sure, I'd like that. But not until I get you clearance, understand?"

"Yes, Mom."

"And I think your father would like some time with you as well. Do you think you can go out with him without getting gassed again?"

Elissa rolled her eyes and grumbled, "I'll try."

They got into the main living room and Diana raised her chin as she saw Alfred approaching. "Is Bruce still here?" she asked.

"Down in the cave," Alfred replied. He turned his attention to Elissa and offered a smile. "I believe you wanted pizza with everything, right?"

Her eyes lit up and she raised her brow, clasping her hands together as she asked, "Did you order one?"

"Even better," he said as he reached her. "I made two, myself."

She squealed and threw her arms around his neck, hugging him tightly as she offered, "Thank you! Thank you! Thank you!" with her usual girlish enthusiasm.

Diana grasped her shoulder and informed, "I'm going to go find your father. Go ahead and grab a bite and get some rest. I'll catch up."

"Okay, Mom," she assured as she pulled away from Alfred and took his hand, leading him back toward the kitchen. "I've seriously got to try this!"

As they entered the kitchen, he patted her hand and assured, "I can make more if you..."

They both looked ahead and Alfred raised his chin.

A well dressed young man was sitting at the small table in the kitchen and half turned as they entered, resting his elbow on the back of the chair he sat in. Dark blue eyes found them quickly and he smiled. His black hair was well groomed and he wore a black dress shirt and tan trousers.

On the table in front of him was one of the pizzas Alfred had made, and one slice was already gone from it.

"Master Dick," Alfred declared. "It is good to see you home!"

"Just blowing through," he informed, his eyes leaving Elissa for only a scant second. He finally stood and turned toward them, folding his arms as he looked her up and down. He was very tall, very broad shouldered and square jawed, a very handsome young man who appeared to be in his mid twenties. "And who is this?"

Stepping away from her, Alfred introduced, "This is Miss Elissa, a special guest of Master Bruce." Looking to the handsome young man, he continued, "Miss Elissa, this would be Dick Grayson."

Elissa's eyes widened and she breathed, "Nightwing!"

Dick nodded in slight motions and confirmed, "That's me. And you must be Golden Angel."

She nodded, still staring at his piercing eyes.

He finally approached and extended his hand. "Well it's good to finally meet you. I've heard a lot about you over the last few months."

She took his hand and smiled. "I've heard all about you. You were Robin years ago and you were at Batman's side for a long time! That must have been so awesome!"

"It had its moments," he confirmed. Half turning, he extended his hand to the table. "Alfred's made some good pizza and I don't think we should let it go to waste."

They approached the table and he pulled a chair out for her. She turned and smiled at him before she sat down and he pushed her closer to the table before taking his own seat.

Alfred approached the counter across the kitchen and informed, "I'll just get started on another."

"Thanks, Alfred," Dick offered. Pulling another slice from the pizza in front of them, he slid it onto a napkin and offered it to the girl, and when she took it, he took a slice for himself and asked, "So how are you liking Wayne Manor?"

She had taken a bite already and chewed back some of what she had before answering with a nearly full mouth. "It's beautiful here, but kind of cold at night. This is a really big house, too."

He smiled. "Have you seen the basement?"

Elissa's eyes slid to him and she nodded, then she took another bite of her pizza.

Between the two of them, they managed to consume all three of the pizzas that Alfred made for them. Getting acquainted was very easy. Dick was very charming and very easy to talk to and they found themselves laughing with each other even after the pizza was gone. At some point they retired to the sitting area where Dick took a deep cushioned recliner and Elissa perched on one end of a love seat closest to him, pulling her feet under her as she always did. The two talked for some time, and finally Dick looked down at his watch and raised his brow.

"Well, darn," he said absently. "I hate to cut this short, but there's somewhere I have to be soon."

She nodded. "No problem. It looks like I'll be around for a while so I'll be easy to find."

He stood. "Wish I could look you up again, but I'll be leaving after tonight. Big operation going on that we're trying to get shut down."

Elissa slid from the love seat to stand in front of him, folding her arms as she looked up at him with a lean of her head. "Big operation? Could you use a hand?"

Looking away, Dick shrugged and shook his head. "Really I'm just looking into something here in Gotham. If I'm able to disrupt something and maybe take down one of the local bosses then that could compromise what they're doing in Chicago." His eyes shifted back to her. "Besides, I'm sure Bruce has plans for you already."

"We could go ask," she pressed.

Dick raised his brow and shrugged again. "Well, if you're that determined, I guess I wouldn't mind some company. It might be several hours of boredom, though."

She folded her hands behind her, absently swinging her shoulders back and forth as she said, "Oh, it won't be a problem. I've been told I need to learn patience and stuff and this sounds like a good time to start."

He smiled and shook his head. "You're just too cute to say no to."

Moments later saw them emerge into the Batcave with Dick embracing the idea of having her at his side for the night.

"Just remember," he warned, "*you're* the sidekick tonight."

Elissa laughed and bumped him with her shoulder. "Okay, I get it, Mister Nightwing. I get it!"

They paused as they heard voices.

In the distance, near where the Batmobile sat awaiting its next mission, they could see Batman and Wonder Woman facing off in what looked like a heated argument. They could not make out what was said, but when Diana poked him in the chest, Elissa was sure she heard her name.

This was not something either of them was accustomed to seeing, but as Dick looked down at Elissa, he saw the distress in her eyes, the arching of her brow and how her lips slowly parted. She began to tug on one finger and ever so slowly she drew her shoulders up. Dick knew what was happening and turned his attention back to the fighting heroes, then he took Elissa under his arm and bade, "Come on. Let's give them some space."

WW

Hours later, the sun had set and Nightwing and Golden Angel were on a rooftop that overlooked a popular restaurant, one that was very high class and catered largely to those of less than scrupulous reputation, those who ran Gotham's underworld. Peering over the two foot high wall that surrounded the rooftop, Nightwing stared through his binoculars, waiting for his target to arrive. Golden

Angel sat beside him with her back to the wall, her legs drawn to her, her arms wrapped around them and her chin resting on her knees. She stared blankly forward, obviously still upset about seeing her parents at odds and openly fighting. She had sensed tension, but she did not know until that moment that it had escalated so.

Pulling his eyes away from his binoculars, Nightwing looked to the girl and asked, "You okay, kid?"

She simply shrugged and did not even look his way.

"They'll work it out," he assured. "They're two of the most level headed people I know."

"I guess," she replied softly.

He turned his attention back to the restaurant, looking through his binoculars again. "It's just how it works out sometimes. They just have to get it out of their systems and then they'll be cool with each other again."

She lowered her eyes and nodded.

"I could really use you in the game right about now," he informed. "I think that's Falcone's limo coming."

Elissa finally perked up a little and turned to look over the wall, squinting slightly as she peered through the darkness. A new found ability was one that enabled her to see small details at a great distance and her eyes strained lightly as she brought distant images in very close. "That him in the gray hat?" she asked.

"No," Nightwing replied, "he's in a really dark blue hat. That's him getting out now, kind of a big guy with the gray sideburns."

"I see him," she confirmed, then she glanced at Nightwing. "Um, so we just watch him have dinner?"

"We need to get closer," he answered. "If I can record him talking about the Chicago operation then we've got him."

"Will that hold up in court?"

He shrugged as he watched them enter the restaurant. "Usually does. We get a little more leeway than the police do on these matters. Sometimes they out-lawyer us, sometimes they know we have them and want to make a deal, and this guy knows he's been in Batman's sights for years. He'll want to deal."

Resting her arm on the wall, she laid her chin on her hand and looked back down to the activity across the street. "So you have a plan to get closer?"

"Fast and silent," was his reply. "I'm afraid this is where I go in alone."

She smiled and cut her eyes to him. "I bet I can get a whole lot closer than you."

Nightwing finally turned his full attention to her, his eyes narrowing.

WW

In only about ten minutes they were in a back room behind the stage in the restaurant where the performers got ready for their shows. This was the private dressing room of one of the star attractions, a young woman who was about five foot seven with bright red hair who called herself Star. She was very well made and had legs that she liked to show off to the crowd as she performed her act. It was not a huge room and had a dressing table with a well lit vanity, a couple of deep cushioned chairs and a very comfortable leather couch that Nightwing laid her on as she slumbered away.

Golden Angel sorted through her dresses and asked, "How long will she be out?"

"Three or four hours," he replied as he covered her with the white blanket that had been thrown over the back of the couch.

"Great," Elissa said as she pulled a sparkling red dress from the rack and held it against herself, looking down at it as she saw how it fit her. "Plenty of time." Looking around her, she saw a privacy screen set up in the corner and strode around behind it.

Turning toward her, Nightwing folded his arms and complained, "I still don't like this."

"You said it's a good idea," she countered from behind the screen, throwing her top half over it.

"If something happens..." he started, then he trailed off as her pants were laid over the screen as well.

"Risk is our business," she explained. "It seems like you would get that by now. I mean, you've worked with Batgirl, haven't you?"

He cleared his throat and turned away. "Batgirl isn't Batman's daughter. She also isn't Wonder Woman's daughter."

"And I happen to be both," she laughed. "Dang! This is a little too long!"

Dick turned back as she strode around the screen wearing the red dress she had picked out. It was rather low cut in the front, full

75

sleeved and had a slit all the way up one side that showed all of one leg as she walked, and part of her hip. She was also barefoot and the dress swept the ground as she moved.

She turned an unsure look to him as she held the skirt up from the floor and asked, "What do you think?"

He swallowed hard as he looked her up and down. The dress fit her very tightly, moving with her almost like a second skin and showing off her generous curves as it was supposed to. The low cut front also displayed her chest in a very seductive, very suggestive way. He had a difficult time looking away from her, but finally nodded and managed, "You look fine."

"What about the extra length?" she hissed.

"I would imagine that Miss Star's stilettos will take care of that," he replied, "or did you intend to go out there barefoot?"

She looked down at her feet, raising the skirt higher, then declared, "Oh, yeah!" Glancing about, she saw the shoe rack, with about two dozen different pairs on it, over by the make-up table and strode to it, the dress ruffling loudly as she walked. Picking out a red pair, she sat down in the chair and pulled the first one on, buckling it with care around her ankle.

Dick found himself watching her, then came to his senses and turned away. "Okay, Angel. What's the plan?"

She pulled the other shoe on and explained, "I'll work on getting their attention and give you a chance to get as close as you need to. You might pose as a waiter or something or just use that stealth thing you were talking about earlier."

"And then?" he prodded.

Elissa finished with the other shoe and looked up at him. "I thought I was the sidekick! Don't you have a master plan for all of this?"

He nodded and turned back to her. "Okay, I'll work on my part, but if we get discovered and any shooting starts—"

"Um," she interrupted, raising an arm and pulling the sleeve back to reveal her gauntlet. "Hello! Amazon, remember?"

"Oh, yeah. Right. Okay." He looked toward the door. "I'll go out first. Just tell them that Star is ill and you'll be entertaining them tonight."

She stood up and saluted him. "Yes, sir!"

"I'll be out there," he went on, "but I won't be visible. If it goes bad, just make for the back and I'll cover you."

Golden Angel smiled as she pulled her long hair out of the ponytail it was in and shook it out. "Yeah, like I need you to cover me."

WW

Peeking out onto the stage, which was not very big and had only a high stool and single microphone right in the middle, she remained focused on what she was really there to do, yet she felt herself becoming anxious about performing in front of an audience. At the back, near the door she looked out of, was what appeared to be a karaoke machine, what looked like it would provide the music when she sang, and she was a little disappointed. "No live band?" she grumbled. No matter. This would greatly simplify things.

With the red curtain still drawn, she took the opportunity to slip out onto the stage and examine the machine, turning it on to check the music selection, and she smiled as she saw one of her favorites, one that she used to sing for her mother and grandmother when she was a little girl, something left over from long ago. Making this selection and then another, she pushed what she assumed was the queue so that she could start her numbers as soon as the curtain opened.

The sound of the curtain pulling behind her and the sudden rush of light had her entire spine go rigid and her eyes widened. Very slowly, she looked over her shoulder.

The curtain had opened and there were more than two dozen people staring at her. Deep cushioned booths lined the walls and many small, round tables were carefully distributed about between them, and most had patrons occupying them. All were very well dressed in expensive suits and nearly all were men. Of these men, it was clear that many of them worked for those who operated outside of the law for the most part, though she thankfully did not recognize any of them and prayed that none recognized her. One thing that was abundantly clear was that everyone out there, including the wait staff, had stopped what they were doing when that curtain had unexpectedly opened. She also realized that she was still bent over the machine and that everyone's first impression of her was of her backside. It was time to just go to work.

As she looked back to the controls to start the music, she realized that what she thought was the queue was the curtain control, and she ground her teeth a little as she looked to find the queue.

Someone in a white shirt and with black trousers and a white vest rushed onto the stage from the side and stopped right beside her, hissing in her ear, "What are you doing? And where is Star?"

"She's not feeling well!" Elissa hissed back. "How do you work this thing?"

"You aren't supposed to start for twenty minutes. Just get on stage!" he ordered. Huffing a breath, he shook his head and grumbled, "Just once I'd like to be notified when there's a change."

"I'm sorry, okay?" she offered in a whisper. "I have a couple of songs in there to get me going."

"Go on," he insisted. "I have this."

She stood fully and turned, her eyes glancing about at the unforgiving faces she had to entertain. There was that nervous crawl in the pit of her stomach as she slowly strode to the microphone, and as she stumbled in shoes she was not used to wearing, that crawl got a little worse. Finally reaching the microphone, which was on a thin chrome stand and already adjusted to her height, she forced a smile and waggled her fingers at the people who watched her, greeting, "How's it going?"

No response.

Elissa swallowed hard and grasped the microphone stand as she looked back to the man who worked with the controls, and finally heard the music softly roll from the speakers hidden around her. Now was the time to relax and allow herself to become what they needed to think she was, and she closed her eyes and drew a deep breath as she allowed the music to sweep her into its current. As the music played, her body began to sway with it, and for a few seconds as she rolled her head back and danced in slight motions where she stood, she seemed lost in it.

Drawing the microphone close to her lips, she did not open her eyes as she started the first words of the first song, instead grasping the microphone almost tenderly in both hands as she began to sing.

"If you ask my beating heart to stop beating, it just can't start missin'..."

Her voice snared the attention of everyone in the room, and many exchanged looks beneath high brows and nods.

"If you ask me not to think about you, I'll never listen. I can't think of life without you, , but I know there's nothing I can't do, with you at my side..." She finally opened her eyes and unleashed the true power of her voice. "Along this path we walk, when all we do is talk and you're holding my hand so tightly in yours, I never feel afraid, I know I've got it made, when I'm with you my spirit soars..."

Surely, with their attention fixed on her so, Nightwing would be able to get in, get close, and do whatever it was he intended to, and she was determined to give him all the time he needed. Removing the microphone from its stand, she turned slightly and strode with slow, sultry strides toward the steps at the front of the stage, and she had the side with the slit in the skirt turned strategically toward her audience. As she neared the steps, a passing waiter who was dressed much as the man who had helped her with the music was held his hand to her, and she gently slipped her hand into his as she descended from the stage, one slow step at a time. Once down, she flashed the waiter a big smile before spinning around and continuing her song on a walk among the men at the tables. Seeing their reactions to her, she could not help the big smile that overpowered her mouth. Sure she had a job to do, but she found herself lost in the fun of the moment, and she also rather enjoyed the attention.

When her song ended, she had made her way back to the stage, sat on the edge and swung her legs up onto it, crossing them there as she propped herself on one arm and really powered out her last notes. She was not completely aware of the reasons the men watching her responded to her so, she only knew that they did, and she liked it.

This was not a crowd to applaud with much enthusiasm, but applaud they did, and many stood up to do so.

Elissa stood up on the edge of the stage with a giddy smile on her face as she looked about at them. When the second song started, she raised a brow and looked about at the booths, finally seeing the large man in the expensive blue suit who also watched her with great interest, and her eyes were fixed on him through the first words of her next number. "Let me entertain you. Let me, make you smile..."

Once again, she left the stage and wandered among the tables as she sang, very slowly and sharing her attention among the people who watched her, and for that fleeting moment it did not matter that they were underworld crime bosses.

Her eyes found Falcone once more before she turned back to the stage.

As the song ended, she climbed back onto the stage and made her way to the control panel. She definitely did not want songs played that she did not know!

The man who had helped her before met her there and she graciously allowed him to work the controls this time.

Giving her a sharp look, he informed, "You aren't getting a break early, by the way."

She smiled and assured, "Don't need one. I'm having a really good time out there."

"Just keep having a good time. I think they like what..." He trailed off and looked over his shoulder.

Elissa felt the man walk up behind her and turned to face him as he reached her, looking up at him as he leered down at her.

He was a big fellow, broad shouldered and rather thick all over. He was rather well groomed but still pretty rough looking, and a little snarl took his mouth as he informed in a deep voice, "Mister Falcone would like for you to join him."

She raised her brow and asked, "Seriously?" Looking to the man helping her, she stammered, "Um, do I go ahead and take that break now?"

"Yes!" He hissed.

Falcone's eyes were hard and scrutinizing as she approached, looking her up and down with no readable expression.

As she reached the table, one of the men sitting across from him stood and offered her his seat.

"Thank you," she offered with a smile as she sat down. Settling herself with care, she finally folded her hands in her lap and looked to the mob boss across from her, beaming him a big smile as she greeted, "Good evening, Mister Falcone."

He just nodded back and stared at her.

A little anxiety began to show its way through as her brow arched and she asked, "Am I doing okay out there? I mean, you like my singing, right?"

His voice was cruel and betrayed years of smoking as he replied, "You have a wonderful voice." He leaned his head slightly and asked, "What happened to Star?"

"She's not feeling good," Elissa answered straightly, looking him right in the eye. "She's asleep in the dressing room and might get to come out later if she's feeling better. Um, it's okay that I came out in her place, isn't it? I'm not trying to push her out of her job or anything, I just wanted..." She turned her eyes down to the table before her. "I just wanted my chance, is all."

Falcone lounged back slightly and looked to the waiter who stood nearby, then to Elissa and asked, "You want something to drink? Bring her something to drink."

She looked up to the waiter and sheepishly said, "Chianti, please. Thank you, Mister Falcone."

"You know who owns this club?" he asked suddenly.

Shaking her head, Elissa replied, "No sir."

"Huh," huffed from him. "You don't know the owner, but you come in here to sing anyway."

She drew her shoulders up slightly. "You don't have to pay me for tonight or anything. I really just wanted to come out and perform."

"Ya got good manners, kid. I like that."

"Thank you," she offered with a shy smile, her eyes still on the table before her. When a glass of wine was set before her, she glanced at the waiter and offered a smile and a nod. Taking the flute of the glass gingerly in her fingers, she stared down into it, and finally managed, "So, um, you like me?" This was starting to become more than a diversion for Nightwing. She found herself really getting into her role.

With a slow nod, Falcone confirmed, "You got good pipes, kid, good pipes. With the exception of one little detail I think you could make it in this business."

She turned her eyes to him and picked up her wine glass, raising it to her lips as she asked, "What detail is that?"

When he glanced at one of the men standing beside the booth, the man laid Golden Angel's trousers and top, neatly folded, on the table with her tiara on top of them. He set her boots down beside her on the floor and threw her utility belt over his shoulder.

Elissa took a dainty sip of her wine before setting her glass back down. With her eyes locked on her crime fighting garb, she drew a deep breath, raised her brow and absently said, "Well this sure is awkward."

"You really thought we wouldn't check out the dressing room?" he spat.

"Well," she stammered, "I was hoping you wouldn't." She finally shifted her gaze back to Falcone and asked, "So aside from this little problem, did you really like how I sing?"

Falcone looked to his henchmen and they all laughed, and Elissa smiled and took another sip of her wine.

"I got to hand it to ya, kid," he said with a complimentary tone, "ya got moxy."

She looked back to her wine and shrugged. "Well, you can imagine how much I actually get to do this. You know, sing for an audience and stuff. My other life usually gets in the way of what I'd rather be doing."

With a nod, Falcone admitted, "I can see where that would be very inconvenient. Now you want me to believe that you just happen to come in here, make Star take a nap, and all because you just want to sing for a club where my associates and me are going to be talking business. That's too much of a coincidence, baby doll. You know what I think? I think you are here to find something out."

Elissa picked up her wine glass and raised her brow. "Well, if you're talking about the thing in Chicago, I already know about that." As she drank, she noticed the men around her exchanging uneasy glances, and she set her glass back down and looked back to Falcone. "Oh, come on. Your so-called partner there has been bragging all over the place about this stupid little scheme and how you guys here in Gotham are going to take the fall for the whole thing. I mean, you can't be *that* naïve."

Falcone set his jaw and glared at her.

"I just came here to see if I could head off the inevitable bloodshed that is to follow when it goes bad for you," she went on. "Well, that and sing a little." Her eyes darted from one to the next and widened. "Wait a minute. You mean you didn't know, did you? I thought for sure you knew!" She shook her head and looked down to her wine. "Oh, boy. Not good."

"So what exactly are they saying in Chicago?" he demanded.

Elissa took another drink of her wine before she answered. "Um, well…" She vented a deep breath, then looked to him with uncertain eyes. "Yes, Mister Falcone, I was sent to watch you, but I'm supposed to report in when you and your gang load up in your cars to go get what's-his-name in Chicago. That's what I'm supposed to report." She looked down to her wine, holding gingerly with the fingertips of both hands. "I guess I managed to screw this one up, too."

Falcone looked up at one of his henchmen, the man who stood beside the girl with her belt over his shoulder. When the man's eyes narrowed and he nodded, the mob boss looked back to the girl and folded his hands on the table. "So you expect me to believe that Goldwin is planning a double cross?"

With a little shrug, Elissa simply advised, "I guess you'll believe what you want to."

Tapping his lips with his finger, Falcone stared at her for a long moment, watching her movements as she took another sip of her wine. He looked to his henchman again as the man handed him a bat-arang, and he looked it over for a few seconds.

"You can have that if you want it," she offered. "I know where to get more."

"Yeah," Falcone confirmed as he looked it over. "I'll bet you do. So you're workin' with the Bat, huh? Let me tell you somethin' about the Bat." He turned his eyes to her and found her looking attentively back at him. "The Bat had it in for my old man. In fact, everything was great before the Bat showed up. Now my old man's dead. You think Batman didn't have nothin' to do with that?"

"Batman doesn't kill people," she pointed out.

His expression hardened.

Elissa looked down to her wine glass, turning it slowly in a circle for long seconds before her attention strayed back to Falcone, and with a sympathetic tone she offered, "I'm truly sorry for your loss."

He looked away from her. "It was a long time ago, kid." He huffed a breath. "The old man never thought much of me, anyway. He ended up leaving most of the business to my brother. Always said I was too weak to run it."

Taking a sip of her wine, Elissa listened attentively.

His eyes shifted to her. "You know how to run a business like this? You come in under the radar. My old man never figured that out. He strong-armed or paid off everybody from cops to judges to get what he wanted, and that's when the Bat showed up."

Elissa nodded. "Batman came as a result of the corruption, so it sounds like your father may have been partly responsible for Batman becoming what he is."

Falcone nodded slightly.

She looked back to her wine and smiled an innocent smile. "I wasn't even born yet when a lot of that happened. These days I find myself standing in some pretty big shadows." Her eyes shifted to him and she added, "Just like you are."

"I make my own shadow," he informed with a little smile of his own.

Picking up her wine glass, she asked, "So what's your secret? How are you different from the other mob bosses?"

"You'd really like to know, wouldn't you, kid?"

She nodded and took a sip.

"Okay," he conceded, leaning forward and folding his hands on the table. "Here's how it works. Most of my business is legit. I own clubs and video stores, cleaning agencies, apartment buildings, cab companies... I'm into a little of everything. You want to make money, diversity is the key. And you know what? The feds watch everything that goes on with all of them. They're too stupid to realize that my *other* business has nothing to do with them, they just assume they're covers for... Let's just say my more colorful occupation."

She nodded. "Huh. Do you make very good money with the legal stuff you do?"

"Well yeah. There's a fortune to be made out there if you're savvy enough to find out where."

"What about the more colorful business. Does it make good money?"

He nodded. "Yeah, pretty good."

"As good as the not so colorful stuff?"

Falcone glanced at the man he had standing at Elissa's side, then he looked back to her and shrugged. "I guess that depends on what you mean by as good."

"In other words it doesn't," she guessed. "With Batman and the police and the FBI watching you, it seems like the risk simply wouldn't be worth it, especially if you're already getting rich doing legitimate business." She raised her brow. "And it's all about making money, isn't it?"

"Not all, kiddo," he corrected, "not all."

"The thrill?" she said with a smile. When he smiled back, she went on, "Yeah, I know what you mean. I don't always follow the letter of the law, myself."

"Get out," he scoffed.

"Really," she assured.

"You've actually broken the law," he said with disbelief in his words.

She nodded. "Yup. Doing it right now." She took another sip of her wine.

"How's that?" he questioned.

She took another sip of wine before answering, "I'm a minor."

Falcone stared at her for long seconds, then he broke out in hearty laughter.

WW

The huge computer console of the Batcave was always well lit when occupied. There was the huge screen right in front of the user with the keyboard beneath it, but there were four smaller screens, two on one side at sitting eye level and two on the other of the concave work station, that acted as secondary data displays. Each was tied into the main terminal, but they also each had keyboards and data entry ports of their own. This was one of the best computer terminals in the world, rivaled only by those used by the Justice League, which were merely newer models of this same design.

Batman, his cowl pulled down from his head, sat in the big chair right in front of the main terminal. With his thumb and index finger, he massaged his eyes, his head bowed as he drew a deep breath.

Standing behind him, Golden Angel and Nightwing exchanged uneasy looks. Both had their hands folded behind them and both were nervously silent as they awaited what seemed like the worst.

With a deep growl, Batman finally raised his head, looking up to the words on the main display in front of him for long seconds before he spoke. "Let me get this straight," he began, his voice deep and growling and laced with aggravation. "My daughter went into a club owned by one of Gotham City's worst crime bosses, sang for him all night, got caught, had a nice little chat with him, and I'm supposed to be okay with this?"

Elissa took a deep breath and declared, "That's what we're hoping."

Slowly, Batman swiveled around in his chair, his brow low over menacing eyes that found Nightwing and remained locked on him.

"Yeah," Dick stammered, "um, it looks like the Gotham part of the operation has been at least stalled."

"No," Elissa corrected, "he's pulling out completely. I might have made him think it was a double cross, so we came up with a plan to make the criminal underworld look like they were going to betray Mister Falcone and he's a really nice guy down deep and I don't think he's going to stay a mob boss. I mean, he's got a lot of legitimate businesses going and he already—"

"Angel!" Batman barked. He stood and loomed over her. "I've been trying to put him away for more than ten years, and now you're telling me that you are a close personal friend of his?"

She cringed and drew her shoulders up, lowering her head as she stared up at him like a scolded child.

"Bruce," Nightwing defended as he stepped toward him. "She stopped this end of the operation, which was more than I was hoping for tonight. She also broke up what could have turned into a nationwide crime syndicate that could have been a lot of trouble for all of us."

His eyes found Dick again and he growled, "Why was my daughter in that place to begin with?"

And now it was Nightwing who postured, countering, "She did great in there! You're just going to have to trust that the kid knows what she's doing."

Batman looked away from him.

"I might add," Dick went on, "that we also stopped two robberies and a couple of assaults. She went right after the bad guys, Bruce, and she kicked butt out there!"

Bruce had his teeth clenched and just stared across the Batcave.

Nightwing spun around and strode toward the elevator. "I'm going to grab a shower. I'll pull out in the morning." He paused and turned one more time. "By the way, when I saw her in action, she kind of reminded me of you."

Finally, Bruce looked to him, and still he did not look happy.

Raising his chin slightly, Dick informed, "She blindsided them without warning, just like you do." He turned and strode to the elevator, finishing, "Thought you might like to know."

They both watched him enter the elevator, and watched even after the doors closed.

Batman huffed a breath and wheeled around, sitting back into his chair as he reached for the controls.

Elissa felt trapped, as if powerful hands were closing around her throat. Turning her eyes to the floor, she did her best to compose herself, then she turned and silently approached the Dark Knight, gingerly laying her hands on his shoulders as she offered in a meek voice, "I'm sorry, Daddy." When he did not respond, she bowed her head and turned, striding away with light, quiet steps.

"Angel," he suddenly called.

She froze where she was, her gaze on the floor before her.

Bruce stared blankly at the computer keyboard and huffed what sounded like another angry breath. In a more gentle voice, he summoned, "Come over here."

She tensed, but turned and complied, sitting gingerly in the chair to his right.

He just stared at the keyboard for a time and she could see the strain in his eyes, on his features. She did not speak, fearful of any sound that might shatter the deafening silence of the cave.

"I always worried," he finally said, staring at the controls before him. "Every time I sent out Dick or Tim or Barbara, Cassandra or Stephanie... Of course I worried about them. Anything could happen out there. But, I trusted them. I trusted that they would have their training to call on and that they could handle anything that presented itself."

Elissa watched him intently and with her every nerve pulled taut, not knowing what to expect from him.

He cut his eyes to her, turning his head her direction just barely. "I suppose I have to find that same trust for you."

Her lips tightened and she conceded, "That can't be easy with me being your kid and all."

"That makes it a hundred times harder," he admitted. "Believe me, Angel, I don't want this life for you."

"I'm kind of stuck with it now," she informed gently. "I can't just walk away."

"Any more than I could," he confessed. "I'm still new at being the father of a headstrong teenage daughter. I suppose you'll have to expect me to be a little overprotective for a while."

She finally relaxed and allowed a smile to curl her lips. "A while? Like fifty years?"

"Maybe longer."

Elissa giggled and lunged toward him, wrapping her arms around his neck as she moved her chair right up against his. Closing her eyes as she laid her head on his shoulder, she whispered, "I'll be careful, Daddy, I promise. I won't let you down."

His arm slid around her back and he replied in a whisper, "I know you won't, Angel."

WW

Elissa found herself nearly exhausted. The sun was finally up and she realized she had not slept since the previous morning. She also realized that staying up all night just felt… right.

Dressed in light pink shorts and a thin white tee shirt that had a pink skull and crossbones on the front, she padded downstairs with her hand gliding gingerly along the handrail and her eyes on the carpeted steps before her.

Nearly down, she stopped as her eyes caught movement off to one side, near the cavernous room where the two staircases met. Bruce had just emerged from his study and this was one of the very few times she had ever seen him dressed comfortably. He was wearing thin, loosely fitting trousers that appeared to be pajamas and a tightly fitting black tee shirt. He was shoeless, walking with weary steps and was rubbing his eyes. Under his arm was a newspaper.

As he turned fully away from her, apparently to the big sitting area around that huge fireplace, she crouched down and watched him, then noiselessly crept down the steps, slipped around the last post at the bottom, and padded on the carpet that ran down the middle of the hardwood floor behind him. Her eyes were fixed on him, how he carried himself, how he held his head, and her steps quickened. She was half crouched, holding her arms ready, and as he approached the back of the huge leather couch and she found herself only about six feet behind him, she crouched and raised her arms to spring into him.

He turned slightly to go around the couch.

Time to make her move. Without making a sound, she leapt at him, her hands grasping for his shoulders. Taking him high, she would easily be able to pull him over the back of the couch.

Just as she grabbed his shoulder he spun around and raised his forearm into her belly, effortlessly redirecting her.

With a loud scream, she tumbled over the back of the leather couch, bounced off of the cushions and made a loud thump as she hit the floor between it and the coffee table flat on her back. Taking a second to collect her wits, she grasped the couch with one hand, the coffee table with the other, and pulled herself up, looking up to the smiling face of her father as he leaned on the back of the couch on his crossed arms with his newspaper in his hand.

She just glared back at him for a few seconds before grumbling, "Not cool."

He huffed a laugh and shook his head as she got to her feet, turning toward his favorite chair which was on the right side of the couch. As he sat down, Elissa curled up on the end of the couch closest to his chair, leaning on the arm of the couch as she stared at him with eyes that betrayed annoyance. As he opened the paper and looked into it, casually crossing his legs as he read, she rested her chin in her palm as she kept him locked in her sights.

A moment passed in silence.

He turned the page, and finally said, "Did you ever give much thought to watching your own shadow?"

"I will from now on," she snarled.

He chuckled.

"So did you make up with Dick?" she asked suddenly, then she bit her lip as he drew a loud breath.

"We're okay," he assured. "We talked it out like we always do."

Elissa nodded. "Yeah, that's good that you guys can talk stuff over." Looking down to her fingernails, she hesitantly asked, "Are you and Mom doing okay?" He took a moment to answer and this sent a crawl through her stomach.

"We're fine, Angel," was all he would say.

She nodded again and observed, "You guys seem to be… Where is she, anyway?"

"Germany," he replied.

Her eyes snapped to him. "Germany?"

"The Justice League is a global organization," he informed as he read. "We go wherever we are needed."

"Cool," she said absently. "So you didn't go with her?"

"She didn't need me along," was his reply.

His answers about Diana were very brief, almost curt, and Elissa took full notice. Time to change the subject.

"So, um, you going to work tomorrow?"

He raised his brow and looked to the other page of his paper. "I have some meetings late in the morning and a working lunch to discuss a project merger with Cybermed Corp."

"Sounds fun," she observed. "Can I come with you?"

Bruce finally turned his eyes to her.

She shrugged. "I just want to watch you work. It's okay if you don't want me to. I don't want to be in the way or anything."

His long, expressionless stare could have meant anything, but finally he ordered, "Go get some rest. I'll have Alfred wake you when it's time to get ready."

With a big smile, Elissa sprang from the couch and went to her father to tightly hug his neck. "Thanks, Daddy!"

As she got up to her bedroom, she strode to the night stand where her cell phone lay. She put in some numbers and held it to her ear, then greeted, "Hi, Mom. Busy?"

CHAPTER 4

Alfred had his eyes on the road and both hands on the wheel of Bruce Wayne's late model limousine, but still he smiled and shook his head.

"I know I can get this right," Elissa assured. The morning found her in the seat across from her father, facing the rear of the car. She was dressed in a light gray business suit with a white blouse and a knee length skirt that was the light gray of her jacket. Black, thin strapped high heeled shoes did not look comfortable, though she did not complain. Her hair was worn in a bun; she had new oval glasses on and a pencil behind her ear, another in the bun of her hair. In her lap was what appeared to be a leather bound schedule with a couple hundred pages within.

Bruce sat across from her wearing a very expensive black suit with a dark gray tie and white shirt. The armrests at his sides were folded down, his elbows rested on them and he had his fingers laced in front of him as his eyes scrutinized the young woman in front of him.

"Okay," he began. "Let's do it again. I need to make an appointment with Wayne Finance to discuss the numbers before we make the next move."

She opened the schedule and grabbed the pencil from her ear, her eyes on it as she scribbled something. "Yes, Mister Wayne."

"Do you have the notes from the last stockholder meeting?"

"No, Mister Wayne. I can have your office fax them to me right away if you like."

"What about the production and safety reports from the Medical Laser Division?"

She opened the little binder to the last pages and pulled a blue envelope out, reporting, "Right here, Mister Wayne."

"And what is your name?"

"Lisa Summers," she replied, "from the Corporate Intern Pool."

Bruce smiled. "Great work, Angel. Just keep that up."

"And keep my mouth shut as much as I can," she added.

"Just remember that you're an assistant," he said. "These negotiations are pretty important and I'd like things to run smoothly, and in my favor."

One of her eyebrows cocked up. "How smoothly? Should I..." She unfastened the top two buttons of her blouse.

His eyes narrowed.

"If I wasn't your daughter," she pointed out, "you'd tell me to go for it and you know it!"

He growled and looked out the window. "Make that as far down as you go."

Elissa smiled and answered, "Yes, Mister Wayne."

The limousine stopped at an extremely affluent restaurant that clearly catered to those of great wealth and importance and a young valet in black trousers, a white shirt and red vest rushed to the car and opened the door, standing beside it as he watched the occupants step out, and he greeted, "Good afternoon, Mister Wayne."

Bruce looked to the door of the restaurant and said, "Good to see you again, Randy."

The Valet's eyes widened a little as Elissa stepped out, and his attention remained on her as she followed her father toward the door. In fact, many eyes found her.

Inside, the place was all about atmosphere. Tables were covered with red cloth, the lights were relatively low and expensive paintings hung on the walls. The staff all wore tuxedoes and hurried about. The floor was a thin red and green carpet in complex designs that would make the eye want to stray from it. Deep cushioned booths were on the far side and a wall separated another section that could barely be seen from the entrance.

A podium just inside the door was manned by a middle aged man with slicked back hair and a thin mustache, one who seemed to light up as he saw Bruce Wayne approaching him. Stepping around the podium, he greeted, "Mister Wayne! It is a pleasure to have you in our midst again."

Bruce shook his hand and nodded to him. "Thank you. Are they here?"

"I took them to the private table in the back," the man informed, "and I've served them a round of drinks as you instructed."

Nodding again, Bruce commended, "Good work. We'll go on back now."

Half turning, the man snapped his fingers and ordered, "Escort Mister Wayne to his table."

A young woman in a tuxedo who looked to be in her twenties rushed to them, holding her clipboard to her as she smiled and said, "Right this way, Mister Wayne."

Elissa marveled at how her father stepped into a room and completely took control of all around him. She was used to seeing Batman do this, but the charisma that surrounded Bruce Wayne was something entirely different and she began to feel herself swept up in it. It was no wonder her mother had fallen for him so many years ago!

The meeting was going much as Elissa had imagined it would: Boring. Cybermed Corp. had sent four representatives, but not the promised CEO and this had not gone unnoticed by Bruce. He listened to what they had to say, sipped on his drink and ordered them all something to eat. Cybermed seemed to be trying to talk him into funding for some kind of gadget they intended to manufacture, but she could not be sure. She was only listening enough to catch what she needed to. After a while, she found herself glancing frequently at her watch. Bruce didn't know it, but this meeting needed to end soon!

After a sip from his glass, he nodded and looked to the older fellow who sat right across from him. "And I should go ahead and just sign off on this," he guessed with just a hint of suspicion in his voice.

"It's ground floor," the older fellow informed, "and will make billions in the next couple of years."

Setting his glass down, he looked to it as he reminded, "I still haven't seen your test records, or application to the FDA for approval."

"All of that is pending," the fellow in the blue suit sitting to the older man's right assured. "Everything has been filed, but these things take time. I can assure you, Mister Wayne, that once word of this leaks out then we'll have everyone climbing on board."

Bruce's eyes were pools of mistrust as they shifted to this man.

"But for some reason you want Wayne Enterprises to sign on early. Would you mind telling me why?"

"Partnerships can do great things," he explained, "but great partnerships between two powerful partners can change the world."

A smile almost emerged on Elissa's face as she finally realized that Cybermed's plan had unraveled from the beginning. They came to the meeting having her father outnumbered. They had their facts and figures and would surely be able to brow beat him into what they wanted. It just was not happening. Bruce took total control from the moment he sat down, and these four men found themselves on the defensive and fighting an uphill battle, and not doing well.

"So you don't have the reports yet," Bruce accused.

"They aren't yet available," The older fellow started.

"Miss Summers," Bruce ordered.

Elissa opened the folder she had and pulled out the blue envelope that she knew her father wanted, not saying a word as she offered it to him.

Bruce slapped the envelope down in the middle of the table. "I have the reports. Here's your copy."

All four of the Cybermed representatives stared down at the envelope with nervous eyes.

Checking her watch, Elissa bit her lip. This meeting had to end, very soon. She looked to Bruce as the Cybermed representatives stammered for an answer and interrupted, "Mister Wayne, I'm sorry to butt in, but you have that other meeting here in fifteen minutes."

Turning his head only slightly, he cut his eyes to her and offered, "Thank you, Lisa." He folded his hands on the table, looking to each of the four men in turn. "Well, gentlemen, it looks like we have a problem. You'll find more in that report than the production estimates and the safety tests." His eyes narrowed. "I've also uncovered exactly how much of your program is a direct result of Wayne Enterprises research." As the men exchanged nervous glances, his eyes narrowed. "Now, gentlemen, you can go back and tell your CEO, who I was expecting to be here today, that we will go ahead and finish testing and that Wayne Enterprises will be fully on board, just as soon as the bugs in safety are worked out and just as soon as I see a signed and notarized document that gives Wayne Enterprises eighty-five percent of the project."

The man in the darker suit took on a more challenging posture as he also folded his hands on the table and warned, "That simply will not happen, Mister Wayne. We know that several W. E. projects are on hold pending—"

"Your information is not entirely accurate," Bruce interrupted. He glanced at Elissa, then picked up his glass. "Thank you for coming, gentlemen. I think we're done here."

Silently, they all stood and without a word turned and just walked away.

Bruce took a sip of his drink and looked to his daughter, and found her smiling at him.

She picked up her own drink, a glass of milk, and held it to him. "I only thought you were amazing before. Wow!"

He touched his glass to hers and they both drank.

Elissa glanced at her watch again and was quick to blurt out, "Do we have time for dessert?"

With a little nod, he replied, "I think we do. Considering how much you eat, aren't you worried about your figure?"

"Do I look worried?" she countered. "Besides, I'm a kid *and* an Amazon."

Bruce huffed a laugh and shook his head. "So what do you want, Angel?"

"Bruce?" Diana summoned.

They both looked, and Elissa sprang up.

Diana was dressed in a loosely fitting, light blue blouse that was trimmed in white lace around the neckline and the cuffs of the long sleeves. Her skirt, which was knee length, was a darker blue and a very thin, satiny material that showed off the shape of her legs as she moved. The high heeled shoes she wore accentuated the shape of her legs further. Diamond earrings dangled from her ears and she had her long black hair worn back and restrained behind her with two jeweled barrettes that sparkled even in this dim light. She also wore thin rimmed glasses before her eyes, and an expression of surprise with them.

"Mom!" Elissa declared as she darted around the table to meet her. "What a surprise! Come on and sit down. We were just about to order."

As the girl took her hand and pulled her around the table, Diana asked, "Surprise?"

"Here," Elissa offered as the reached Bruce. "Take my chair." She pulled the chair out, then strode quickly around her mother to the other side of the table. "I'll just sit over here."

Diana met Bruce's eyes, and she did not look comfortable. More than that, she could see that he did not feel so comfortable, either. Still, she hesitantly sat down, then looked to her daughter who did the same on the other side of the table.

"Wow," the girl declared. "I'm totally starving! Anybody else hungry?"

"You just ate lunch," Bruce pointed out.

"Yeah," she countered, "but that was like a half hour ago. I'm a growing girl. Got to keep my strength up." Looking around, she mumbled, "Where's that waiter?" She looked to her mother and smiled. "He's really cute! So, are we going to get appetizers or what?"

Bruce rubbed his eyes. "Elissa..."

"We need menus!" she declared with quick words. "Should I go find someone?"

"No, Angel," he replied. Looking to Diana, he raised a brow, and she just shrugged in response.

Looking to her mother, Elissa suddenly asked, "So how was Germany? I hear it's great this time of year."

"It was fine, Junior," Diana assured.

A loud clearing of his throat announced Bruce's disapproval of something and they both looked to him.

His eyes were locked on Diana as he said in a low voice, "Identities."

"I don't think my calling her that here is going to cause any problems!" Diana hissed.

"We don't take those kinds of chances and you know it," he grumbled back.

Elissa sensed the hostility between them growing and loudly cleared her throat.

"Didn't I just hear you call her Angel?" Diana snapped back.

Reaching across the table to grab her glass of milk, Elissa asked, "Anyone need a refill? I need a refill." She finished the last couple of swallows and looked around her, holding her glass up as she announced, "Dry here!"

Diana snapped, "I thought we understood that she was not to be seen publicly with Bruce Wayne."

"Nobody knows her," he countered. "All anyone sees is an assistant."

Her eyes darting from one to the other, Elissa desperately said, "Guys, seriously, it's okay. Why don't we just—"

"And you tried to scold me for running on the beach with her," Diana barked.

Bruce raised his chin, his narrow eyes locked in a challenging stare on her. "You both also changed right out in the open, and just a few miles from my house!"

Elissa pushed away from the table and slowly stood as they argued on, and when they argued on and did not notice her get up, she turned and hurried away from them.

Outside the restaurant, she looked around for the limousine, but it was not to be found. She walked a way down the sidewalk. Around the corner, there was a parking garage about a block away, concealed behind the restaurant and a couple of the other businesses, and as she saw valet drive into it with a rather expensive looking car, she headed that way.

Inside, she wandered for a while, and finally she saw the car she was looking for. Alfred was outside of it, leaning against the closed door and talking on his cell phone, and when he looked up and saw her, he said his farewells to the party on the other end and quickly hung up.

"Miss Elissa?" he greeted hesitantly as she reached the car.

She turned and leaned back first against the car, her gaze finding the dirty concrete floor before her as she drew her shoulders up and folded her arms. Huffing a short breath through her nose, she seemed lost in her thoughts, though she was clearly aware of the man right beside her.

"Are you all right?" he asked with concern in his words.

She only shrugged in response.

"Where is Master Bruce?" he asked with the same concern to his tone.

"Still in the restaurant," she grumbled in the voice of someone much younger. "They're arguing again."

Alfred nodded and looked away from her. "I see. Perhaps they'll get it all out of their systems this time."

"They never will," she complained. "I thought having Mom meet me here to surprise him would... It was just a bad idea."

"Still a noble effort," he commended, turning his eyes to her.

"They used to love each other," she whined, trying not to cry. "And then I came along." Shaking her head, she was clearly fighting tears as she whimpered, "It isn't supposed to be this way!"

Alfred slipped an arm around her shoulders and was about to deliver some wise words to her when she turned onto him and buried her face in his shoulder. Her body quaked and it was clear that she was trying not to cry. "There there, Miss," he comforted. "They'll find their way. This can't go on forever." When she nodded, he kissed the top of her head and assured, "It will be all right. It really will."

Elissa fought off crying, but still reached up to wipe a stray tear from her cheek.

WW

When darkness fell she was supposed to go deep into Gotham City with Batman, but he found himself called away, leaving from the Batcave in his small jet. Her mother had been called to the Watchtower, the mysterious orbiting station that hung high in orbit. From there, the Justice League seemed to conduct most of its business, even though the official headquarters was in the city somewhere. She had not seen either place but had always dreamed of seeing both.

Spending the night alone in that big, dark and lonely mansion was not an appealing thought at all, so Golden Angel would travel into Gotham City alone, the same as she had done as Wonder Woman, but this time she would take along many of the tools her father used. She had become very accurate with the bat-arangs and had borrowed a few little smoke bombs and a grapple, not too much to weigh her down, but just a few things that might come in handy.

The dark streets of the older part of Gotham were hunting grounds for those of ill intent, and their prey was any who carelessly strayed that way. Elissa knew this and so became bait for her own needs. Wearing a well kept khaki overcoat that was draped over her shoulders served two purposes. One was against the chill that hovered in the damp air at night. The other was to conceal who she really was.

Many street lamps were out and few people shared the sidewalk in this run down and dirty part of town. On the roadside she would occasionally encounter an old car that had been left to die. Each one had all of the wheels and tires gone and many of them were missing parts here and there. A few had been burned and one or two that still had the glass intact were still inhabited, mostly by those with nowhere else to go. A few homeless people had dwellings built of boxes and pallets and whatever discarded materials they could find.

There were many eyes on her. She could feel them, could almost hear the thoughts of those who watched her. Her insight was on full alert and she found her nerves pulled taut, anticipating the battle that could be a second or a moment or an hour away.

Almost an hour later nobody had even approached her. Scanning the area, she knew that this *had* to be the worst part of town. There were plenty of eyes on her, plenty of bad guys down here, yet nothing was happening.

A group of rough looking young men ahead of her caught her eye and she watched them as she drew closer, and this time she dared to stop as she reached them. There were five of them, three in old leather jackets, one in a trench coat and all of them no doubt armed to one degree or another. They studied her with a hungry intent, and yet they would not move on her, would not advance.

Raising her brow, she asked in an innocent voice, "Why so standoffish?"

They all stared back at her for long seconds, then they exchanged looks and simply walked away from her, in the direction she had just come from.

"Huh," she huffed as she watched their cool retreat from her, then she shrugged and turned to resume her stroll.

Only a block was put behind her and her attention shifted to someone across the street, a man in ratty attire who had not shaven for some time. He was not walking well nor in a straight line and in his hand was a bottle wrapped in a small paper sack. She shook her head and continued on, toward an abandoned store that had the windows and glass doors broken out. This got but a glance when she noticed movement on the other side of the street again. There she saw a man and a woman walking side by side, nervously glancing about them. They did not belong in this area and keeping a discreet eye on them seemed like a good idea.

A woman standing in the doorway of the abandoned store observed, "So you're why the pickings are so slim tonight."

Elissa drew a gasp and spun to face her.

Stepping from the shadows, this was clearly a very tall woman, about Wonder Woman's height, though she did not have quite the Amazon Princess' build. Her boots were a satin black and were knee high, leaving her thighs bare all the way to the lavender leotard she wore. This leotard also left her sides and belly bare like it was designed for maximum freedom of movement and covered her chest and shoulders, where some kind of armor or padding was in place. Long black gloves covered her hands and forearms and ended just past her elbows, leaving her well toned upper arms bare. She wore a belt that reminded Elissa of Batman's with many dark purple pouches and a few throwing weapons mounted to it. A single hand crossbow was mounted to her right thigh and a dozen bolts for it were on the other. Long black hair was left unrestrained and was very long down her back, shimmering in the dim street lights. She wore a lavender colored mask that concealed most of her upper face and kept her hair in check with two long points that rose from her temples to add more height and menace to her appearance. As she approached, her blue eyes never left Elissa's.

With the woman only about six feet away, Golden Angel took a step back merely to assume a more combat ready posture. She retreated no more as she looked up at the tall woman who finally stopped right in front of her.

Raising her brow, the woman only hinted at a smile as she commented, "Nice costume. Did you stay up all night thinking it up?"

Elissa's eyes narrowed.

The woman's eyes shifted upward to the girl's forehead. "The headpiece just brings it all together."

Hesitantly, Elissa reached to her head, and she clenched her teeth as she felt her tiara still there.

With her eyes locked on the little Amazon's, the tall woman took a few purposeful steps back, and in an instant the crossbow was in her hand, though held downward.

Throwing her arms back, Golden Angel shed the overcoat and held her arms ready, her wide eyes locked on her tormentor. When the crossbow was aimed and shot in one fluid motion, she swept her arm and easily deflected the bolt.

In an instant another was loaded and shot and the results were the same.

Elissa raised a brow and dared to say, "I can stop bullets and you think you can take me down with that."

"Not at all," the woman corrected with a smile. She shot one more, then her other hand swept from her belt and sent a throwing knife right at the little Amazon.

Golden Angel calmly swept her hand in a quick blur seemingly to ward it off, then she set one hand on her hip as she raised the other hand before her—with the throwing knife between her fingers.

The woman watched as the girl casually dropped the knife, then she smiled and holstered her crossbow. Without warning, she charged and spun around, sending the heel of her boot right at Golden Angel's head.

Elissa easily blocked the kick, then spun the other way to sweep the woman's leg from under her, a maneuver that was thwarted with a quick jump and backward flip.

Landing in a crouch, the woman's brow was low over her eyes, and yet she was smiling as she observed, "I see you've been really well trained, too."

Assuming her battle stance, Elissa's eyes narrowed and she confirmed, "By the best."

"Only if you had the same teacher that I did," the woman corrected. With amazing speed, she sprang up and attacked again.

And this time Golden Angel met her head-on!

The two sparred for some time, neither managing to get the upper hand. Elissa was much quicker, much stronger, but experience favored the woman she fought and so did reach. The people hiding among the shadows and down the alleys of the dilapidated street slowly emerged as the battle raged, watching with nervous attention as the two fought.

Sometime later the more experienced of the fighters landed a kick to the girl's side in a move she did not anticipate and Elissa barked a shout as she staggered back, reaching for her side. The woman pursued and spun around to kick again, but this kick was blocked and in an unpredictable move of her own Golden Angel lunged and head-butted her opponent hard right between the eyes.

The woman slammed onto the ground flat on her back and lay there for a second as she covered her head with her hand, and unexpectedly she laughed.

Her eyes narrowing, Elissa half turned her head and stood ready.

Finally looking up at the girl, the woman shook her head and insisted, "You must have picked that up from Diana!" She offered her opponent her hand and was pulled to her feet as she held the other hand to her forehead.

"You mind telling me who you are?" Golden Angel demanded.

Taking a step back, the woman extended her arms and barked, "Come on, girl!"

Elissa looked her up and down a couple of times, then her eyes widened and she raised her chin, announcing, "Huntress!"

"Scariest thing on the streets," Huntress confirmed.

Golden Angel folded her arms and countered, "Yeah, when Batman's not around."

"Now that stung," the tall woman chided. She set her hands on her hips and asked, "So aside from showing off that really bad costume you were wearing, what are you doing out here?"

With a shrug, Golden Angel replied, "Just looking for bad guys." She glanced across the street and added, "And maybe looking out for the honest people out here."

"Don't let them fool you," Huntress advised. "Not everything is as it seems around here. They're just waiting for some poor bonehead to come along and offer to help them."

Clenching her teeth, Elissa turned her full attention to the couple as they strolled nervously down the sidewalk on the other side of the street. "That is about low, preying on other people's good will. We should go kick their butts."

"We can't do anything until they actually break the law," Huntress informed grimly, "and if we do, then we're the criminals." She slapped the girl's shoulder. "Come on... It's Golden Angel, isn't it?"

Nodding, Elissa confirmed, "Uh huh." Her eyes snapped to the tall woman. "Wait a minute. You know who I am?"

"I like to stay current," Huntress replied. A beep from her belt alerted her and she looked down as she removed what looked like some kind of smart phone. As she read the text on the small screen, she smiled and declared, "Score! Come on, Golden Girl. We have somewhere to be!"

Elissa followed her down the street, and found herself walking briskly and with quick steps just to keep up. "Where are we going?"

"Bank robbery across town. The Justice League's been called out which means there's a major bad guy involved."

Her brow dropping, Golden Angel asked, "Aren't you in the Justice League?"

Hesitation found the tall woman's steps and she started to look back at her young companion, but as the girl finally caught up to her, she simply strode on. "I'm as much a part of the Justice League as I want to be."

That seemed like a sore subject that Elissa decided would be best left not discussed.

Down an alley a block away, Huntress kicked some old crates aside to reveal her black and lavender motorcycle. As she pushed it into the open and climbed on, Elissa backed away a step as she watched her start the machine.

"Um," the girl started, "my bike's a couple of blocks the other direction."

"No time," Huntress insisted. She looked to the young heroine and barked, "Climb on if you're coming or stay here."

Golden Angel hesitated for just a second, then she threw caution aside and climbed onto the bike behind the tall woman, hesitantly slipping her arms around her waist as the machine roared and they took off.

The ride was a fast one as Huntress swerved through the scant traffic on the Gotham streets, disregarding traffic signals on her high speed chase to arrive at the crime scene.

There, across town, dozens of police cars and vans surrounded a block. SWAT teams were deployed and barricades were in place, and these Huntress negotiated around with apparent ease.

Arriving just behind the police line, she stopped the bike and lowered the kickstand, her eyes on the front of the new looking granite building that had lights trained on it from many trucks and cars. The front doors had been smashed in and some kind of armored truck was backed up to it. The whole building was street level and landscaped all around where people would approach the front. There were windows to the inside, but these had been blocked by something.

Golden Angel followed Huntress to what appeared to be the command area, right across the street from the front doors of the bank. There, many uniformed police officers and SWAT team members had their weapons trained on the bank.

Standing beside a rather large man in a trench coat, who Elissa recognized quickly as Gotham City's Detective Bullock by his voice and build, was a much shorter but muscular fellow in the unmistakable, tight fitting costume of the Atom. She glanced around, hoping to see some of the other Justice League there, and as they stopped behind Bullock and Atom, she overheard the grim news from the Detective.

"I don't know what we're supposed to do when he comes out of there," he grumbled. "The guy's bullet proof and I don't think a bazooka could stop him."

Atom added, "And there are the hostages to consider."

"Yeah," Bullock growled.

Folding his arms, Atom informed, "We need a plan and we need it fast. Metallo isn't going to wait for us to make our move."

Elissa's eyes widened. Metallo? That nervous crawl resumed in her belly and she glanced about, finally stammering, "Um... Should we wait for the Justice League to send more help?"

Everyone turned their attention on her, and nobody looked pleased with her.

Bullock took the ever present toothpick from his mouth and spat, "By the time the rest of that freak show gets here he'll—"

"Easy!" Atom barked. Looking back to Golden Angel, he explained, "We don't have time. We have to do something to get those people out of there now."

Her brow arching slightly, Elissa protested, "But that's Metallo! What are we supposed to do against him? We should call Superman or someone!"

"He's on the other side of the world," Atom informed impatiently, turning to look back to the bank. "Everyone's already called out.

This one's up to us."

As everyone else shifted their attention to the bank, Elissa's eyes slid that way and she swallowed hard. Resurfacing in her memory was that first encounter with Red Panzer less than a year ago and how ineffective she was against him. The thought of facing another mechanically enhanced opponent, especially one of Metallo's power, was simply horrifying.

Swallowing hard, she reached for her cell phone and informed, "I'm going to call Wonder Woman."

Huntress cut her eyes to the girl as she folded her arms, and there was no patience in her voice as she said, "She'll never get here in time. We're on our own."

Elissa had already entered the number and pressed send, and she stared dumbly down at her phone for long seconds before putting it away and looking back to the bank. As the older heroes and the police discussed quickly what to do, indecision whirled within the young Amazon, and good judgment abandoned her again as she asked, "Are you sure Superman isn't—"

Huntress wheeled around, looming over her from less than a foot away as she barked, "Look! We're on our own here! If you are too scared to help then get back behind the police line with the onlookers. Otherwise, it's time for you to grow up, put on your big-girl panties and do your job! Got it?"

Staring up into the tall woman's eyes for long seconds, Elissa sheepishly nodded, and when Huntress turned around and folded her arms, the girl glanced around to see other people, including Atom, taking their attention from her and looking back to the bank. She felt near tears. In this moment, she did not feel like a heroine, not even a sidekick, just a whiny, scolded little girl. Turning her eyes down, she looked aside and briefly thought about walking away. She drew a breath, trying to reason out what her mother would do.

No, not her mother, not Wonder Woman. Her father! He would find a way to outthink his opponent.

She looked back to the bank, to the armored truck backed up to it. She slowly strode to Bullock's side and set her hands on her hips, raising her chin as she asked, "How many hostages are inside?"

His eyes slid to her and he sneered, "About a dozen. You want their names too?"

"Nope," she snapped back. Half turning, she looked to Atom and asked, "How small can you go?"

Atom and Huntress exchanged looks.

WW

Metallo and his men had been thoughtful enough to completely disable the alarm system, so quietly entering through the back was rather easy. Batman had taught Golden Angel the art of picking locks and she proved to be a quick study, so even the security lock into the back of the bank proved to be no match for her.

Once inside, she quietly negotiated her way through the back offices, cubicles and the office equipment and crept toward the front where she expected to find the hostages. Freeing them was her top priority and Atom and Huntress had agreed. In fact, they had surprised her by embracing her plan.

The lobby was ahead of her and her eyes narrowed as she crouched down and silently approached. This small hallway emptied out behind the teller's stations and she could see some activity out there, but no hostages. Peering around the corner, she saw the door to the vault standing ajar, then she saw movement out of the corner of her eye and shifted her attention directly ahead—right as a man dressed in all black with a black mask walked around the corner into the hallway and saw her.

Wide eyed, he froze and dropped the empty sacks he was carrying as he made contact with the young Amazon.

Elissa only hesitated for a second before she sprang forward and delivered an uppercut to his jaw that knocked him out cold. She watched him fall straight back and slam onto the floor, then she peered around the corner and into the teller's stations, seeing two more of them cleaning out cash boxes. This was predictable and for some reason they did not seem to be in any hurry. Apparently, with Metallo on their team, they did not fear the guns of the police.

Swiftly and silently, she rushed the two and dispatched them with quick and expert moves, delivering a kick to the head of the first one, then wheeling around and slamming the heel of her boot into the jaw of the second. With a little smile, she looked down at her work, setting her hands on her hips, then she turned around and froze.

Two more of the men in the black gear were standing there with their guns trained on them. Not usually a problem, but Metallo stood right behind them, his mechanical arms folded and his glowing eyes locked on the little Amazon.

He was also dressed in black, the same clothing the others were dressed in, but he wore no mask over his head. His head and face were skull like and reminded her of Red Panzer, though he was not quite as big as the mechanical Nazi that had almost killed her less than a year ago. Mechanical workings could be seen melded in with the armor that was his exoskeleton and old memories made her heart race and pump fear throughout her.

Metallo casually leaned his head as he studied her, then he shook his head and observed, "I guess the real members of the Justice League are all busy, so they are sending in the children now." His accent sounded British and his voice synthesized, much like Red Panzer's.

Elissa swallowed hard and backed away a couple of steps, her eyes locked wide on the big cyborg before her.

"Put the guns down, boys," Metallo ordered. "This little girl is an Amazon. Bullets are something she knows how to deal with." As the men lowered their weapons, the big mechanical criminal slowly strode forward, slowly lowered his arms. "So are you their response, or are you some kind of diversion?"

"Um..." she stammered, her eyes locked on his.

"You weren't sure what you would find in here, were you?" he pressed as he drew closer.

Elissa backed away and was stopped by the teller's station only three steps behind her.

Metallo raised his chin. "Do you know who I am?"

Hesitantly, she nodded.

He folded his arms. "So. You know who I am and what I can do. What do you intend to do about it?"

Her lips were parted in fear as she stared up at him, and with a tiny voice she admitted, "I, uh... I don't know."

"I didn't think so." Metallo looked to the men who took his sides, then back to the frightened girl.

She shrieked as he brutally took her arm and spun her around, bending her over the work station.

"Give me that pathetic guard's handcuffs," he ordered.

Elissa half turned her head as her arms were forced behind her, and she tensed as she felt the cold steel of the handcuffs close around her wrists with loud, quick clicks. In seconds she was subdued and was turned with the same brutality to face him again. As he held her by the arms, she just stared up at him and she did not resist at all.

"Taken without a struggle," he chided. He slowly reached to her face and his metal finger stroked her cheek. "You are a lovely one, aren't you?"

"Thank you," she offered in a wisp of a voice.

He took her tiara gently from her head and looked it over, then he turned his attention back to her. "Amazon warrior, huh? Not Amazon enough to challenge me, though."

Turning her eyes down, Elissa softly admitted, "I guess not."

Metallo turned and pulled her by the arm toward one of his waiting henchmen. "Put her with the rest, and take her little tool belt."

Two men took her arms, and one of them was rubbing his jaw, and he did not have a pleasant look for her.

They took her to the vault, which strangely had a red carpet on the floor. This was a large vault, easily thirty feet deep and twenty wide with four round tables down the center. One wall was lined with safety deposit boxes, many of which were left open and empty. The other side was a bare concrete wall that was painted, and there is where the hostages all sat, lined up on the carpeted floor.

Elissa scanned the room once more, seeing four large safes at the end of the vault, all of which were open. As she was pulled to a stop, she turned her attention to the two dozen hostages, noticing quickly that they all bore looks of people who had lost all hope, especially at seeing someone who was supposed to be a superhero taken prisoner as well.

The man she had kicked in the jaw had her belt slung over her shoulder, and he stepped in front of her, glaring down at her as he was at least six feet tall. With a scowl and a growling voice, he informed, "I got something for you."

His fist slammed into the side of her face and she spun around and collapsed, unable to break her fall.

He pointed down at her and shouted, "You just lay there and think about that for a while. I'll be back to settle up with you when we're done!"

Raising her head, she looked over her shoulder as she watched the two turn and leave the vault, and this time they closed the door as they left.

"They didn't lock it," she observed aloud in a slight voice. Laying her head back down, she found herself facing the hostages.

One of them, sitting about the middle of the line, was a rather big man, a plump man who was losing his hair and seemed to be a rather rough fellow. He was wearing a plaid shirt and dirty trousers, and a disgusted look on his face.

"Great," he grumbled. "Now we're never going to get out of here."

Elissa smiled at him. "No, everything's going according to plan." She looked down at herself and said, "It's clear, guys."

Atom had a firm hold on Huntress' hand as they both jumped from the middle of her top. Each was less than a quarter of an inch tall, but as soon as they hit the carpet they rapidly grew to their normal sizes, each enveloped in an eerie glow that emanated from him.

Pulling a small lock pick from under one of her gauntlets, Elissa looked up at him and flashed a big smile as she said, "You'd better not let my mother find out where you were hiding."

He looked down at her and chuckled. "It's not like I've never been down *her* shirt."

Elissa's smile yielded to a horrified gape.

"So now what?" the same man demanded.

Huntress pointed at him and hissed, "Keep it down!" She looked to the door, then to Golden Angel, who was sitting up and had already freed one hand. "Okay, Angel. It's time for phase two."

Elissa nodded.

Sometime later, the vault door opened and four of Metallo's henchmen strode in, holding their weapons ready as one barked, "Okay, people it's time to..."

They all looked around, scanning the now empty vault with wide eyes.

"Where did they go?"

They all ran from the vault and to the lobby where Metallo and the other two waited with several full canvas bags.

The same one barked, "They're gone!"

Metallo spun to face him and demanded, "What? How did they get out of there?"

"I don't know, Boss. They just aren't in there anymore."

Looking that way, Metallo grumbled, "That's impossible." He strode to the back, followed by his men, and once he reached the vault he grabbed onto the edge of the door and pulled it open. Storming in, he looked around, carefully scanning the room, and he declared, "They couldn't have gotten out. They couldn't have." Turning to his men, he ordered, "Search the bank! Search everywhere!"

"Don't bother," Huntress advised from outside the vault.

The seven men turned toward the vault door just in time to see it close, and the sound of a mechanical lock engaging confirmed that they had been locked in.

Outside the door, Elissa turned the huge wheel one more time for good measure, then she dodged aside and pressed her back to the wall beside the door, right beside Huntress.

"Working so far," Huntress complimented. "You sure we should stick around?"

Something banged into the vault door hard enough to shake the whole wall.

Golden Angel looked to her and replied, "I'll take off and get them to chase me. You can take his henchmen from behind. Can you handle six of them?"

With a confident smile, the tall woman simply answered, "Oh please. There are only six of them."

A second bang and the wall around the door began to buckle.

"I wonder where they left my belt," Golden Angel said absently.

With the third impact, the vault door exploded from the wall and slammed onto the floor with a heavy thud.

The two heroines looked to each other and said together, "Phase three."

Elissa darted away, spinning around right before she made it to the lobby and raising her arms before her. Two of the men fired and she easily deflected their bullets.

"Stop shooting!" Metallo ordered, his attention fully on the little Amazon who defiantly stood her ground before him. "I'll take care of the little girl."

When he charged forward, Elissa barked a scream as she wheeled around and ran from him.

The six men he left behind never knew what hit them, and Huntress left nobody standing.

A chest high writing station with a black granite top that was about eight feet long was right in the middle of the lobby. Beneath it were many of the forms people could fill out before going to see the teller. Many pens were connected by short chains, but these were of no consequence. Golden Angel stopped at one end, grabbed it with both hands and wrenched the granite top off, then she wheeled around and slammed it into Metallo's head with everything she had.

It exploded into hundreds of little bits as it hit him and he stumbled sideways across the lobby.

The piece she still held was only about two feet square, and before he could get his bearings, she threw it at him with a good aim and hit him in the head again, and this time he stumbled into the teller's station, crashing into it and almost all the way through it.

As he steadied himself and emerged from the mess of the teller's stations, Elissa set her hands on her hips and demanded, "Where's my tiara?"

He took a couple of steps toward her, then set himself and countered, "Come and take it, little girl."

She snarled back, "You so don't know how much I hate to be called that." She still feared him, but she was also sure that stronger heroes would be along soon and all she had to do was fight a hit and run battle against him, using her speed and agility to keep him busy until help arrived.

Predictably, he strode toward her, but this time she did not retreat.

As he neared, he asked, "What did you do with my guests?"

"They're safe," she replied, "but I can't say the same for you."

"We'll see," he countered.

When he grabbed for her, she ducked under his arm and rammed her shoulder into his midriff, quickly driving him backward and to the teller's windows again. Before they got there, she grabbed onto one of his legs behind the knee and drove him as hard as she could onto the tile floor. Many of the tiles shattered as he struck back first, but he was not stunned and got his hand around her forearm, her gauntlet, before she could get away from him. She punched at his arm but could not break his grip on her as he stood. She tried to pry his fingers loose, but this only gave him the opportunity to get his other hand around that wrist. Now she had a problem.

Standing fully, he picked her up and stretched her arms in opposite directions. Golden Angel struggled in his grip and eventually kicked at him, catching him in the head, but this was to no avail.

"You are a spirited one," he commended, "but I'm afraid that spirit will not help you today." When she only responded with a defiant glare, he leaned his head and wondered, "Which of your arms do you think will tear away from you first?" Slowly, he began to pull her arms apart.

Elissa screamed as she felt her arms beginning to dislocate and pulled back with everything she had, but there was simply no hope of matching his strength.

A crossbow bolt hit him in the back of the head and his head swiveled around.

Standing behind him, Huntress had already reloaded with a bolt with an unusually large head on it, and her eyes narrowed as she snarled, "Let's see if you can take one of these." She shot the bolt with a good aim and it exploded between his shoulders.

As he stumbled forward, he lost his grip on one of the girl's arms and she took the opportunity to kick against him and free the other.

Huntress backed away, quickly reloading as he advanced on her. With a quick aim, and from only about twenty feet away, she shot him with another exploding tip bolt, but he only lurched backward and kept advancing on her.

Golden Angel acted quickly, slamming into his back and wrapping her arms around his metal waist. With a savage yell, she picked him up and arched her back, throwing them both backward and slamming him head-first onto the tile floor. Once again the tiles shattered as he struck, but this time she rolled away from him before he could turn on her. By the time he stood, she had backed away and stood beside Huntress.

"Okay," Elissa said, her attention locked on their enemy as he began to stride toward them again. "How many of those exploding arrows do you have left?"

"One," Huntress replied, "but it's not like they're doing any good, anyway."

"Headshot," Golden Angel mumbled, then she charged right at him and darted away right before she was within striking distance.

His attention turned to her as she readied herself about ten feet away from him. The last exploding crossbow bolt slammed into the side of his head and he staggered sideways a few steps from the blast, and Golden Angel struck hard, slamming her shoulder into him and driving him toward one of the huge windows. He turned and warded her off and she darted away again.

Looking to Huntress, Golden Angel shouted, "Get out of here! I've got him!"

Hesitantly, the tall woman nodded, then she backed away, turned and fled.

Metallo and Golden Angel faced off again.

"Alone at last," she observed with a coy smile.

"Yes," he drawled. "I don't make a habit of underestimating my opponents more than once. I know you are up to something or you would not have dismissed your little friend."

She slowly backed away as he stalked toward her. "Yeah, three's a crowd and stuff. So, are you afraid of me yet?" When he laughed, she grumbled, "Didn't think so." Looking past him, she saw what she could use, and smiled ever so slightly. "Well, then we should play before the grown-ups get here." She darted toward him again, and when he grasped for her she fell to the floor and under his arm, sliding on her leg and backside past him. Once behind him, she stood and darted to the vending machine that stood on one end of the lobby in a waiting area that had two rows of comfortable looking chairs facing a long coffee table that had magazines lying all over it. She hurtled over the table and landed right in front of the machine, glancing over her shoulder to see him advancing on her again. Reaching down, she grasped the bottom of the drink machine and rocked it up onto her shoulder, turning slightly as she looked to the approaching robotic bad man. Her eyes narrowed as she took careful aim, then with a mighty yell she threw the vending machine at him with all her might.

He simply batted it away and kept advancing.

Wide eyed, she watched it slide to a stop near the teller's stations and mumbled, "Well that sure didn't work." She was cornered again and they both knew it, but to her surprise he stopped on the other side of the table.

"You sure are a strong little girl," he observed.

"Thanks," she said, her eyes locked on his, "and please quit calling me that."

He folded his arms. "I already know who your mother is. Perhaps you'll tell me who your father is."

"That's none of your business," she spat.

"Process of elimination, then," he informed, slowly lowering his arms. A thick plate on his chest opened to reveal a glowing green stone that was mounted in place between four triangular metal keepers.

Golden Angel's eyes widened as she was bathed in the glow of the green stone. She knew immediately that it was kryptonite, and as he strode toward her again, kicking the table aside, she backed into the wall behind her, raising her palms as if to ward it off. She began to shake and breathe in quick gasps, and this told Metallo exactly what he wanted to know.

"Well," he drawled as he drew closer. "It would seem that Wonder Woman and Superman are more than just friends after all, wouldn't it?"

"Please," she implored in a whimper, "keep that away from me."

He slowly advanced, his hand clenching into tight fists. "This is a surprise. On the up side, it means I won't be killing you tonight after all. No, you are much more valuable to me alive."

She tore her wide eyes from the kryptonite and trained them up on his, her lips parting in fear as she pressed herself against the wall behind her.

He stopped only a foot away from her and set his hands on his hips. "Yes, you will be very valuable. Feeling weaker, my dear?"

Her knees shook and almost buckled, and she pled, "Please stop!"

"Too much of this will kill you, won't it, little girl?"

Elissa raised her brow and corrected, "Well, no, not really." Her hand darted into his chest, grabbed the chunk of kryptonite and retreated before he realized what had happened, and before he could react her other palm slammed hard up into his midriff and knocked him over the chairs behind him. She watched him slam onto the floor about twenty feet away, and she smiled as he slid to a stop. Looking to the kryptonite, which was about the size of a softball, she tossed it up and caught it a couple of times before turning her attention back to the big cyborg as he staggered to his feet. "Not so full of yourself now, are you?"

Clenching his fists, he ordered, "Give me that."

"Or what?" she challenged. "You'll kill me? You kind of want to do that anyway, don't you?"

He stalked forward. "Little girl, believe me I can make it quick and painless or—"

"Blah blah blah!" she barked back as she strode slowly forward to meet him. "I've done some reading on you, Mister Metallo, and we both know that this is what powers you."

He stopped.

Elissa raised a brow. "It seems to me that you're going to run out of juice here pretty quick without this, so you'd better start thinking about giving up without giving me any more trouble."

The door in his chest closed and he folded his arms again as she slowly neared. "You're a pretty smart girl."

"Thanks," she said sweetly. "I like to think so,"

"But not smart enough to think that I might have a backup power supply."

About ten feet away, Golden Angel stopped and for a few awkward seconds just stared up at him.

"I can go on for weeks without that," he informed, "and I have before."

She looked down to the kryptonite and mumbled, "Oh. I did not know that."

"Now you do," he pointed out. Extending his hand, he said, "Now be a good little girl and give Metallo the nice kryptonite."

Her brow slowly lowered and just as slowly she turned her eyes up to his, reminding through bared teeth, "I said don't call me that!" In quick motions she knocked his hand away and half spun, kicking him as hard as she could in the midriff.

Metallo landed on his back on the other side of the lobby, clearly taken by surprise by this attack, but he was quick to lunge to his feet and face her as she advanced again.

"Yeah," she spat. "Now you're going to have to tell the other bad guys you got your butt kicked by a little girl!"

"Not quite," he countered as he strode toward her again. "I think it's time for you to learn a little lesson. Now give me the kryptonite!"

She shook her head. "I so don't think so." When he charged, she evaded him easily, back-pedaling away and circling around behind him. He turned on her again and she dared to smile at him. "Too slow, metal man."

He tried again, this time side stepping to corner her, but she was simply too quick, and it was all too clear that she was just toying with him, buying time.

Turning to face her again, he reached into his pocket and conceded, "Very well. You have something I want," He produced her tiara. "and I have something you want. Shall we just trade?"

Her eyes narrowed and she raised a brow. "You must think I'm really stupid."

He slowly strode forward, holding the tiara toward her. "No, I just need to end this nonsense and be on my way. Now take your headpiece and give me the kryptonite."

"Keep the headpiece," she offered, backing away. "I have another one."

Metallo tossed the tiara away and shouted, "Little brat!" as he charged at her again.

She dodged away and he corrected and managed to get a hand around her upper arm. With speed she did not anticipate, he wheeled around, jerking her from the ground as he did and hurled her into the granite tiled wall about twenty feet away.

She slammed back first into it and barked a yell as she hit, then she crumpled limply to the floor, but somehow kept her grip on the kryptonite. Lying face down with her hair sprawled about around her head, her wits returned to her slowly and she struggled to pull her hands under her and push herself up. She drew a knee under her, planted her foot and tried to stand, but his fist came down on the back of her head to send her back down, and down she stayed.

Metallo stared down at the unconscious girl for a few seconds, then he bent down and plucked the kryptonite from her grasp, informing, "I'll just take that." Looking over his shoulder, he saw that two of his men had recovered and were staggering toward him, then his attention returned to the girl and he ordered, "Collect this foolish little girl. We'll take her with us. And make sure you bind her better this time. I want no more surprises."

One of the men falling to the floor near his foot caught the corner of his eye and he looked down to see the man lying unconscious face down. Wheeling around, he saw the other already down, and Huntress standing over him.

Staring up at him, she smiled as she announced, "Surprise!"

"This ends my patience," he growled as he strode toward her.

Backing away, Huntress pointed behind him and advised, "Don't tell me! Tell her!"

He stopped. Slowly, he looked over his shoulder, then he spun around to face Wonder Woman.

She was less than ten feet away and just standing there with her hands set on her hips. Glaring at him as she was, she appeared to be Death personified and for the first time Metallo found himself racked with hesitation.

Diana turned her eyes down to her unconscious daughter, then those deadly eyes shifted back to the cyborg who had knocked her out.

Finding his confidence, Metallo raised his chin and guessed, "I have to go through you as well? No matter." He strode toward her. "I'll make this quick." He swung as hard as he could.

She caught his fist in her palm and replied with her own, right into his chest.

This time, Metallo crashed all the way through the teller's stations and was finally stopped by the wall behind them, though he penetrated it about a foot before crumpling to the ground.

Diana strode after him, glancing at Huntress as she ordered, "See to Golden Angel."

Huntress kept her eyes on the Amazon Princess who strode with purposeful steps after Metallo, then she turned her eyes to the unconscious girl and hurried to her. Kneeling down beside Elissa, she first checked for a pulse, then she brushed her hair aside, looking for her face, and finally finding it.

"Angel?" she summoned, stroking the girl's cheek. "Angel. Can you hear me?" Hearing a crash behind her, she looked over her shoulder as Metallo flew over the teller's stations and slammed into the now topless table where people were meant to fill out their forms, smashing it to pieces as his metal body drove through it.

He stood turning to face the Amazon Princess as she pursued him with heavy, menacing steps, her eyes locked on him in that deadly glare.

Diana paused and looked to her daughter, to Huntress and asked, "Is she okay."

With a glance down at the girl, Huntress looked to Diana and nodded, assuring, "She's out, but I think she'll be okay."

Nodding back, Wonder Woman turned her predator's gaze back on Metallo and said, "Well, it looks like this is your lucky day." She held her hands before her and cracked her knuckles, snarling, "But not *that* lucky."

WW

Morning was only a few hours away and now police and investigators milled around the bank lobby and all marveled over the damage caused by the battle between Golden Angel and Metallo. Commissioner Gordon looked over the wreckage of the teller's stations as Detective Bullock reported what had happened.

Gordon, who faced the teller's stations with his arms folded, half turned his head and asked, "So how long were they in here?"

"We think about six hours," Bullock answered. "They hit the place a few minutes before it closed and had everyone locked in the vault. We didn't even know about it until we were responding to missing persons calls and found out most of them were last known to be here."

Watching them, Diana sat on the floor near where her daughter had slammed into the granite wall tiles. Her back was against the wall and her legs outstretched and crossed at the ankles as she listened for the detective's report. Golden Angel slumbered peacefully, her head lying on her mother's lap and her arms drawn to her as she was curled up on the floor next to her mother, and Diana slowly, gently stroked the girl's hair.

When the girl whimpered and rocked her head ever so slightly, Diana looked down to her and gently combed her fingers through her hair right over her ear.

Golden Angel drew a deep breath and rolled her head to look up at her mother through eyes that were open only to thin slits. She blinked and slowly brought the world around her into focus.

Wonder Woman smiled. "How did you sleep, Junior?"

Unable to answer, Elissa drew another breath and blinked, holding her brow low as she tried to remember where she was, and as that realization hit her she gasped loudly and sat up, bracing herself up on her palms as she looked around her with wide eyes. Seeing that it was over, she bowed her head and grumbled, "I got my butt kicked again, didn't I?"

"Afraid so," Wonder Woman confirmed. "Have you thought about taking on bad guys who are not so..."

"Mechanical?" Golden Angel snarled.

"Well," Diana sighed, "I was going to say out of your weight class, but that would be a good start."

"I thought I had him," Elissa said softly. "I really did."

Wonder Woman roughed her daughter's hair. "Cheer up, little warrior. We don't win every battle."

Drawing her legs to her, Golden Angel wrapped her arms around them and laid her chin on her knees. "Lately I just want to win one."

"You got the hostages out of there safely," Diana pointed out, "and Atom tells me that was your main goal. You saved lives tonight."

"Except my own," the girl mumbled.

A police officer approached and offered, "Excuse me." When the Amazons looked to him, he offered Golden Angel her tiara and informed, "I found this and thought you might like it back."

"Thank you," she said softly as she slowly reached to him and took it.

He smiled at Diana and went about his duties.

Elissa laid her chin back on her knees, staring blankly ahead of her.

Wonder Woman simply stared at her for a moment, then she drew her feet to her and stood, slapping the girl's back with the back of her hand as she bade, "Come on, Golden Angel. Let's get going."

Reluctantly, Elissa stood, then she barked, "Whoa!" as she grasped for her mother's arm. Her eyes were wide and she was clearly having some problems with balance, then she squeezed her eyes shut and reached for the back of her head, whining, "Ow."

Grasping the girl's shoulders, Wonder Woman asked, "You okay,

Angel?"

With a hesitant nod, Golden Angel replied, "I think so. My head hurts really bad."

"Maybe we should get you checked out," the Amazon Princess suggested as she turned with the girl toward the door.

"I'm okay," Elissa assured, walking more on her own, though not with steady steps.

Outside, police cars were still everywhere, an ambulance or two, a fire truck and many people in uniform, mostly police officers. The armored truck had been taken away from the front of the bank and the way was clear to the perimeter line the police had set up. And, of course, the ever present news cameras.

Seeing the media on the other side of the police line, Elissa pulled fully away from her mother and walked on her own, holding her head up as best she could as her eyes darted about at the all the activity.

A very big, dark blue van was backed up about fifty feet from the bank and its doors hung wide open, and Elissa tried not to look that way as they passed.

There, at the back of the van, Metallo had been secured to a heavy, metal table of some kind by thick, form fitting metal brackets across his chest and belly that kept his arms down and under control. Similar metal restraints held his legs down. Mounted on a wheeled dolly of some kind, it held him nearly standing and leaning back on the steel platform that would be used to load him into the van and later transport him from the van to whatever facility they saw fit. As he saw Wonder Woman and Golden Angel stride by, his head followed their movement with evil intent, and finally he called, "Hey, little girl."

Elissa stopped and could only stare forward for long seconds as she fought to suppress that nervous crawl within her. Slowly, reluctantly, she looked toward him, her lips parted a little fearfully as she did.

His mechanical eyes simply glared at her for a few seconds after, and he growled, "This isn't over, you little brat."

She could not purge all of the fear from her voice as she spat back, "It looks pretty over to me." She flinched as he wrenched his shoulder up as if trying to escape the restraints that held him.

His head drew toward her as far as his mechanical neck would allow and he warned, "They won't be able to hold me forever, little girl, and when I get loose..." His attention shifted slightly away from her.

Wonder Woman strode around her, right at the robotic villain, right up to him.

He was a little taller and stared down into her eyes with wicked purpose, but he was silenced by her approach.

Stopping only about a foot away, Diana stared back at him. Slowly, she reached up and stroked his cheek with the back of her finger. "You can't feel that, can you?" When he pulled his head away from her, her eyes narrowed and she continued, "You can't feel anything, can you, John Corben?"

He looked away from her.

"Oh," she drawled sympathetically, "but I guess there is no more of John Corben left in you, is there? The man you used to be has been replaced by this piece of junk you live inside of now."

His mechanical eyes slid to her.

"A pity," she sighed as her fingers stroked across his robotic face. "I'll bet you were once quite a handsome fellow. Now you're just... this."

"Don't think that you are off my radar, you Amazon wretch," he warned. "You and that little girl are—"

She grabbed onto his neck and slammed his head back onto the solid platform he was strapped to. "Threaten me all you want, but if you go near my daughter again I will tear you into so many pieces they'll never be able to put you back together! I suggest you remember that!" She released him and turned to walk away, finishing in a softer voice, "John."

He glared back as she took the girl under her arm, then he spat, "And your pal Superman? He'll be feeling the brunt of what that little girl should the next time I meet him."

Diana paused and looked over her shoulder at him. "Rest assured, Mister Corben, that you may be a problem to him, but now you have your own nightmare to worry about." Her eyes narrowed. "Me." She continued on, leading the girl away as she added, "You're under my full attention now, so just pray that you never, ever get paroled. Prison is the only place you'll ever be safe from me. I catch you on the outside and I will finish what I started tonight."

Wonder Woman led her daughter past the police line.

Elissa vented a hard breath through her nose, then she shook her head and grumbled, "Why do mechanical bad guys always seem to have it in for me?"

Laughing under her breath, Diana shook her head and replied, "I just can't imagine, Junior."

WW

They entered the mansion through the Batcave, careful not to be seen by unwanted eyes. As they walked side by side toward the staircase at the back of the mansion, Diana ordered, "Just get changed. We'll talk about it later."

Elissa cut her eyes up to her mother's and informed, "She said we did really well together. I don't see why we can't hang out from time to time."

"I'm not saying no," Wonder Woman informed, "just not tonight. You need to get some rest and recover from your big evening, and I'm sure you have another concussion so you are to go right to bed."

"Yes, Mother," the girl grumbled. "I guess the Justice League just got a little further away, didn't it?"

Diana smiled and slipped her arm around her daughter's shoulders, brutally pulling the girl into her as she replied, "You thought of the safety of the hostages first, and having Atom shrink them down so that they could all hide in a safety deposit box was simply brilliant."

Leaning her head against her mother's shoulder, Elissa also smiled and offered, "Thanks."

"That's the kind of thinking you'll have to have in the Justice League," Diana informed. "It's not all about brute force and fighting bad guys. Much of it is what you did tonight."

"So," the girl stammered, "a little closer?"

"A little," Diana assured. "Now go change and get cleaned up."

Elissa changed quickly and bounded back downstairs to bid her parents good night. Surely Batman had made it back and she headed straight to the clock to greet him in the Batcave, only wearing white running shorts beneath a long, pink tee shirt that read *Princess* in big white, sparkly letters.

The cave itself was cold and very damp, not well suited for a scantly clothed girl in bare feet, but she barely noticed as she strode into the cave. Stopping abruptly, she looked ahead of her, to the massive computer console some distance away. Batman was there, and Wonder Woman. They faced each other in front of the big monitor of the computer where some unfinished research was still displayed.

And they were arguing.

Cold quickly began to penetrate Elissa and she crossed her arms over her chest as she watched them. She could hear their voices, and while she could not make out what was said, she could hear the anger in their voices. She had only seldom seen them together and not fighting, only then it was because of work, of having to take on bad guys or something like that.

She lowered her eyes and slowly turned away from them.

Back upstairs, she closed her bedroom door behind her and padded to her bed. Alfred had pulled the covers back for her and she slipped under the sheet and blanket, pulling them up to her neck as she curled up on her side and stared into the darkness, a darkness her gift of night sight penetrated with ease. Tears rolled from her eyes and a deep breath entered her in broken gasps. Finally closing her eyes, she curled up tighter and hugged her pillow to her. And she wept.

"It isn't supposed to be this way. Why can't they just love each other again?"

WW

Hours later she had finally managed to fall asleep, though it was a restless one. Lying flat on her back right in the middle of the huge bed, she was largely sprawled under the covers with her head rocked over to one side, one arm curled over her head and the mother lying straight out from her.

Slow, rhythmic breathing began to succumb to deep, hard breaths, then quick shallow ones. A whimper escaped her and she rolled her head the other way, her lips parting and her brow tense. She sucked a hard breath and whimpered again, drawing her legs to her and grasping the edge of the bed tightly in her hand: her other hand clenched into a tight fist.

Quick, short breaths shrieked into her and she cried out, then she sat up and screamed, "No! Get it out of me! Get it out!" as she grasped her belly with both arms. Her wide eyes were locked across the room as she struggled to catch her breath and realize where she was.

When the door to her bedroom burst open she screamed and looked that way as her entire body convulsed with shock.

Wearing a long red tee shirt that went almost to her knees and her hair loose and flowing behind her, Diana strode into the room and hurried to her daughter's side, sitting beside the girl and enveloping her in her arms.

Elissa found herself crying and clung to her mother, burying her face in Diana's neck as she tried to separate reality from dream.

"Shh," Diana soothed. "It's okay now. It was just a bad dream."

Hesitantly, the girl nodded, still clinging to her mother like a frightened child. She found herself covered in finely beaded sweat and trembling, and she concentrated on overcoming that.

Even after Elissa had finally calmed herself, the two just sat there and held each other, and Diana continued to slowly stroke the girl's hair to soothe and reassure her.

"Are you okay now?" Diana asked with a gentle voice.

Drawing a deep breath, Elissa just nodded again, then she pulled away, turning her eyes down as she offered, "Sorry. Really bad dream. I guess I kind of freaked out a little." Intermittent tremors still racked her body despite her best efforts to control them.

"You want to talk about it?" Diana asked as she combed her fingers through the girl's hair.

Elissa shook her head. "No. Not now."

"Okay," the Amazon Princess said in a whisper. "Do you want me to lay with you for a while?"

Turning away from her mother, Elissa shook her head again and scoffed, "I'm seventeen, Mom. I don't need to—"

"Elissa," Diana barked. When the girl looked to her, she raised her brow and asked, again, "Do you want me to lay with you for a while?"

Tears welled up in Elissa's eyes and her trembling mouth curled downward in a little girl's frown, and hesitantly, she nodded.

"Go on, then," Diana ordered as she pushed the girl back into bed.

Elissa faced away from her mother, curling up on her side, and Diana pressed her body to her daughter's and pulled the sheet and blanked over them both, then she wrapped her arm around the girl and held her closely to her. Elissa felt a little ashamed about this, being as old as she was, but this was comforting, and finally she felt safe.

Loosing a hard breath, Elissa offered, "Sorry I'm such a wimp tonight."

Diana laughed under her breath and kissed her daughter's head, then settled back down and assured, "You're no wimp, Junior." She stroked her fingers through the girl's hair right about her temple and whispered, "I will never regret these moments. Just be my little girl a while longer."

CHAPTER 5

Late morning brought a new day and new possibilities. While sleep had been elusive, she had finally drifted off and slept soundly through the rest of the night. The sun was climbing high and shining through her window, making bright ribbons of white and yellow light through a gap between the curtains.

Having forced herself to forget about the most recent fight between her parents, she sat up and a little smile found her lips as she stretched. Slipping from beneath the blankets, she stretched more, this time falling into more of an athlete's regiment as she fell into a daily routine of stretching each muscle group to prepare it for the coming day. Her head no longer hurt. Her Amazon metabolism and healing power had taken stock of the injuries from the night before and she felt as fresh as ever. Still wearing the running shorts and pink tee shirt, she found the morning rather chilly and padded to the wardrobe across the room when she had finished her stretching regiment, opening it to find the thin red robe within. She slipped into it and tied off the sash as she headed for her door, looking forward to the freshness of a new day. Leaving her bedroom, she strode to the baluster and grasped the hardwood handrail as she looked down into the living area below, toward the big sitting room. All of the joy left her features as she saw her parents there, both standing in front of the big fireplace, now cold.

Bruce was dressed in a satiny blue business suit with the shirt open three buttons down. He had no tie on, and his hair was, as always, perfectly groomed. Diana wore a red blouse and white slacks, and her hair was down.

And this time, Elissa could hear what was said.

"Do you want me to just take her back to Themyscira?" Diana barked with angry words. "She's already seen this part of the world and she'll never be content to spend the rest of her life among the safety of the Amazons."

"She wasn't content before," he countered "and I know it is too late for her go be isolated on that island again."

"Then what do you propose we do, Bruce? She wants to join the Justice League, or at the very least take on a crime fighting crusade on her own again. Or with one of us!"

"I know she does," he assured, "but allowing her to go head to head with those like Metallo will eventually get her killed and you know it!"

"Have you no confidence in your own daughter?"

"I have every confidence in her, Princess, but there are certain realities to face. She is simply no match for many of the enemies we have out there."

Folding her arms, Diana turned away from him and growled, "You would have her just sit, then."

"No, I wouldn't, but we have to be more responsible about what she is put up against. If you keep thinking she'll be able to take those like Metallo and Bane then you're going to end up getting her killed!"

Elissa could simply hear no more and she wheeled around and rushed back into her bedroom.

Moments later, dressed in blue jeans and a black tee shirt, she sped through the front gate of Wayne Manor on her motorcycle.

A fast bike ride down the roads on the outskirts of Gotham City was not clearing her head. Only one thing would, and she turned her direction toward a private but heavily guarded air strip where Themyscira's most advanced jets awaited her.

She had changed before approaching the hangar and now it was Golden Angel who came for the aircraft. No one questioned her as she strode into the hanger, opened the doors and started the engines of the crescent shaped aircraft. It was small for a two seat fighter, especially one with the seats side by side and was something of a quarter moon shaped flying wing with the two engines embedded in the wings at the sides of the cockpit. Intakes and exhausts were difficult to see and the fluid lines of the wings joined into a long, thin tail that trailed behind and offered extra control and maneuvering surfaces.

Taxiing to the one runway seemed to take forever but she made it finally and throttled the powerful engines to full as she easily lifted it from the ground.

Her helmet lay on the seat beside her, leaving her long, obsidian black hair free and pulled over one shoulder to keep it out of her way. Her blue eyes darted to the instruments frequently and automatically, but mostly scanned the cloud strewn sky outside of the airplane.

She flew ever higher, knowing that her airplane would adjust for higher altitudes and eventually space. This was a trans-atmospheric craft, though leaving the atmosphere was something she had never done before and she was actually forbidden to do so. No matter. In the moment, she simply did not care.

In short order, the crescent shaped airplane left the safety of the atmosphere and found itself in orbit, and Elissa found herself streaking across the sky much faster than she had ever gone. A little smile found her lips as she looked out the side of the canopy and saw the curvature of the Earth for the first time, beholding something that very few people would ever see. It was time to simply enjoy being aloft and away from all of the troubles that plagued her.

She did not know how long it had been since she had taken off, probably a couple of hours. She had orbited the Earth many times by now and finally felt her head clearing. An alert from her radar drew her attention. There was a craft approaching, very fast. It was in a higher orbit and would cross her path less than a mile ahead, and would do so in only a few seconds. Operating only on thrusters, she slowed the IJ121 and looked to her right, and a little smile found her lips again.

It was a huge, broad bodied craft, a trans-atmospheric shuttle with blunt wings near the rear. Its shape was one she recognized from the many pictures she had studied. The Javelin 4 was a resupply shuttle used by the Justice League's Watchtower, a place she had always dreamed about seeing someday.

Turning the IJ121, she made the impulsive decision to follow the Javelin and fell in behind it.

The flight to the Watchtower was much quicker than she thought it would be and her lips slowly drew apart as she saw it. Slowing her fighter, she allowed the Javelin to make its approach and just watched as a huge hatch opened on the massive saucer shaped center body of the station, the hangar deck.

"If only," she whispered as she watched the shuttle disappear into the Watchtower. Her eyes danced about, studying every line she could about the station as she daydreamed about the day she would be welcomed aboard as part of the Justice League.

"Themysciran craft," a deep, monotone voice called to her over her speakers.

Elissa flinched. She had not expected to be contacted and was not sure what to do.

"Themysciran craft," the voice repeated. "This is Watchtower. Please respond."

"Comm system," she ordered. After it replied with three beeps, she answered, "This is Themyscira one two one four. Go ahead Watchtower."

"Stand by to receive approach telemetry," he ordered.

Her eyes widened and she breathed, "No way!"

"Repeat last," the Watchtower said.

"Um," she stammered, "ready to receive telemetry." She swallowed hard as she checked her scope and prodded her fighter forward, assuring, "I have telemetry. Approaching on thrusters."

WW

The doors to the hangar deck slid open and she hesitantly strode out into the circular corridor. People in blue jumpsuits, many carrying clipboards and other paperwork, milled about on their respective tasks, and few even acknowledged her. Turning left down the corridor, she walked slowly, just taking in as much of her surroundings as she could.

She wandered for a while, dodging aside as supplies and equipment were moved from place to place, and finally she realized that there was more activity on this deck than she was comfortable with. Finding an elevator, Elissa pushed the green up button and waited for the door to open, and when it did, she found two other people already in there, one with a clipboard and one pushing a covered cart. Hesitantly stepping in, she backed herself against the wall furthest from them and watched the doors close.

"Yeah, I tell you," the man said in a laugh, "that Flash has a million of 'em. Did he tell you the one about the weasel and the rat?"

The woman with him, carrying the clipboard, laughed and

nodded. "Yes! It was great!"

They both looked to Elissa.

She offered a shy, nervous smile back before turning her eyes down. They had ID badges on, and this was a quick reminder that she did not belong here. Long, tense seconds of silence followed.

Mercifully, the car stopped and the doors opened, and out they went.

Elissa drew a breath and leaned her head back against the wall, closing her eyes as the doors began to slide shut, then a chill ran through her as they opened again.

"Because that's how it was assigned," Green Arrow explained as he strode in. "J'onn knows what he's doing. Just give it a rest already!"

When Black Canary entered behind him, Elissa felt herself near panic, and swallowed hard as the doors closed.

"I know he knows what he's doing," Black Canary complained as she folded her arms and turned toward the door, "but he has to realize that some of us have lives beyond the Justice League."

They both looked to Golden Angel.

Elissa's eyes darted from one to the other and a nervous smile found her lips again as she raised a hand before her to waggle her fingers in greeting.

Green Arrow raised his chin and asked, "So who is this?"

Turning fully, Black Canary declared, "Wait a minute. Golden Angel?"

Elissa nodded.

With a broad smile, Black Canary observed, "So Diana let you come to the watchtower, huh?" She turned to Green Arrow and went on, "This is the kid we read about a few months ago, the one that took down Red Panzer's stupid little war against the Justice League."

"Oh!" Green Arrow said. "I thought you looked familiar. You're Wonder Woman's little girl, aren't you?"

Elissa nodded again and shyly confirmed, "Yes sir."

He extended his hand to her. "Well it's good to meet you. Welcome to the Justice League."

She took his hand and shyly offered, "Thank you." She also shook Black Canary's hand, still trying to shake off that feeling of panic.

"So where are you going?" Green Arrow asked.

Swallowing hard, Elissa struggled to answer, "Um, I, uh... I just got here."

The two heroes looked to each other and Black Canary said, "I'll take her to Control since I'm going there anyway." She looked away and complained, "Again."

"Oh, quit griping," he growled. When the doors opened, he assured, "I'll see you later."

"Yeah," Black Canary grumbled. As he left and the doors closed, she looked back to Elissa and informed, "I'm glad to see us getting some help. We're all stretched so thin lately that it's getting hard to have anything that resembles a real life. So have you been put on the schedule yet?"

Elissa shook her head.

"I'll bet you're anxious," Black Canary guessed. "I remember my first few months with the League. I couldn't wait to get up here and get to work." She leaned against the wall on the far side of the car and propped one of her boots against it. "We usually go in teams these days, almost never alone." Another smile found her mouth. "Anxious to work with your mom again?"

Just that thought sent new tremors of anxiety through Elissa and she hesitantly shrugged as she turned her eyes down.

"Yeah," Black Canary drawled. "You don't want to be under Mom's shadow. I get it."

The doors slid open again and Black Canary strode confidently out, and Elissa held her head up as best she could as she followed. She had to look confident, had to look like she belonged here. If she was accepted by the others in the Justice League before her parents found out then perhaps it would be too late for them to tell her no.

The main control console was ahead and Elissa's eyes widened as she recognized the tall, caped figure who stood at it.

Martian Manhunter turned slowly, and his attention found Elissa immediately. His eyes seemed to narrow as he looked her up and down, as he studied her.

"J'onn," Black Canary introduced, "this is—"

"Golden Angel," he finished for her in that deep, monotone voice. "I was not informed that you would be joining the League."

Black Canary pointed out, "You knew it had to be coming. She saved Wonder Woman, saved Superman, and brought down a major bad guy all in day one, not to mention taking on Metallo last night. I'd say she's proven her metal."

He hesitantly nodded. "Indeed."

Elissa could sense that he could see right through her and avoided eye contact, instead glancing about her and absorbing the details of the cavernous control room.

An alarm on the control consol drew his attention and he looked down to it.

Black Canary strode toward him and asked, "What do we have?"

His eyes narrowing again, he replied, "I'm not sure. There appear to be multiple alarms at Star Lab's West Coast facility. Take Flash and Hawkgirl and investigate."

She set her hands on her hips and barked, "Flash?" When he simply looked to her, she huffed a hard breath and turned to the elevator, grabbing the communicator from her belt as she ordered, "Hawkgirl and Flash to Teleporter One." She did not seem happy about the assignment or at least one of her team members and her body language made no secret of it. Looking over her shoulder, she bade, "See you later, Golden Angel."

Elissa waved back at her. In a moment, she found herself alone with the Martian Manhunter, and found his attention on her again. She offered a nervous smile and asked, "So how's it going?"

Slowly, his attention turned back to the consol and he punched a few keys. "It is a relatively calm day. Hopefully it will remain so."

She nodded and looked to what he was doing.

A long, silent moment passed, one that grew more and more tense with each passing second.

Elissa was not sure what to do and was too afraid to ask or wander off, so she just stood there and watched the Martian's activities. Sooner or later Wonder Woman or Batman would come through those doors and then her reckoning would be at hand.

Another alarm sounded and the Martian Manhunter worked the controls.

"What's up?" Superman asked from right behind Elissa.

She gasped and spun around, looking up at him with wide eyes and her lips open in surprise.

Standing there with his arms folded, he looked down at her and smiled, greeting, "Hi there."

"Hi," she replied dreamily with a broad smile and a slight lean of her head. Without realizing, she raised her hand to a lock of her hair that hung over the side of her tiara and absently began to twist it around her fingers.

"It's good to see you again," he said with a nod.

That giddiness welled up inside of her and she drew her shoulders up slightly, gently biting her lip as she replied, "You, too."

J'onn raised his chin. "Several people have disappeared in a mine in Central America. According to the report there was a partial cave-in and a number of people are trapped, mostly scientists who were studying reports of strange creatures that live down there." He half turned and looked to Superman.

The Man of Steel nodded. "I'll check it out, but I could sure use a second set of eyes down there."

"I'll go!" Elissa barked without realizing.

Superman and J'onn looked to her, then to each other, then back to her.

Her gaze shifted from one to the other, then she shrugged and assured, "It sounds routine, and besides, I see perfectly in the dark."

Superman looked back to the Martian Manhunter and raised his brow.

Venting a deep breath, J'onn conceded, "Very well."

"Come on, kiddo," Superman ordered as he turned toward the elevator.

Elissa followed, now feeling giddier than she ever had. This was for real! She was going on a mission for the Justice League! With Superman! She could not control the little bounce in her steps as she followed him, but her heart jumped as the Martian Manhunter called, "Golden Angel." Hesitantly, she stopped and turned.

He tossed her a Justice League communicator and ordered, "Stay in contact."

She caught it with one hand and a broad grin overtook her face and she nodded, assuring, "Yes sir, we will."

WW

The site looked just like one would expect. Police cars and fire trucks were parked around the entrance, many people in uniform milled about as did many miners who wore jumpsuits and hard hats.

There was wooden bracing piled near the entrance to the mine and much rock and debris. When Superman and Golden Angel strode toward the mine entrance, two ambulances raced from the scene with their lights and sirens going.

As they reached the entrance, Superman folded his arms and looked down to the collapsed pit, asking, "What can we do?"

A man in a well decorated police uniform that had a white shirt and brown trousers looked up at him and said with a Spanish accent, "We know that there are about eleven people down there. A little girl was seen going in this morning right before the entrance collapsed. She lives locally and her name is Christina. She is who we are most concerned with at the moment. The scientists all disappeared almost a week ago and rescue teams have reported being attacked by strange creatures with very long hair, very powerful creatures. A few came out injured." He looked back down to the pit and shook his head. "And I don't think this was an accident."

Superman squinted slightly and his gaze swept along the ground around the pit. "Hmm. The entrance has collapsed for a good twenty or thirty feet, and it doesn't look that stable down there until well into the first tunnel." Backing away a few steps, he ordered, "Everyone get back."

Elissa watched him leap into the air, hover there for a moment, then he began to spin, faster and faster until he was nothing but a blur. Angling downward, he plunged back to the ground, drilling himself through the earth and rock and disappearing below ground. Dust, dirt and chunks of rock were spat from the tunnel he made at a high rate of speed and in great volume as he drilled deeper and deeper, and in less than a moment the eruption of debris stopped. Knowing that this meant he had reached an open tunnel below, Elissa strode into the settling dust cloud and looked down into the neatly cut tunnel left by the man of steel. It was at a good angle for her to climb down comfortably and she looked to the police officer Superman had spoken with, ordering with all of the authority in her voice she could muster, "Wait here. We'll check it out."

She was able to see perfectly in the pitch black below ground as she slid down the dusty tunnel on her backside, watching her path of travel carefully.

Down in one of the mine shafts, which was about fifteen feet wide with a ceiling that was arched and about eight feet at the highest point, she slid out of the tunnel Superman had drilled and came down perfectly on her feet, falling to a crouch with one hand down to help break her fall. Looking around her, she saw Superman about ten feet away as he half turned to see her land.

Elissa stood and dusted off her behind as she walked to him, asking in a low voice, "So do you see anything?"

He looked forward again and shook his head, answering in a normal tone, "Not a thing, not yet, but something doesn't feel right down here."

"Can you see okay in the dark?" she asked.

He looked to her and smiled, tapping his temple as he reminded, "X-ray vision."

They followed the shaft for some time, noting that the floor angled downward and they descended deep into the Earth. Although she had excellent vision in the dark, something about this place made Elissa's skin crawl. They eventually reached a juncture with another shaft branching off of the one they traveled down, and here they stopped.

Superman's eyes cut down the branch tunnel, then ahead again and he asked, "Do you see anything?"

Her eyes shifting from one tunnel to the next, Elissa admitted, "Not a thing, but I sure sense something. We aren't alone down here."

"Let's split up," he suggested.

Elissa suddenly felt near panic and her eyes widened. "What?"

"We can cover more ground if we split up," he explained. "I'll take the main shaft here. You take that one to the right and yell if you see anything."

As he strode fearlessly down the main shaft, she mumbled, "How about I scream if I see something?" Looking down the tunnel that branched off, she did her best to swallow back her fear, drew a deep breath and headed down it.

Her gift of insight was, for the first time, speaking very loudly. She knew she was being watched by something that did not want to be seen and her walk was a slow one as her eyes scanned her surroundings, seeing perfectly in the pitch blackness of the mine. Turning her eyes up, she studied the arched ceiling as she slowly put one boot in front of the other, holding her hands down as she strode ever deeper into the dark recesses. Though she sensed that the presence closest to her meant her no harm, she also sensed others with more malicious intent, hungry intent.

About a hundred yards down the shaft she stopped as she heard something. Her eyes darted about to search for whatever was there. She did not sense anything wicked from it, but she did sense that someone or something was afraid of her approach.

Setting her hands on her hips, Golden Angel assured, "I won't hurt you. I'm here to help. Please just come out where I can see you." Something shifted ahead of her and she trained her gaze that way. Hesitantly, she strode forward, then she heard soft foot falls running away from her. She pursued, calling, "Wait! I won't hurt you, I promise!"

About ten yards ahead the tunnel came to a dead end. Fallen rock, piles of debris and a few old crates and some digging equipment littered the area. This far down the shaft was about fifteen feet wide and ended suddenly at a solid wall that had been worked recently, but not by tools. It had been drilled to be blasted by explosives and dozens of holes pocked it from ceiling to floor. She stopped and looked left, seeing what looked like claw marks on the wall. To the right, the wall had been dug out in a round tunnel that looked to be about three feet wide and high, and inside something moved.

Elissa's insights were fully alert and she slowly approached the hole, crouching down to look in. Leaning her head, she softly called, "Hello." Something in there growled, but she did not feel afraid. "Oh, come on," she prodded. "Come out here and let's talk."

Without warning, the creature in the hole burst out and knocked the girl to her back, landing on top of her. Before Golden Angel realized what had happened, she found herself pinned beneath something of tremendous weight. Her wrists were in the powerful grips of heavily clawed hands and held firmly to the ground at her sides.

Getting her wits back to her quickly, Elissa looked up to the flat faced creature that held her down. It was covered with long course hair that was a dark blue and had rigid and very sharp quills over its back and shoulders, and more quills in its forearms that faced forward. Large, solid black eyes stared down at her as wide nostrils flared in quick snorts. Its thick lips were parted to reveal a mouthful of heavy, pointed teeth that were tightly clenched. It was very broad shouldered, but it had short legs that were very strong. This was a powerful creature, very formidable looking, and yet it hesitated and did not seem intent on hurting her.

Elissa only struggled for a few seconds as she tried to twist free of this creature, but finally lay still and looked up at it, raising her brow as she complimented, "You sure are strong." She squinted slightly, looking to the side of the creature's head. It had small ears that were laid back against its head that were barely visible beneath all of that hair and she might not have seen it at all but for something that dangled from its long lobe: An earring! It was gold and in the shape of an angel, and this irony was not lost on her. Looking back to the creature's eyes, she breathed, "Christina."

The creature's brow lifted slightly.

"Are you Christina?" Golden Angel asked.

It released her and backed away, keeping its attention trained on her.

Elissa sat up and drew her legs to her, planting her palms on the ground behind her as she stared back in disbelief. "It's okay. I came to find you."

It made a series of chirps, then cooed in response, and it seemed to understand her.

Pushing herself up, Golden Angel stood and then knelt down right in front of the creature, whispering, "What happened to you?"

It looked down at its hand and brushed the quills on its forearm.

Leaning her head, Elissa guessed, "You got stuck with one of these and it made you this?"

The creature chirped twice. Something seemed to alarm it and it looked up the shaft, screeching as it backed away from her.

Springing to her feet, Golden Angel spun around and took her battle stance as she saw the same kind of creature bound into view, but this one was much bigger, more than twice the size of the first and with a far more muscular build, and a much more aggressive stance that resembled how a gorilla might stand on all fours.

As it bared its teeth and stalked forward, Elissa murmured, "Oh, crud," as she backed away. "Christina, get behind me."

The bigger creature's huge forearms began to swell and it thrust one at her. There was a loud pop and three of its quills streaked forward at great speed.

As she would with bullets or arrows, Golden Angel deflected them easily with her gauntlets, then deflected again as it sent another barrage toward her, then another.

The big creature seemed to grow angry and howled at her through bared teeth. Christina responded and stepped around Elissa on all fours in a clear attempt to intervene, but she backed down as the larger creature growled at her.

Stepping away from the smaller creature, Golden Angel stood ready as she called upon her gift of insight to see what she was up against. To this creature she was an enemy that had to be turned to its side, but its thoughts were straying from that idea and pursuing another about her, that she was food!

With another loud roar, it lunged forward with amazing speed. Golden Angel dodged away, raising her arm as it swiped at her. She took its claws on her gauntlet and was thrown off balance, and as she stumbled backward it turned with speed and agility she did not know it possessed and attacked again, swiping at her with its other clawed hand. Backing away, she took its claws on her gauntlet again, then again, then she kicked straight up and slammed the toe of her boot into its jaw.

It stopped and shook its head, then bared its teeth and growled as it looked back to her.

Elissa raised her brow and observed, "Yeah, you're kind of tough, aren't you? That didn't look like it hurt at all."

With an angry howl, it lunged at her again, and as she raised her arms to ward off its claws it grabbed both of her forearms and drove her backward into the shaft wall, slamming her hard into the stone. Elissa cried out as her back and head impacted, and while she was stunned it wheeled around and threw her the other direction.

Golden Angel hit the far wall with her back even harder than the first time and the air exploded from her. As she crumpled to the floor she tried desperately to summon her wits back to her, sweeping her arm just in time to ward off another spread of its quills. She had barely gotten to her feet when it slammed its shoulder into her and crushed her to the wall again, and this time consciousness nearly slipped away. As her knees buckled and she collapsed, it grabbed onto her gauntlet and hurled her the other way, and this time she crashed into a stack of old crates.

Elissa moaned weakly as she lay in the splintered wood of the crates, which were thankfully empty but for the paper packing within. She rocked her head back and forth, blinking her eyes open. She knew quickly that the fight was not going well for her and heard it charging her again. Even before she saw it, she drew her knees to her chest, and when it was upon her she kicked it with both legs as hard as she could.

This time the creature found itself hurling backward through the air. Its head slammed into the ceiling and then it hit the far wall and crumpled to the ground. A little rock and dust that had been knocked loose rained down on it for a second later as it lay on its belly.

Taking the opportunity to get back to her feet, Golden Angel staggered backward through what was left of the crates and into the wall, and for long seconds that was all that kept her upright as she rubbed the back of her neck. Looking across the tunnel, she saw that the creature was also getting to its feet, and it looked even angrier.

It thrust its arms again, there was a series of pops and the little Amazon swept her arm to ward off more of its quills. With an angry growl, it turned and picked up a stone that was twice the size of its head and hurled that at her.

Quick to dodge away, she stumbled over one of the broken crates and fell, raising her arm against still more quills as she lay on her side. She could not move well like this and could not protect her entire body. As it shot more quills at her she drew her legs to her and deflected the quills as best she could. One struck her boot and stuck and she gasped as she felt it pass close to her skin inside the boot.

It stopped.

She stared back at it, too afraid to move but knowing it was going to charge her again any second.

A deep growl rumbled from it and it took an ape-like crouch, its solid black eyes fixed on her as it dug its back claws into the ground beneath it, preparing to pounce.

Breaths entered the little Amazon reluctantly and she forced each one as she slowly pushed herself up with one arm, holding her other ready as she braced to defend herself.

The creature roared again, shooting more quills at her as it charged.

Golden Angel's boots could not find good footing and she kicked frantically to move aside as it closed the distance between them in seconds, and she raised her arm as it was upon her, bracing for the impact that was an instant away.

Air whooshed by and the creature was slammed into the end of the tunnel.

Superman backed away, landing halfway between Elissa and the creature as he watched it crumple to the ground. Half turning, he looked to the little Amazon and barked, "Are you okay?"

She nodded and assured, "I'm good." She stood, but did not advance as she offered, "Thanks."

Looking back to the creature as it rose to all fours, the Man of Steel set himself to receive his opponent.

With an angry roar, it thrust its arms and sent a barrage of quills at its new foe, all of which bounced off of Superman's chest and belly.

A tense moment followed.

It growled, and Superman's eyes narrowed.

This time when it lunged it was met by an enemy of vast strength, and the fist of the Man of Steel slammed squarely into its face. It impacted the wall again, fell limply to the ground and this time did not get up.

Spinning around to face the smaller one, Superman ordered, "Stay behind me, Angel."

"Wait!" she cried, darting around him.

The smaller creature cringed and backed into the tunnel wall right below the hole it had emerged from.

Elissa darted to its side, kneeling down beside it as she carefully put her arms around it, careful of the quills on its back, insisting, "It's okay. We don't want to hurt you."

Setting his fists on his hips, Superman leaned his head and eyed her suspiciously.

"I know what you're thinking," she admitted as she stared back at him, "but they aren't what they seem to be." She maneuvered herself around to face the creature, and gently she framed its face in her hands, staring into its eyes as a golden light sprayed from between her fingers.

Slowly raising his chin, Superman watched the transformation in amazement.

In a moment, a frightened girl about twelve years old sat huddled and frightened in front of Golden Angel, her black hair a bit of a mess and her eyes wide with fear. She was wearing nothing but that fearful look, and gold earrings in the shape of angels.

Elissa combed her fingers through the girl's hair and assured, "It will be okay. We are going to take you home now."

Hesitantly, the girl nodded.

Looking over her shoulder, Golden Angel asked, "Can I borrow that cape?"

When the girl was wrapped in Superman's cape and cradled in his arms, Elissa turned to the unconscious creature and slowly strode to it, knelt down and placed her hands on it. Venting a deep breath through her nose, she shook her head and observed with regret, "It's too late for this one. There's nothing left of the person he used to be."

Superman looked down to the girl he held. "You mean these creatures were..."

"Yes," she answered softly, still staring down at the creature. "The quills turn people into them. I got to Christina in time, but it seems to be too late for the others." She looked over her shoulder and suggested, "We should go, and we should make sure they aren't disturbed by anyone again."

Superman nodded.

WW*

The mission was much quicker than Golden Angel had expected it would be and only a couple of hours after leaving for it she and Superman walked side by side down one of the corridors of the Watchtower. She was still dirty from her action in the mine, but she was smiling and the hero beside her had her full attention.

"Believe me," he assured, "they are only rarely that quick and easy."

She raised her brow and barked, "You call that easy?"

He glanced at her and smiled. "Well, it could have been a lot more complicated. I'm glad you saw them for what they really are. It made things much simpler."

Elissa finally turned her eyes forward and shrugged. "Just something I do." She was unconsciously twisting a lock of her hair that had fallen over her tiara as she asked, "So, how about lunch or something?"

"The commissary's up ahead," he replied. "I thought you might like a bite after all of that."

"Well thank you," she offered sweetly. "I guess I can clean up after lunch unless you want me to before."

"You're fine," he assured.

"I'd love to hear more about some of the stuff you've done," she said with a girlish enthusiasm. "You're the only one I haven't heard talk about what you do."

Superman laughed. "Well, I don't like to brag. Everything we do here is a team effort, and that's how I like to keep it."

"You're still amazing," she said dreamily.

From ahead of them, Atom turned into the corridor, pointed to her and greeted, "Hey! Golden Angel! What's the good word?"

She waved her fingers at him as they passed and said, "Hi."

"Feels good to be recognized, huh?" Superman asked as he smiled down to her.

"Yeah," she confirmed.

"Golden Angel," Batman summoned from behind.

She tensed and suddenly felt a little ill as she added, "Usually." Looking up at Superman, she took his arm and said, "Hey, I'll catch up to you, okay?"

"Sure," he assured. Looking over his shoulder, he raised his chin and greeted, "Good to see you two are back."

Elissa stopped in her tracks, watching as Superman strode on. Two? Slowly, she turned around, her eyes widening as she saw Batman and Wonder Woman standing side by side. Batman's arms were folded. Wonder Woman had her hands set on her hips. Both of them had their eyes fixed on her, and both looked extremely annoyed.

With a nervous smile, Elissa waggled her fingers to them and bade, "Hi, guys."

Wonder Woman's expression did not change as she pointed to the open doorway she stood beside.

Drawing a breath, Elissa cringed, drawing her shoulders up as she strode toward the doorway, no longer able to look at two of the Justice League's founding and senior members.

The room they entered was a conference room of some kind with four comfortable looking chairs surrounding a round metal table. A computer station was on the far wall, a communication terminal to the right and nothing notable on the left.

Elissa stopped at the table, folding her arms across her belly and closing her eyes as she heard the door slide shut behind them. It locked, and she knew her moment of reckoning was at hand. She knew to expect this, but still found herself completely unprepared for it. "I know what you are going to say," she started.

Wonder Woman barked, "No, you really don't."

Venting a hard breath, Elissa turned toward them, keeping her eyes on the floor before her and her feet close together as she shrugged her shoulders up, trying to occupy as little space as she could. She hated being in trouble with them, and hated more that they were angry with her.

"We have been sick with worry over you," Wonder Woman declared. "You just disappeared, you did not answer your phone... What were we supposed to think but the worst?"

"I guess I was kind of out of cell range," Elissa admitted softly.

Batman added, "Even the members of the Justice League check in with others to make certain someone knows where they are. That's the mature thing to do. Taking off like that without a word was very irresponsible."

Elissa nodded.

"What are you doing here?" Batman asked in a harsh voice.

She shrugged and replied, "It's kind of a long story."

"We have time," Wonder Woman assured.

Drawing another shaky breath, Elissa explained, "I just needed to get away and clear my head, and I do that best when I fly, so I took the airplane I brought from home and..." She glanced at Wonder Woman, seeing quickly the hard and angry expression she wore. "I just flew, and I kept going higher and higher and..."

"Are you supposed to go out of the atmosphere?" Diana barked.

Elissa cringed again, staring at the floor as she sheepishly replied,

"No, Mom."

"And how did you get aboard the Watchtower?" Batman demanded.

"Um..." she stammered. "I... I was just flying along to clear my head and, well, I saw a Javelin and I kind of followed it." She glanced up at him. "I was just looking at the Watchtower and I watched the Javelin land..." She glanced at Wonder Woman. "I think they thought I was you flying here, Mom."

Batman growled, "And you didn't correct them."

"No sir," she replied in a low voice, just over a whisper.

Diana rubbed her eyes. "Skip ahead to the part where you were sent on a mission with Superman."

Once again she drew a deep breath, trying to collect her thoughts, and finally answered, "I think they thought you said I could join. Um, we were in the command room..."

"Oh, Hera help me," Wonder Woman hissed as she massaged her temple.

"Um," Elissa continued, "this... Martian Manhunter got this call and Superman said he would check it out and that he could use someone watching his back and... I might have..." She looked up to her mother. "I really thought my ability to see in the dark would be helpful. It was in a cave and stuff and... We did really well. We made a good team. Mom, you know how I've always wanted—"

"I know," Diana assured, raising a hand to the girl. "I know." She looked away, blowing a breath from her before she asked, "Why did you leave the mansion to begin with?"

Batman also turned his eyes away. They both seemed to know the answer already.

Backing into the chair behind her, Elissa turned her eyes to the floor and could not reply for a moment, but she finally managed, "I... I couldn't be around you two. I so hate when you fight. I just know it's my fault that you fight so much."

Diana folded her arms and looked to the floor.

Reaching to his head, Batman removed the cowl to reveal his face, something he almost never did aboard the Watchtower. Closing the distance between them with two steps, he took the girl's chin and turned her face up, her eyes to his. "Nothing about that is your fault, Angel," he assured. "Sometimes grown-ups fight."

"But it's always about me," she pointed out in a meek voice. "It's all my fault."

Diana finally stepped toward her and took her shoulder. "No, Little One, it isn't." She looked to Bruce and did not seem to know what else to say.

Elissa looked to the side, across the room as she whimpered, "I'm the reason you don't like each other anymore. If I'd never been born then you..." A tear rolled from her eye. "You would still be in love with each other."

"Elissa," Batman corrected with harsh words, "no problems we have between us are your fault."

As if summoned by the tense moment, all of their communicators blared to life with J'onn's voice ordering, "All active members report to the Watchtower command center, priority one."

Batman was quick to pull the cowl over his head again and looked to Wonder Woman, observing, "This sounds major."

"Let's go," she bade, and as the two turned toward the door, she ordered, "Come on, Junior."

Elissa followed them to the command center where almost all of the Justice League was already gathered. She was content to stand between Batman and Wonder Woman and folded her arms as she listened to J'onn.

"They struck multiple installations simultaneously," the Martian Manhunter explained, "almost all to the exact minute, and all over the world. This was a very coordinated attack made by someone with an organization to handle the logistics of such an operation. Assemble your teams and report to your assignments. Batman. Batgirl, Nightwing and Robin are already awaiting you in Gotham. Just be careful. All of the inmates of Arkham were released, and we know how many enemies you had there."

Batman's eyes narrowed and he asked, "What about Metallo and Bane?"

J'onn reported, "Both of their transports were attacked at the same time. They are both missing now."

"Ah, come on!" Elissa declared in a loud voice.

Silence suddenly gripped the control room and all attention was turned to her.

Glancing around, she shrugged her shoulders up and mumbled,

"I'm just saying."

Superman patted her shoulder from behind, and when she turned and looked up at him he smiled and shook his head.

"I'll see to it we can send help if you need it," the Martian Manhunter added.

The Dark Knight nodded and turned toward the elevator.

The Justice League members assembled into their teams and disbursed, but Wonder Woman approached the Martian Manhunter, and Elissa stayed on her heels.

Someone took her arm from behind and turned her around and her wide eyes turned up to Batman's as he bent close to her.

Grasping her jaw in his gloved hand, he ordered in a low voice, "Watch your mother's back, Angel."

She nodded and assured in a whisper, "I will, Daddy."

He offered her a little smile and a wink, then wheeled around and swept toward the elevator again.

Wonder Woman nodded to J'onn and informed, "We'll need a couple of teams here on standby. Something tells me that they'll try and surprise us once they think we're all in the field."

"I'll bring up the reserves and assemble a few teams here," he agreed. "Hawk Girl is awaiting you in Teleporter Three."

Spinning around, Wonder Woman had a powerful intensity in her eyes as she raised her communicator to her mouth and called, "Wonder Woman to Hawk Girl. We're on our way." Putting it back to her belt, she strode on, ordering, "Come on, Junior."

Raising her brow, Elissa said, "Really?"

"Come on!" Diana barked, her voice laced with impatience.

Darting to her side, Golden Angel asked, "You aren't putting me on the reserve team?"

"I need you at my side," Wonder Woman replied. She gave the girl a sidelong glance and a little smirk. "And I heard what your father said to you."

Staring at the elevator doors as they stopped at them, Elissa also smiled. "I'd better not let him down then. I totally don't want to get into more trouble than I'm already in."

"No you don't," Diana warned with an ominous tone.

CHAPTER 6

Normally, four heavily armed men would not be much of an issue. The corridor they strode down was rather wide, poorly lit and obviously underground. Three men could comfortably walk abreast, but the four soldiers in black body armor were content to walk behind him. The arched, stone or concrete ceiling was nine feet high and Bane glanced up a couple of times, tempted by something from a lingering boyhood to reach up and bat at one of the lights that hung from the conduit that ran along the peak of the ceiling. Still dressed in the orange jumpsuit of the maximum security prison facility he was destined for, he still had the size of the mercenary who had been created in the Caribbean many years ago. Since then, his augmented strength had remained with him, though not at the level the super steroid Venom had given him. While it had helped make him what he was, he loathed it now. Still, he would continue to use the strength it had given him, and his almost super human intellect. There were jobs to do, and now new scores to settle.

They approached a heavy, steel door, one that was very high, over eight feet, and about four feet wide. It was painted black and trimmed in red, and looked out of place in this subterranean complex.

When they arrived, he stopped at the door and one of the guards reached around him and turned the gold colored handle, pushing it open ahead of him.

Bane turned and looked to the four men who escorted him, and when one of them motioned with his head to enter, he casually turned and entered the room.

Inside, the red carpeted floor was something else that was out of place. The room was rather large and in the center was a long conference table that was built of dark stained oak and surrounded by seven chairs of the same material and construction. The walls were dark stained, hardwood paneling and the ceiling was formed metal tiles. Ornate lights hung from the ceiling. On the far end was

a huge, oak desk. Shelves along the walls bore the weight of old
books and many items that appeared to be war memorabilia from
World War Two. Behind the desk was a shield with swords crossed
behind it, a red shield with a black Swastika in the center, and this
gave Bane pause.

Looking to the one man who sat at the conference table, he met
his eyes coldly. The man had well groomed blond hair and wore a
black business suit and tie, and a white, silk shirt.

In a slight, British accent, the man in the suit informed, "Our host
appears to want us to be comfortable."

When the door closed behind him, Bane looked over his shoulder,
then back to the man and folded his arms.

With a shrug, the man in the suit leaned back in his chair and
informed, "I don't really care how comfortable you are. I'm sure at
some point our host will make himself known and we'll know why
we've been brought here. In the meantime, you have nothing to fear
from me.

Bane's eyes narrowed and he growled, "Why would I fear you?"

The man's eyes slid back to him, and he smiled slightly. "Believe
me, my friend, at your best you could never match me."

Bane huffed a laugh.

"We can, perhaps, posture with one another later, Mister Bane,"
the man in the suit informed.

Raising his chin, Bane set his jaw.

The man laced his fingers in front of him and turned his attention
to them. "One thing is clear: Someone broke us out for a reason.
The way I see it, we are valuable to someone with enough power to
stand up to the feds." His eyes shifted to the big man. "I intend to at
least hear him out."

Bane drew a deep breath as he considered, then he strode forward
and sat on the other side of the table. A moment later, when he and
the man in the suit had been staring at each other seemingly without
blinking, he informed, "I do not like to be kept waiting."

As if cued, the door opened and four armed men strode in, taking
up their positions on either side of the door. The weapons they
carried were huge and fed by very big magazines.

Two well dressed women also entered, both with blond hair and
both generously made and dressed in black. Each carried a tray

covered with a silver dome, and each tray was placed before each man at the table. Bane and the man in the suit looked down at the domed trays, then to the departing women, then to each other.

Bane stood and demanded, "You will tell us why we are here!"

They left without responding, as if he had not even spoken.

Someone else filled the doorway, and this time the man in the suit also stood, his eyes locked on the huge form who entered with heavy steps.

"I will tell you," a deep, synthesized voice assured with a German accent, "and I will make you a generous offer, one that will make use of both of your unique skills and talents."

The man in the suit simply folded his arms, asking, "And if we should refuse this offer?"

Mechanical workings could be heard as the huge form strode into the room. Almost seven feet tall, he wore a long, red overcoat and the black uniform of an army defeated long ago beneath it. Over his head was the helmet of this army, also black with a skull and crossbones emblem right in the middle. The lapels of his overcoat bore the ominous insignia of an old and evil order, the SS, and beneath these was a silver dollar sized red pin, each with a black Swastika in the middle. Black gloves covered his huge hands and big, polished black boots found the floor with purpose and completely covered his shins and calves, and buckles on the outsides where his ankle would flex were perfectly polished. His head was metal and his face was a metal human skull with chrome teeth and black lenses in the eye sockets covering his eyes.

His head pivoted to Bane, then to the man in the suit, and he assured, "You do not want to refuse me, Herr Corbin." He half turned his head. "Or do you prefer Metallo?"

"Metallo is just fine," the man in the suit replied. "Since you know who we both are, what makes you think we won't take you out and fight our way out of here?"

Looking over his shoulder to the guards at the door, the huge Nazi ordered, "Leave us." As they complied, closing the door behind them, he strode to the end of the table and folded his hands behind him, raising his metal, skeletal chin as he offered, "If you mean to do this, then it is best to get it over with."

"You seem to know I'm not at full power," Metallo informed.

"One piece of kryptonite to get me back to full charge would…" He trailed off as he watched the huge figure remove a large green stone from his coat pocket, and his attention remained on it as it was slid down the table to him.

"Plenty of kryptonite to bring you back to form," the big Nazi informed. "Install it, and let us get this foolishness out of the way."

Metallo hesitantly opened his coat and shirt, then the hatch on his chest opened and he picked up the kryptonite and shoved it into the mounts that would hold it in place with a series of loud clicks. A whine was heard as his systems powered up to maximum. "Feels good," he observed as he buttoned his shirt. "I suppose I should be thanking you Mister…"

The huge mechanical form replied. "You may call me Red Panzer."

Metallo slowly turned and strode to him, nodding as he admitted, "Yes, I believe I've heard of you. And you've clearly heard of me. So, if I don't like this offer I suppose I just have to kill you and—"

"Not likely," Panzer interrupted. "But try if you must." He strode right up to the smaller cyborg, holding his arms to his sides as he just stood there.

"Suit yourself," Metallo sighed as he threw a hard punch at Panzer's chest.

Much quicker than he looked like he should be, Red Panzer caught Metallo's fist in his hand and clamped down with a powerful, mechanical purpose. Metallo tried to wrench his fist free, but it was not to be. He threw a punch at the huge Nazi's head and this time connected, but Panzer's head was only knocked around slightly. His other hand slammed into Metallo's neck, his throat, and gripped him there like a vice. As Metallo struggled to free himself, Red Panzer slowly lifted him from the floor and raised his head nearly to the ceiling.

Watching this, Bane raised his brow.

"Now," Panzer started, "we have two choices. I can crush your neck and tear the head from you, or you can sit down and hear what I have to say." Slowly, he lowered his opponent to the floor and released him, and Metallo backed away.

Nodding, Metallo agreed, "Okay, Panzer. I'll hear you out. Just know that I have no love for Nazis."

"Noted," Red Panzer said before looking to Bane.

Bane took his seat and folded his hands in his lap, his eyes on the big Nazi as he said, "Let us hear this offer of yours."

CHAPTER 7

Help was needed in Gotham and it was the Dark Knight himself who grudgingly requested it. Closest were Wonder Woman, Hawkgirl and Golden Angel, who responded with great haste.

Most of the frightened citizens of Gotham City had locked themselves in their homes and businesses. All of the police were out and many were conducting door to door searches for the wayward criminally insane of the city.

Topping Batman's list was the Joker, the brilliant, unpredictable madman who had always been his most troublesome nemesis. He intended to deal with Joker personally, but Robin would not leave his side and could easily run interference if and when the Joker's sidekick, one Harleen Quinzell came to her employer's aid. Joker had many henchmen in the dark underworld of the city and a few more who had escaped with him, but his unpredictable nature made him not only very dangerous, but extremely hard to find.

Against her mother's wishes, Golden Angel struck out on her own and disappeared into the dark alleyways of the lower side of the city near the docks. She did not expect to find anyone important, but surely some of them would choose to hide here and she could drum up some action and capture a few of them. The noteworthy bad guys were being actively hunted by the more experienced heroes of the Justice League and the entire police force, but perhaps she could make some small difference.

Even the ruffians who normally inhabited the dark streets of this roughest part of the city could tell that the girl who strode fearlessly down the sidewalk was more than a force to be reckoned with, and while they all paused to watch her, none would dare to approach. There was just too much of Wonder Woman's look in this one for their comfort.

Approaching an old, run down pizza buffet, she absently wished that it was still open. Having not eaten that day, she was famished!

Stopping about fifty yards away, she squinted slightly and first saw that the doors had been forced open, and a little smile found her lips as she strode that way.

Neither door protested as she opened them and here she hesitated. Her hand found her communicator and she raised it to her mouth, calling, "Golden Angel to Batman."

"Batman here," came the reply. "What do you have, Angel?"

"A pizza place with the doors forced open," was her reply. "It looks like it might have been one of those Funland places that shut down some time ago. I just get the feeling someone's hiding in there."

"Proceed with caution," he ordered, "and observe only. Do not engage. I'll be there in a few minutes."

"Yes sir," she replied before pushing the communicator back into its place.

Elissa still was not in control of the gift of insight within her, but she did know how to read it. She could sense four people inside. Only four.

She strode slowly inside, looking around her at the abandoned tables, drink station, and the serving bars that were dirty and in disrepair, and most of them had broken sneeze guards. Garbage was strewn about, the floor was clearly not the same color it had been when the place was open, and some of the suspended ceiling was lying about on the floor. The walls were painted with fun colors and images and led to the large rooms where diners would go to have their meals. It was a familiar layout, abandoned for years, but for some reason the smell of freshly made pizza lingered in the air. Knowing that the game room would be at the far end, she was fairly certain that whoever was hiding in this place would be there, as far from the glass doors and windows as possible to avoid detection.

A maniacal laughter ahead made her stop and look that way, confirming her suspicions about the locations of the people she sought. Her eyes narrowing, she noiselessly strode that way, passing the bathrooms as she did.

As she reached the door to the men's room, a big man in an orange jumpsuit had just emerged—and froze as he saw her only three feet in front of him.

Golden Angel also saw him, stopping as she turned her head that way. Before he could react or raise the alarm, she kicked straight out to the side, slamming the bottom of her boot right into his chest. With a loud grunt, he flew backward back into the rest room and landed flat on his back on the dirty tile floor. She just stood there and watched him as he slowly got to his feet and met his eyes as he glared at her. Predictably he charged and she did not move a muscle until he was only a few feet away, and she spun around and slammed the heel of her boot into the side of his head.

This time he hit the floor out cold.

She stared down at him for a moment, leaning her head as she watched him slumber, then that maniacal laughter drew her attention back to the game room.

One down, three to go.

She strode forward again, pausing as she heard a woman talking, and laughing with the voice that belonged to the strange laughter. Her eyes narrowed. It was time to call Batman.

No. She would do this herself.

Reaching the doorway of the emptied out game room, she peered inside and found that a booth and table had been moved back there, that and many other things that looked like they belonged in a carnival. A bouncy castle was inflated in the middle of the room and its blower motor was announcing its labors as quietly as possible.

"So what do you think, Harl?" a man's voice asked from the far side to the right.

She looked that way, seeing a pale, green haired man in a purple suit spinning around and holding his hands up.

"That is so you, Mista J," the woman replied. "How did you come across this place, anyway?"

"I know the guy who owns it," he replied, then he laughed that loud, horrible laugh of his. "He had a little accident and I told him I'd take over the operation until he's feeling better." He laughed again. This time, they both did.

Elissa turned into the room and leaned her shoulder on the wall by the door, folding her arms as she crossed her legs at the ankles and just watched them. The woman was still in the jumpsuit she wore at Arkham and Elissa reasoned out quickly who she was: Harleen Quinzell, better known as Harley Quinn. She was sitting in the booth with her adoring attention locked on the man in purple as he sat down across from her. Batman was scouring the city for him, and here he sat, the Joker, right in front of her. He was one of Batman's most notorious enemies, but he sure did not look like much.

Harley asked, "So what kind of accident did he have, Puddin'?"

"Oh, it's such a funny story," he chuckled.

Another big man in a jumpsuit entered behind Golden Angel and she turned her head to look at him as he stopped beside her. His hair was black and straight and bowl cut around his head. He had small eyes, was clean shaven and wore a white apron from the kitchen. He was also carrying a pizza tray as a waiter would, and his full attention was locked on her. She offered him a smile and waggled her fingers to him.

"Anyway," Joker continued, "we couldn't quite agree on—"

"Uh," the man stammered, "Mister Joker?"

Joker's whole disposition changed in that instant and he turned an angry look to the man, barking, "Moe! Can't you see I'm in the middle of a story?" His brow shot up as he noticed Elissa and he said, "Well hello there!"

She dared to smile at him, waggling her fingers at him too as she greeted, "Hi."

He stood and slowly stalked toward her. "So who might you be?"

Elissa turned her eyes to the pan of pizza that Joker's henchman carried, reached up and carefully removed a slice, then she raised her other hand to catch the cheese that clung stubbornly between the pie and her piece. "You don't know me?" She looked back to him and raised her brow, gingerly taking a bite out of the pizza with her lips curled back.

Joker stopped, setting his hands on his hips as he looked her up and down. "Let's see. I was thinking that you want to have a Wonder Womanish look, but the symbol across your chest screams..." He smiled, very broadly and showed off his yellow stained teeth. "Batman."

She took another bite and grabbed for the strings of cheese that were left dangling from her mouth. Chewing for a few seconds, she admitted, "Yeah, I hear that a lot." She finished chewing and swallowed before asking, "So you don't know who I am?"

"I sure wish I did," he replied. "You are an absolute doll!"

Smiling back at him, she shyly offered, "Thank you," then she took another bite of her pizza.

Not unnoticed was Harley Quinn, who strode up behind the Joker with her brow held very low over her eyes, and when she reached him, she folded her arms, holding her shoulders up slightly. Everything in her body language from how she stood to the angry glare in her eyes told all who saw her that she simply did not approve of this new young woman who had the Joker's attention.

"This is really good pizza," Elissa observed with a half full mouth.

"I am so glad you are enjoying it!" the Joker declared as he took a couple more steps closer to her. Shaking his head, Joker folded his arms and asked, "So is this the part where I am supposed to give up quietly? Surely you have some heroic and absolutely corny thing you would like to say."

She chuckled and shook her head. "No, I don't do corny."

"You know," he started slowly, "by this time Bat-boy would be telling me to give up and come along quietly. After all these years, he still says it! Can you believe?"

Golden Angel finished her slice of pizza. "Yeah, he still likes to give law breaking jerks like you a chance to give up peacefully. So why do they call you Joker, anyway? I mean, I've been here for at least five minutes and you haven't said anything even close to funny yet."

He frowned and his brow lowered, and in a deep, grumbling voice he said, "What?"

"If you're really the Joker," she challenged, "say something funny. I mean, you're kind of boring me to tears."

Joker growled and looked to his henchman, who just shrugged, then he looked back to the insolent girl and unexpectedly smiled. "So who does your hair? I hope for your sake someone was able to stop him before he strikes again."

Her brow arching, Elissa slowly turned her eyes to Moe, then she shook her head as she looked back to the Joker. "That was sad. Do you have any jokes that aren't totally lame?"

"Hmm..." rolled from him as he stroked his chin. "Tough room. Oh, I know. How many bats does it take to clean up Gotham?"

Golden Angel folded her arms and countered, "How many Jokers does it take to come up with jokes that don't suck?"

He growled and approached her, stopping only about three feet away. Quinn followed him, and Elissa could tell by her body language that her boss was plotting something.

"Everyone's been telling me how funny you are," she said almost in a sigh. "If you're really the Joker, then make me laugh. Do something funny."

"Something funny," he repeated as he reached up with both hands to straighten his purple jacket. "Oh, if you want to laugh, then I'd be just giddy to give you something that is sure to work." His hand moved to the plastic flower on his lapel.

And Golden Angel was ready!

As soon as he squeezed the flower to release the toxic laughing gas, she grabbed onto Moe's arm and pulled him in front of her. She moved aside and backed away in one motion and watched as the gas fully enveloped the big man's chest and face.

Moe coughed and choked, dropping the pizza tray as he covered his mouth and backed away.

"Hey!" Elissa barked. "We were going to eat that!"

Falling to the floor, the big man curled up and began to laugh uncontrollably.

Joker pointed down at him and shouted, "Bad Moe! That pizza was for company!"

Moe laughed harder.

"At least *he* thinks you're funny," Golden Angel chided.

"At the moment," Joker countered, "he thinks a root canal would be funny."

Elissa giggled. "Yeah."

"Ha!" the Joker yelled as he pointed at her. "You laughed!"

"I did not!" Elissa denied. "Okay, I giggled."

"A laugh by any other name is still a laugh, says the clown."

She raised her chin slightly. "Is that Shakespeare?"

"Oh, no," he replied, setting his fists on his hips. "That's classic Joker! Just think of me as a pit bull with clown makeup and a joy buzzer."

Golden Angel smiled. "A pit bull? How about a poodle?"

"With green hair? Good luck pulling that look off!"

Giggling again, she nodded and conceded, "Yeah, okay."

"You know," he started, stepping toward her, "you aren't such a bad kid after all!" He extended his hand and offered, "Put 'er there."

As he knew she would, she took his hand to shake it, and the joy buzzer in his hand responded with a loud buzz and about fifty thousand volts of electricity that hit her glove with bright arches of power, and all of it was absorbed by the contacts in her gloves and sent right back!

Joker screamed and convulsed as the shock he had intended for his young victim instead lanced through him, and for long seconds Golden Angel squeezed his hand tightly and gave him a good dose of his own medicine.

She finally released him and he fell forward to the floor, smoke rising from him in thin ribbons from all over as his body quaked from the shock. One was left.

"Puddin'!" Harley shouted as she stared down at her fallen Joker. Her lips curled back from her teeth and she reached behind her. "You're going to get it now, Toots!" She trained a small, two barreled palm gun on the young Amazon and took careful aim with both hands.

Golden Angel did not even turn fully to her. She only slid her eyes that way, and when Quinn fired the first shot, her arm was a blur as it swept up and deflected the small bullet.

Harley drew a gasp, her wide eyes locked on the girl, then she aimed and fired her second round, only to have it deflected by the same arm.

They stared at each other for long seconds after.

Raising her brow, Elissa asked, "You got anything else you'd like to try?"

With a snarl on her mouth, Harley tossed the gun aside and assumed some kind of battle stance, and she circled her young opponent as she replied, "I'm going to beat you down the old fashioned way, Toots."

Elissa loosed a breath and set her hands on her hips, following Quinn's movements with her eyes and not moving otherwise.

When Harley was beside her young opponent and slightly behind her, she struck, moving in with a barrage of clumsy punches and a loud, "Hi-yah!" as she attacked.

The young Amazon's arm swept too quickly for Quinn to see and easily knocked her attacker's fists away over and over. Not a single blow was landed and Elissa's hand lanced toward Harley's neck, grabbing the jumpsuit in a solid grip, and in one motion she pulled the slightly taller woman to her and half turned, head-butting her right between the eyes.

When Golden Angel released her, Harley staggered backward, her eyes crossed as her head rolled back.

Elissa watched her fall and shook her head. "Hi-yah? Seriously? That *had* to be a major blond moment."

"Now that was funny!" Joker yelled from behind.

Spinning around, Golden Angel raised a hand to defend herself, but this time he grabbed her arm at the elbow in a firm grip, and this time the electricity lanced all the way through her!

Elissa convulsed and threw her head back as she screamed. Her body would not respond to her at all and in seconds she was drained of strength and collapsed as soon as the shock ceased.

Joker caught the barely conscious girl and held her tightly to him, and he giggled evilly. "You are just a delight." He raised his chin and smiled broader. "Larry! Good to see you up from your nap. Get Moe to the alley and bring me some of that rope from the kitchen."

Harley stirred and sat up, rubbing her forehead as she struggled to get back to her feet. When she was finally standing, she found the little Amazon held up by Joker's arms, and her lips slid away from her teeth anew as she stormed to them and shouted, "Hey! Get your grubby little paws off my man!"

Struggling to find consciousness, Elissa whimpered and raised her head, and she had barely opened her eyes when Quinn punched her hard on the side of the head. The blow knocked Elissa out cold and her head rolled back as her body went completely limp, and in a second she was held upright only by the Joker's sinister embrace.

WW

Golden Angel moaned weakly and struggled to open her eyes. She found herself staring down at her lap and blinked her eyes to clear them. The first thing that came into focus was the bright yellow rope that was wound a half dozen times round her knees, binding them tightly together. Awakening fully, a gasp shrieked into her and she raised her head, looking around her. She was still in the emptied out game room, but now there were crates and pallets piled up everywhere—and she could smell gasoline! Looking down at herself again, she found that she was securely bound to a chair, and as she struggled to free herself, she discovered that her legs were tightly tied together above and below her knees and to the chair, that more rope was wound many times around her chest. Her wrists were crossed behind her and tied with expertise that she had not attributed to the crazy clown. With her gauntlets touching and bound so, she found her Amazon strength and abilities had drained away, and for the first time in her life she was mortal, and quite helpless.

Harley's voice said from one side, "Wakey wakey."

Her eyes cutting that way, Elissa was slow to turn her attention to the Joker's crazy girlfriend, but when she did she found Quinn dressed in her red and white jester's attire, complete with bells and white face paint with black lipstick and a black mask painted around her eyes.

Looking to the only door in or out, Harley yelled, "Mista J, she's awake!"

"Oh, how fun!" he yelled back from somewhere. That maniacal laugher sounded from him, coming from beyond the doorway.

The two big men entered first, and both were glaring at her, and were clearly thinking about what they could do to her.

Joker entered behind them, his hands folded behind his back and that huge grin on his face as he sauntered in. The certain spring in his step had to belie his intentions and she could feel that those intentions were as wicked as she could imagine. Her eyes remained on his as he approached and she simply could not purge all of the fear she felt from her face. He stopped right in front of her and bent down to bring his face close to hers. She did not move and kept her head low and her wide eyes locked on his.

"Well now," he said in a jolly voice. "Looks like you'll be getting that final punch line after all."

Elissa was forcing breaths into her and her chest heaved as far as her restraints would allow.

Half turning his head, he barked, "Moe. Go find Curly and see if he's finished with those charges."

Drawing a gasp, Golden Angel watched Moe as he turned and strode out of the big game room, her lips ajar and her jaw quivering.

Joker bent closer to her and grabbed onto her jaw with a painful grip. "This is a fun place. Of course, everywhere I go is a fun place."

"Like Arkham?" she asked with shaky, defiant words.

Unexpectedly, he laughed that loud cackle of his. "Oh, Arkham was a laugh a minute, but I'm not going back. Not now, not ever. No, I'm out here to have a good time, have a few laughs. In fact, in about five minutes, we're going to have an absolute blast!"

When he laughed, Harley and Larry laughed along with him.

"Oh, but not to worry," he assured. "I'm not going to blow you up. You're too hot a dish to blow up." He bent closer and touched his nose to hers, his brow lowering over her eyes as he growled in a horrifying voice, "And you're going to get a whole lot hotter!"

He released her and she watched him turn around and fold his hands behind him. For a moment he just stood there, tapping his fingers, then he looked to Harley and growled, "What's taking so long?"

She shrugged. "I dunno, Puddin'."

"Larry," he barked. "Go find out what's holding them up."

"Hey," Harley summoned.

Elissa looked that way, and as Quinn twirled around, she noticed the jester woman wearing her utility belt.

"You like?" she asked with a girlish enthusiasm. "It's just my size, too."

"It fits you a little tight," Golden Angel spat.

Once again that hateful look overtook Harley's features and she snarled and set her hands on her hips as she glared back.

"Uh, oh," Joker declared as he stared out of the doorway. "Harl, they aren't coming back." He slowly turned and looked down at his helpless victim. "I think we have company."

She squeaked a loud gasp and raised a hand to her mouth as she looked to him. "You mean..."

"Afraid so, Poo," he confirmed. "I think we have a pointy-eared rodent problem again." He reached into his pocket and withdrew a gun of some kind, one with a huge barrel. It looked like a flare gun, and for some reason it had a big cork stuck in the muzzle. His other hand darted into his other pocket and emerged with a little black box that had a short antenna protruding from one end, and a red button right in the middle.

With her eyes locked on the remote detonator, Golden Angel spat, "You aren't even going to give me a fighting chance?"

"Where is the fun in that?" he countered. He looked down at the detonator and that smile returned to him. "Oh, what the heck." His eyes slid to Harley and he raised an eyebrow.

She reached into her pocket and withdrew a red bandanna. She closed the distance to their bound victim with two steps and ordered, "Open wide!" Golden Angel did not entirely cooperate, so she forced the middle of the bandanna into the girl's mouth and tied it behind her head. Backing away, she clasped her hands together and squealed, "Aren't you pretty?"

"Let's go, Harl," he ordered. They started to one of the secured emergency exits on one end of the room and then paused to look back at her. "Oh, by the way, one of the exits will be wired with explosives, so if you want to leave you'll have to figure out which one." He aimed at the pile of gasoline soaked pallets and crates on the other side of the room and fired the flare gun, sending the burning cork and flare right into the middle of it.

Elissa's eyes widened as she watched flames quickly engulf that end of the room only forty feet away, then she turned a desperate look to the Joker as he reloaded the flare gun.

"Try to stay cool," he advised as he pushed Harley on her way. "Give Batsy my regards."

He laughed all the way to the door, and she heard the flare gun fire again before the door closed behind him. The only sound left was that of the fires on both sides of her, and already the heat was becoming unbearable. Screaming behind her gag, she looked over her shoulder and struggled to free her hands, finding this to be in vain. In less than a minute she was drenched in sweat and found the air becoming unbreathable. Pulling against her bonds as hard as she could, she knew she only had another minute to get out of there. She could not even reach under her gauntlets for the small blade and pick set that was hidden there.

Even as far away as they were, the flames began to burn her skin and she screamed behind her gag in desperation.

A horrific explosion devastated the front of the old restaurant and a blast of hot air and smoke rushed in and slammed into her, rocking the chair back. As it settled back, she blinked to clear her eyes, then she looked around her and realized that the explosion had knocked down the fires in the arcade room, and she felt it bought her precious seconds. Joker may have unwittingly saved her. Still, she could barely breathe and found herself growing weaker. She began coughing and this became more and more uncontrollable.

Sirens drew her attention and she looked through the doorway. That was where they were coming from.

Looking down, she saw that the smoke was much thinner at floor level and her struggles changed tactics. Rocking as hard as she could, she finally toppled the chair and found herself on her side, and in cleaner air.

Still, even as she had bought herself another moment of life, the fire began to flare up again, consuming what was left of the air in the room and increasing the temperature more very second.

Part of the ceiling and roof collapsed in the doorway.

The air was becoming too thin to breathe. Slowly, her eyes closed and her body began to succumb to the heat.

A muffled voice shouted, "I have one here in the back!"

Elissa's eyes flashed open and she looked to see a firefighter kneeling beside her. He appeared to be a big man in dirty yellow bunker gear, a yellow helmet and an air mask over his face connected to a tank on his back by metal shrouded tubes. The hiss of his breathing brought her a little more alert and she tried to say something to him, but gagged as she was she could not make words.

"Don't worry," he assured, reaching to his belt to retrieve a black handled knife. "I'm going to get you out of here."

She nodded and laid still as he reached to her legs with the knife to cut her loose.

He was quick but careful with this task, freeing her legs in a couple of seconds before turning his attention to the ropes around her chest. When she coughed again, he pulled the helmet from his head, removed his air mask and put it to her face, ordering, "Just breathe normally." Holding the mask to her face with one hand, he laid over her and worked to free her hands.

Once her hands were freed and he had cut the rope that bound her body to the back of the chair, she reached around and pushed the mask away from her face.

The firefighter grabbed her wrist and put it back in place, saying, "Just leave it there and get some clean air into your lungs."

Her Amazon strength returned quickly and she was able to push it away again, this time reaching to her face with her other hand and removing the gag from her mouth. Looking up at him, she desperately said, "The emergency exits are wired with explosives!"

He nodded and assured, "We won't use them then." Looking over his shoulder, he studied what was behind him, then he turned his attention back to her and put the mask back over her face. "Can you make it through there?"

Elissa nodded.

Taking her arm, the firefighter stood and pulled her to her feet. He held the mask to her face and held her close to him with his other arm as he led the way out of the burning room and toward the rubble of the front of the restaurant. There was some burning debris from the ceiling in front of them that he kicked out of the way. When they were clear of the doorway into the arcade and in the wreckage of the rest of the place, she tapped him on the back, and when he looked to her she offered him his helmet.

He smiled as he took it from her and laid it on his head.

Halfway out, she could see the activity on the outside. The front wall and part of both side walls were gone, as was much of the roof, some of which they negotiated around on the floor. News cameras had already arrived and were filming the scene with special lenses on their cameras.

Looking to her right, Elissa saw two more firefighters clearing some debris from the roof, and she paused as she saw someone moving beneath it! As a large slab of asphalt roofing still attached to the roof decking was cleared, she gasped as she saw a battered Batman pull himself from the pile of debris that had him buried.

In a panic, she pushed away from the firefighter who was helping her and, "Daddy!" exploded from her as she tore away from her rescuer and darted to her father as he stood.

Batman looked stunned and burnt and was coughing as he staggered from the pile of wrecked roof and tables, helped by the two firefighters.

She was quick to push past them and get her arm around him, pulling his arm around her neck as she helped him out of the restaurant.

Once out of the danger zone, the firefighters who had helped them guided them to a waiting ambulance. Elissa was coughing, but did not seem to notice her own discomfort.

Turning as he reached the ambulance, Batman grabbed the coat of one of the firefighters and said in a raspy voice, "There are three more in there!"

The firefighter took Batman's shoulder and assured, "We'll find them, Batman. Don't worry. We've got it." He motioned to the other two, then turned and headed back to the restaurant.

Golden Angel raised her hand to Batman's cheek, terror and concern in her eyes as she looked up to his.

"I'm all right, Angel," he assured.

The firefighter who had rescued her shouted to another, "I'm going to get a fresh tank and I'll be in there in a minute." He looked to Elissa and took her shoulder, and when she turned to him he asked, "Are you okay, Miss?"

She coughed again before answering and struggled to reply, "Yes, thank you."

He looked back to the building, then down to her again, and he smiled. "It's not going to be easy to walk away from you, pretty lady, but I gotta go."

With another nod, she offered, "Thank you."

He stroked her cheek, then he turned and strode with quick steps to one of the fire trucks.

Elissa watched him, then she turned her eyes to Batman as he coughed, and she raised her hand to his face again. "Are you sure you're okay? Should you go and get checked out?"

"No," was his curt answer. "Come on."

When he turned and just walked away from her, she could sense something was wrong.

The Batmobile was just across the street and had collected the attention of a number of people and one news crew.

Batman reached to his belt and pushed a button, and the car responded by starting and opening the canopy. He said nothing as he climbed stiffly in, then he looked to Golden Angel and ordered, "Get in the car."

"Yes sir," she answered as she jumped in the other side.

In a moment they were on the way down the road and out of the city. Batman did not speak and kept his eyes on the road.

Elissa looked to him often, growing more and more uneasy at his silence, and finally she reached to him and took his shoulder, asking, "Are you sure you're okay?"

He did not answer.

She withdrew her hand. Something was definitely wrong and instinct told her to just remain quiet.

The ride to the Bat Cave seemed like a long one, but they finally stopped on the turntable where the car rested, and as the engine shut down, it slowly rotated the car back the way it had come. When the canopy opened, Batman got out immediately, and his daughter watched him with hurt eyes as he strode toward the computer console.

Slowly climbing out of the car, Elissa hesitated beside it once her boots hit the ground. She was dirty and sore, but did not notice as her attention was consumed with her father. Hesitantly, she strode toward him, making her steps soft, quiet ones as if she did not want to be noticed. He was leaning over the console, his hands planted firmly on the edge and his head bowed. When she finally reached him, she slowly laid her hand on his shoulder.

"Daddy?" Her timid voice echoed slightly through the cave.

He did not respond.

She stepped closer to him, beside him, and she looked up at him with concerned eyes.

Batman just stared blankly down at the console.

A long moment passed.

When he finally spoke, it was in a low voice, an ominous voice. "I told you to wait for me. I told you to observe and not engage."

Elissa lowered her hand and took a half step back. Her expression was now that of a fearful child who was awaiting a good scolding. With wide eyes and her brow arched over them, she tensed as he slowly turned his eyes to her, and she braced for the worst. She could not see her father glaring back at her. She could only see Batman, and he looked really angry.

He drew a breath, his hands clenching into tight fists.

She found herself trembling and softly asked, "Are you mad at me?"

Batman clenched his jaw and finally pushed off of the console, and as he stepped toward her, she backed away, and a step and a half later had backed up into the other side of the computer console and reached back to it with both hands.

He stopped less than a foot from her and grabbed onto her shoulders as he roared, "What were you thinking? You can never underestimate the Joker! That's why I told you to wait for me!"

Tears filled her eyes and she offered in a meek voice, "I'm sorry, Daddy."

He shook her and shouted, "He almost killed you! Don't you understand? What if I hadn't been there? What if I hadn't already called the fire department and what if they hadn't gotten to you in time? You can't take chances like that! You can't! Are you listening to me?"

Broken breaths entered her as she stared up at him with eyes that streamed tears, and she managed a slight and timid nod.

"Bruce!" Wonder Woman shouted from the elevator.

Both of them heard her, but neither could respond even as she strode toward them.

Batman's hands slid up the girl's shoulders, up her neck and to her face where he grasped her and pulled her toward him, gently touching his forehead to hers as he closed his eyes.

Elissa took his wrists gently in her hands, sobbing as she offered again in a meek voice, "I'm sorry."

When Wonder Woman reached them, he gently stroked his hands over the girl's hair, then he wheeled around and strode with quick steps toward the elevator. Wonder Woman and Golden Angel both watched him enter, and they watched for long seconds after as the doors slid shut behind him.

Diana cut her eyes to the girl, and Elissa bowed her head and began to cry.

Turning to her daughter, Diana took the girl's shoulder and gently asked, "What is it?"

Elissa could not answer and instead wrapped her arms around her mother's waist and fell into her, holding her as tightly as she could as emotions and tears poured from her.

Slipping an arm around the girl's back, Diana gently stroked her hair and held her close, and she kissed her on top of the head. "Shh," she soothed. "It is all right Little One."

"No it isn't!" Elissa cried. "Mom, I failed again." She cried harder. "He's so mad at me." She drew a broken breath and stomped her foot. "Why can't I listen? Why?"

As her daughter wept, Diana simply stroked her hair and held her tightly. She knew this would pass, and she knew that it had to come out.

In a few moments Golden Angel's hard crying was subsiding and she began to feel weak and numb, staring blankly at the computer console as she slowly raised her hand to her mouth and nibbled her thumbnail.

"Can you tell me what happened now?" Diana asked with soft words.

Elissa was a moment in answering, but finally did so in a meek voice more befitting a girl half her age. "I found the Joker. Daddy told me to wait and... He told me to wait for him, but I thought..."

"You thought you could take him," Diana guessed.

Closing her eyes, Elissa nodded and drew a broken breath. "I did okay at first. I had them all down, and then the next thing I knew he was back up and he grabbed me and shocked the heck out of me. Mom, if a mortal can do that to me..."

"Joker isn't just any mortal," Diana informed. "He is extremely dangerous to anyone who meets him. He can't be predicted and you should not try." She drew a breath all the way in. "Your father was right to tell you to wait for him."

"I know," the girl admitted. "Joker almost killed me. He had me tied to a chair and left me there with the place on fire, then he blew up the front part. He knew Daddy was there. Somehow he just knew." New tears streamed from her eyes. "Mom, I almost got us both killed!"

"Then you need to learn from this," Wonder Woman ordered. "Remember what I've always taught you. We learn more from defeat than victory."

"I learn nothing if my opponent kills me," Elissa countered, frustration in her voice.

Diana pushed the girl away from her and held her by the shoulders at arm's length. "He didn't, and I promise you, *that* will come back to haunt him."

Her jaw shaking, Elissa looked toward the elevator and said in a meek, little girl's voice, "He's so mad at me."

"Just give him time," Diana advised. "This will all pass, Little One. You'll see."

"Watchtower to Wonder Woman," Martian Manhunter's voice called over her communicator.

Diana looked aside and raised a hand to her ear and replied, "Wonder Woman here. Go ahead, J'onn."

"You are needed aboard the Watchtower," he informed. "I cannot raise Batman or Golden Angel. Are they nearby?"

Looking to her daughter, Diana raised her brow.

Elissa turned her eyes down and admitted, "Joker took my utility belt and communicator."

"I'll inform them," Diana advised. "We'll be there shortly. Home in on my signal and bring us up in five minutes. Wonder Woman out." She turned with quick motions, her hair flailing out as she ordered, "Come on, Junior. Let's get upstairs."

WW

Wonder Woman and Golden Angel strode into the conference room of the Watchtower and found most of the senior members already there and half sitting on one side of the table opposite the huge monitor on one wall while the other half stood behind them. Elissa's eyes found Superman, and when she saw him looking her way, she averted her gaze, feeling overwhelming shame for her recent failures. Her feelings about him, for him, confused her and she did not want him to see her as some pathetic failure. Backing up a step, she put her mother between herself and as many eyes as possible. She knew she was dirty and smelled of smoke and soot and even aside from that just did not want to be seen.

Superman was not the only senior member in the room, though he was the one most noticeable to Elissa. Flash was there, Hawkgirl, Green Lantern, Aquaman, Black Canary, Green Arrow, Atom, Firestorm, Martian Manhunter… All of the senior members were there, and all of them had been watching the monitor.

A moment of quiet thickened the air in the room. No one spoke and expressions were mixed and difficult to read.

It was Superman, standing behind Black Canary who was seated at the table, who finally shattered the silence with, "Diana, you're going to need to see this." He looked back to the monitor.

J'onn standing at one end of the table, pushed a button on his console.

The Monitor lit up with a news reporter, a middle aged man in a blue suit who reported, "Police are now saying that it was notorious escaped criminal the Joker who caused the explosion that nearly killed Batman. But that's not the end of the story. There was apparently another member of the Justice League who was being held captive by the Joker at the back of the restaurant, one identified as Golden Angel."

Elissa's brow arched and she mumbled, "Ah, crud."

"In this footage," the news reporter continued as the image changed to the scene she had just left, "we see her being helped out of the ruins of the structure by a firefighter, identified as Ronald Larson. Watch what happens when she sees Batman being pulled from the debris as well."

"Oh, no," Elissa breathed.

The image closed in on her being helped out, then she looked to her right and loudly screamed, "Daddy!" as she ran right to Batman.

Covering her mouth, she continued to watch with wide eyes and a tense brow.

"We know she is the daughter of Wonder Woman," the newsman went on, "and now it seems that her father has been identified. You might remember a few months ago when—"

The monitor suddenly went black as the door slid shut behind Elissa and her mother.

Batman strode to the table and sat down about halfway down the other side. He was not looking at Wonder Woman or Golden Angel, instead keeping his attention on the other members.

Diana folded her arms and looked away from her as well, announcing, "This is a problem."

"To say the least," Superman confirmed.

"To be honest," Hawkgirl said, "this comes as just a big a shock to the JL members as it no doubt does to the rest of the world." Her eyes shifted from Diana to Bruce and back. "I mean, most of us didn't have any idea!"

"Most of us didn't," Batman confirmed as he looked down at his hands, folded on the table before him. "Question is what now?"

The Justice League members were quiet as they all took their seats at the conference table, and Wonder Woman was careful to sit as far from Batman as she could.

Golden Angel just stood there and stared at the floor, her arms crossed over her belly.

"I don't see what the big deal is," Black Canary said with a dismissive tone. "So you guys have a daughter. It's not like the world doesn't expect us to have a life outside the League or anything."

"Security's the issue," Aquaman informed, his eyes finding the girl in a hard stare. "That little slip could come back and cause some big problems."

Elissa shrugged her shoulders up slightly.

"It happens," Batman countered. "We've all had problems like this."

"I think this one's kind of unique," Firestorm argued. "Look, I'm not the kind of guy to point fingers, but—"

Batman interrupted, "We can all agree that it's a problem, but I think we can deal with it. She made a mistake. We all have."

Wonder Woman turned a narrow eyed glare on him and snarled, "A mistake, yes, but one that did not warrant the dressing down she got from you."

He did not look her way as he shot back, "It warranted more than that, Princess. Our identities are our only real defense in the real world and she needs to learn that."

Elissa bit her lip, turning her head slightly away from them.

Standing, Wonder Woman leaned on the table and loudly said, "You could be more a teacher and less an angry bear! If you're going to be a leader of this League *and* a father then you'd better learn to control how you talk to people."

Batman also stood, and his voice was much louder as he countered, "I didn't seem to have the opportunity to teach her what she most needs to know, and believe me she needed all of the teaching I could give her while you were keeping her a secret from me!"

"We've been over this!" Wonder Woman shouted.

Elissa could take no more. She spun around and in an instant was out the door. Fighting back tears, she strode down the corridor, oblivious to the people who passed by and gave her long stares, oblivious to the activity around her.

She did not seem to make it far when she heard a woman behind her shout, "Hey, Angel!" She did not want company, did not want to talk to anyone and just strode on.

At a run, Black Canary caught up to her and took her arm, ordering, "Would you wait up?" She pulled the girl to a stop and half turned her, asking, "You okay?"

Keeping her eyes down, Elissa simply shrugged.

"Looks like you've had a hard day," Black Canary observed.

"Yeah," the girl confirmed. "It seems like I can't turn around without making some monumental boo-boo. I can't seem to do anything right."

"Oh," Black Canary drawled as she folded her arms. "You must be looking for the League of Perfect Heroes. I think it's on the other side of the galaxy, a place called Fantasy Land." When Golden Angel's eyes snapped to her, she raised her brow and asked, "Did you think you were in a room full of people who have never made mistakes? We all have, Angel, and we learn from them. And you know what? We're all going to make more. We don't win every fight and we have huge ways of screwing up. You learn to accept it."

"I was supposed to keep my parents' identities a secret," Elissa pointed out. "I couldn't even pull that off."

"So people know that Batman is your father. If you ask me it just makes him that much sexier."

A little smile broke through Elissa's somber expression and she turned her eyes down again.

"Hey," Wonder Woman called as she strode to them. "Angel, you okay?"

"I guess," she mumbled. "You and Dad through fighting?"

"Quit worrying about us." Wonder Woman ordered. She removed a card from her belt and offered it to the girl. "Here. This will get you into my quarters. Get a shower and drop your clothes down the laundry chute as soon as you get there. They'll be able to have it cleaned and returned in about a half hour."

Taking the card, Golden Angel nodded and meekly complied, "Yes, Mom."

"And stay there until I call you," the Amazon Princess ordered.

"I will."

"I'll show her where it is," Black Canary offered.

Nodding, Wonder Woman said, "That's fine, but get back to the conference room as soon as you can. We have an issue to clean up." She turned and strode the other way, warning, "Don't leave my room a mess, Junior."

"I won't, Mom," the girl assured in a voice with strained patience.

WW

Wonder Woman's quarters were as Spartan as her room on Themyscira. It was spacious and had a big bed that was perfectly made, a dresser across the room, and a few Themysciran weapons hanging on the walls. Across the room from the door were two comfortable looking chairs that flanked a small table, on which a candle sat. To the left was the door to the bathroom, and it was there that Elissa went.

After a long shower, she emerged from the bathroom wrapped in one of the big white towels she found as she dried her long black hair with another. Events were still weighing heavily on her and she flopped down on the big bed and just lay there on her back for a while, staring at the ceiling as she reflected on the events of the day, the last few days. She refused to cry again and forced back the feelings that brought that on. Everyone was right. It was time to grow up and start learning from her mistakes.

Two beeps from the clock by the bed drew her attention and she heard her mother's voice summon, "Angel."

"Yes, Mom?" she replied.

"Remember what we talked about?" Wonder Woman snapped.

With a sigh, she looked back to the ceiling and mumbled, "Sorry. Wonder Woman."

"Better. We need you back in the conference room," Diana informed.

"Just waiting on my clothes," Elissa reported.

"Very well," Wonder Woman replied. "Get here as soon as you can."

"Okay," the girl complied.

Sometime later, the door to the conference room slid open and she hesitantly entered. All of the senior members were still in there, seated in their places at the table, and all of them looked her way as she slowly entered. When the door slid shut behind her, she suddenly felt trapped and stopped where she was only a couple of feet inside the room.

That tense silence was there again and her eyes darted nervously about.

Superman was sitting in the chair closest to the door and had turned it around when she had entered, and he shattered the silence with, "Come on in, Angel."

She drew a deep breath and strode further in, stopping a few feet away from him. Looking away from the group, she tried to explain, "Look, I... I know I can't seem to keep from screwing up—"

"That's why we called you here," Superman informed.

Her heart sank and she turned her eyes down.

"You have a lot to learn," Green Lantern informed.

"You also have a lot of potential," Black Canary added. "It's time you learned to work as part of a team. That's something you never quite figured out with the Titans."

Martian Manhunter raised his chin slightly. "You seemed to have a difficult time taking orders from your peers. That is most likely what led to your failure there."

Elissa nodded.

Batman added, "That doesn't seem to be as much of an issue here, but you still have a problem following direction."

"I know," she grumbled. "I'm trying." She looked to her father with desperate eyes and assured, "I know I can get it right."

"And you have our every confidence there," Atom said straightly.

"But," Wonder Woman added, "there is the issue of your little slip-ups, your underestimating dangerous opponents and your carelessness under stress. You act far too impulsively sometimes."

Elissa would not meet her mother's eyes and instead looked to the floor.

"And there's the issue of the loss of your equipment," J'onn added, "as well as one of the Justice League's communicators. There is also the damage to the bank you fought Metallo in, the restaurant that was blown up when you were going after Joker, and the stolen van you overturned fighting Rhino."

Heaving a heavy breath, Golden Angel could only nod.

Firestorm pointed out, "You bite off more than you can chew, go right after bad guys who outclass you..."

Aquaman added, "You tend to be cocky and arrogant..."

Atom interjected, "You come up with these off the cuff plans..."

Staring at her, Flash rested his chin in his palm and observed, "Yeah, she sounds like Justice League material to me."

Elissa's wide eyes snapped to him, her mouth agape.

Superman stood. They all stood.

Her eyes met the Man of Steel's.

He smiled. "Congratulations, kid. You're in."

When everyone applauded, Golden Angel felt like she could not breathe and her eyes darted about from one hero to the next.

When the applause ended, Wonder Woman pointed out, "There will be conditions and you are on a probationary period for the next ninety days. I suggest you spend that time learning all you can and get out of some of your old habits."

Nodding in quick motions, she assured, "I will! I... I don't know what to say!"

"It's probably better that way," Black Canary warned.

Folding his arms, Superman informed in a hard voice, "Now we're going to lay out the ground rules."

Holding her head low, Elissa raised her brow and stared back up at him, drawing her shoulders up slightly.

"First," he started, "you're not going at it alone anymore. You'll be assigned to a team and you'll stick with that team, got it?" When she nodded, he continued, "Second, you're going to have to learn to follow orders and follow your team leader, and you can't keep volunteering information when you're faced with a high stress situation."

She turned her eyes down and mumbled, "I know."

"But," he added, "you are going to have to think on your feet and be ready to improvise when you have to, and that's where you seem to be most gifted. We're all assuming you're ready for this, and while we all like you and we've all come to appreciate your bubbly personality and playful nature, you'll have to know when to act grown up and do the job."

"Yes sir."

He smiled and roughed her hair. "You're going to do just fine,

Angel. We'll get you on the schedule for tomorrow."

A smile curled her mouth and she looked up at him. "Can I go with you again?"

Superman shrugged. "Yeah, I don't see a problem with that."

"Just no more splitting up!" she barked.

Everyone laughed and he roughed her hair again. "Yeah, okay."

J'onn informed, "I'm going to be making sure that we can maximize your talents and play to your strengths, so I'll be scheduling you accordingly." He strode around the table and made for the door. "Come with me. I'll equip you with a new communicator, then we should see about replacing your other equipment."

Nodding, she complied, "Okay." She looked to Batman and raised her brow.

"I'll take care of it," he assured.

She nodded to him, then looked to Superman again and smiled, unconsciously reaching to a lock of her hair that she began twisting loosely around her fingers. Waggling her fingers at him, she said in a shy but flirty voice, "I'll see you later."

"Okay," he replied as he watched her follow the Martian out.

Black Canary took his side, Hawkgirl the other side, and Wonder Woman beside her, and all of them were staring out the door the girl had just left.

Shaking her head, Black Canary observed, "Yeah, she's got it pretty bad."

He turned his eyes to her and asked, "What?"

"You can't see it?" Hawkgirl barked. "Come on! How can you miss that?"

"Miss what?" he questioned. "What are you talking about?"

The three women looked to each other, then shook their heads and strode to the door, and Black Canary chuckled as they left, "Super-man, super-clueless."

Superman stared at the door after it slid shut, turned his palms up and demanded, "What!"

Other members began to leave. Flash paused to pat Superman's shoulder and he laughed and shook his head as he did.

Batman was the last to leave and he stopped and turned toward the Man of Steel with narrow eyes. Approaching to within a couple of feet, he jabbed a finger into Superman's chest and coldly informed, "You and I are going to have a long talk, Kent!"

Superman watched him leave, and as he stood alone in the conference room, he set his hands on his hips and barked, "Is anyone going to tell me what's going on?"

CHAPTER 8

A more exciting week Elissa could not remember! She was kept busy in day long shifts with the Justice League, and while on watch she stayed in her mother's quarters there. She had a new utility belt and collected the assortment of tools and weapons she preferred, and this time Batman had given her two exploding Bat-arangs, and he had warned her to use them very carefully. There were times when Diana was on the schedule at the same time, and when they were not on missions or studying clues to the whereabouts of some of the escapees from prisons and asylums they spent as much time as they could together, and when Batman was on the schedule she spent time with him. Knowing that her attempts to bring them together were simply dismal failures, she abandoned that plan and worked to keep them apart as much as possible. Even when they were just in the same room she could sense the tension, and just that tension was enough to upset her, so keeping them from having any contact with each other became her priority.

Many times, she found the opportunity to spend time with Superman, and it was during these times that she found the giddy little girl in her rampaging into the open. She never was worried about looking foolish around him and really did not even think about it. She just loved being around him and made every excuse she could think of to be so. The time she spent with him was not lost on her parents, nor did it go unnoticed by the other members of the League, who did not miss any opportunity to give Superman a good ribbing about it.

For a while, there were no other great tests for her, no super villains for her to engage in one on one combat. While she would face crisis situations on three occasions, she was always a part of a team, twice with Superman, and on none of these occasions was she sent in to face off with the strongest adversaries, instead serving more of a support role. Meetings between on-call members were more frequent than she would have liked, but she did her best to pay attention and not allow her mind to wander much while she attended them. Always during these meetings, she sat or stood beside Superman, and when he was not on call, one of her parents. When both of her parents were there, she avoided them both, not wanting to show favorites.

She was falling into the Justice League routine nicely and even persuaded J'onn to put her on the flight roster should a Javelin need a pilot, though she realized that she was more a reserve than anything.

Roused early one morning, she sprang out of bed and dressed quickly to get to the conference room where an important meeting was about to start. The senior members were assembled and many others would attend this one, and she was excited to be included in something that seemed so important.

As she stepped into the elevator, she had barely enough time to push the up button before a red streak and a gust of air announced that Flash had arrived, and as the door closed, he folded his arms and beamed her a big smile.

She smiled back and greeted, "How's it going?"

"I'm late as always," he sighed. "Just woke up two seconds ago."

Elissa covered her mouth and giggled.

The car stopped and the door opened, and she smiled as she saw Superman standing there waiting for it. He stepped in without a word and the two occupants moved aside to give him room.

Turning back to the doors as they closed, he folded his arms and waited in silence.

"Hey, Big S," she greeted. "What's up?"

He just glanced at her, trying to be polite and finally answered, "We've had a situation come up. Things are about to get real interesting."

Elissa could tell that he was very tense about something. She had never seen him nervous before, did not even know that was possible, and she wanted to help him overcome it. "Oh boy!" she said with her usual enthusiasm. "Sounds like it's going to be fun."

"Let's hope so," Flash cut in. "I'd hate to think that this is another one of those villains that I have to just run circles around."

"You know you love it," Golden Angel scoffed.

The door opened and they filed out, eventually walking abreast of one another down the wide corridor with Superman flanked by Golden Angel and Flash, and still very quiet.

When they entered the conference room, they found almost everyone there. Superman sat in the chair closest to the door where he always did, all of the senior members took their seats and the others stood behind them around the table. There was a nervous buzzing of conversation and Elissa could sense that this was big as she stood behind and a little beside the Man of Steel. She took the opportunity to read the body language of everyone, seeing that those who already knew what the coming crisis was were uneasy about it, and her gift of insight only confirmed this.

Apparently, the meeting had already started and all eyes found Green Lantern as he said, "It looks like this was more than just a terrorist plot. We've confirmed that most of the more dangerous escapees are starting to organize and we're sure the ones we haven't heard from have already."

Steel, a very tall man encased in robotic enhanced armor and carrying a rather large hammer pointed out in a deep voice, "Then picking them off one or two at a time is going to be a problem long term, especially if the organized cells are able to break them right back out."

Finding her voice, Elissa asked, "What about taking down whole cells?"

"We thought of that already," Batman informed. "In fact, we're trying to nail down a few of the smaller ones."

She shrugged. "I personally would go after the biggest first."

"I agree," Aquaman concurred. "We need to hit the biggest ones first and in force."

"We have to find them first," Green Arrow pointed out. "These guys have become experts at hiding."

"What if we bait them out?" Black Canary suggested. "If one of the bigger cells hears about something that's way too good to pass up, a gold shipment or something like that, they're bound to try and hit it."

"Draw one out that way," Batman countered, "and you'll have the rest looking for that tactic."

"Unless we change tactics each time," Green Arrow pointed out. "It sounds like a viable plan."

Elissa grumbled, "Assuming they're not up to something else."

A few people looked to her.

Superman looked over his shoulder at her and said, "You need to speak up, Angel."

"It's nothing," she assured, turning her eyes down.

Captain Atom raised his chin to her and ordered, "Don't be afraid to speak your mind here, kiddo. We could use some fresh ideas."

She shrugged and hesitantly turned her eyes to him. "I… I was just thinking that they may not just be returning to business as usual. It could be that this was planned so that they could organize for something much bigger than what they were doing before."

Silence gripped the room for long seconds.

Flash suggested, "What if they're trying to rebuild the Legion of Doom or something? That could be trouble."

"I've looked into that," Batman informed. "There doesn't seem to be that kind of pattern to their activities."

Martian Manhunter folded his hands on the table and offered, "Unless their activities are meant to deceive us. It bears another look, I think."

"Whatever happens," Wonder Woman finally said, "we need to be ready to hit them in force. There is no telling the preparations they've made to meet us."

Superman looked down to the table and asked, "Did Metallo ever show up again?"

"No," J'onn answered immediately. "He and several other very formidable enemies of ours have disappeared completely."

Golden Angel grasped Superman's shoulder, just to show him she was behind him no matter what.

"That may be the real threat," Green Lantern said grimly. "While we're off chasing these smaller groups of escapees they could be reforming the Legion of Doom, or worse."

Elissa's imagination strayed to what could be worse, then her eyes widened and she slowly raised her head. Looking to Wonder Woman, she called out, "Mom!" before she realized.

"Angel!" Batman barked.

She grimaced and offered, "Sorry, but…"

Wonder Woman, sitting a quarter of the way around the table, snapped, "It's not like everyone doesn't know I'm her mother by now.

For Hera's sake, the whole world knows!"

"We should still be careful about sticking to protocols," he growled.

"Right!" Golden Angel agreed in an effort to head off another argument. "I totally agree and I'll be sure—"

Standing, Wonder Woman glared at Batman and informed in a loud voice, "Protocols are not going to help anyone get this situation under control! We need to focus on the issue at hand."

Looking back to her with narrow eyes, he countered, "We need to make sure security is maintained and that all members—"

"Would you be doing this if she wasn't your daughter?" Wonder Woman shouted.

Batman finally stood and turned fully on her. "All league members are held to the same standards and regulations."

"Of course," she chided. "No double standards for the Batman."

"I've never withheld anything from you," he snapped. "Can you say the same?"

She slammed her fists onto the table, leaning on it as she countered, "Perhaps we need to go over the whole thing again!"

Elissa backed away, shaking her head as she whimpered, "Mom, please."

"We've been over it enough," Batman assured, "and nothing you've said has convinced me—"

"Stop it!" Elissa suddenly screamed, backing away more.

Everyone's attention was suddenly trained on her.

Drawing a hard breath that shrieked all the way into her, she backed away more as she shouted, "For Hera's sake just stop it! Can't you stop fighting for two seconds? You are so obsessed with your animosity toward each other that you've completely forgotten how you used to feel about each other and you are so determined to fight and hurt each other that you can't see that something beautiful came from the relationship you had."

Her brow tensing, Wonder Woman softly asked, "And what was that?"

Elissa locked tear filled eyes on her mother and whimpered in a meek voice, "Me."

Silence consumed the room and the heroes all around them exchanged pitiable looks as the girl wheeled around and fled. The door slid shut behind her, and that silence thickened the very air all around.

Diana sat down, her eyes on the table before her in a bewildered stare. Her mouth hung open and the conflict she felt was all too clear to everyone in the room. Batman showed no emotion as he stared down at the table himself.

"Well," Flash started, "somebody had to say it. You guys have been at each other for weeks now. I thought we were going to have to send you to your rooms without any supper."

With her gaze still locked on the table before her, Diana softly scolded, "Now is not the time."

"I think it's the perfect time," Flash disagreed. "The kid's right. You guys have been so preoccupied with fighting with each other—"

"Wally!" she shouted, then she looked to Batman. "Oh, sorry. There's another breach of protocol. Do you intend to tear into me as well?"

Superman slammed his fist onto the table, caving in the thick metal and buckling half of the tabletop with a horrific bang. All attention went his way as he stood and shot an angry glare at Wonder Woman, then Batman, then back to Wonder Woman as he shouted, "I've had about enough of both of you!" He half turned and pointed to the door. "She's right! You're so obsessed with fighting that you can't see anything around you, especially what you're doing to that little girl who wants nothing more than to just see you get along!" His eyes shifted from one to the other and his voice lowered to an ominous growl. "This ends now. End it, or I will."

"We will," Green Lantern added. "You two have been behaving like children instead of trying to raise one."

Wonder Woman turned her full attention to him and she started, "You can't..." She vented a hard breath and looked to Batman. "Can you at least..."

He was gone.

Diana stood and hit the table with both fists, yelling, "I hate when he does that!"

"Hang on," Hawkgirl advised, deploying the consol from in front of her. "If Superman didn't knock the whole system out... Here we go. Tracking him now." She turned her eyes to the monitor.

Everyone did.

"The observatory," Martian Manhunter said.

The image they saw was not of Batman, even though that is where he was located. The first image was of the teenage girl who sat huddled on the steps to the lower level where the Earth could be seen. Her legs drawn to her, her arms were crossed over her knees and her face was buried in her arms, and she wept.

Diana's heart broke and she slowly sat down as she saw her daughter crying. "Hera," she breathed. "What have I done?"

In the observatory, Elissa simply could not compose herself, and after a time she gave up and just cried. Everything seemed lost and the penned up emotions could no longer be contained.

Feeling a presence behind her, she slowly raised her head and looked over her shoulder to see her father standing behind her, one step up from where she was and a little to her right. Looking back to the Earth through the observatory window, she set her chin on her arms and just stared at it, not knowing what to say, not caring to say anything, but at least the awkwardness staved off her crying for the moment.

Moving as quietly as always, he sat down beside her, also turning his gaze to the Earth. He also did not seem to know what to say, but finally managed, "Looks like a full Earth tonight."

She just nodded.

He vented a deep breath and turned his eyes down. "I'm sorry, Angel. There's no excuse for how we've been acting around you."

She still did not know how to respond, but she did not want to provoke any ill will toward either of them, though her anger with her mother was beginning to surface. Finally, she lifted her head and asked, "Why couldn't she just let it go?"

"I don't know," he said softly.

Elissa shook her head and cried, "Why couldn't she just—"

"This wasn't her fault, Angel," he interrupted. When she finally looked to him, he forced his eyes to her and confessed, "It's mine."

Still watching from the conference room, Diana's eyes widened and she raised her chin, her lips slowly parting in surprise.

Bruce looked away from his daughter. "She kept you from me for sixteen years. All that time I didn't know I had a daughter. And then one day there you were. I missed out on your entire childhood." He looked back to the Earth and heaved another breath. "I look back on the relationship we could have had with each other, you and I. There is so much I had to offer, so much I still want to give you."

"I know," she agreed softly. "It was wrong of her to keep me from you."

He cut his eyes to her. "To be honest, I can't say I would have done things differently in her place. I would have done anything to protect you, to keep you out of the sights of our enemies." He looked to the Earth again. "To keep you from this life."

She wiped the tears from her eyes and informed, "I like this life. Sure it's dangerous, but I'm warrior trained and I'm ready for this, and you have to remember that I worry about you guys, too. I don't want to lose either of you."

Bruce turned his full attention to her, and a slight smile curled his mouth. "You are a remarkable young woman, Elissa. You need to know that your mother did a fantastic job raising you."

Her eyes locked on the monitor, Diana raised a hand to her mouth as tears filled her eyes.

Batman slipped an arm around the girl's shoulders, wrapping her in his cape as he pulled her to him, and she laid her head on his shoulder and snuggled into him.

"I won't fight with her anymore," he assured, "especially in front of you. I wish we both could have seen how incredibly wrong it was to do that."

Elissa closed her eyes and nodded.

They just sat there for a time and for that time they did not speak. He held her, and she snuggled as close to him as she could.

Hawkgirl turned off the monitor and the conference room was consumed by a deafening silence.

Flash wiped his eyes and asked, "Does anyone else feel all warm and fuzzy?"

WW

Hours later the station seemed quiet. Diana stayed in the conference room with many others to discuss the issue of the escapees, many of the Justice League were out on missions and a few had gone home for the night.

Answering a call, Golden Angel stepped from the elevator to the control room and strode toward the imposing form of the Martian Manhunter. He still intimidated her, but she remained friendly and light hearted around him.

Reaching the console where he stood, watching the main monitor, she folded her hands behind her and looked up at the monitor as well, asking, "What's up?"

"Disturbances at two museums in New York," he replied. "Someone has broken into both of them and stolen very specific artifacts."

She nodded and said, "I'll check it out."

"There's more," he informed. Bringing up a map, he highlighted all of the museums, then pointed to the left one. "He hit that one first, then this one, and he was last seen heading toward this one."

Her brow lowered. "Heading in a straight line from one to the next. It doesn't sound like we're up against someone who is very smart. He has to know we'll head him off."

J'onn looked down at her. "Or he is not worried about being stopped."

She looked back at him and nodded. "I still think I can handle it. It's just one guy."

He raised a brow.

"I won't get in over my head," she assured. "If it's serious and I don't think I can handle him then I'll call for backup. I promise."

"Very well," he agreed reluctantly. "I'll send you down to the third museum. He should be there any moment. Stay in contact."

Elissa smiled and complied, "Yes, Uncle J'onn."

WW

Everything seemed quiet as she approached the museum from about a block away. The chill in the air did not go unnoticed but the little heroine ignored it, even though she could see her breath every time she exhaled. Daybreak was still a couple of hours away and street lamps lit the way to the museum. It was very well lit by landscape lighting and lights from the ground that were aimed to illuminate it, and it was a really big structure that reminded her of some of the Greek style architecture of Themyscira. Police cars had already arrived and had set up a perimeter and it was clear that the perpetrator had already arrived. Hearing shots fired near the front door, she quickened her pace.

Rounding a SWAT van, she saw a police car overturned and an ambulance attending to some injured men, and she hesitated. More shots drew her attention to the front of the museum and she ran that way.

Nearly to the museum there was a secondary perimeter set up and she paused, turning her eyes up as a police car flew into view and crashed to the ground just on the other side of the line of waiting cruisers. Many uniformed police and SWAT were taking cover behind these cruisers and all turned their eyes to her.

She heaved a breath, then ran that way.

Circling around the main sidewalk, she ran across the small courtyard and darted up the steps to the front door, which had not been breached yet. Standing right in front of the glass doors, she looked toward the police line, raising her chin as a tall, thickly made figure stormed around an overturned van and brushed aside the policemen who tried to stop him. Other police were shooting at him, and their bullets simply bounced off. Trotting down the steps to the wide concrete walkway, she saw a number of police officers taking up their positions between him and the museum.

Grasping one's shoulder, she ordered, "Get everyone out of here. Your guns aren't working, anyway."

He turned and nodded to her, then he shouted to the others, "Fall back!" As they departed, Elissa set her hands on her hips and watched her big opponent stride into the lamps that illuminated the walkway, and she found herself turning her gaze upward as he neared.

About six foot six, he had a titanic build with massive arms and chest, a thick but solid waist and huge legs. His hair was blond and very long, dropping in flowing locks down below his shoulders. He wore a headpiece that was made of some kind of tanned leather with polished steel plates riveted in place all around it and many different colors of jewels mounted into the plates. He had dazzling blue eyes with his heavy brow carried low between them. Clean shaven, he had strong features and a big jaw and chin, and from the look of him he was very young, no older than twenty. His big arms were bare but for the polished metal gauntlets that he wore around each forearm. He wore a blue jerkin over his bulging chest that was trimmed in elaborate silver embroidery and held open at the front. His trousers were black and met heavy, knee high black leather boots that were topped with white fur and had many silver buckles on the outsides that held them snug to his massive calves. A mantle on his back was the same color as his jerkin and was fastened at his neck by a silver chain. It too was trimmed in that elaborate silver embroidery, and as he neared she could see that it looked Celtic.

He stopped only about three feet away and towered over her.

Looking him slowly up and down—twice—Golden Angel finally looked up to his eyes, seeing that he had also been studying her. When their eyes finally met, she absently said, "Wow, you're gorgeous!"

He raised his brow.

Raising a hand to her head, she mumbled, "Okay, Elissa. Focus." She drew a breath and set her hands on her hips, looking up at him with a challenging stare this time as she observed, "So you're the one causing all of the noise over here. You mind telling me what you're doing?"

His eyes narrowed and his fingers curled inward.

Tamping her foot, she barked, "I'm waiting!"

In a young but deep voice and with a thick Germanic accent he ordered, "Do not stand in my way, daughter of the Amazons."

She raised her brow. "Seriously? You know I'm an Amazon and you're still going to talk trash?"

A snarl took his mouth and he growled, "Do you mean to challenge me for the right to enter this temple?"

Elissa shrugged. "Sure, whatever. So what's your name, sweetie?"

He set his jaw, raising his chin slightly as he replied, "I am Beowulf, champion of the Norsemen."

"Champion of the Norsemen," she repeated. She had learned to hate the German accent during her encounters with Red Panzer less than a year ago. Now she was changing her mind about that. "So would you mind telling me why you are busting up museums?"

His expression hardened. "These temples hold stolen items belonging to my people, and I have been sent to retrieve them."

"What kinds of items?" she asked sweetly.

"I haven't time to stand about making words!" he barked. "Move aside, kleines mädchen, or you must challenge my right to enter!"

Her eyes narrowed and she dropped her arms to her sides, clenching her hands into tight fists. "Look, pal, I know some

German, and if you call me 'little girl' again in *any* language, I'm going to knock you on your butt! Oh, and you are not busting up another museum on my watch!"

He clenched his jaw again and growled, then he strode forward and ordered, "Move aside."

Demonstrating her Amazon strength, she stepped into him and slammed her palm into his very solid chest, stopping him cold as she shouted, "You do *not* want to mess with me! Now back off!"

With a single swing of his arm, he easily brushed her aside and she fell as gracefully as she could as he strode by. Slowly, she pushed herself up, lying half on her side as she turned her eyes back up to him. As he just walked away, her lips slid away from her teeth and she yelled, "Oh, no you didn't!"

Springing up, she charged, grabbed his arm and swung him around. Her right hand balled into a fist, she swung as hard as she could to deliver a blow that could kill any mortal she struck. Her fist slammed into his jaw and snapped his head around. As he recovered, her other came and knocked it the other way. An uppercut connected with his chin with killing force and he stepped backward. Spinning around, she slammed the sole of her boot solidly into his gut, then she spun the other way and sent the same boot toward his head, connecting with his cheek, and he sidestepped.

Wheeling fully around, she assumed her battle stance, surprised to see him still standing, then her eyes widened as he slowly turned his full attention on her, and he looked angry.

Taking a step back, she held her fists ready and mumbled, "Ah, crud," as she saw he had not hurt him at all. When he bared his teeth and advanced on her, she backed away.

Breaths entered him in heavy heaves and he shouted, "You would challenge me?"

"I would," she replied, "but I'm sure starting to have second thoughts about that."

"The challenge must be answered," he informed. "You must yield or fight."

She stopped and held her palms to him. "Wait a minute. You can't go in unless you fight me and win?"

He stopped right in front of her and raised his chin. "Ja. The challenge must be answered. Do you yield, or must I fight you?"

"No, I don't yield!" she barked, setting her hands on her hips. "I just want to know the rules. We fight and if I win you have to go away, right?"

Beowulf nodded. "I must win the right if I am challenged. That is what honor demands."

"Okay, then," she accepted, holding her hand out. "May the best fighter win." When he took her hand, she clamped down on his and yanked him toward her, half turning as she did and slamming her knee into his gut. This time he doubled over slightly and she released him and jumped straight up, and when she came down she slammed her elbow right into the back of his shoulder.

He lurched over and she took his arm, spinning around to throw him over her shoulder, but this time his experience prevailed and he wrapped his arm around her neck and pulled her brutally in to him.

With her throat locked into the crook of his elbow, she found her air supply and the blood flow to her brain being seriously compromised. She grabbed onto his arm with both hands, trying to pull his arm away, but he was far too strong. Kicking back, she slammed the heel of her boot into his shin, then again, and again, but still she could not break free, and she was slowly lifted from the ground. She slammed her elbow into his solid gut a few times, but it was like striking a wall and did not hurt him. Consciousness began to slip away. She had to do something! Reaching into a pouch on her belt, she removed a small metallic orb, took a second to calculate where his face was, and threw it over her head with all her strength.

It hit him in the forehead and exploded with a loud bang and a blinding flash and he yelled and reached for head, and his grip on her loosened just enough.

She broke free and quickly wheeled around, slamming her boot hard into his chest while he was distracted. When he stumbled, still holding a hand over his forehead and eyes, she kicked him there again, then spun and kicked him again. She was driving him toward the street, away from the museum, and was succeeding until she spun around with a well aimed kick at his head, and he blocked it.

He had recovered fully from the flash-bang and when she threw a punch at him, he grabbed her forearm and wheeled around, hurling her toward the street.

Golden Angel slammed back-first into the side of the van hard enough to cave it in almost a quarter of the way. It lurched over and threatened to overturn before righting itself again and she crumpled face down to the street, struggling to regain her wits. She pushed herself up and shook her head, then she looked up to see him standing over fifty feet away. Every time he breathed out his breath could be seen as smoke in the cold air, and this gave him the look of some kind of ominous demon as he slowly strode toward her.

Staggering to her feet, she stumbled into the van and reached for her communicator, her wide eyes locked on him as she raised it to her mouth and called, "Golden Angel to Watchtower!"

"Watchtower here," J'onn's monotone voice replied.

"Um..." she stammered. "Uh, this guy's really strong. Can you go ahead and send backup this way please?"

"I'll dispatch someone now," he assured.

"Thanks," she offered. Putting her communicator away, she turned and reached for the door handle of the van, opened the door and planted her foot just on the edge. Looking over her shoulder, she saw him less than fifteen feet away and she grabbed the door with her other hand and wrenched it off of the van, then she spun completely around with a mighty yell and swung the door at him as hard as she could.

He blocked it with his gauntlet, grabbed it with his free hand and yanked it out of her grip.

As he tossed it away, Elissa backed up against the van, pressing her back and palms to it as she watched him close on her. When he grabbed at her, she quickly ducked under his hand and lunged into him, planting her shoulder low into his abdomen and trying to drive him backward. With a savage yell, she picked him up, then lunged forward and drove him as hard as she could into the road.

Asphalt and concrete shattered as his head and shoulders slammed into them.

He was finally down and she would not wait for him to recover. She leaped onto his chest, grabbed his jerkin and raised a fist, bringing it down with all her might.

Beowulf simply raised his hand and stopped her fist solidly in his palm.

She met his eyes, and did not expect what she saw there. His were not the eyes of a furious warrior, rather someone who was almost… patient. They were frozen where they were for long seconds, her holding his jerkin and him holding her fist.

"Yield," he ordered.

Her eyes narrowed and she countered, "Don't think so."

His other hand found her belly, pushed her off of him and hurled her into the van again.

She slammed into it and crumpled to the ground where she had been before, this time rising a little slower. Before she had her wits about her, his big hand was wrapped around her throat and she was pushed back into the van. Raising both hands to seize his wrist, she found herself looking into those cobalt blue eyes again, and once again she froze.

"Yield," he said in a low voice. "You don't have to fight on. We both know you cannot beat me and there is no dishonor in yielding to a superior warrior. Please, just yield."

It finally occurred to her that he had not struck her even once, that he had not even tried to. Aside from throwing her into the side of the van a couple of times, he seemed to be doing his best not to hurt her. For the first time in her life her heart thundered at the sight of a young man, at his proximity to her. Still, she had to find some way to stop him. That had to be first and foremost. It had to.

His grip on her throat gently loosened and his fingers glided up the side of her neck.

Chills were sent through her at his touch and she closed her eyes as his thumb gently caressed her lips. She finally realized she was not breathing, and made herself take a breath.

"Will you yield?" he asked softly.

Opening her eyes, Elissa looked into his for long seconds before shaking her head and insisting, "No."

He stroked his fingers through her hair, right above her ear and new chills swept through her.

With a regretful look in his eyes, he told her, "Then understand I will do as I must." Backing away, his expression hardened and his hands clenched into tight fists. "If you will not yield, then you must fight me."

She folded her arms and defiantly raised her chin. "What if I don't wanna?"

He hesitated and appeared to not know what to do or say for a few seconds, then his brow lowered and he shouted, "Fight me!"

"No," she spat.

Shaking his head, he insisted, "Then yield!"

"Nuh uh," was her answer.

"Then..." he started. "Then you force me..."

"To what?" she asked in a challenging tone. "Hit a girl?"

"Fight me!" he yelled. The threw a hard punch that crashed into the van right beside her head.

Cringing, she closed her eyes for a couple of seconds and was trembling when she opened them again, her chest heaving in frightened breaths as she gave him a defiant glare and insisted, "I won't." She flinched as he punched the van on the other side of her head, but this time kept her gaze locked on him.

He bent close to her, bringing his nose only an inch from hers as his eyes bored into her. With a regretful tone, he growled, "Then I will do what I must."

"So will I," she informed. Without warning, she reached up and grabbed the sides of his head with both hands, pulling him to her, and she closed her eyes as she pressed her lips to his.

Clearly surprised by this move, Beowulf did not close his eyes and he pushed against her and finally separated their mouths.

She opened her eyes to look up into his and once again she struggled to catch her breath. Raising her brow, she asked, "Do you give up yet?"

He shook his head and answered, "No." He grasped her neck and pulled her to him.

Elissa sucked a breath right before their lips met. She had no experience with this, but he clearly did. She whimpered as he took her mouth with an experience she had never imagined and sensations she had never known waged war inside her. When she felt his other hand slide up her waist and around her back, she whimpered again and raised her chin to surrender to his kiss, her first. She felt his strength as he crushed her to him and her hands slid around the sides of his head, her arms wrapping around his neck. He had been bending over to bring their mouths closer, but now he stood, lifting her effortlessly from the ground.

Beowulf finally drew away and met her eyes, and for long seconds they just stared at each other.

"You're really good at that," she gasped, unconsciously and slowly kicking her dangling feet back and forth in opposite directions.

"You don't seem so experienced," he observed.

A little smile touched her lips and she nodded. "Yeah, but I'm a quick learner." She closed her arms tighter around his neck, pulling herself closer to him.

They kissed again and he pressed her up against the van, and she tightened her hold on him.

He drew away again, drawing a deep breath before asking, "Will you yield now?"

With a coy smile, Golden Angel shook her head. "Oh, don't count on it. I can keep this up all night."

"Can you, now?" he asked with a teasing tone.

"Yeah," she assured. When he kissed her again, she purred, "Mmm…" and simply gave in, and learned quickly. This time, she kissed him back as best she knew how.

She drew away and demanded, "Okay, *you* give up."

Beowulf smiled and shook his head. "Oh no, mein schatzi. I can do this all night, too."

One of her eyebrows cocked up and she challenged, "Prove it."

Elissa did not allow inexperience in this matter to give her pause. She found herself consumed by this first taste of passion and kissed him more and more hungrily, and soon found her hand running through his long hair, hair that was soft as silk and very strong, very pleasing to the touch. As he pressed his body harder to hers, she found feelings within her that ignited in such ways that she had never imagined. Somehow, this new and exciting moment was just perfect.

Wonder Woman loudly cleared her throat nearby.

Golden Angel and Beowulf pulled away from each other, staring fearfully into each other's eyes, then they looked to the side.

And there stood Wonder Woman, her hands set on her hips and a furious glare in her eyes. Superman stood beside her and Hawkgirl on her other side, and those two wore bewildered expressions.

"Uh oh," Elissa mumbled. She looked back to Beowulf, swallowing hard, then she whispered, "I think we're kind of in some major doo-doo."

His eyes cut to Wonder Woman.

Elissa looked that way, too, her brow high over her eyes as she tightened her grip around his neck and declared, "I got him!"

"I see that," Diana confirmed in a hard voice.

"It's a good thing you showed up, too," Golden Angel went on. "I was just about to make my move."

"Looks like you already have," Hawkgirl observed.

Wonder Woman clenched her jaw and turned a look of daggers on Hawkgirl, who cringed under her attention.

When her mother looked back to her, Elissa mumbled to Beowulf, "You really need to put me down now."

He wisely set her down and backed away and the two of them turned to face the three heroes who were now approaching them.

Wonder Woman stopped about six feet away and folded her arms, locking the big Norseman in a deadly glare. Though he was both taller and much bulkier, she was not intimidated in the least.

Golden Angel's eyes darted from one to the other, finally locking on Superman as she cleared her throat and observed, "So you guys sure got here in a hurry."

"Not fast enough," he grumbled.

Beowulf held Wonder Woman in his gaze, also not showing any intimidation as he raised his chin and asked, "Would you tell me your name?"

"Tell me yours," she demanded.

He answered with strong words in his thick accent, "I am Beowulf, champion of the Norsemen."

"Beowulf died long ago," the Amazon Princess pointed out.

"I was given my father's name," he explained. "Now I am sent on a quest by Odin himself to collect the lost treasures of my people and return them home."

Wonder Woman exchanged glances with Superman.

"I will face many more tests," he continued, "before I earn my place in Valhalla and stand next to my father and the Gods. I cannot fail at a single one. If I do, the gods will laugh at me and I will be cast out forever."

With a slight nod, Wonder Woman said, "I see. So, is one of those great tests kissing my daughter like that?"

Slowly, Beowulf turned his attention down to Golden Angel.

"Oh, yeah," she declared nervously. "That's my mom." Her brow arched as he just stared at her, and she extended a hand to her mother. "Beowulf, meet Wonder Woman."

His eyes slid back to her, wonder and suspicion there as he demanded, "I would know your name, Amazon."

"She just told you," Wonder Woman snarled.

"No," he corrected, "your name."

Raising her chin, she eyed him with authority and replied, "I am Diana, Princess of the Amazons."

Beowulf's eyes widened, his chest heaving as he drew a breath. He took a long step toward her, then he knelt, folding his arms over his knee as he bowed his head. "I beg forgiveness, your Highness."

Elissa's wide eyes shifted from him to her mother several times.

"On your feet, Beowulf of the Norsemen," the Princess ordered.

He complied, towering over her. He was careful to keep his arms at his sides and no longer met her gaze so confidently.

"You will return home," she commanded, "and tell Odin if he wishes to have these artifacts, he can come and speak to me himself."

His expression hardened and he informed, "I will not fail in my task, Princess Diana. I will return in victory, or I will die in the attempt."

Her eyes narrowing, Diana cracked her knuckles.

Golden Angel rushed between them, placing a hand on Beowulf's chest to push him back a step. "Wait, guys. We don't need to fight anymore." Giving her mother a desperate look, she asked, "Can't we help him finish his tasks? Isn't that what we're about?"

Hawkgirl folded her arms and pointed out, "You know, she might be a little more sympathetic if we hadn't caught you sucking face with him just now."

Wonder Woman raised her brow and turned an infuriated look on Hawkgirl.

Backing away, Hawkgirl raised her hands before her and assured, "I'm just saying!"

Superman folded his arms, his eyes shifting from the girl to the big Nordic champion. "She's right, Diana. We should help." When she turned a bewildered look on him, he casually looked back and pointed out, "Why fight a pointless battle with him when we can just help out and send him on his way?"

"You guys won't have to do a thing!" Elissa assured. "I'll stay with him and keep him out of trouble and we can—"

"Leave you alone with him after what I just saw?" Diana yelled. "Are you out of your hormonal little mind?"

Defiance took the girl's features and she folded her arms. "Oh, like you've never kissed a guy."

"Not at sixteen I didn't!" Diana replied.

Elissa heaved a breath and grumbled through clenched teeth, "I'm seventeen, Mom."

Superman took Wonder Woman's shoulder and informed, "I'm going to give the police an update and get them to stand down." When she nodded, he took to the sky.

"I'll make some calls and get the other curators here," Hawkgirl stated. "I'm sure they'll want to know what's going on." Looking to Wonder Woman, she suggested, "How about we give these young lovers some privacy?"

Diana's patience was lost when her eyes slid that way and she warned, "Shyira, I swear to Zeus—"

With a playful smile, Hawkgirl opened her wings and backed away. "I just remembered I have this thing I have to do. See you guys later." She turned and swept her wings, lifting herself into the sky.

WW

Sunup was only an hour away or so and colder air was moving in from the east ahead of it.

Standing at the bottom of the front steps of the museum, they watched the glass doors anxiously and in silence. Elissa had her arms crossed over her chest, her shoulders drawn up as she shivered just a little from the chill in the air. Beowulf, standing closely at her side, looked down at her and could see her discomfort in the cold air. Being a Norseman, the chill did not bother him, but he found sympathy for the young Amazon. Reaching to his neck, the unfastened his mantle and pulled it from his shoulders, then he turned to throw it around hers. The girl was a little surprised and looked over her shoulder as it settled into place, then she looked up to him as he gently took her arm and turned her toward him, reaching for the chain that would fasten it high across her chest.

"There you go," he said softly. "Maybe this will keep you warm, ja?"

A little smile curled her mouth and she offered, "Thank you." Reaching from within the cape, which dropped to her ankles, she pulled it to her, feeling how soft it was against her bare skin. It felt right on her and narrowed itself to fit her shoulders better and somehow made itself smaller, suiting her nicely.

Once again they stood side by side as they watched the door of the museum.

A moment later he observed, "She has been in there for a while."

"Yeah," Elissa agreed. "She's talking to the curator. That and the guys from the other museums you busted up are in there talking to her." Her eyes slid to him. "You couldn't just wait for them to open?"

Beowulf shrugged. "I don't know your ways."

"You know, it doesn't hurt to just ask sometimes."

"I have fought many battles, Schatzi," he informed. "Not once would asking—"

"This isn't a battlefield," she interrupted. "Not everything has to be. If you need something then just ask, and if they give you a hard time, *then* you kick their butt."

He smiled. "Does this work for you?"

"Yeah," she confirmed, "it usually does."

The door opened and Wonder Woman emerged, looking to them for a second before she beckoned them inside.

They watched her go back inside, then Elissa drew a breath and sighed, "Well, here we go."

Together, they walked up the steps, and when they reached the top and were almost to the door, she threw an arm across his chest and stopped him, then she stepped in front of him, very close.

With a flirty little smile, she looked up at him and folded her hands behind her as she informed, "You still haven't won the right to go in there."

A little smile curled his mouth too and he took her shoulders. "Oh, haven't I?"

She shook her head. "Nope. I still haven't yielded."

"So how do I make you yield?" he asked in a low voice, bending over slightly to bring his face close to hers.

Leaning her head, she raised her chin, half closing her eyes as they found his mouth. "Well I don't know, Handsome. What do you think would work?" Her long lashes slid down over her eyes as his lips touched hers ever so gently

Elissa slid her arms slowly around his waist. His glided around her back, one high at the back of her neck, and he pulled her to him in a very tight embrace. They did not know how long they enjoyed this moment as everything around them, everything they had to do just melted away.

"Junior!" Wonder Woman shouted from the door.

They both flinched, meeting each other's eyes.

"Okay," Golden Angel conceded. "I give." She looked over her shoulder and assured, "Coming, Mom!"

Under Wonder Woman's watchful, irritated gaze, Beowulf and Golden Angel strode into the museum, offering her only nervous glances as they strode by her.

The cavernous first room of the museum was where several massive skeletons of extinct animals, ancient suits of armor and paintings along the far wall were displayed. The floor was some kind of marble tile and the ceiling looked to be more than thirty feet high, most likely to accommodate the massive mammoth and dinosaur skeletons that were assembled in this room. Right across the room, about eighty feet away, was where tickets were purchased and people could go into the main museum where the really spectacular exhibits awaited.

Only about twenty feet inside, four police officers and three men in expensive suits waited. Two of these men were older with white hair and one had a beard while the third looked like he was in his forties with gray around his temples. None of them looked pleased.

In a show of support, Elissa reached from within Beowulf's cape and took his hand, and when he looked down at her, she offered him a confident little smile and a nod.

They reached the men there and Wonder Woman took Elissa's side, setting her hands on her hips as she assured, "I'm sure we can come up with a resolution to this problem that does not involve more conflict."

Golden Angel added, "He really just wants what belongs to his people, anyway."

The older gentleman with the beard raised his chin and barked, "So we should just give up tens of thousands of dollars in exhibits on your word? Like it or not, those Nordic artifacts are a draw for thousands of people a year to these museums."

"He doesn't want all of them," Elissa assured, "just the few he was sent to collect."

The three men exchanged disbelieving looks.

She looked up at her mother, then to the Nordic champion beside her before her eyes drifted to his belt. There, one of the pouches he wore looked a little heavy. Freeing her hand from his, she opened the pouch and her fingers darted in, returning with a huge gold coin that looked like it had been struck in ancient Greece. Her eyes darted back to the older bearded fellow and she suggested, "What if he has something to trade?"

Beowulf had watched her retrieve the coin from his pouch, and he gently took it from her fingers. Looking to the men, he offered it to the bearded fellow and said, "I can offer you each one of these."

Hesitantly, the older bearded man took the coin, looking it over before he reached into his coat pocket to retrieve his glasses. When his glasses were on his nose they made his eyes look huge and he raised his brow. The other two men leaned in to get a closer look, then all three turned wide eyed looks to the big Nordic warrior.

Bartering worked and the museum curators were ecstatic about what Beowulf had to offer. Hours later found him with Wonder Woman and Golden Angel at the waterfront where a small, sleek ship awaited him. Seemingly powered by oars, it also had a sail on its single mast that depicted a dragon emerging from the clouds. It was a beautiful ship, and Elissa noticed quickly that it did not float on the water; rather it hovered right above it on a cushion of mist. Seeing the ship also gave her a heavy heart. It meant that he would be leaving soon.

Turning first to Wonder Woman, Beowulf bowed to her and offered, "You have my thanks, Princess Diana. My quest has succeeded, and my test has been passed."

She nodded to him. "Odin will be very pleased, Beowulf. You are an honorable man and a great champion."

"So," Elissa began hesitantly, "are you actually Beowulf? I mean, didn't..."

He turned to her and took her hands. "I am, Schatzi, but not the Beowulf of legend. Not yet. I was given the name of my father by the Goddess Zisa, mein mother."

"You're a demigod," Diana observed with a lean of her head.

Looking away, he shrugged and admitted, "No, no place in Valhalla yet. I hope soon." Still holding on to Golden Angel's hand, he looked to the Amazon Princess and continued, "I'll not be accepted into Valhalla until I can return home a true champion of mein people, and a hero."

Diana folded her arms and smiled. "A hero is one who knows when to fight, and when not to. You've demonstrated that today."

He smiled and bowed his head to her. Looking back to Elissa, he was tight lipped as he softly said, "I must go, Princess."

Seeing tears fill her daughter's eyes, Diana stepped to their sides and patted their shoulders. "I'm going to go call Superman and touch base with him."

They watched her walk away, taking her communicator from her belt, then they looked back to each other.

"You can't just stay?" she asked in a soft, vulnerable voice.

Beowulf shook his head. "I cannot, Princess. Even if I could, it would be only for one reason."

Raising her brow, she asked, "What's that?"

"You already know," he assured.

"Me?" she asked, hopefully.

With a nod, he softly confirmed, "Ja." He released her hands and took the headpiece from his brow. Looking down at what he did, he pried an oval sapphire stone from it before putting it back in place. Gently, he took her tiara from her head, and under her watchful eye he pressed the sapphire to the star in the middle of the tiara. The stone liquefied and it flowed out into the blue star there, covering it, and in seconds it had become solid again to become a bright, star shaped blue sapphire that covered the blue star that was there.

Her lips slowly parted as she watched him put her tiara back into its place above her brow.

"It is a shard of the Eye of Odin," he explained. "It has special powers, but only when worn by a descendent of a Nordic God. As long as you wear it, I will feel you in my heart." He looked into her eyes, more deeply than anyone ever had. "When you need me, I will be in your heart, Schatzi. When you are in your greatest peril, I will come and I will unleash all of the fury that I am to take your side in battle and smite down your enemies. We've had but a few hours, but..." He looked away.

"Yeah," she confirmed in a whisper. She bit her lip and informed, "I'd never kissed a boy before."

He smiled. "I am honored to be your first."

"Will I ever see you again?" she asked hopefully.

"You will," he assured. "I wish I could tell you when. My heart is yours, little Amazon Princess, but we have all the time of the world, you and I. Find your adventures and your romances and fill your heart with all you can. Deny your heart to no one."

Tears filled her eyes anew. "What if I want only you to have it?"

He raised her hand to her mouth, touching his lips to her fingers. "I will always be, mein Schatzi, and so will you. I beg you do not deny this world that wonderful heart behind your breast. The world needs your heart far more than I."

"So don't wait for you?" she asked in a whisper.

"Destiny will call us together when it is time," he assured. "Your gods and mine remain at odds, but one day there will be peace between them again."

She nodded.

He pulled her to him, slid his arms under the cape she still wore and around her back, and her arms wrapped around him. She raised her chin, leaning her head as she closed her eyes.

Diana stood some distance away and had turned to watch her daughter, and a little smile found her lips as she watched the two join in one last, passionate kiss.

This kiss took a while, but he finally pulled away, holding onto her hand as he backed away from her, and finally their hands slipped apart. He turned and jumped onto the ship, bounding to the mast in the center. Holding onto the mast, he turned back and waved to her, shouting, "Until our paths cross again, Daughter of the Amazons, be well, and know that a champion's heart beats strong with each thought of you."

Waggling her fingers to him, she called, "Be well, Champion of the Norsemen." Her eyes darted to her shoulders and she drew a gasp as she realized she still wore his cape. "Beowulf!" When he looked to her, she grabbed part of it and held it up.

As the ship rose higher off the water on the mist that now glowed blue, and he called back to her, "Let it keep you warm in my absence, Schatzi!"

Elissa watched with tear filled eyes as the Viking ship climbed higher and began to speed toward the horizon, leaving behind it a fading trail of glowing blue mist. She raised her hand toward the departing Nordic Champion, and as the ship found a burst of speed and streaked out of sight, her fingers curled inward and slowly her arm lowered to her side. As Beowulf disappeared, the sun broke the horizon in a brilliant orange and yellow explosion of light, right where he had vanished toward the horizon. The little Amazon stood there for a while, watching the horizon, the sunrise. Her heart ached, and yet it felt full and beat within her with a strength she had never known before.

After a time, Wonder Woman's arm slipped around her shoulders. Elissa turned her head to look up at her mother, and she smiled as a tear rolled from her eye as she slipped an arm around her mother's back.

Diana pulled the girl close to her, laying her cheek on the girl's head, and they both looked to the rising sun. For a time they just stood there and enjoyed the sunrise, and slowly a mother's fingers combed through her daughter's hair.

Finally, Diana asked, "You okay, Junior?"

"Yeah," Elissa breathed with a little smile. "I wish I had given him something to remember me by."

"I saw that kiss, little girl," Diana informed. "Believe me, you did."

WW

A few hours later Golden Angel sought refuge in the Watchtower's observation deck, right in front of the window that overlooked the Earth. She still wore Beowulf's cape as she sat on the steps where she had before. In her hands was her tiara and she stared down at it with all of her attention, mesmerized by the sparkle of the blue sapphire that had replaced the star there.

Wonder Woman approached slowly, quietly. She knew the girl would feel her coming and her silent approach was more to not disturb her thoughts. Sitting beside her, she slipped her arm around her shoulders for a gentle hug, and when she saw the tiara in her daughter's hand, she commented, "That sure is pretty."

Elissa nodded. "He said it is a shard of the Eye of Odin. He took it from his headpiece and gave it to me, and when he pressed it to my tiara it took the shape of the star." Leaning her head into her mother, she went on, "He said he would know when I am in my greatest peril and he'll come and fight by my side. He said destiny will bring us together someday, but not to wait for him. That's so confusing."

"Yeah," Diana said just over a whisper. "Men can be."

Turning the tiara slightly to make the lights sparkle off of the facets of the stone, Elissa informed, "He told me our gods are at odds with each other. Do you know what he's talking about?"

"I sure don't," Diana confessed. "I'm sure Granna knows more about that than I do and if you can get a straight answer out of her about it there is much you could learn."

With another nod, the girl just stared down at the tiara, once again lost in thoughts.

"You want me to leave you alone?" Wonder Woman asked with gentle words.

"No," Elissa answered softly. "I'm just kind of thinking, I guess."

Diana tugged at the cape. "And how long are you going to wear this?"

"I never want to take it off," Elissa replied with a strange little smile.

The door to the observatory closed and many sets of boots approached with loud clops.

Wonder Woman and Golden Angel turned to see who had entered.

Behind them were Hawkgirl, Black Canary, Huntress, Fire, and Maya striding to them.

Elissa slipped her tiara back onto her brow.

They all stopped, and Black Canary, who was closest to her, set her hands on her hips and demanded, "Come on, Angel." She and Fire reached down and took the girl's arms, helping her up.

"Where are we going?" Elissa asked nervously as she was escorted to the door.

In a Spanish accent, Fire replied, "We're going to the commissary."

Hawkgirl added, "And we want to hear all about this guy you were kissing."

Looking over her shoulder as they left, Black Canary met Wonder Woman's eyes and asked, "You coming?"

Raising her brow, Diana stood and turned toward the door, striding after them as she mumbled, "I'm not missing this."

CHAPTER 9

In no time Elissa was back to her usual fun, bubbly self and everyone in the Justice League was glad of it. While she did not forget about the dashing Nordic Champion, she went on as he had instructed and filled each day as best she could. Training with Batman proved to be quite an education. He knew things, how to move and avoidance maneuvers that she had never even dreamed of! More than that, he taught her to move silently and quickly and together they worked to overcome her fear of heights. When she was with him, her mother was conspicuously absent, and had in fact left Wayne Manor, presumably to give Elissa and her father more uninterrupted time together.

Often, she spent many long hours aboard the Watchtower, and only rarely was she selected to go on a mission. She did not allow this to bother her, though, as she saved her energy for outings with Batman, which proved to be just as hard to get through as those quiet times aboard the Watchtower. He spent most of his time simply gathering information, and a few times sent her on her own to do so. As his trust in her grew, so did the intensity of the training he had waiting for her almost daily.

There finally came the night where she found herself aboard the Watchtower with both of her parents present. This always ran tensions very high, though good to their word they had not fought with each other for nearly a week.

The control room of the watchtower seemed to be where the action was for the most part so on a quiet evening, after much studying and strength training with her mother, she left the commissary with a huge drink and headed that way. Though very hungry, she did not want to take the time to sit down and eat anything. She could feel something was up and wanted to be in the middle of it. Striding into the control room, she found only four people there. J'onn was, of course, at the main station. Batman was seated at one of the secondary consoles with Wonder Woman and Question behind him. They were all staring at the screen in front of Batman, and all were quiet.

Elissa joined them there, squeezing in beside her mother and behind her father's shoulder. Taking a suck from her straw, she read the script on the page:

Riddle me this, and Riddle me that, can a riddling genius outfox a bat? What you seek is not safe, but held safe until, the bat finds it hiding, if ever he will. Only if time runs backward it seems, 8 minutes past midnight, on vertical lines. Afternoon falls flat on any army's watch, three times 3 PM with 12 minutes to spare. When two hundred four million gold is dropped in the sea, no more will you search for so elusive me. Drop it in line with Gotham the same, fifty miles out will perish the game. Eight minutes past midnight a splash will save a thousand its true, but silence will send many more deep into blue.

"Pew," she mumbled as she raised her straw to her mouth.

Everyone slowly turned their attention to her.

"What is this, anyway?" she asked as she read it again.

Batman looked back to it and replied, "One of Riddler's sick games. It's clear he means to put lives in jeopardy, but he gives two different times to do so."

"An army's watch," Question commented. "That's got to mean he's going to do something to a military base near Gotham. Three times in the afternoon… No, that doesn't make sense. They'll be on full alert after the first time."

Wonder Woman shook her head. "The only thing he makes clear is he wants two hundred four million dollars in gold dropped in the ocean fifty miles off of Gotham at a certain time, but the other times don't give us much to go on."

"He's getting more meticulous with these," Batman observed, "and this is the longest riddle he's sent in a while. The other times he indicated could be a diversion."

"They aren't," Golden Angel corrected. "They're coordinates."

All eyes found her again.

She met their gazes one by one, then declared, "Oh, come on, guys! You can't see it?" She looked to the screen and pointed to the third line. "These lines are the only ones that don't rhyme and the only ones he used numerals on instead of writing out the number. Eight minutes after midnight… On vertical lines… That's twelve degrees, eight minutes latitude. An army's watch doesn't mean an army base, he's talking about a watch that tells time. Military time."

Batman's eyes narrowed and he started entering information. A map appeared.

"Wait," Question barked, grasping the console with his hand. "Only if time runs backward."

"On it," Batman assured.

The map changed, a map of the world, then it turned and an "X" appeared in the middle of the ocean.

"That can't be right," Wonder Woman grumbled.

"Computer," Batman ordered. "Chart all current shipping lanes on or near the coordinates shown."

Many lines appeared and many of them intersected at or near the X.

"Computer," Question said, "eliminate freighters and tankers. Show cruise ships in red."

All of the lines disappeared but four.

Batman raised his chin. "Computer, which ships will pass within ten kilometers of the given coordinates tonight?"

A name appeared under the X.

Wonder Woman's lips parted and she raised her head. "The *Golden Princess*. She's one of the biggest in the world."

Martian Manhunter turned to the main console and worked the controls before calling, "Martian Manhunter to Aquaman. We have a situation. I am sending you coordinates. Assemble a team that can work in deep water."

"I'm on it," Aquaman replied over the comm system.

Wonder Woman turned and strode with hurried steps toward the elevator. "I'm going down and warn the ship away from that area." She looked over her shoulder and smiled at her daughter. "Nice work, Junior!"

Elissa smiled back and took a drink from her straw.

The faceless Question turned toward the girl and leaned back against the console, folding his arms as he shook his head. "I can't believe it. Four of us stared at that riddle for two hours and you solved it in two minutes."

Golden Angel smiled at him and nudged Batman with her elbow. "I guess I'm just a chip off the old block."

Still staring at the screen, Batman's eyes narrowed again and he said, "The question is, who really sent this?"

They all looked to him.

"This is way out of Edward's comfort zone," he informed, "and the riddles have always been more to the point, cryptic, but to the point. Someone wants us to go there."

"To a random spot in the middle of the ocean?" Question asked. "If he went to that much trouble, I'm thinking he wants us to look into that ship."

"Where is Riddler now?" Golden angel asked.

Batman punched in some data and the information came up on the screen almost immediately. "He was paroled eight months ago."

Elissa's eyes narrowed. "So he wasn't part of the big escape."

"No," Batman confirmed. "His last known address is in Gotham. He's been pretty quiet since he got out." He looked down to the keypad and entered more data. "I wonder..."

"If he's on the ship?" Golden Angel guessed.

"You read my mind, Angel," Batman said as he typed. He looked up at the screen, which now showed the passengers on the ship in question, and he nodded. "There he is. Edward Nigma."

Golden Angel glanced aside. "So, he gets out of prison and goes on a cruise eight months later?"

"That's not as odd as you would think," Question pointed out. "If these guys have a lot of money when they get out then they want to live it up for a while to make up for lost time."

She raised her brow. "I guess that makes sense." Her eyes widened. "Batman, can you bring up that riddle again?" When he did, she read it, then again, then a third time. "That's an unusual amount to be demanding."

They all looked back to the screen.

"I agree," Question said. "Why not two hundred million, or two hundred fifty? Why two hundred four?"

Martian Manhunter stepped forward, folding his arms as he ordered, "Computer, what is the displacement of the *Golden Princess?*"

A diagram of the ship, including views from three angles,

appeared on the screen, as did its dimensions and its displacement: One hundred two thousand tons.

Elissa squinted slightly. "One hundred two... Two hundred four million pounds. Great Hera! That's the gold he means to drop in the ocean!"

"Computer," Batman summoned. "Display the current cargo manifest for the *Golden Princess.*"

As the manifest was uploaded, Elissa turned and took a couple of steps away from them, raising her communicator to her mouth as she called, "Golden Angel to Wonder Woman." Long seconds of silence passed. Desperation entered the girl's voice as she called again, "Golden Angel to Wonder Woman. Please respond."

Everyone was silent.

Reaching to the main console, J'onn activated the main communication console and called, "Martian Manhunter to Wonder Woman. Respond please."

Again they were met with silence.

Elissa's mind whirled around the riddle and she said aloud, "Eight minutes past midnight a splash will save a thousand its true, but silence will send one more deep into blue." Slowly shaking her head, she drew a gasp and wheeled back to them. "You've got to get me down there! Something is bad wrong!"

"Wonder Woman could be in danger," J'onn suggested.

"Problem is," Batman pointed out, "if a bunch of us show up suddenly there's no telling what could happen. The riddle indicates that they mean to sink the ship which tells me they have the means to do so. We also don't know exactly what we're up against." He looked to Golden Angel and ordered, "Get to your quarters and get changed."

She started to go, barking, "Right!" Then, she hesitated and turned back to him. "Wait! What?"

"They shouldn't see any more of us on the ship," he explained, then he looked to Question. "They may not notice one or two more passengers."

"I'll go with her," Martian Manhunter said. "Computer. How close is the *Golden Princess* to the port at Gotham City?"

The data came up quickly.

Question absently read, "Two hundred miles, and at her speed she's expected to make port about two AM."

"They're going to sink her before she ever gets there," Golden Angel mumbled.

"Nothing unusual on the manifest," Batman observed absently. "He has to be after something one of the passengers has, or after one of the passengers. I'll check it out."

Wheeling around, Golden Angel rushed toward the elevator, insisting, "I'm going to get changed and I'll meet you in teleporter one!"

WW

The ship was largely dark, but even with many of the lights off it was clear that it was built for luxury. From the Watchtower, it could be seen that the rear deck near one of the swimming pools was deserted and did not appear to be patrolled by one of the roving bad guys who were keeping watch. They made for cover as soon as they could, darting to a wall on the superstructure that had an awning hanging over it.

Elissa had changed quickly into her pink running shorts and a black tank top that read *2 hot 4 u* in red across the front. She could not decide on shoes and reasoned quickly that finding a barefoot teenager on a cruise ship would not be that unusual. Her long black hair was down and worn loose and her gauntlets again looked like gold cuff bracelets.

Martian Manhunter had taken the form of an older man with short white hair who wore a flower pattern dark green Hawaiian shirt and black trousers, black socks and sandals. Still very tall, he towered more than a foot higher than his young companion.

Pressing their backs to the wall, they scanned the deck for unwanted eyes.

Looking the Martian Manhunter up and down, she hissed, "You couldn't disguise yourself as a hot boy or something?"

He glanced at her. "I'm going forward. Check the decks aft as quickly as you can and report in as soon as you've found something. Our highest priorities are Wonder Woman and the passengers."

She nodded and they took off in different directions.

Elissa wanted to start from the bottom up, so she took elevators and stairs as low as she could go, found a utility entrance and took the stairs behind that door to the lower decks and toward what she thought might be the engine room. The place was a maze and she did not encounter anyone, friendly or otherwise, but she quickly realized she was lost. Much of the area here was very dark and it was clear that nobody was here.

Heading back up, she moved swiftly and silently through corridors and carefully checking every door she encountered. Foremost in her mind was finding her mother.

She found nothing in the lower part of the ship, but twice she eluded armed men who were patrolling down there, and as she hid in the shadows and waited for them to pass by, she wished she had dressed in all black.

On the upper decks where passenger activities were located, she was careful to slink about in the shadows to avoid detection. There were still many lights on here and a few times, behind closed doors, she could hear voices. Still, no sign of any of the passengers. She checked many of the cabins, finding that every one she looked into had been hastily abandoned. They had to be in an area where they could be watched in great numbers. That answer had to be the dining hall.

Following the signs, she was quick but very quiet as she headed that way. It was up one more deck and she made for the stairs, fearing that an opening elevator door could reveal some unfriendlies.

The stairs were behind a door at the end of the corridor where some of the doors to passenger's cabins still stood open. About twenty feet away she heard voices coming from the stairwell and she froze, her eyes locked on it as the shadows of many men darkened the steps. Before she could react, a strong hand covered her mouth and a powerful arm wrapped around her and she barked a scream behind the hand as she was pulled into one of the open cabins.

Dragged backward into the shadows of the dark room and into an open closet door, she heard him order, "Shh," as she was taken into the darkness of the closet.

Elissa knew that she was much stronger than this man, that she could easily and quickly take him down, but there were two other things to consider. First was the issue of the gunmen in the corridor who were going to pass by the open door any second. Second, her instincts were speaking loudly, and they were telling her that the man who held her had no ill intent.

Slowly, he withdrew his hand from her mouth. That arm reached across her chest and gently grasped her shoulder.

Outside the cabin, they heard several men casually talking amongst themselves as they walked by. They waited a moment longer just to be sure everything was clear. He was holding her tightly against him and she could feel his heart pounding hard in his chest. He was clearly very frightened, and yet he risked being discovered to get her to safety.

"Stay here," he ordered in a whisper.

Gently maneuvering her aside, he slipped out and approached the door, peering cautiously out one way, then the other.

Elissa did not need light to see him clearly as she peered out of the closet to have a better look. He was rather big, broad shouldered and tall. Thick legs and a heavily built trunk told her that he was somewhat athletic, and his arms were very bulky as well. He was wearing a tightly fitting tee shirt, a black one with some kind of rock band image on the back. His shorts appeared to be swimming trunks and were blue with white stripes on the outsides. Brown hair was worn down past his neck and nearly to his shoulders, and appeared to be in disarray. He also wore no shoes, telling her that he had little time to prepare when the ship was taken. When he turned around, he had a very pleasant face, though concern was dominating his features at the moment. His chest was a bulgy one and he had a little bit of a belly. About six foot one, he was much taller than she was, but a little acne betrayed that he was young.

He crept back to the closet and held his hand to her, and when she slipped hers into it, he raised a finger to his mouth, then turned and headed back toward the door with the girl in tow.

Elissa allowed him to lead the way and take her to safety, even though she needed to go the other way. Perhaps he knew something, where the passengers were being held and how many bad guys she and J'onn would have to deal with.

Turning down another corridor, they went nearly to the end and he looked up at a door and stopped. Reaching into his back pocket, he withdrew a card and inserted it into the door lock. There was a beep and a click and he turned the handle and opened the door.

Inside, this was a modest cabin with one bed, a small bathroom and a little closet that stood open. A small dresser was on the opposite side from the bed with a TV on it and a desk was right beside it. One chair was in the far corner, a small but comfortable looking chair. There was no window or porthole and light was offered by one globe that hung from the small ceiling fan in the middle of the room.

He gently closed the door, then backed away from it, all the way to the bed and he absently sat down.

Elissa looked around her and nodded. "Nice digs."

Slowly, he turned his eyes to her. The stress on his features was clear as was the disbelieving look at her apparent lack of concern for the situation.

Her insight spoke loudly about him when she met his eyes. He was terrified and unsure. More than that, he seemed to feel obligated to protect her.

With a little smile, she offered, "Thanks for doing that."

He nodded. Drawing a breath, he seemed to poke his chest out a little as he asked in a voice befitting a man not quite mature, "What's your name?"

"Um," she replied hesitantly, "Angel." She approached and sat down beside him, still looking up into his eyes as she asked, "So what's yours?"

"Zack," he replied. "Zack Wilson."

"You from around here?" she asked with a teasing little smile.

He did not seem to get her humor and just arched his brow, then slowly shook his head.

"I'm trying to lighten the tension," she informed. "Do you know who these guys are?"

"No," he replied, seeming as if he was still dazed by what had happened. "They just kind of showed up tonight and caught almost everybody still in bed."

"They didn't get you," she observed.

"I wasn't in my cabin," he informed. "I was out by the pool, in the hot tub." He looked to the floor. "There were a few girls there who go to my school. A bunch of us from Dent High School got the opportunity for this weekend cruise with our parents. I was kind of trying to ask one of them to prom." He shrugged. "I guess I wasn't her type or something. Then we heard all of the screaming and the shooting start. I tried to get them to safety but they just wouldn't listen to me and got caught."

"Serves them right for not going to the prom with you," Elissa spat.

His eyes slid to her. "I'm an offensive lineman, not a quarterback. I mean, why would they want to? Would you have gone with me?"

She shrugged. "I don't know. Why would you want me to go with you?"

"Do I really have to say it?" he countered in a low voice. "What guy wouldn't want to go with you? I mean, you're hot, you're beautiful..."

Her cheeks almost glowed red and she looked away from him, unable to control the little smile that forced its way onto her mouth.

"So," he stammered, "um, which school group are you here with?"

Hesitantly she started, "I'm, uh... I..." Her attention snapped back to him. "Wait, what? How many school groups are on this ship?"

He shrugged. "I don't know. Most of the major schools in and around Gotham had people on this offer."

Her attention strayed from him and she stared blankly ahead. "The riddle," she breathed. "It wasn't... It was a warning!"

"What are you talking about?" he questioned.

"Somebody planned this," she informed, reaching behind her to find her communicator. She looked down at the display and shook her head. "We're too deep in the ship." Springing up, she grabbed his hand and pulled him from the bed and toward the door. "Come on. We've got to get topside!"

Zack did not seem to understand but he did not protest as she pulled the door open and peered out.

They quietly made their way down the corridor and toward the stairs, Elissa leading the way with Zack in tow by the hand. Once at the stairs, she released his hand and silently bounded up them as he watched from below. Near the top, she hesitated and looked around her, then beckoned him to follow. The next level up was also lined with passenger's cabins and ahead of them another corridor intersected from the right. Once again they were as quiet as they could be as they made their way toward the stairs on the other end and the rear of the ship.

Nearly to the corridor that emptied into theirs, they froze as two big men in ski masks, thin green long sleeved shirts and black trousers rounded the corner. They both carried compact machineguns and both stopped about three feet in front of the two teenagers. And both trained their weapons on them.

Elissa moved too swiftly for anyone to respond to her and a sweeping kick knocked both guns aside. She spun around and slammed the back of her fist into the first man's head, knocking him into the other.

Zack seemed stunned by this and took a step back, and his eyes widened further as he saw a third man turn into the corridor, his eyes on Elissa. Without thinking, he charged with a mighty yell, ramming his shoulder into the gunman's gut at a dead run and knocking him off of his feet. They slammed into the floor and the machinegun slid down the corridor. Not waiting for his opponent to get his wits about him, Zack slammed his big fist hard into the gunman's face, knocking him out cold. This done, he pushed himself up and wheeled around to help Elissa, his brow lowering as he saw her standing over the other two who lay unconscious on the floor.

She looked back to him and shrugged. "Mom always insisted that I train hard to take care of myself."

They made it another deck up without incident, and as she turned to go down the corridor, he grabbed her arm and stopped her.

"Not that way," Zack insisted. "The Lido Deck dining hall is over there, and they have a few hundred people they're holding in there."

"How many bad guys?" she asked.

"Don't know," he confessed, "but I know there are a lot of them in there watching people."

They heard something down the corridor, the buzzing of men talking.

"Not good," Elissa mumbled.

Zack took her hand and they hurried the other direction. They wheeled into a gaming room, one of the ship's casinos that was a big place with lots of colorful lights and a long bar along the far wall twenty feet away, and they pressed their backs to the wall just to the right of the door. Elissa was not used to hiding like this, but she found the excitement of dodging about with this boy beside her rather fun. They would wait for the men to just pass by. Both of them tensed and ice ran up their spines as the three men entered the casino!

Dressed as the others had been, two had their machine guns slung over their shoulders and the third, who only carried a pistol, holstered his weapon as they approached the bar.

And Elissa's eyes narrowed as she saw the man in the middle, the one with the pistol, had her mother's lasso and belt slung over his shoulder. A little snarl took her mouth. Now she knew where her mother was, and it was time to go to her aid.

She lowered herself to the floor and scrambled quietly to a gaming table.

Zack followed.

Looking to him, she motioned left, held up two fingers, then pointed to herself. Motioning right, she held up one finger and pointed at him. He seemed afraid, but still nodded.

The three men sat at the bar as if expecting drinks to be served to them, and they talked casually amongst themselves as they waited.

Staying behind cover as much as they could they silently approached their intended targets, and when only one gaming table remained, Elissa pounced! A swing of her fist slammed into the head of the man who had her mother's equipment, and as he went down she wheeled the other way and delivered a hard kick to the other as he turned on her and reached for his machine gun. The third also turned toward her and never saw Zack as he swung a stool from one of the gaming tables. After a single blow to the head, the man went down. Elissa finished hers quickly with a knee to his face, then she set her hands on her hips and turned to face her companion with a big smile.

He set the barstool down and nodded to her.

She nodded back, then looked down to the man who had her mother's lasso and belt as he moaned and planted his palms to push himself up. Kneeling down beside him, she took the lasso from the floor, grabbed the back of his shirt and lifted him just high enough to get the loop around him down to his elbows, then she pulled it tight and demanded, "Where is Wonder Woman?"

He replied, "Lido Deck dining hall."

Elissa jerked on the lasso. "What happened to her?"

"She gave up," was his answer.

With her palm, she slammed him down to the floor and barked, "She wouldn't just give up! What happened to her?"

This time the answer was a little more forced. "We told her we would shoot a hundred of the hostages if she didn't. We could cut down at least that many before she got more than one of us."

Her mouth tightened as she clenched her jaw. "Is she okay? Is she hurt?"

"No," he replied. "She's not hurt."

"That's good," she commended angrily. "Is she restrained?"

"No," he replied again.

With a slight nod, Elissa tightened the lasso around him and ordered, "You are going to sleep now and you will not awaken until sunup. When you awaken you will not sleep again until you turn yourself into police, understand?"

He nodded, then fell to the deck and was out.

Taking the lasso from him, she looked up to Zack as she rolled it again. "Okay, now we..." Movement by the door caught her eye and she dropped the lasso.

Another man had entered the room and this one trained his pistol on them, on Zack!

"Ah crud," she mumbled as she saw him squeeze the trigger. Her speed was something not even she realized she was capable of; she darted in front of him and swept her arm in a blur and a flash of golden light. The bullet sparked as it was deflected. In a second, she stood there with her gaze fixed on the gunman and a gauntlet on her left arm.

The gunman's eyes narrowed as he slowly lowered his gun. Coming to his senses, he aimed again, this time at her.

She charged and leapt up onto the table, sweeping her arm again as he fired at her, then she jumped to the table closest to the door, deflecting another bullet. Spring-boarding from that table, she deflected one more as she spun in a blur in mid-air and golden light exploded from her.

Golden Angel hit the ground boots first right in front of him, took his arm and wheeled around with him, slamming him into a row of slot machines near the other side of the door. As he rolled unconscious to the floor, she darted around the tables to where her companion watched her with wide eyes and a gaping mouth. She picked up her mother's equipment, throwing the belt over her shoulder and securing the lasso to her belt as she smiled up at Zack. "Still want to take me to the prom?"

He watched her turn and stride toward the door, then he came to his senses and followed at a quick pace, assuring, "Well yeah!"

She giggled as she grasped the doorway with one hand. Peering out, she looked one way, then the other, then back to him. "It looks clear." She leaned back against the wall, planting the sole of one boot on it as she folded her arms. "So now what?"

Zack was looking her up and down still, and shrugged. "So, you want to go with me or what?"

She raised her brow. "We're on a hijacked ship with an unknown number of gunmen, some of whom have already tried to kill us, we have to rescue Wonder Woman, and you're still looking for a prom date?"

He smiled. "Got to keep my priorities straight."

"You're cute," she complimented with a smile.

Zack glanced at the door and dared to take another step toward her, closing to about two feet. "So, if we get out of this—"

"We will," she assured. Taking her communicator, she looked down at it and shook her head. "We have to get to a higher deck." She put it away, then nudged him backward a few steps as she advanced into the room. Holding her arms out, she spun around again, and after another golden flash of light, she was dressed in the pink shorts and black shirt she had been before. "Okay, now do you think we can get up to the deck without being seen this time?"

"Maybe," he guessed, looking her up and down again. He cleared his throat and looked away, out the door, then back to her. "So, you know Wonder Woman?"

"Yes," she replied almost impatiently. A little moan escaped her as she raised a hand to her eyes.

"You okay?" he asked, grasping her shoulder.

She nodded. "Yeah, I'm... I'm good." Looking up at him, she asked, "Do you know where the bridge is?" When he nodded, she insisted, "Let's get up there. If we can at least stop this thing and call for help then we'll greatly increase our chances of stopping these guys and getting everyone to safety."

WW

The gunman hit the deck unconscious and Golden Angel stepped over him on her way to the control center. Zack followed her as they approached the huge windows at the front and the big control console that was very ornate and trimmed in brass and chrome. There were three computer stations with monitors that were flat against the console. An ornate wooden steering wheel that was about four feet in diameter was right in the middle and many other controls were on the other side of it.

They stared down at the console for a moment, their eyes darting from blinking lights, to monitors that displayed different information, to control knobs and switches... It was a confusing array!

"I fly airplanes," Elissa grumbled, "I don't drive ships."

"There," he declared, pointing to a silver lever that was next to a display that showed power from green to red. "Looks like we're going full speed."

She reached for it, informing, "Well I can sure fix that!"

He grabbed her wrist before she had the handle.

"It has to be done slowly," he said, "otherwise they'll feel the ship slowing down." He took the handle himself and gently began to pull it back, pausing from time to time as he did so.

While he did that, Elissa raised her communicator to her mouth and called, "Golden Angel to Martian Manhunter."

"Go ahead," J'onn replied.

"Found Wonder Woman," she reported. "There are lots of guys on this thing with guns! They have most of the passengers in the dining hall on the Lido Deck and I'm sure they have others in other places."

"I found a group of them," he informed. "They have the passengers in many places and they communicate with each other frequently. Do not engage them."

Zack and Elissa slowly looked over their shoulders to the man who lay unconscious on the floor behind them.

"They check in with each other about every fifteen minutes," J'onn continued.

"Um," Elissa stammered, "uh, we already kind of took eight of them out."

"I'm calling for reinforcements," Martian Manhunter said. "See if you can get to Wonder Woman. I'll send help as soon as I can."

"Okay," she complied. Putting the communicator away, she looked to Zack and informed, "We're running out of time."

As he pulled the throttle down to zero, Zack nodded and said, "Maybe this will buy us some more."

She patted his arm and smiled. "You up to some serious hero stuff, big guy?"

They made their way quickly but quietly back toward the Lido Deck, trotting or running where they knew the way was clear. As they got down the stairs to that deck and made for the casino, Elissa paused and raised her hands to her eyes again. Looking down the corridor, everything appeared to blur, then sharpen and blur again. Her head was beginning to hurt and her heart was racing.

Taking her arm, Zack asked, "Hey, you all right?"

She drew a breath and nodded. "Yeah, I think so. I've never been on a ship before so I guess I don't quite have my sea legs yet." She combed her hair back and assured, "I'm fine. Come on and let's do this."

WW

The dining hall on the Lido Deck was one of the biggest rooms on the ship. Very colorful and ornate carpet was wall to wall and a number of crystal chandeliers hung from the high, domed ceiling. All of the tables and chairs had been moved from the middle of the room and were stacked and piled against the walls on all sides and all of the six doors in or out were closed. Under the watchful eyes of a dozen gunmen, who were in groups of two or three at the entrances, hundreds of people were in the middle of the room and sitting on the floor, more than half of them children and teenagers. Many were in robes and pajamas. They were formed into circles that grew ever larger from the one woman who was on her knees in the middle of them.

Wonder Woman's mind scrambled, her eyes constantly darting about. Her fingers were laced behind her neck and she knew she dare not make a move. She could easily take down all twelve of the gunmen, but not before they killed all or most of the people they held hostage. Foremost in her mind was that the Justice League did not know what was going on and with her communicator in the hands of the bad guys she had no way to warn them.

Looking to her left, she saw one of the gunmen wading through the hostages toward her. He was dressed like all of the others were and held an automatic pistol. His eyes were on her with some wicked intent as he approached, and Diana's narrowed as he neared her.

He kicked one of the hostages and ordered, "Out of the way!" The man moved over and he continued on, finally stopping about eight feet away from her.

Wonder Woman's expression was one of fierce rage and defiance as she stared back at him.

He dared to smile at her. "You comfy?" When she did not respond, he continued, "We're taking you with us, babe, along with about a hundred others. You get out of line even once and we're going to shoot people. You want that on your conscience?"

She looked away from him.

"And here I was hoping..."

A door burst open and Diana looked to her right, seeing the black haired girl in the pink shorts and black shirt who froze in the doorway. Her eyes widened, her lips parting in fear, and she breathed, "Oh, no."

Elissa glanced around, terror in her wide eyes as she breathed in shrieking gasps. Shaking her head, she backed away and cried, "No! Oh no!"

One of the gunmen grabbed her arm, but she tore away and fled.

"Get her!" one of the gunmen shouted.

Three of them, those three closest to that door, charged out after the girl.

What is she doing? Diana thought.

WW

With three bad guys following close behind, Elissa ran just fast enough to keep a comfortable distance ahead of them. Ahead was a corridor that entered hers from the right side and when she reached it she cut hard and ran down it.

Predictably, all of the gunmen followed, and a second after the last one made that turn, Zack slammed into them all low and they were knocked backward and driven into the wall on the other side of the corridor.

Before they could recover, Elissa was upon them as well, grabbing the first one she reached and spinning around with him, slamming him hard into the wall and almost through it. Zack picked one up on his shoulder, throwing him backward and into the corner. The third barely had time to stand when he kicked straight up, catching the masked man under the chin and snapping his head back. The one behind Zack, though stunned, scrambled to his feet and fumbled with his gun. Elissa spun around and slammed her heel into his belly, and when he doubled over she leapt up and came down hard, driving her elbow into the back of his head.

The fight lasted only seconds and Zack was ready to continue as he looked to the girl, fear taking his features as she stumbled sideways and into the wall, holding a hand to her head again. She appeared to be barely conscious and he reached to her, grabbing her arms to help hold her up.

"Angel!" he called.

She blinked and did not appear to be able to catch her breath. She shook her head, then looked up at him and nodded. Seeing movement behind him, her eyes widened as she saw another of the gunmen only about twenty feet away—and taking aim with his pistol. She shoved Zack as hard as she could down the cross aisle as she shouted, "Watch out!" Fatigue washed through her and consciousness tried to slip away. Her eyes closed involuntarily and she staggered, fighting hard to bring herself around.

The gun fired with a loud pop and this time she was too dazed to respond. The blunt bullet slammed into her shoulder, through it and knocked her from her feet. Screaming in pain, she fell and hit the floor flat on her back, and everything went dark.

Elissa's next realization was Zack kneeling down beside her and she looked pitifully back at him as unimaginable pain surged through her shoulder and worked to rob her of consciousness still again.

He gently laid her left arm over her belly, slipped a hand under her knees, his other carefully behind her shoulders, and as gently as he could he picked her up, and she winced as he stood with her.

Breathing in short gasps, she turned her head toward his shoulder.

He turned and hurried toward the stairs, holding her to him as he informed, "I'm getting you out of here."

Elissa nodded, and as sweat began to bead all over her, her eyes closed despite her efforts to keep them open and consciousness slipped away entirely.

CHAPTER 10

Outside of the Watchtower infirmary, Wonder Woman sat in one of the three chairs that were lined up across the hallway from the operating room. Her arms were folded over her belly, her eyes fixed on the metal tile floor before her. The lights were very bright here, but she longed for darkness and solitude.

A dark form sat down beside her.

Her lips tightened.

Batman asked, "Did Doctor Groege make it in there?"

She nodded.

"She's in good hands," Batman assured. When Diana remained silent, he informed, "I talked to the boy she was with. He said she was acting sick off and on and she looked like she was about to faint right before she was shot."

She finally looked to him, distress in her eyes.

He watched the door and heaved a heavy breath. His voice was deep and largely monotone as he went on. "He kept saying that her first concern was you and the hostages and that she stayed in contact with J'onn as much as she could." He turned his eyes down. "I suppose we'll find out what happened when she's out of surgery."

"What was she doing there?" Diana breathed.

"She reasoned out that something was wrong," he replied. "She and J'onn went to check things out. I'm not sure what happened after that."

"She lured four of them out of there," Wonder Woman informed, "and seven others went out to patrol and did not return. I know she had a hand in that."

"I'm sure she did," he agreed.

Silence swept between them for a time and they both just stared at the floor.

"I'm sorry, Bruce," she offered softly.

He cut his eyes to her.

"You were right," she continued. "Keeping her from you all that time was for my own peace of mind, to appease my own fears. It was horribly selfish. I can never, ever make that up to you, no matter what I do, no matter how hard I try, I will still have done this to you both."

Slowly, he slid his arm around her shoulders and pulled her to him, enveloping her in his cape. "I can hardly blame you for doing what you knew how to protect your daughter."

"Our daughter," she corrected in the wisp of a voice.

"I need to know something," he said.

She finally looked to him and assured, "Anything."

"I want to know about her," he insisted. "Everything. Her childhood, how she did in school, was she happy, what she likes, fears… Everything."

Diana stared blankly at him for long seconds, then she leaned back, angling into him as she reached to her shoulder and grasped his hand. "I remember vividly when she was a baby. Sometimes, she liked to be up at night." Her eyes narrowed. "*All* night."

He smiled.

"It hurt sometimes," she continued with a more nostalgic expression. "She so much reminded me of you, how she always wanted to know how things worked, how she was so curious about so many things. She was only nine years old when she convinced my mother that it was time to head up an expedition to explore the mountains on the east side of the island we lived on. They were out there for three days! She stopped at every stream and tree, every time she saw a stone that looked out of place." She laughed under her breath. "She had learned Morse Code a year earlier and she and my mother spent the entire second night on different mountain tops flashing messages to each other with lights. People always told me how she reminds them of me, how she looks like me, but she's always reminded me of you, nearly everything about her."

When she turned her eyes down, he squeezed her to him. "Tell me more."

A little smile took her mouth. "I don't know if you've heard her sing, but she has a beautiful voice, a siren's voice. She loves to dance and has done so since she could walk." Diana went quiet again, then closed her eyes and slowly laid her head on his shoulder.

"Bruce, I did not want this life for her. I was so afraid for just this reason!"

"She's a strong girl, Princess," he assured. "You saw to that. She always talks about the wonderful childhood she had. She'll shrug this off before you realize and start bugging you about the next thing she wants to do."

Diana nodded and whispered, "Yeah."

The door opened and Wonder Woman sprang up, stepping halfway across the corridor. Batman stood and calmly took her side.

Dressed in blue scrubs, Doctor Groege was not wearing a surgical mask or gloves anymore and reached up to take the cap from her blond hair. Looking to them in turn, she raised her brow and offered, "Sorry to keep you waiting so long."

"Is she all right?" Diana asked desperately.

Groege smiled and took Wonder Woman's shoulder. "She's fine, Diana. The surgery went very quickly. She lost a little blood but I got the bullet out of there in about ten minutes. It shattered her collar bone, but it began to mend as soon as the bullet was out. In fact, I had to ice her shoulder to slow her recovery enough to allow me to finish. She'll be up and around by this afternoon and I'll bet in a week or so she won't even have a scar to brag about. You Amazons are simply amazing." Something more serious took her features. "Can you tell me something about her diet?"

Diana blinked, glanced at Batman. "What would you like to know?"

"What kinds of foods does she eat most often?" the Doctor asked.

"Just about everything," Batman replied. "I've never seen someone her size eat so much."

Doctor Groege nodded. "So she eats a lot and often?"

Both parents nodded.

Venting a deep breath, she extended her hand to the chairs across the hall and went to sit down herself.

Batman and Wonder Woman sat down as the Doctor pulled the third chair in front of them.

Groege drew a deep breath, looking to the floor as she collected her thoughts. "Okay, I may be able to answer both your questions at once. The reason she eats so much is because she has a rare form of hypoglycemia. I don't recall the exact name, but to sum it up, she doesn't store energy the way we do. Nothing she eats goes to fat and she burns it almost as quickly as she eats it. She stores sugars in her liver and releases them almost every waking moment." She looked to Diana. "When she was under my care before, I couldn't get her fever down. This explains that. She has such a high metabolism that she runs at a higher temperature, over a hundred most of the time. What happened on the ship is she had not eaten as much as she needed to most of the day. She was running out of gas and her body was trying to tell her to stop and eat and rest. I'm guessing she was barely conscious when she was shot."

Diana's teeth clenched.

"This isn't life threatening," the Doctor continued, "unless she runs herself down like this again. We just need to make sure she eats balanced meals several times a day, and I can't believe I'm saying this but she would do very well with a lot of sugar in her diet as well. Some people are just like that, eat whatever they want and never put on a pound and the rest of us hate them for it. However, she's going to have to have a balanced diet, lots of complex carbs, lots of protein... You know how it goes." She loosed another deep breath and looked to the floor before she spoke again. "Diana, she's seventeen, isn't she?" When the Amazon Princess nodded, she continued, "I gave her a full examination after I operated. Chronologically she is seventeen, but anatomically she's no more than fourteen, and that's pushing it."

Diana raised her chin. "I don't understand."

"There's no way you could know about this. I'm sure you don't remember even being her age. You look twenty, but we all know you are far older." The Doctor looked to Batman. "It works like this: We know that Amazons are immortals, but Elissa was the first baby born to the Amazons in more than a thousand years. They had no way of knowing what to expect from her and no mortal babies to compare with her. While her early childhood was what we would consider normal, as soon as she came of age, as soon as she started to become a woman, her aging began to slow, and it will continue to slow. She could likely be anatomically and even emotionally a teenager for the next forty or fifty years, maybe longer."

Batman and Wonder Woman exchanged grim looks.

"I know this isn't easy news," Doctor Groege said

sympathetically, "but you really needed to know. It might make understanding her a little easier."

"Thank you, Samantha," Diana whispered, unable to muster her voice.

Doctor Groege grasped Wonder Woman's shoulder. "This changes nothing, Diana. It just gives you a couple of things to look out for. She's a delightful girl and will continue to be, and the best advice I can give you is to let her be who she is. If that means she is a heroine in the Justice League, then so be it. Believe me, the only thing you owe her is guidance, understanding and love." She stood. "I need to get some rest. They're going to set me up with quarters nearby in case I'm needed. I suggest you two do the same."

As the Doctor turned to leave, Diana anxiously asked, "Can we go and see her?"

Groege stopped and half turned. "She was taken the back way to recovery. You can find her in room three, they said. She'll probably be asleep, but you can go see her for a little while."

Batman asked, "Was she still out when she was taken to recovery?"

A strange little smile took Doctor Groege's mouth. "She walked."

As the Doctor turned and walked away, Batman and Wonder Woman turned wide eyes to each other, and both smiled.

"That's our little girl," Batman said proudly.

WW

The recovery room was a cold and sterile place. The artificial lighting gave it nothing but a feeling of gloom. White walls, white linins and a white tiled floor were just too, well, sterile. Only the one bed and an array of medical instruments broke up this eight by eight by eight foot cube, that and the power supplies on the wall at the head of the bed and valves for oxygen and pressurized air. A metal night stand was beside the bed with a blue plastic cup about half filled with water.

Lying on the bed on her back was the sleeping Golden Angel. Not redressed after surgery, she was covered to her shoulders with a sheet and blanket, also both white, and her head lay on a plush pillow and was rocked to one side and facing the only way in or out. Her hands were lying across her belly and her left shoulder was tightly bandaged.

Batman and Wonder Woman stood by her bedside, silently staring down at the slumbering girl.

Diana raised her face, looking to the ceiling as she blinked to hold back tears.

Bruce looked to her, and his gloved hand took hers.

"I'm okay," she whispered.

"No, Diana, you aren't."

She turned her gaze to him as a tear streamed down her cheek. "How would you know?"

"Because I'm not," he replied.

Diana turned toward him and pulled her hand from his, then she reached to him and slid both hands around his back, closing her eyes as she laid her chin on his shoulder. Bruce enveloped her in his arms and cape and held her tightly to him, and he kissed her cheek.

They would not know how long they held each other, but the moment ended abruptly.

Elissa slurred in a weak voice, "If I'd known that this is all it would take to get you guys back together I'd have gotten shot weeks ago."

They slowly pulled away from each other and looked down to the wounded girl.

She was staring at them with sleepy eyes, and smiling.

Diana reached down and took the girl's hand, offering her a forced smile as she asked, "How are you feeling, Junior?"

Her smile broadening, Elissa replied, "Great!" She did not look like she could focus well as her eyes danced from one of her parents to the next. "Did you know I got shot again? Oh! And there was this guy I met! He's cute and really tall and stuff. Is he still here somewhere? You should meet him."

"I did already," Batman informed.

"Oh, that's good. Hey, did you know I got shot again?"

"Yes, Little One," the Amazon Princess confirmed, "we know. Are you in any pain?"

"I don't know," the girl sighed. "I can't really feel much of anything." Her eyes widened. "Hey! Did you know Samantha's here?"

Nodding, Diana assured, "We saw her, Little One."

"It was so good to see her again. It was like, wow! There she was!"

Bruce also reached to her, stroking her hair as he said, "You should get some sleep, Angel."

"Yeah," Elissa drawled. "Sounds like an idea." She closed her eyes and slurred, "See you guys at breakfast."

Diana stroked the girl's cheek. Her mouth was quivering as she fought the urge to cry.

"Come on," Bruce ordered, turning the Amazon Princess toward the door.

While she did not resist, she did protest, "I need to stay. She'll need me here with her."

"She's been pumped full of pain killers," Batman pointed out. "She's not aware of anything. Let's go get some rest."

They stopped just outside the door as it slid shut and she turned fully toward him.

"Bruce," she said in a meek voice, "I... I don't want to be alone tonight."

He stared almost coldly back at her for long seconds, then his hand stroked through her hair. "Let's get something to eat. We have some talking to do."

CHAPTER 11

Elissa's eyes opened slowly. At some point she had been taken to
Wonder Woman's quarters and was tucked into her large bed there.
She blinked to clear her vision and hesitantly sat up, wincing as she
did so. Looking to the night stand, there was a note there, folded
neatly over itself with her name written in big letters and in a
handwriting she did not recognize. Carefully reaching to it, she laid
back down as she opened it and held it above her head, and she
smiled as she read aloud, "Hi, I hope you're feeling better. I had a
great time with you until you got shot. Let's think about doing
something sometime where people aren't trying to kill us." She
giggled. "I hope I get to see you again, and my offer to take you to
prom still stands. I can't see taking anybody else after meeting you."
She sighed, "Aw!" Then read on, "Here's my phone number if you
want to do something sometime. I'll be thinking of you every
minute. Zack." She closed the note and laid it on her chest.

She just laid there for a while, staring at the ceiling with a little
smile on her lips. Looking to the side of the bed, she saw her outfit
laid out and waiting for her. It was time for Golden Angel to get up.
As she sat up and swung her feet over the bed, she winced as her
shoulder announced that it was still not fully healed, and she looked
down to the bandage that still encased it, gently running her fingers
over it.

WW

Elissa had loved the design of her top as it left her right shoulder
completely bare and free, and it did not cover the left much, either.
The look just appealed to her. This day, with that shoulder wrapped
in bandages, she wore Beowulf's cape over her shoulders as she
strode down the corridor toward the commissary. Surely this would
not draw much attention, seeing as how half of the heroes aboard the
Watchtower wore capes. Besides, she liked wearing it. It gave her a
certain sense of mystery about herself, some kind of hidden menace

that might make the bad guys think twice about challenging her. If only it was black.

As she entered the line for the cafeteria, which was deserted but for the people in white who worked the other side, she found herself walking with a certain air of confidence. The cape just made her feel powerful somehow.

To those in white who worked on the other side of the counter, this was mostly just a job. They had grown accustomed to feeding superheroes who regarded them as what they were: Workers. Very few of the heroes who came through the line seemed like they were anything but indifferent. This bothered Elissa at times, but she had resigned herself to things being as they were. She also knew that when she was seen the workers behind the stainless steel and glass counter would, for some reason, light up.

And sure enough, the first to see her did just that, smiling a broad smile as he loudly greeted, "Hey! Golden Angel!"

She waggled her fingers at them as they all shouted greetings and said, "What's up?"

They went to the task of filling plates and bowls for her, and as she took a tray from the stack they handed these over the sneeze guard to her.

"We missed you," a woman informed as she handed over a huge bowl of fruit.

"Thanks," the girl offered. "I missed you guys, too."

A burly looking man who looked like he needed a shave informed in a gruff voice, "I made a special beef tips and gravy for ya, kiddo." He handed a steaming plate over to her. "Let me know what you think."

She closed her eyes and smelled it before she set it down, offering him a smile as she declared, "It smells yummy. Thanks."

Making it through to the end of the line, she looked to the robust, older woman who set her hands on her hips. "Okay, Missy. I've made two deserts with just you in mind. Which one do you like the best?" She picked up two plates and held them to the girl to allow her to choose.

Elissa took them both and set them down on the already crowded tray, offering a smile and a sweet, "Thanks. I'll let you know." as she moved on.

The woman watched her leave, and she shook her head.

The commissary itself was nearly deserted. Apparently, this was an odd time to be taking meals as only a few people were out there, and most of them were gray shirt workers who kept the station running.

She stopped at a table for six that had three women and a man sitting there, and she shyly asked, "May I join you?"

They all looked up at her, and all smiled. Two of them moved over to allow her to sit down between them. Usually, the heroes of the station either kept to themselves or ate in groups, and almost never with the workers. Golden Angel was a very rare exception.

Of course, conversation centered around the incident the night before and everyone was concerned with how she was, but eventually this strayed to Flash's latest joke, the gossip that abounded around the station and woes with work that everyone seemed to have. Elissa listened politely and attentively and spoke when addressed. There was just something about being accepted by adults that she found thrilling.

Her communicator buzzed and J'onn's voice ordered, "Golden Angel to the conference room."

Looking down to her nearly finished meal, Elissa swallowed what she had and grumbled, "It never fails."

The people at the table laughed softly.

She raised her communicator to her mouth and replied, "I'll be there in a few." Putting it back, she insisted, "I am finishing this chocolate cheesecake first."

After one bite, her communicator buzzed again and this time it was her mother's voice. "Wonder Woman to Golden Angel."

Elissa loosed a hard breath, her brow low over her eyes as she reached behind her again.

"Lonely at the top?" one of the women at the table asked.

"If only," the girl grumbled as she raised the communicator to her mouth. "Go ahead, Wonder Woman."

"Are you eating?" Wonder Woman asked.

"Yes Ma'am," she replied.

"Go ahead and finish, Junior. We'll wait for you."

A little smile touched the girl's mouth and she offered, "Thanks, Mom." Putting it away, she raised her brow and mumbled, "Well *that's* new."

WW

As expected, Golden Angel entered the conference room and found most of the senior members already there. Most of the Justice league was there, and all of them were laughing. This made her freeze only a few feet inside.

Wonder Woman, sitting between Superman and Batman, wiped her eyes as she composed herself and continued, "Oh, it was a sight. I looked up and there's my three year old daughter, stark naked except for my tiara that she was holding on her head with one hand and she had my lasso in the other and she was dragging most of it down the beach behind her shouting, 'I am Wonder Woman and I'm here to save the day!'"

Everyone laughed again, and when Golden Angel was finally noticed and Flash greeted, "Hey there, kiddo!" they all turned to see her standing there with her mouth hanging open, her eyes wide and her brow arched high over her eyes.

Wonder Woman finally turned around and worked hard to control herself as she said, "Junior. Your father was just asking about your childhood and—"

"Mom!" she shouted. "Seriously?" When everyone laughed again, she covered her eyes and mumbled, "Oh, Hera help me." She pointed a finger at her mother and assured, "I am so getting you for this, Mom!"

Diana shook her head and assured, "That's not the first time I've heard that, Little One. Now come in here. We have to debrief you."

WW

Later, Elissa sat in the control room at the main console as she stared down at the note left for her by Zack.

Black Canary sat at the main console that was usually monitored by Martian Manhunter. She was half turned and facing the young Amazon, her legs crossed, her elbow resting on the edge of the console and her cheek resting in her palm. She just watched Golden Angel struggle with such an easy decision, and after a while she barked, "Just call him!"

Elissa flinched and looked to her, then back to the note. She heaved a heavy breath and conceded, "Yeah, I should. He's probably wondering how I am or something. Did I mention that he wants me

235

to go to his prom with him?"

"About four times," Black Canary dryly replied.

"I'll bet he's in school or something," Elissa guessed. "I should wait."

"What school did you say he goes to?"

"Dent High School outside of Gotham."

Shaking her head, Black Canary stood and worked the controls on the main computer, looking up at the monitor as she did so. Activating the communicator, she called, "Come in, Fire."

"Go ahead," Fire replied in her pleasant Spanish accent.

"I have somewhere to go," Canary informed. "Can you relieve me for a while?"

"Sure."

"Okay, thanks." She turned to Golden Angel and set her hands on her hips. "Come on, you."

Elissa looked up at her and raised her brow. "Where?"

WW

Black Canary and Golden Angel stood side by side on the steps of Dent High School on the outskirts of Gotham City. This was a big building at the front, one constructed of steel and brick and one that was as inviting as a high school could be.

Elissa drew a deep breath and turned unsure eyes to the imposing woman beside her.

"Come on," Black Canary prodded. Seizing the girl's arm, she started up the last few steps and into the massive main building of the high school.

Their first stop was the office to find out where to find the boy. From then on, Elissa would be on her own, and after a few words of encouragement and a brief lecture on demonstrating strength and self-confidence, off she went.

Lockers lined most of the walls and the place was a bit of a maze, but following directions, she found the room to the chemistry lab, Room 121, and paused there. Looking around her, everything was quiet. Very quiet. She felt that awkward squirming in her stomach, but this time was able to dismiss it. She was not a teenage girl among a group of tall and beautiful Amazons nor was she that same teenage girl among a group of world renowned superheroes. This time, *she* was the hero!

Still, she did not want to interrupt the class, so she leaned back against the lockers across the hallway from the door, folded her arms and waited.

And waited.

Looking down at herself, she worked the cape off of her right shoulder, just to be sure that everyone could see her shoulder and arms.

Elissa actually jumped when the bell rang.

Doors all up and down the hall opened and hundreds of students seemed to crowd into the hallway all at once.

She watched the ones who filed out of the chemistry room, and many of them paused to get a good look at her. Naturally, Zack and two of his friends, all big boys in their own right, were the last to exit the room. All dressed in blue jeans and black tee shirts that had different rock band logos on them, they were indeed a sight.

One of Zack's friends punched him in the arm and assured, "Come on, man. You know she ain't gonna call you! Why would she?"

Zack was staring at the floor as he walked and just shrugged. "I don't know."

All of them walked by without noticing and Elissa shook her head as she watched them. Reaching behind her, she withdrew her phone and his note and quickly entered the number he had given her, and she held the phone to her ear as she watched them slowly negotiate the crowd down the hallway. She smiled as she heard his cell phone ring and he reached into his pocket for it.

"Hello?" he greeted.

"Tell your friend he was wrong," she ordered.

He froze and raised his head. "Angel?"

His two friends stopped as well.

"Go ahead," she prodded. "Tell him."

He looked to his friend and complied, then he put the phone back to his ear and nervously asked, "So how's it going?"

She smiled again. "Not too bad considering I got shot last night. How are you?"

"Better now," he reported.

"Why don't you and your friends turn around," she suggested.

Slowly, Zack complied.

"Golden Angel!" someone announced from her other side.

A crowd of teenagers began to form around her and Zack and his friends hurried to push through them.

Elissa closed her phone and put it away, then folded her arms as the boy she had come to see finally reached her. She glanced at the two boys who were with him, seeing that they were staring at her with expressions of absolute shock and disbelief.

Zack strode right up to her, stopping only a foot or so away as he greeted, "Hey."

"Hey," she replied with a little smile. "So I guess our story has circulated around school?" When he nodded, she raised her brow and asked, "How many people believed you?"

"Not many," he grumbled.

The crowd of people grew quiet so that they could hear the conversation.

"I guess they will now, won't they?" she said. "Look, I don't want to keep you from anything and I do need to be getting back, but I just wanted to stop by..." She looked away and down, then back to him, stepped up to him and raised a hand to his face, rising up on her toes to give him a kiss on the cheek. "Thanks for saving my life, Zack."

The crowd rumbled with gasps and new found gossip.

Elissa smiled at him once more, then turned and strode slowly down the hallway, and people moved out of her way as she approached.

Zack did not watch her long before he raised his hand to her and bade, "Angel, wait!"

She stopped and half turned, looking back at him over her shoulder.

He approached apprehensively, rubbing the back of his neck as he stammered, "So, uh... You know... Remember when I asked you about the prom?"

Elissa turned fully and folded her arms. "Yeah, but I thought you would have all kinds of girls fighting over the chance to go with you by now."

Shaking his head, he corrected, "No, not really. So, it's three weeks from Friday and I was hoping you were free that night."

With a little shrug, Elissa assured, "I don't have any plans that I know of, unless Martian Manhunter puts me on the schedule for that day." She looked down to her right shoulder and pulled the cape over it again. "Of course, nobody's formally asked me to do anything that night." Her eyes shifted back to his with a blink and her brow held high over them.

He drew a deep breath and vented it slowly before he asked, "Do you want to prom with me?"

A little smile curled her mouth and she stared up at him for a second before she replied, "It sounds fun. Yeah, I'll go with you."

A collective gasp swept through the crowd of onlookers.

"Great!" he declared, smiling back at her.

"But," she added, poking him with her finger, "you have to remember that this can only be a onetime thing, okay? You have to understand that what I do makes having a steady relationship kind of a problem."

"I'm cool with that," he assured. "So..."

"I'll call you," she told him as she straightened out his collar. "And you'd better be ready for me. I can dance for hours without stopping." She kept her attention on him as she turned to leave again and a flirty smile returned to her mouth. "Catch you later, Zack."

As she strode away and disappeared down the hallway, someone shouted, "Zack! You da man!"

Arriving outside, Elissa had a very self-satisfied smile and a familiar spring in her step as she bounded down the front steps. She saw Black Canary leaning against a tree outside and headed that way.

"I'm guessing you found him," Black Canary said with a little smirk.

Elissa's nod was an absent one and she simply looked across the street. "Yeah, I found him."

"So what happened?"

"He asked me to the prom."

"And you said..."

Smiling an excited little smile, the girl clasped her hands together and bounced up and down, squealing, "Yes! I said yes! I'm going to my first prom ever!"

Black Canary raised her brow and nodded. "I see. So, how is your mother going to feel about this?"

The bouncing slowed and in a few seconds stopped. Elissa's

smile faded and her eyes became a little blank. She glanced about for a second, then she vented a deep breath and replied, "She's going to kill me."

WW

The doors to the conference room slid shut behind Elissa and she was slow to approach the table where her mother and several others were discussing something. Her steps were small and hesitant and her attention was fixed on the Amazon Princess who sat right between Superman and Green Lantern, and all of them had their backs to her.

Black Canary entered behind her and as the door slid shut she followed closely, giving the girl a little nudge with her fingertips.

About ten feet away, she finally stopped and watched Black Canary stride around her toward the table. Swallowing hard, she looked back to her mother and sheepishly greeted, "Hi, Mom."

Diana looked over her shoulder and smiled. "Well hi, Junior. Did you find that boy who helped you on the ship?"

Elissa turned her eyes down and nodded. "Yes, I found him. We talked for a little while..." She trailed off as Wonder Woman stood and approached her and folded her arms. "Um, I thanked him for saving me and gave him a little kiss on the cheek and... Oh, yeah, he asked me to his prom and I told him I'd go." Raising her brow, she forced a smile and continued, "I mean, he saved my life. How could I tell him no, right? You know, it's just a dance and..." Frustration took her features and she set her hands on her hips. "Come on, Mom! I've never been asked to one of these before! And he saved my life for Hera's sake! I really wanna go and I know I should have asked you first but it was just one of those things! I *had* to say yes! Please, Mom! It's just a bunch of kids..." She stopped as Wonder Woman raised her palm to her.

"Would you calm down?" Diana barked. "It's okay. I think it is great that you have the opportunity to go." She raised her brow. "But, you're the one who has to ask your father."

Elissa threw herself into her mother, wrapping her arms around her as she squealed, "Thanks Mom!" Pulling back, she wore a much more serious, almost fearful expression. "Wait! What? Ask Daddy?"

Raising her brow again, Diana nodded.

Backing away, Elissa smiled and dismissively said, "No problem. I'll just turn on the girly charm, give him a big hug and my very best puppy dog eyes and he'll never say no to me."

"Oh really," Wonder Woman chuckled.

"Hey, I'm his little girl and it's his job to spoil me, right? I'll have him wrapped around my little finger and... He's right behind me, isn't he?"

Once again, Wonder Woman raised her brow and nodded.

Heaving a heavy breath, Elissa looked aside and mentally prepared herself for the worst. She turned slowly, seeing Batman only a few feet behind her, just standing there with his arms folded and a very hard look in his eyes. Slowly, very humbly, she lowered her eyes to the floor and approached him, drawing her shoulders up as she neared.

He lowered his arms, setting his fists on his hips as he stared almost coldly down at her. His elbows caused his cape to flare out, giving him a much more imposing look.

Very sheepishly, Elissa looked up at him, then unexpectedly she threw herself into him, wrapping her arms around him as she cried, "Daddy, please! I never get to do anything! It's just one dance and he's a really nice boy! He saved my life and I just couldn't tell him no. Just let me go to this one prom and I'll never, ever ask for anything ever again!" She nuzzled into him and appeared to be sobbing as she held him.

He shifted his hard eyes to Wonder Woman with a blink.

Diana smiled. "Welcome to *my* life for the last sixteen years."

Batman's eyes narrowed, then he looked down to his daughter, gently taking her by the waist and pushing her away from him. When she turned her famed puppy dog eyes up to him, eyes that were full of tears and when she stuck her lower lip out just a little, he vented a breath and grumbled, "It's okay with me."

Elissa screamed and threw herself at him again, hugging him tightly as she squealed, "Thank you, Daddy! Thank you!"

"But," he started with an ominous tone.

She slowly pulled away and stood before him with a fearful look, her head held low and her wide eyes locked on his.

"There will be two conditions," Batman informed.

Elissa nodded in quick motions.

"One," he growled, "I want to talk to the boy before you go anywhere with him."

She nodded again, tensing up more.

"Two," he continued, "your mother will be there to pick you up at ten."

Backing away, she set her hands on her hips and cried, "Ten? That's totally not fair! It doesn't end until midnight! Why can't I..." She stopped as Wonder Woman grasped her shoulder.

Diana whispered in the girl's ear, "Think hard about what you say, Little One. He can still change his mind."

Elissa looked aside, swallowed hard, then looked back up to her father, continuing in a much calmer voice, "Like I was saying, ten sounds awesome. I mean, I'll have to get some rest for patrols and stuff the next day, right?" She forced a smile and tugged on one finger. "Thanks for letting me go, Daddy."

He bent down close to her, his eyes narrowing as he growled, "Call him. I will speak to him tonight."

She nodded and watched after him as he turned and left. When the doors shut, she turned around with a self-satisfied smile and folded her arms. "Like I said. No problem. Daddy's little girl."

Wonder Woman looked to Black Canary, shaking her head as she said, "At least she didn't throw her dignity by the wayside this time." Turning her attention back to her daughter, she asked, "Have you given any thought to what you are going to wear?"

Elissa's eyes widened and her brow popped up and she gasped, "I don't have a dress!"

WW

The Justice League members generally took turns standing the watch in the control room. With J'onn deployed on a mission with Fire, it fell to Wonder Woman to keep watch on the world and be ready to assemble teams and send them into action. Alone in the cavernous room with only the computer screen for company, there was just too much time to think.

This night, she sat at the console with her elbow resting on the edge of the control panel and her cheek in her palm as she stared blankly at the screen as the map shifted automatically from place to place. Lost in thoughts, she did not notice the door to the elevator open and close, and was barely aware of the soft footsteps that grew louder as the caped figure neared. Finally drawing a breath, she greeted, "Good evening, Junior."

Golden Angel stopped behind her, placing her hands on her mother's shoulders as she replied, "Hey."

The two were silent for a time, just watching the screen.

Wonder Woman looked down to the keyboard and entered some information with her free hand.

"So," Elissa started, "Stacy's supposed to be home tomorrow. I was hoping we could go and see her."

"Sure," Diana agreed absently.

"I thought we might spend a couple of days," the girl went on. "We could all have some serious girl time together, maybe go to that spa that Stacy likes so much. It's really awesome. They have massages and pedicures and stuff. Oh, and I have to go and see Terrance about my gown. Stacy said that they had already been talking about a formal dress for official stuff and this would be a good time to unveil it."

Nodding, Diana said, "That sounds fine."

Elissa stared down at her for a moment, then asked, "Can I get my ears pierced while we're there?"

"Sure," Wonder Woman said with only a wisp of a voice.

Crooking her jaw, Elissa finally reached to one of the other chairs and pulled it close to her mother, sitting down as she looked into her mother's face and grasped her arm. "Okay, Mom. You're never this agreeable! What's wrong?"

Diana could not look at her daughter and instead turned her eyes down to the computer keyboard. "I'm fine, Junior."

"Bull!" the girl barked. "We have never kept things from each other and I'm not going to let you start now. Talk to me, Mom!"

Drawing a deep breath, the Amazon Princess tapped at the spacebar, and slowly her eyes glossed with tears.

Elissa's hand slid down her mother's arm, over her gauntlet, and she took her mother's hand.

"I'm sorry," Diana whispered.

"For what?" Elissa demanded.

Closing her eyes, Diana confessed, "I was so hard on you your whole life. I pushed you so. I pushed you away. For Hera's sake I could have trained you to death!"

"You didn't know, Mom! Neither of us did! You pushed me to make me a better woman, a better warrior, and I am! You pushed me to prepare me for what I would meet later. I can't imagine what would have happened to me without you training me so hard my whole life!"

A tear slipped from Diana's eye. "I could have spent more time with you, just being your mother."

"I guess you don't remember all of the fun we used to have together. Sure, we trained hard. Everyone on Themyscira does." Elissa reached to her mother's face, grasping her jaw and turning her mother's eyes toward her own. "You can wallow in guilt all you want, but you were a great mother then and you are a great mother now. I wouldn't change a thing, Mom. I wouldn't."

Diana stared at her daughter for a moment and another tear slipped down her cheek. "I still have regrets, Little One."

"So do I," the little Amazon admitted. "There *were* times I could have trained harder and there were plenty of times I just didn't want to listen, but I can't keep looking back at that. I'm listening now. I understand now, Mom. I finally understand."

Reaching to her face, Diana took her daughter's hand, and she closed her eyes as she bowed her head. "There is so much more to this, Little One. I kept you isolated most of your life. Your father knew nothing about you because I was afraid. He was right. I kept you from him to appease my own fears more than to protect you. I didn't want this life for you."

Elissa squeezed her mother's hands. "Well, first of all, you kept me isolated on an island that's called Paradise. They call it that for a reason. I had a great childhood that I'm still enjoying. As far as that eating thing I have, I've made peace with it. I mean, come on! I get to eat as much as I want now. No, I *have* to. How cool is that, right? And she said I'll be a kid for like fifty more years! Who doesn't want that? These aren't the liabilities you seem to think they are. They are wonderful gifts."

Diana turned her eyes to the girl's with a blink. "And your small stature?"

With a shrug, Elissa replied, "I'm pretty sure that's Dad's fault. So, um, can I get a tattoo?"

A long stare followed, then Diana smiled and slowly shook her head. "I don't think so, Junior."

"I knew I'd find it!" the girl declared.

"Find what?" Wonder Woman asked with a lean of her head.

"Your smile," Elissa replied. "I knew it was in there somewhere."

Combing her fingers through the girl's hair, Diana informed, "That always worked on you when you were little."

The girl shrugged. "It probably still does, and I'm still kind of little. So, no tattoo, but can I still get my ears pierced?"

"Of course," Diana confirmed.

Elissa drew her head back. "Seriously? You're really going to let me?"

"Why wouldn't I? I got mine pierced a long time ago. I'm a little surprised that you haven't already."

"I thought you would throw a fit!" Elissa barked.

Diana smiled again. "I don't throw fits, Junior, I throw little Amazons."

Smiling back, Elissa added, "And bad guys, and cars, and trucks..."

"All of the above," the Amazon Princess confirmed with a laugh. "So you want us to spend a couple of days with Stacy, do you?" When the girl nodded, Diana nodded back. "Sounds okay. Your father asked me to come back to the mansion for a while. I guess we still have a lot to talk about, but—"

"Best news ever!" Elissa confirmed. "You're going, right? I mean, Stacy and I will be fine with you going to spend time with Daddy."

"I'm also sure he would understand if I want to spend some time with you girls," Diana informed.

Batman confirmed, "I would."

Elissa screamed and wheeled around, her chair sliding back-first into the console as she turned wide eyes up to her father's. Grasping her chest, she drew a calming breath, looking up at him with much annoyance as she snarled, "Not cool, Daddy."

He smiled. "That insight doesn't work so well when you're distracted, does it?" His expression becoming more serious, he looked to Wonder Woman. "I have a situation in Gotham and I could use a hand."

She leaned her head. "What kind of situation?"

"Nigma was not on the ship," he replied, "but we know the message we got was sent from the ship. He's made some enemies so under the circumstanced I don't know if someone's setting him up or if this was just part of a more elaborate scheme."

Wonder Woman stood. "Do you have an address for him?"

"I do," he confirmed, "but there's also been activity with three others, and my sources tell me that something big is supposed to go down soon. I have Nightwing checking out the last known location of Two Face and Batgirl is tracking down Poison Ivy, but I could use a hand with a couple of others."

Elissa sprang up and barked, "Sweet! Let's go—"

"Observe," he interrupted. "This is information gathering and we can't let them know we're watching them."

"Why not just take them down?" the girl asked.

Wonder Woman answered, "We have to catch them doing something, otherwise they get right back out and we end up the bad guys. Do you think you can do this without being seen this time?"

Golden Angel confidently folded her arms and replied, "I'll be like a grain of salt in a snowstorm."

WW

Elissa's assignment turned out to be the notorious Penguin, and after a briefing on him and a lengthy lecture by both parents about underestimating him and more importantly not being seen and to avoid combat until her shoulder was completely healed, she was dropped off at the rear of the Iceberg Lounge.

Only after arriving did she realize that her plan to go in as a patron and watch the place had one fatal flaw: She did not have a gown that would allow her to go in unnoticed, and it was too late in the evening to go shopping for one. It was so late, in fact, that the club would be closing shortly, and people were trickling out, presumably on their way home.

The back door was an old steel door with a lock that was easy to pick. As she quietly opened it, she reached to a pouch on her belt and retrieved a small plastic bat, one about the size of a quarter. Holding the middle of it, she rotated the wings a quarter turn to activate it, then stuck it over the door on the outside in a shadowed area where it would not be seen. If she did not report back to Batman for some reason, this would tell him where she had entered the club from a great distance.

With her blue cape on over her shoulders and nearly closed around the front of her, she snuck into what appeared to be a storage room of some kind. Shelves lined the walls and were laden with liquor bottles, mixers and boxes of cans and dry food items. Pallets of other boxes were also left in the room almost randomly. The lights were off, of course, but the darkness in the room was not an obstacle for someone with the gift of night sight.

She made her way to the door without any problems, and as she heard activity outside, she pressed her back to the wall right beside it.

Light swept in and bathed a wedge of the floor in a fluorescent glow from the outside and a hand reached along the wall, groping for the light switch and finding her chest instead.

"Hey!" she barked.

The hand quickly withdrew and she backed away.

Two men in white peered inside, and one hesitantly reached for the light switch a second time.

As the fluorescent lights inside the storage room came on, they slowly crept in, both of them eying her with looks of surprise.

Golden Angel set her hands on her hips and barked, "You need to be very careful where you touch people! That's a good way to get your butt kicked!"

They escorted her out of the storage area, through the kitchen and, joined by two large henchmen in tuxedoes, she was taken out to the cavernous banquet hall. It seemed to have a glacier theme about it with a high ceiling that looked to be over thirty feet from the floor. It was in a semi-circular arrangement with a long bar at the back near the entrance to the kitchen. What appeared to be long icicles hung from the ceiling and provided light. The walls were lined with booths white and blue, deep cushioned booths, a small stage with white and blue curtains was on the far end and tables were distributed around a granite tiled dance floor in the middle of it all. It was spectacularly decorated and the ice theme actually made her feel a little cold.

Her eyes sweeping along the hundreds of icicles that hung from the ceiling, she smiled and declared, "Wow this is pretty!"

"Why thank you, my sweet," someone offered from behind her

and slightly to the left.

Elissa and her escorts stopped and turned, seeing a rather short, plump man just getting out of one of the deep cushioned booths. He wore a black top hat and a well pressed and well made tuxedo. He had a very long, pointed nose and did not have pleasing features about his face. Almost a foot shorter than Golden Angel, he approached her with a commanding gaze and walked with the help of an umbrella that he used as a cane.

Stopping right in front of her, he held the umbrella to the ground between his feet with both hands, hands that had independent thumbs and index fingers, but the other three fingers were fused together into what looked like flippers.

He stared up at her, politely keeping his eyes on hers and not scanning her body as every other man seemed to do.

Neither afraid of him nor repulsed, Elissa extended her hand to him and greeted, "Hi. You must be Penguin."

He hesitantly took her hand in his own flipper-like hand and did not take his eyes from hers as he nodded once, confirming, "Oswald C. Cobblepot."

"I'm Golden Angel," she introduced.

"Charmed," he responded. He drew her hand close to his mouth and gently kissed her knuckles.

She smiled.

Taking his cane handle with both hands again, he raised his chin and asked, "So what would bring such a lovely dove like yourself to slink about in the back rooms of my lounge?"

She shrugged. "Well, I don't know how well I slink. I kinda got caught." She motioned with her head to the man behind her on the left. "This guy reached in for the light switch and got a handful of... Well, something else."

With a nod, the Penguin said, "I see." He half turned his head, leering up at her. "So why were you in the storage room again?"

Elissa hesitantly raised her brow. "Health inspector?" When he just stared at her, she added, "Not buying it, huh? Okay, fine. I was sent to keep watch and make sure you aren't doing naughty things tonight." She folded her arms and looked across the room. "I also wasn't supposed to be noticed." Her eyes slid back to him. "Look, I'm already kind of on the bubble with Batman, so can we just, like, not tell him that you caught me?"

He seemed a little confused by her behavior, but nodded and assured, "I suppose it can be kept between us. So, what does the Batman think I'm up to this time?"

With a shrug, Golden Angel replied, "I don't know. He wasn't real specific, he just said to come here and keep watch on things." A little smile touched her lips. "I guess he just assumes that you're going to do something bad."

"His assumption wouldn't be the first," he assured.

Elissa looked around her. "So this is your place, huh? Nice! I'll bet you throw some serious parties here, don't you?"

"I've been known to," Penguin replied.

She looked back down to him, almost relieved to find an opponent who was actually shorter than her for a change. "So, what do we do now? We both know I can take your thugs here out with no problem." She looked over her shoulder. "No offense, guys."

They all nodded.

Turning her attention back to Penguin, she set her hands on her hips and raised her brow.

He stared up at her for long seconds, then raised his brow also. "Well, before you arrived I was going to have dinner. I don't suppose you would care to join me."

A smile touched her lips. "Why, Mister Cobblepot, are you asking me on a date?"

He shrugged. "Perhaps just dinner. Since you mean to keep watch on me tonight we should at least be comfortable." Half turning, he held his arm to her. "Shall we retire to my private booth?"

She took his arm and nodded to him. "I think we shall, kind sir."

In true gentlemanly form, he reached to her shoulders to remove her cape before they sat down and he handed it to one of his men before extending his hand to the booth, inviting her to sit. They took their seats and he hooked his umbrella on the edge of the table, well within quick reach. Looking up to his henchmen, he waved them away and ordered, "That will be all, gentlemen."

As they left, Elissa rested her elbows on the table, lacing her fingers and resting her chin on them as she asked, "So what's for dinner?"

"I ordered kippers already," he informed, "and a nice dinner salad. You do like kippers, don't you?"

"I love kippers," she drawled with a smile.

"Simply splendid. I like to give mine a nice Italian flair, so they are in an oregano marinara sauce of my own concoction."

She smiled broader. "Sounds yummy."

Dinner was served a moment later and light conversation passed between them.

Slipping another of the small, marinara covered fish into her mouth with the long, two pronged fork provided, she looked down at her plate and shook her head, chewing only a few times before she said with a half full mouth, "Mister Cobblepot, these are absolutely delish." She turned her eyes to his. "The salad was great and this tea is simply wonderful." She reached for her glass. "Mint, you said?"

"Yes," was his polite reply as he reached for his own. "A mint and Ceylon variety. I find a little mint to be a good idea when dining on fish, especially in the presence of a lovely young lady."

She smiled at him and took a drink.

"So what does a girl fancy these days?" he asked as he set his glass down. "Do you attend banquets and dances when you are not nabbing nefarious ne'er-do-wells?"

"Well," she began as she picked at her kippers, "I finally got asked to a dance in a couple of weeks. Well it's a high school prom." She unknowingly blushed a little. "A boy I met while I was working… Okay, he's kind of cute, really brave and we sort of hit it off. He said he didn't have a date yet and asked me if I would go with him and he gave me his number."

"Sounds like the rumblings of a budding romance," Penguin observed with a smile.

She smiled broader, staring down at her plate as she picked at her kippers with the long fork. "No, just a prom date. Considering what I do… Well, having any kind of a steady relationship is kind of a problem."

"To be happy," he announced, "one must give up the things that makes one happiest."

Elissa raised her brow. "Sounds about right."

"Have you all of your proverbial ducks in their rows?"

"I guess so," she sighed. "I have a dress lined up and I'll be meeting him there. I wish he could come by and pick me up but, you know, security issues and stuff."

"And your dancing steps? One would assume that you have mastered whatever the minstrels would muster."

She looked to him and asked before slipping another kipper into her mouth, "You mean like hip-hop?"

He picked up his tea. "One would assume that they would play a more heterogeneous selection."

Elissa stopped chewing and stared at him with concern on her features, finally asking, "Like what?"

"Well," he replied in a sigh as he set his glass down, "this being a formal event, they're bound sneak in the occasional ballroom number, perhaps a waltz. Surely you've some experience in those forms."

Her brow arching, she looked down to the table and slowly shook her head.

Staring at her for long seconds, he tried to reassure her, "It may not be likely that they will play such numbers. Your younger generation simply does not—"

"But what if they do?" she interrupted, desperation in her voice. "I've always just danced, kind of done my own thing. What if I go in there and look like a total doofus?"

No one had ever seen pity on Penguin's face before, but this night it emerged. He took the napkin from his lap, wiped his mouth, then struggled from his seat.

Golden Angel turned her eyes to him as he stood, and she raised her brow as he offered her his hand.

WW

When Batman arrived behind the Iceberg Lounge, he found Nightwing leaning against the wall beside the slightly open back door with his arms folded, and a strange smile on his face.

As he met Batman's eyes, Nightwing slowly shook his head and said, "You just aren't going to believe this."

Batman looked to the door, his eyes narrowing as he grumbled, "She got caught again?"

"You know," Nightwing started as he pushed off the wall, "I'm not real sure what happened." He pulled the door open and strode in.

"You just aren't going to believe this."

They arrived to the lounge on the inside, staying to the shadows of the darkened back area, they found a good vantage point just outside of the kitchen where they could scan the restaurant and dance floor. Several of Penguin's white clad employees were still there, standing just outside of the kitchen and in the light and watched the dance floor.

"No," Penguin scolded, "your left foot. Don't step, glide."

One of his hands was around her waist while the other held hers out from them. Music started and the unlikely pair turned and began to move with the strings of the symphony that played. Golden Angel was looking down at her feet as she moved, and once again this provoked the Penguin's ire.

"Look at me," he ordered, "not at your feet. Feel what you are doing on the floor, don't watch."

She turned her eyes to his and nodded.

Batman looked on in disbelief.

Two of Penguin's big thugs, both dressed in black tuxedos, approached from behind the duo, and one of them grabbed onto the Dark Knight's shoulder.

Batman half turned his head and asked, "Are you sure you want your arm broken tonight?"

The thug was quick to release Batman's shoulder, and he glanced at the other as they both backed away.

Elissa squealed, "I'm doing it!"

"Remember to let your feet glide along the floor," Penguin reminded. "Your date should lead so you should remember to follow his steps and let the music do the rest." When one of his thugs approached and tried to get his attention, he glared at him and barked, "What is it? Can't you see I'm..." He stopped dancing and his eyes shifted behind this henchman, finding Batman standing there with a cold stare in his eyes and Nightwing standing beside him with his arms folded. Heaving a heavy breath, he released Golden Angel and took a step back from her. "It would seem that your carriage has arrived for you."

She looked to Batman, to Nightwing, and forced a smile, waggling her fingers at them as she bade, "Hi, guys."

Batman's eyes narrowed and he ordered, "Wait for me in the car."

"Okay," she complied in her usual bubbly tone. Looking to Penguin, she smiled at him and offered, "Thanks for showing me some moves, Mister Cobblepot, and thanks for dinner."

He smiled back and took her hand, kissing her fingers before he replied, "Thank *you* for a wonderful evening, my dove. Now practice those steps I showed you until they are instinct."

"I will," she assured. Throwing her arms around him, she hugged him tightly enough to make him groan, then she kissed his cheek before spinning toward the Dark Knight and the door at the back. Halfway there, one of Penguin's henchmen offered her the cape and she stopped to allow him to drape it over her shoulders, then she half turned and waved to Cobblepot one more time, giving him a big smile as she said, "I'll see you later."

Penguin returned her smile and waved back to her, and he watched after her even as she disappeared into the back of the club.

Batman and Nightwing strode toward the much shorter bad guy, their gazes locked on him almost curiously.

"Nightwing," Batman said in his deep, low voice. "Make sure Golden Angel finds her way to the car."

Without responding, Nightwing turned and strode out after the girl.

Penguin turned his eyes up to the Dark Knight, observing, "She is a remarkable young woman."

"That she is," Batman confirmed almost coldly. He kept his gaze fixed on the Penguin, watching him approach his booth, and the umbrella that was still hooked there. "She goes out of her way to see the best in everything and everyone around her, sometimes to her detriment."

"I can see that," Cobblepot confirmed as he stopped at his booth. Slowly, he looked down at his hands, turning them palms up as he did. "Tonight, it is what she did not see that I find refreshingly relevant."

"And what was that?" Batman asked almost harshly.

Penguin balled his deformed hands into tight fists, closing his eyes as he replied, "A monster." Taking his umbrella, he turned the other way, heading toward the far end of the club and toward the back corner. "Good night, Batman."

His henchmen both followed.

Batman watched them until they disappeared around the bar on the far end, then he turned and headed out himself.

Outside, Golden Angel stood by the Batmobile, which was parked in the middle of the alley, and Nightwing was on his black motorcycle beside the car. As Batman approached, Nightwing gunned his engine, nodded to the Dark Knight as he sped away.

Batman reached the car and removed the remote control from his belt, pressing the button that would open the canopy. The whole time his eyes were on Golden Angel, and hers were on him.

When he was quiet like this, Elissa had learned to tread lightly around him, and as he strode around to the driver's side of the car, she slipped into the other seat and reached for her seat belt.

In a moment they were away, speeding down a quiet back road toward the hidden entrance to the Bat Cave. Neither spoke for a time, though there was much to say.

Batman finally glanced at the girl as she stared out the window beside her, and he broke the silence with, "Dinner and dancing with the Penguin?"

She turned and looked to him and pointed out, "You wanted me to keep an eye on him so I kept an eye on him."

He glanced at her again and seemed to be a little irritated at her response.

Resting her elbow on the center console, she leaned toward him and went on, "I did exactly what I was supposed to do."

"Except not be seen," Batman pointed out.

She stared at him for long seconds, then straightened in her seat and looked out the window beside her. "Yeah, I might have blown that again." Her head whipped to him and she was quick to add, "But it wasn't my fault this time!"

"How so?" he asked.

"Well," she started hesitantly, "um, I was in the storage room about to come out and look around and someone opened the door so I hid against the wall so they wouldn't see me. I figured they would come in for some stuff and I could slip out when they did but one of them reached in for the light switch and grabbed a handful of, well, me instead!"

Batman's eyes slid to her.

"I know it was an accident," she continued, "but I still let him have it. I didn't hit him or anything I just kind of chewed him out. I mean, come on! There are certain places you just don't touch a girl! Then we went to see Mister Cobblepot."

"And he was okay with you being there?" Batman guessed.

She admitted, "Well, not at first. We talked for a minute and then he asked me if I like kippers… Oh, they were good! And that dinner salad had everything! Have you ever had mint tea? Anyway, we were sitting there having dinner and talking and the prom came up and he asked me if I knew how to dance ballroom and stuff and I don't. I've just always kind of done my own thing and he offered to show me some steps. You wouldn't think but he's really light on his feet and he knows what he's doing on the dance floor."

"I wouldn't know," Batman grumbled.

That her father was upset was clear. Elissa could sense it even without her gift of insight. She gave him a hard stare, then she looked out the windshield and folded her arms, frustration in her voice as she pointed out, "You told me to keep watch on him and I did."

"I also told you not to be seen," Batman pointed out.

She huffed a breath and conceded, "I know." Her eyes shifted to him. "But I did okay anyway, didn't I?"

Batman glanced at her. "More than anything, there are times you need to be invisible. That doesn't mean having dinner with those you are supposed to be observing."

"You told me to lay off the combat for a few more days," she reminded, "and I don't see how having dinner with him and keeping him preoccupied to prevent him from plotting and planning is a problem." She shook her head. "Oh, crud, now I'm talking like him. Anyway, he didn't have any malicious feelings toward me and I think he genuinely wanted to help."

"Did your gift of insight tell you that?" he asked.

Golden Angel turned her eyes down and nodded. "Yes sir."

They rode in silence for a time, and finally he glanced at her again and observed, "You have a way of bringing out the best in most people. Truthfully, if your instincts told you to trust him as far as you did, then I'm good with that."

She turned her head slightly and looked at him.

"However," he went on, "*my* instincts tell me that your mother is better off not knowing about this."

Elissa smiled. "Our secret, Daddy. So, um, did that thing go down tonight that you heard about?"

"Armored truck robbery," he confirmed. "Thing is, the trucks they took were both empty."

She raised her chin, her eyes narrowing as she recalled, "That's what Mom and I found the other day when we stopped that truck. They stole an empty truck. But why?"

"We'll know soon enough," Batman replied. "We stopped them this time, but I don't think they'll give up so easily."

She was quiet for a moment, her brow tense as she considered something that had surfaced from her memory. "So, what were the bad guys wearing?"

His eyes slid to her. "What were they wearing?"

Elissa looked to him and nodded.

Staring ahead of him at the coming road, he considered, then replied, "I believe some kind of dark green sweaters and black trousers, black boots, gloves and ski masks."

"Just like the crime sprees last year," she recalled. "All of them were dressed like that. All of them."

Batman considered, then his eyes narrowed and he guessed, "And you think there is some kind of connection with this and what happened with Red Panzer last year."

"And the cruise ship," she added. "All of those guys were dressed the same, too."

"Hmm," rumbled from him. "I'll dig a little deeper while you visit your friend and see what I can piece together. It sure isn't much to go on, though."

"It might help if we knew what they needed empty armored trucks for," she grumbled.

He glanced at her and smiled. "Patience, Princess."

CHAPTER 12

Alfred was the first one in over ten years who could keep disaster at bay in Elissa's bedroom.

Her duffel bag was open and half full as she rummaged through drawers to find the clothes she wanted to take with her. Wearing a black tee shirt with a big, glittery pink heart on the back and red running shorts, she pulled a white shirt out of the drawer and held it up, then she snarled and shook her head as she threw it on top of the dresser and dug into the drawer again. She did not slow down as her phone rang and she reached to the top of the dresser to answer it.

Holding the phone to her ear, she greeted, "Hello?" A big smile took over her mouth and she squealed, "Stacy! What up, girlfriend? Yeah, I'm just about done packing. I should be..." She raised her head, her eyes widening as she asked, "You're in Gotham? Really? Why the heck are you in Gotham? Okay, what hotel? Yeah! I can be there in thirty minutes! Terrance seriously has an event in Gotham this weekend? Huh. Okay, I'll quit packing and get over there. See you in a bit, Stace."

WW

Naturally, the hotel Terrance had chosen to stay in was the best in Gotham City and was as extravagant as its reputation insisted. Just the lobby was an ornately decorated ballroom in itself with comfortable sitting areas distributed evenly about the room. Very comfortable work stations were along the walls with huge desks and deep cushioned chairs. All of the chairs, sofas and love seats that made up the sitting area were bright red and trimmed in dark wood, the same color wood that the tables that accompanied them and were lit by a multitude of crystal chandeliers that were also evenly distributed about the high ceiling.

The marble covered front desk, trimmed in that same dark wood and elaborately paneled at the front, was at the far end of the huge lobby and Elissa strode that way, barely noticing the well dressed people, mostly in expensive business suits, who stared at her the whole way. She also did not even consider that she had not changed clothes, only slipped on her running shoes before leaving, and her muscular legs and Amazon curves were drawing the attention of everyone within eyeshot. Her hair was also not restrained in its usual pony tail and flowed freely to her middle back. She did, fortunately, remember to slip the glasses on her face, not much of a disguise, but better than nothing.

Reaching the front desk, she gingerly grasped the edge of it and looked up to the important looking man in the suit on the other side of it, raising her brow as she greeted, "Hi. I'm here to see Terrance Arthur."

Holding his brow high over his eyes, he looked her up and down and countered, "Yes, I'm sure you are." He looked back to his computer screen and informed, "Mister Arthur is not to be disturbed. Call his secretary and schedule an appointment if you wish to see him."

His condescending tone was not lost on Elissa and she raised her chin slightly, staring at him as he seemed to ignore her. "Um," she started, "I'm a friend of his and—"

"I've heard that one hundreds of times, sweetheart," he interrupted, not even bothering to look at her. "Now I'm going to have to ask you to leave."

She crooked her jaw, feeling her patience drain away. "Can you at least call his room and let him know I'm here? He's expecting me."

The man looked up from the computer and vented an impatient breath. "Miss, he does not want to be disturbed. If you want a modeling job with him then—"

"I'm not a model!" she barked. "Look. I got a call from Stacy Madden and she said to come over here."

His eyes finally slid to her. After a few long seconds of a cold stare, he finally picked up the phone and put it to his ear. "Very well, Miss. Who shall I say is asking to disturb him?"

One of her eyebrows cocked up slightly and she replied, "Tell him his Goddess Elissa is here."

The man rolled his eyes and punched in three numbers. He kept that impatient expression as he turned his eyes to the ceiling while the phone rang on the other end.

It seemed to ring for a while.

Finally, the man behind the desk said, "Yes, there is a," His eyes slid to her, "Goddess Elissa here to see Mister Arthur and she claims to be..." His eyes widened slightly and darted down to his computer for a few long seconds. With a nod, he confirmed, "Yes. Yes, I shall see to it personally." Hanging up the phone, he half turned and snapped his fingers, directing one of the women on the other end to take his station at the desk.

Elissa watched him as he strode to the other end of the desk and disappeared through a door, then he emerged from a door on her side of the desk and she turned fully toward him.

He paused to beckon her toward him. "This way, Miss."

She followed him around the corner, past the elevators, past another elaborately furnished lobby, two restaurants and to two elevator doors that were gold in color, larger than the others and trimmed in dark wood that was ornately carved.

He removed a card from his pocket, one that was attached to a lanyard on his belt, and he waved it once in front of a small scanner between the two sets of doors.

There were no lights above these elevators and no sound came from behind the walls to indicate that the cars were moving.

They stood there in silence as they waited for the doors to open, and Elissa could sense his uneasiness.

Her eyes slid to him.

He was not moving, just standing there with his hands folded behind him, his eyes on the right set of doors, and the card held loosely between his fingers.

The doors mercifully opened and she was quick to stride into the well lit and well decorated car, turning to see him enter with her.

As the doors closed, he turned toward them, waving his card over the scanner within the car, then he entered a code on the keypad beneath it.

Ascending, they were caught in that awkward silence again, an awkwardness that Elissa had never liked. She simply had to end it. Looking to the man with her again, who was almost six inches taller than she was, she turned her eyes up to him and asked, "So, these elevators are for really important people and VIP's and stuff?"

He raised his brow and nodded. "They go to the top level where the penthouses are."

"Oh, so he got a penthouse, huh?"

"Mister Arthur reserves one for his visits to Gotham. Only the elite have ever seen them."

"How many are there?" she asked innocently.

He glanced at her. "There are five, but only four are available to be leased. The fifth is for Mister Wayne's uses and his guests only."

"Wait a minute," she barked. "He has a mansion here in Gotham. Why would he need a penthouse, too? I mean, lease a penthouse when you have a mansion a few miles away? Seems like a waste!"

Glancing at her again, he raised his brow and informed, "Mister Wayne owns this hotel."

Elissa's eyes widened. "Seriously?"

"Seriously," he confirmed.

She looked to the door. "Wow! That's way cool!"

His eyes slid to her and he mumbled, "Yes." Clearing his throat, he continued, "Listen, Miss, I, uh… I apologize for the unpleasantness a few moments ago and I hope we can put it behind us."

She looked up at him.

He went on, "I'm hoping that it can be kept between us. There really isn't a reason for Mister Arthur to know about my one inexcusable indiscretion."

"A second chance?" Elissa guessed with a little smile. When he finally met her eyes, she smiled a little broader and assured, "It'll be our secret."

He looked to her again and asked, "You are not a model?" When she shook her head, he looked to the doors again and said, "A pity. You really should be."

Her eyes slid to him and a smile fought its way back to her mouth. "Thanks."

The doors opened into a simple long hallway that matched the lobby in carpet and wall décor. It was about eight feet wide and very well lit. At the end of the hallway it intersected another and there was a wide dark wood door where the hall ended.

"The door straight ahead," he informed. "They're expecting you."

"Thanks," she offered as she stepped out of the elevator.

Getting to the door seemed like a very long walk!

Finally arriving, she raised her hand to knock but the door opened before she could.

Standing just inside the room and holding onto the door handle was a thin, almost frail looking man who looked to be near thirty. His brown hair was combed back and streaked with blond accents and he wore thick rimmed glasses over his eyes. His long sleeved shirt was open almost to his belly, the sleeves were rolled up and he had a number of pens in the pocket. Tight fitting white trousers were perfectly pressed and wrinkle free.

Setting a hand on his hip, he looked her up and down with an almost disinterested expression as he dryly said, "About time you showed up. Did you expect to keep him waiting all day?"

Elissa's brow arched and she stammered, "Um, well, I didn't—"

Moving aside, the thin man sighed, "Come in."

She hesitantly complied, her eyes on the rude man as she entered the penthouse. Only a few steps in, she stopped and looked around her, her wide eyes taking in the huge room before her. This was not what she expected to see in a hotel. The same elaborate and comfortable furnishings that had been in the lobby were here, but covered in red and gold with lighter wood trimming them Arranged in a semicircle in the center of the room, the sofa was flanked by two comfortable recliners and facing a love seat that was flanked by oak colored tables. There was a rather large kitchen to the left and three big doors through the wall to the right. The carpet was a gold color and sparkled in the generous light. Big windows were along the far wall and let in light from the outside, even though the sky was overcast.

The man who had let her in strode past her and announced, "Terrance, your prospective model has finally graced you with her presence."

Elissa's brow lowered and she snarled, "I'm not a model."

The door farthest to her right burst open and a short young woman rushed out of the room, freezing as she saw Elissa standing there. Dressed in a frilly yellow blouse that was open most of the way down her chest and tight fitting but comfortable looking slacks, she was barefoot and the slacks brushed the ground as she came to a stop. Her blond hair was worn in a pony tail behind her and her thick rimmed glasses were square at the top, round at the sides and bottom.

Elissa turned to face her and the two stared at each other for many long seconds before they both screamed and rushed toward one another. They collided mid way and wrapped their arms around each other, bouncing up and down as their reunion was met in a tight, squealing embrace, and they held each other cheek to cheek.

"I have so missed you!" the blond young woman cried.

"I've missed you, too, Stacy," Elissa assured. She pulled away, holding the slightly shorter woman at arm's reach as she looked her up and down. "Dang, girl! You've dropped some weight! You look good!"

"Thanks," Stacy offered with a little smile. "I've been running my butt off for a couple of months. So how are things with the Titans?"

Her lips tightening, Elissa admitted, "I'm not with the Titans anymore." A smile overpowered her lips and she squealed, "I'm Justice League now!"

Stacy's eyes flared and she drawled, "No! Seriously?"

"Yeah," Elissa confirmed. "It's like I'm a big girl now!"

"My Goddess Elissa!" a man with a Spanish accent declared. Both girls turned to see him enter the sitting area from one of the bedrooms to the right. He was tall and rather thin and was wearing a yellow shirt with a frilly collar, yellow, thick rimmed glasses and tight fitting white bell bottom slacks and no shoes. His blonde colored hair was cut short and spiky with the tips of the spikes dyed a lime green. As usual, he had a drink in his hand and walked with sultry steps, swinging his hips slightly as he strode to them.

"Terrance!" Elissa squealed as she rushed to him. She gave him a quick hug, then pulled away, and when he bent to her she knew to kiss his cheek, then the other when he turned his head, and he did the same.

"And how is Terrance's lovely Goddess?" he asked with his thick accent.

"Doing just great," she replied. "A little panicky about what I'm going to wear to this prom, but—"

"No no no," Terrance insisted with a wave of his hand. "There is nothing to fear for Goddess Elissa. Terrance and his Lamb have provided everything their Goddess will need to enchant everyone at the ball."

She raised her brow, assuring, "You have my every confidence." Looking over her shoulder to the blond young woman, she added, "You both do."

Stacy set her hands on her hips and informed, "Then you need to come see what we made for you."

Elissa drew a gasp and half turned. "You made it already?"

"Of course!" Terrance scoffed. "This business is about rush rush rush! Goddess Elissa's gown needs only a few alterations and it will fit her like a second skin."

"Wow!" Elissa declared. "I didn't think—" Her phone rang and she heaved a heavy breath as she reached for it. Holding it to her ear, she sweetly greeted, "Hello? Roger! How's it going?" There was a pause and she smiled. "Yeah, no problem. Yeah, I'm still coming." Her eyes widened and she raised her chin. "Hearing's in thirty minutes. No! I didn't forget! Yeah, just do like we talked about and I'll see you there, okay? Be good. See you in a little bit." She closed the phone and raised a hand to her eyes as she bowed her head, moaning, "Oh, Hera, I totally forgot!" Looking to Stacy, she grasped her shoulder and begged, "Can you give me about an hour?"

Her friend just smiled and glanced at Terrance. "Go on, Elissa. Justice first and stuff. We'll be here when you get back. Oh, and when you come back, they're expecting Golden Angel at the desk, okay?" She winked.

Rolling her eyes, Elissa turned to the door and grumbled, "Okay, okay." She reached for her cell phone as well, announcing, "I'd probably better call the Watchtower too and see if I can get transported over there."

WW

With Roger's hearing in a city over two hours away, Elissa found herself calling the Watchtower to beg J'onn to transport her to the courthouse. There, in a courtroom that was walled with what appeared to be oak paneling with seating for about a hundred people, Golden Angel pulled both doors open to enter and strode right toward the judge's bench as Roger was escorted there through a side door. She gently nudged the little gate open and walked with purposeful steps to his side.

Wearing a gray, three piece suit, Roger looked to her from between the two bailiffs and offered her a little smile and a nod as he met her eyes.

She nodded back, then looked to the judge, swallowing hard as the judge met her gaze with a hard look.

In her mid to late sixties, the judge was an attractive but harsh looking woman with eyes that told all who met them that she would pull no punches and take no disrespect from those in her courtroom. She wore the traditional black robe, but her collar was white lace, adding a feminine flair to her position.

Her lips pursing slightly as she looked the girl up and down, she narrowed her eyes and asked with harsh words, "And who are you supposed to be?"

Swallowing back the intimidation she felt, Elissa raised her chin slightly and replied, "Your Honor, my name is Golden Angel and I've come to plead to you for leniency." The judge's unblinking stare gave her pause, but she continued, "I've submitted a report to the court with an account of my part and actions in—"

"I read the report," the judge interrupted. She looked down at the bench and moved a few pages from the file before her, finally picking a page up and sliding her glasses on. "From what I see it was Wonder Woman who filed this report, not Golden Angel." Her hard eyes returned to the girl. "So if you filed a report, where is it?"

Elissa tensed. "Um, the report you have... That's the report I turned in, your Honor."

"You don't look like Wonder Woman," the judge pointed out.

With a quick nod, Golden Angel agreed, "I know, Ma'am, but at the time... Um, at the time I was Wonder Woman."

A mumbling rippled through the courtroom.

Somehow, the judge's expression hardened more. "You were Wonder Woman, and now you're someone called Golden Angel."

Glancing away, Elissa hesitantly nodded. She could feel that the judge had only begun to pick her apart.

The judge dropped the report and pulled her glasses off, annoyance on her features as she barked, "Do you really expect me to believe you?"

"I was hoping," Elissa mumbled.

"Young lady," the judge started in a loud voice, "this is a court of law. Do you think I have the time or patience to listen to your fantasies about being a hero of Wonder Woman's caliber? I've never even heard of you and you're telling me that you used to be Wonder Woman. What, did you get demoted or something?"

Elissa drew her shoulders up slightly, lowering her eyes as she found herself unable to answer. She could not even look Roger's way, knowing that she was letting him down.

"You come in here with those nonsense stories," the judge continued, "and you want me to trust you in court. I have a simple rule, young lady: Lie to me once and I don't believe another word that comes out of your mouth. You get me?"

"But I'm not lying," Golden Angel pled meekly.

"Your Honor," a woman from the audience behind Elissa called out. "May I approach?"

Golden Angel, Roger and the bailiffs turned around and the judge looked that way as a tall woman in a trench coat stood and sidestepped into the aisle between the seats, one who wore her hair up in a bun.

Reaching to her obsidian black hair, she pulled the barrette from the back and shook her head as she let it fall to her mid-back, then she opened the coat and flung it behind her in one fluid motion, revealing Wonder Woman's armor beneath.

Elissa's breath caught as she watched her mother approach with long strides and she quickly turned back to the judge's bench, sheepishly directing her eyes there.

Taking the girl's side, Wonder Woman looked fearlessly up at the judge and set her hands on her hips. Her posture was not a challenging one, rather one that showed all she intended to hold her ground. This judge had been a relentless juggernaut on the bench, but now she faced the one woman on the continent she could not intimidate.

"If I may," Wonder Woman started, "Golden Angel's integrity is not in question here."

Raising her brow, the judge corrected, "Oh, it is very much in question. How am I supposed to take the word of someone who is known to have lied to the entire world about being Wonder Woman?"

Turning her gaze aside, Elissa bowed her head slightly, feeling shame and disgrace for what she had done almost a year ago.

Diana set her jaw, her brow lowering over her eyes.

The judge continued, "She wants me to grant leniency to a man who has pled guilty to armed robbery of a bank and taking hostages in the process. I need to know I can trust her word, and if she's willing to lie to the entire world—"

"She didn't lie," Diana interrupted with harsh words. "She wore my armor, my tiara, and she came here to fight injustice and protect the innocent in my absence. In that capacity, she was Wonder Woman."

Folding her hands on the bench, the judge's eyes never wavered as she asked, "Is this the same girl who was almost killed by Red Panzer? You really expect me to believe that she was actually Wonder Woman in your place?"

Her eyes hardening, Diana clenched her hands into tight fists as she took two steps toward the bench, countering, "Now you would question *my* word?"

The judge drew her head back and did not respond.

"Know this," Wonder Woman informed with harsh words. "I trained this young woman myself and taught her about truth and honesty, to hold integrity as dear to her as one of her most cherished traits. I trust her word as my own and I know that what she speaks is only the truth. A true judge of character, a judge of others should be able to see that in her at a glance."

The judge's eyes shifted to Golden Angel.

"And yes," Diana said with a heaviness to her voice, "for those months you question, she was Wonder Woman."

The judge's attention moved back to Wonder Woman. "And who were you during those months?"

Elissa felt that nervous crawl in her stomach, feeling that her mother had been cornered.

She had not been.

Raising her chin, Diana replied straightly, "I was and am Princess Diana, the Ambassador to your country from Themyscira." She raised her brow. "Now that we have straightened all of that out, will you hear Golden Angel's plea?"

Leaning back in her chair, the judge looked to Golden Angel, giving her a long and terrifying stare, then she finally spoke with words that were just as harsh as those before. "So you want me to go easy on an armed robber. You want me to be lenient with someone who went into a bank with a gun and took hostages."

Elissa stepped forward, taking her mother's side as she looked into the judge's eyes. "He was responding to desperation, and responding poorly. The gun he had wasn't even loaded. He just... He... He'd asked for help and nobody listened. Your honor, he's a good man, he really is, he was just desperate. His marriage had broken up, he had lost his job and his home and just didn't know what else to do."

"So he went to rob a bank," the judge concluded. "Miss Angel, if I show leniency to one man who claims he was desperate and didn't have any other choice, what kind of example am I setting? Regardless of the fact that his weapon was not loaded, he broke the law. In this society, we can't just let that go."

Grinding her teeth, Elissa folded her arms as she lowered her brow, countering, "It's happening in this city every day. Armed robbers I've caught in the act and arrested were released the next day with clean records and I ended up catching them again. And they were released again!"

"Not from my court, they weren't," the judge assured with angry words. She leaned forward and folded her hands on the bench in front of her. "You'd better remember something, little girl. This is *my* playground, not yours, and if you're here to convince me to go easy on your bank robbing friend here then you're going about it the wrong way! Do you really think you're going to butt heads with me in my courtroom and win?"

Elissa glared back at her for long seconds, then finally she turned her eyes down and sheepishly answered, "No, ma'am."

"That's a little better!" the judge announced. She leaned back again and stared at the girl for a moment before she spoke. "Look. I get why you came here. I read your report and I get it. But you have to understand that he still broke the law and has to answer for that."

Nodding, Golden Angel turned her eyes back to the judge and assured, "I understand, your Honor, but please. Please remember what drove him to what he did. Putting him in prison for twenty years or whatever will teach him nothing. He knows what he did was wrong. He knows that. But making him a burden for the people to support for decades will not fix what he did."

The judge looked down to the file on the bench before her.

"There has to be another way," Elissa insisted.

Diana raised her chin and said, "Perhaps there is." When all eyes found her, she continued, "Roger was a computer technician before he turned to crime." She glanced at him. "I think he can work off his debt to society in that role."

Her eyes narrowing, the judge asked, "What role is that?"

"We can put him to work at Justice League Headquarters," Wonder Woman replied. "Our computer mainframe is huge and rather complex, and we do find it in need of maintenance more frequently than we'd like, and it has to be kept running twenty-four seven." She looked to Roger. "With the Justice League looking after him, I don't think he'll be able to cause trouble for anyone again."

The judge shifted her attention to him and just stared at him for a moment, then she leaned forward and folded her hands on the bench again. "Mister Merrill it seems that you have some determined people in your corner today. Despite who they are, I'm still not overlooking the fact that you tried to rob a bank and took hostages. Therefore, your guilty plea has been entered into the record and your sentence will be ten years."

He turned his eyes down, bowing his head as he nodded in slight motions.

Elissa's heart sank.

Picking her pen up, the judge wrote something in his file and continued, "You will be remanded to the custody of the Justice League and you will serve your sentence there. You're their problem now. I suggest you make the best of this opportunity and stay out of trouble. You'll be released into Wonder Woman's custody this afternoon." She closed the file and stood, announcing, "Court will adjourn for lunch."

Everyone in the courtroom stood as the judge turned and strode out of the side door behind the bench.

Before the bailiffs took him from the courtroom, Roger turned and looked up at Wonder Woman, smiling slightly as he offered, "Thank you. That was a generous thing you did and I won't let you down."

She nodded to him, a little smile on her lips as she assured, "We just wanted to see justice done. That and I'd heard you were a pretty good computer technician."

"Yeah," he confirmed softly. Looking to Golden Angel, he approached and dared to grasp her shoulder. "Thanks for this. You didn't have to come here and do this and I'll be grateful for the rest of my days."

Staring at the floor, she smiled and shrugged. "I wish I could take credit for what happened here today."

Later, after they all left the courtroom, Diana strode down the courthouse hallway, her eyes panning back and forth until they finally locked on her daughter.

Elissa sat on a marble bench by the wall. Her legs were pressed together from her toes to her knees and she had her forearms crossed over her lap. She was looking down the hallway the other direction and her huddled posture told Diana that something was wrong.

Approaching slowly and with gentle steps, Diana sat gingerly beside the girl, looking to her with a little concern in her eyes.

With a deep breath, Elissa offered, "Thanks for watching my back."

"Sure," Diana assured. "What's troubling you? We won the day in there."

"You won the day in there," the girl corrected. "If I'd been in there by myself she would have sent him to prison forever."

Diana's lips tightened.

Elissa turned her eyes down. "She was right, you know. I wasn't really Wonder Woman. I was just a wannabe. I don't have what it takes to be half the hero you are. I never will."

With a little smile, Diana stroked her daughter's hair gingerly with her fingers. "Little One, you are all the hero you need to be right now. And you have to think about something else. You haven't been doing this for very long. The influence that many of us have comes with time and experience, many years of helping people."

"I was lost in there," Elissa pointed out. "I didn't know what to do or say and I almost failed him horribly."

"You didn't, Angel. You went to his defense when others would have left him to his fate. Isn't that the very definition of a hero?"

The girl shrugged. "I guess."

"Think about something else. I'm not going to be Wonder

Woman forever. When I've parted ways with this role in my life, who do you think will pick up the mantle of Wonder Woman?"

"Aunt Donna," Elissa answered straightly.

Raising her brow, Diana agreed, "Well, yes. Probably. And it's a good thing, too. We would not want the world deprived of an up and coming heroine by the name of Golden Angel."

Elissa finally, slowly turned her attention to her mother, meeting her gaze with very sad eyes. "Golden Angel can't seem to do anything right and she can't do anything on her own. She's not the heroine you think she is."

"Listen to me," Diana ordered. "Think back to when you found Roger in that bank surrounded by his hostages. Think about that day. What would I have done? What would Superman have done, or Batman, or Black Canary or Huntress? Roger would not have been a misunderstood man; he would have been a bad guy to take down. He would have been a target to be dealt with to save the hostages, and he would be on his way to prison right now for a long time. You got everyone out safely, you saved those hostages without a fight. More importantly, you saved Roger." She slowly shook her head. "I would not have thought to try and understand him. He had a gun pointed at people. That's all I would have seen. As much as you still have to learn, believe me when I say the rest of us are learning from you."

Elissa turned her eyes away and considered, and she really did not know what to say.

"Hey," Diana summoned, and when she had her daughter's gaze she asked, "Since when does Golden Angel succumb to self-doubt?"

Staring back at her mother for many long seconds, the girl finally answered, "Since that day Red Panzer kicked the crap out of me." She forced a breath from her. "Mom, that was my first real test and I failed so badly. And then I failed again the next time. And look how many others have—"

"Angel!" Diana barked. "We have all felt the sting of defeat at one time or another. The important thing is to learn from those losses and become better."

"He almost killed me," the girl whimpered as tears welled up in her eyes. Looking down, she shook her head and softly admitted, "I'm still having those nightmares. He's going to come back, I just know it, and he'll come back stronger than ever. I couldn't make it with the Titans, I couldn't beat Joker or Bane or..."

"Superman can't quite hold his own against Metallo," Wonder Woman pointed out.

"I can't either," Elissa reminded.

"Then there's something you two have in common," Diana said with a smile. "There is a reason J'onn selects the teams he does for certain missions, and he's selected you specifically for many of them."

"Yeah," Golden Angel grumbled, looking down at her gauntlets. "Send in the second string to get some playing time when the game is easy."

"Or," Wonder Woman corrected, "send in the most qualified player for the game. One day at lunch he told several of us how much easier his job is with you on the team." When the girl's eyes snapped to her, she smiled and nodded, confirming, "He did. You have to remember that not everyone approaches every problem with pure brawn."

"Like who?" Elissa mumbled with a disbelieving tone.

"Like..." Diana raised her brow. "Batman." She tapped the girl's forehead. "That is his primary weapon, not his weapons or his car or his fighting skill. And when he does need to fight, he still outthinks his opponents. He fights with his brain first and relies upon his skill when he has to."

Elissa looked away again. "I guess he does."

"Do you remember when you beat Panzer in the warehouse?" Diana asked.

"If you want to call that beating him," Golden Angel snarled.

"I do call that beating him, and there is a reason he could not match you that night. You weren't fighting like an Amazon and you weren't fighting like the girl I trained or the girl he had fought before." Diana grasped her daughter's neck with both hands and pulled her to her, touching her tiara to Golden Angel's as she whispered, "You won because you fought like your father."

Elissa's lips parted in surprise.

"And you didn't even know him," Diana informed with a little smile. "You followed your instincts just like he does and you used everything at your disposal, everything around you to prevail—just like he does. Sometimes you are more like him than I'd like to admit, more like him than I've ever been comfortable with, but when you are like him and you call upon your beautiful heart, that is when the greatest hero in you emerges." She kissed her daughter's cheek, then whispered in her ear, "You are the daughter of Batman and you are the best of him and much more."

Grasping her mother's arms, Elissa whispered back, "I think I'm the best of both of you, just a little shorter."

Wonder Woman giggled and hugged the girl's neck. "Yes you are, Little One."

"Excuse me," a man asked from close by.

They both looked to see a bailiff staring down at them with his brow high over his eyes.

"Uh," he stammered, "pardon the interruption," His eyes cut to Golden Angel, "but the judge would like to see you in her chambers."

Elissa felt her heart pound hard behind her breast and she turned uncertain, fearful eyes to her mother.

Diana simply nodded to her, then stood and pulled the girl up with her, ordering, "Lead on."

"Um," he started hesitantly, "she only asked for Golden Angel. Would you mind waiting here?"

Swallowing hard, Elissa drew a breath and turned a less than confident look up to Wonder Woman.

With a reassuring pat on the shoulder, Diana said, "Go on, Angel. I'll be right here." She winked and looked to the bailiff with a hard expression. "And the judge should know that I should not be kept waiting long."

WW

The judge's chambers were exactly what Elissa expected them to look like as the bailiff led her in. The U.S. Flag was on a pole behind the huge oak desk. The walls were paneled in dark wood and bookshelves covered the wall behind the desk and almost all of one side wall. There was no window, but the three lights that hung from the high ceiling lit the room very well. The carpet was deep and well padded beneath, red in color and appeared to have been recently cleaned. Two thick framed chairs faced the desk and a couch of similar design was on the right, flanked by two tables that held heavy looking lamps. This was a nice looking room, and yet was an imposing place.

Very quickly, her eyes found the judge, who sat in a high back, black leather chair behind the desk. Though there was a computer on one side of the desk, she wrote on a pad of paper in front of her and had a stack of files to her left. What she was writing seemed to have her full attention through the glasses she wore.

The bailiff cleared his throat and informed, "Your Honor, I have Golden Angel here like you requested."

Still writing, the judge nodded and offered, "Thank you. That will be all. Please close the door on your way out."

He nodded once and turned to leave.

Pangs of panic began to erupt in Elissa's stomach as she turned and watched the bailiff leave and her breath caught within her as he closed the door. Slowly, she turned back to the judge, standing there near the door with her feet close together. Nervously, she tugged on one finger as she watched the judge write.

"I don't mean to be rude," the judge assured, "but I have to finish this. I'll be just a moment."

Elissa's mouth tightened and she nodded, offering, "No problem. Take all the time you need."

The room became a deafening silence but for the scribbling the judge was doing.

Finally, the judge put her pen down and pulled her glasses off, rubbing her eyes for a second as she set them on the parchment she had been writing on. "I hope you understand why I had to do that in there," she said. Looking to the young heroine, she extended her hand to one of the chairs. "Please. Have a seat."

Hesitant to approach, Golden Angel did so with apprehensive steps and settled herself gingerly in one of the red cushioned chairs. The stare the judge was giving her was one of impatience, almost despair.

Folding her hands on the desk, the judge straightly said, "You struck a nerve with me in there."

"How is that?" Elissa strained to ask.

"The rotating door that the justice system of this city has become," the judge answered. "I found it pretty upsetting when you said it was..." She looked down to her hands. "I pass sentence and the next thing I know the appeals court throws out the case. Not just cases of circumstantial evidence that could be brought into question, but air tight cases. Half of the scumbags they let out don't even have arrest records within a couple of days." Her eyes shifted to Golden Angel. "When you were posing as Wonder Woman... Sorry, when you *were* Wonder Woman the crime rate suddenly dropped. My weekly case files went from thirty or forty to only a handful. Make no mistake, young lady, you were having a huge impact out there."

"Most of those I caught still got right back out," Elissa pointed out.

With a nod, the judge confirmed, "I know. Someone downtown even made arrest records and certain reports disappear. It's like a lot of the people who get locked up were never arrested."

Her eyes narrowing, Golden Angel slowly raised her chin.

"You may not like me," the judge went on, "but let's get one thing clear right now. Something is going on in this city. When you guys took down that Red Panzer character and his cronies, that made a dent for a while, but now it's winding up again. Between you and me, I don't think he's done."

"I don't either," Elissa reported.

"Do you know what you're going to do about it?" the judge asked.

Turning her eyes down, Golden Angel shook her head and admitted, "No. I wish I did." She looked back to the judge and assured, "But I'm not doing this alone anymore. I'm in the Justice League now and we have a lot of resources to go after him with when he resurfaces."

"That's good to know, Golden Angel. Good to know. I don't want to keep you, but I do want you to know that you have an unconditional supporter in this office. I'll do whatever I can to help." The judge raised her brow. "And whenever you get tired of globetrotting with the Justice League, I'll be the first one to welcome you back here. I hope you can consider this city your home."

Elissa smiled, suddenly feeling her confidence surge back in the presence of this imposing woman. "I think I can pull that off, your Honor." She seemed to relax as she leaned back in her chair, crossing her legs and folding her hands on her knee. "So, what can you tell me about Police Commissioner Panetti?"

WW

The Police Commissioner's office was much as it had looked the last time Elissa had visited. The big wooden desk sat directly in front of the window and was cluttered with files and paperwork, an open laptop computer, pens and a lamp. Book cases were burdened with different books, awards hung on the walls, the leather couch looked like it had been slept on recently, the two chairs stood ready in front of the desk and the little refrigerator hummed away to keep the contents nice and cool.

The Commissioner, a thin woman whose short hair was streaked with a little silver and was well styled, was wearing a blue business suit with the collar of her white shirt open and stood from the chair behind her desk, holding her palms to the petite Amazon just on the other side of her desk. "Look. I don't know what you're talking about. I know there's a problem with the court system in this town but I can assure you that my department is not part of that problem! For God's sake, we've been running ragged trying to get the streets cleaned up!"

Golden Angel folded her arms, her eyes locked suspiciously on the Commissioner's. "I have sources who tell me that police reports are disappearing from this building and only someone with high level security clearance could make that happen."

Commissioner Panetti's brow tensed. "Are you trying to accuse me of something?"

Slowly, Golden Angel closed the last of the distance to the desk with two steps and she planted her fists on it, leaning toward the thin woman she stared down. "If you don't have anything to hide, then you don't have anything to worry about."

"I don't have to stand for these accusations," Panetti hissed.

"No you don't," the young Amazon agreed. "Of course, I haven't actually accused you of anything, have I? You just need to be warned, Commissioner, if I find out you are in any way working for Panzer then I'm not going to be in a very good mood the next time I visit here."

"That maniac that killed Pauline?" the Commissioner barked. "If I had my way we'd hunt him down and lock him away forever! You can't possibly think—"

"I think nothing," Golden Angel shouted. "He nearly killed me, too, remember? He'll no doubt try again. He tried to kill other police commissioners as well, and if you aren't working for him then you'd better believe you're a target."

Commissioner Panetti's mouth fell open as she stared back at the young Amazon with wide eyes. She looked down at her desk as she sank slowly back into her chair. "Oh my God," she breathed. "And you couldn't stop him when he killed Pauline."

Those words stung and Elissa found herself clenching her teeth. "Look," she finally said, "we're watching for him, waiting for him. As soon as he surfaces then he'll have to face the brunt of the Justice League."

"He almost killed Superman," the Commissioner pointed out, still staring blankly at her desk. "He almost killed Wonder Woman, almost killed you... Do you really think you can stop him?"

"We're ready for him this time," Golden Angel assured. "Look. You've been losing the confidence of the cops who work for you. You've lost the confidence of a lot of people. It's time to clean up your department, find those who might be working for the other side and deal with them, and find out where the leak is where you are losing these reports on repeat criminals."

Panetti finally looked up at her. "Are you going to come back and help out?"

Elissa averted her gaze, staring over the Commissioner and out the window. "I'll see what I can do."

"Or maybe the real Wonder Woman can spare some time," Panetti added.

With a blink, Golden Angel's eyes shifted back to the commissioner, and she ground her teeth.

Panetti fearlessly met the Amazon girl's eyes. "You weren't all that effective against him. If you had been then Pauline might still be alive. I believe you promised to protect her and I believe you failed."

Pushing off of the desk, Elissa wheeled around and stormed toward the door.

Springing to her feet, the Commissioner barked, "Golden Angel, wait!"

Elissa stopped just short of the door and glared down at the doorknob.

"That was out of line," Panetti admitted. "I'm sorry." She looked down to her desk. "There's been activity in the warehouse district again, north side. I've been too afraid to send investigators. I didn't want to provoke anything." She drew a deep breath. "Look. This guy's gone right through the Justice League's heavy hitters and God only knows what he's up to. Under the circumstances, I just don't want to get in his sights."

Half turning her head, Golden Angel spat, "So let the people you're supposed to be protecting take the brunt of the punishment so that you don't have to get hurt, huh?"

Commissioner Panetti just stared down at her desk for a moment before answering, "How would you feel about going up against him again? I don't have Amazon strength and skill and bullet deflecting bracelets to call upon. If he comes in here again, I'm dead. End of story."

Elissa turned fully and folded her arms.

"I'm afraid," Panetti admitted softly, "just like you were that second time you faced him. I know that's no excuse, but... Golden Angel, I have a city to protect and I have no idea how I'm going to do that with this unstoppable maniac on the loose. I suppose when you left to join the Justice League I lost hope that I could do this with him still out there. Then that Doctor Shipley character who did that to you—"

"It wasn't Shipley," Elissa corrected, "it was Crane. Scarecrow."

Slowly, the commissioner's eyes raised to find the young Amazon.

Raising her chin slightly, Golden Angel informed, "Apparently he's working for Panzer, too, but the last time I saw him he was in Gotham."

"Let's just hope he stays there," Panetti breathed.

Setting her hands on her hips, Elissa asked with harsh words, "So are we going to stay at odds or do you think we can work together?"

Panetti just stared at her for long seconds, then she drew a breath and asked, "What do you need from me?"

WW

Elissa stormed outside of the police station. Her blue eyes were fiery pits of focus and intensity.

"Hey," Diana called from behind.

Stopping, Golden Angel spun around to see Wonder Woman

leaning against the marble wall with her arms folded and the sole of one boot propped against the wall.

Wonder Woman pushed off of the wall and approached the girl, raising her brow as she asked, "So how did it go?"

Her eyes narrowing, the Amazon girl folded her arms and grumbled, "She's hiding something. She talks like she's afraid, but something is definitely up with her. She did spill that there's something going on in the north warehouse district but she also said she's afraid to rock the boat and provoke Panzer into coming after her."

"Did she seem genuinely afraid?" Diana asked.

Elissa looked away and shrugged. "It's hard to tell. She seemed like it and I felt she was to a point, but she's still hiding something."

Wonder Woman nodded. "And you think our answers lie in that warehouse district."

Turning her eyes up to her mother's with a blink, Golden Angel just raised her brow in response.

"We'll check it out, then," Diana assured, taking the girl by the back of the neck to turn her. "But not today. I believe you have somewhere to be."

When they turned to the street, they found themselves swarmed by nearly a dozen reporters and cameramen who rushed toward them.

One, a man in an expensive looking suit, held a microphone to his mouth as he asked, "Wonder Woman, would you care to comment on the identity of your daughter's father being revealed?"

A well dressed woman behind him caught up with her cameraman and also held a microphone as she almost demanded, "Wonder Woman, are you and Batman still dating?"

Other questions poured forth and Diana turned exasperated eyes to her daughter.

With a shrug, the Amazon girl sheepishly offered, "Sorry."

A smirk took Wonder Woman's mouth as she assured, "I've got this, Junior." Turning back to the reporters, she held her hands up and ordered, "Quiet, everyone! And all of you take a step back!" When they complied, she set her hands on her hips and reported, "I know what you all heard, but as usual what was said was taken out of context. I also watched the news report and I can see where you might have been misled. Let me assure you that Batman is not Golden Angel's father."

A low rumbling rippled through the crowd of reporters.

Elissa raised her brow as her eyes slid to her mother.

"The identity of Golden Angel's father is not anyone's business but ours," the Amazon Princess continued. "He was a good man and his anonymity will be protected. Period. When Golden Angel came here, Batman was kind enough to take her under his wing, to be a father figure to a girl who did not know her father, and the fact that she would consider him so, to address him so, is a great honor."

"So her father's dead?" the woman asked.

Diana looked to her, then she scanned the reporters and assured, "This issue is over and I would like to have Golden Angel's private life and mine left as such: Private. If you wish to have any interviews with either of us in the future then you will respect our wishes and allow this issue to rest."

As the two Amazons strode past the mob of reporters, more questions were asked but ignored, and the reporters seemed to know not to pursue them.

Some distance away, Mother and Daughter walked side by side down the sidewalk, and the young Amazon turned her eyes up to her mother again, this time with her brow arched.

"So," the girl began, "Batman's not my dad?"

Diana shook her head. "Nope."

"Then who is my dad?"

Her eyes cutting to the girl, a little smirk took Diana's mouth as she replied in a low voice, "Bruce Wayne is your dad."

Elissa puzzled, then, "Um, aren't they kind of the same guy?"

Looking forward again, a strange little smile curled the Amazon Princess' mouth as she replied, "No, Junior, not even close."

CHAPTER 13

It was a moderately busy week, but Elissa found herself distracted much of the time and the only focus she found was fighting crime. She called Zack a few times just to hear his voice and had many long conversations with him. If those around them didn't know better they would swear that the two were dating, as some of these conversations would last a couple of hours.

Time seemed to accelerate each day and, before she realized, it was the day of the prom.

The sitting room of Terrance's luxury suite had been converted to a large work station with the tools and supplies of the fashion trade distributed about and covering nearly every chair and table in the room. Terrance himself, dressed in white slacks, a light green button-up shirt with huge sleeves that were cuffed at the wrists and black sandals, stood in front of the door to Stacy's bedroom with his hands on his hips as he waited for the door to open. Stacy stood beside him wearing an oversized pink tee shirt and a short black skirt. Wearing her hair up in a bun, she stood beside the fashion guru as she also waited for the door to open.

A knock at the front door drew their attention.

"Terrance will take care of this unspeakable intrusion," he informed as he turned that way. Reaching the door, he seized the handle and pulled the door open with an angry motion, barking, "Who would dare disturb the important work that—" He gulped a deep breath, his eyes widening as they met Wonder Woman's.

She raised her brow and asked, "Is this a bad time?"

"Never for you, Goddess Diana!" he assured as he stepped aside. "Please enter and allow Terrance to make you welcome!"

As she strode into the penthouse, Stacy smiled a huge smile and rushed to her, wrapping her arms around the Amazon Princess' waist as she squealed, "I knew you would come."

Diana hugged her tightly and informed, "There is nothing that could make me miss this."

Terrance closed the door and announced, "Goddess Elissa should emerge any moment in her stunning new gown. The alterations were perfect and Terrance's little Lamb designed every detail to absolute perfection."

"That's the part I came to see," Wonder Woman informed as she turned toward the door to the bedroom.

They all approached the door, stopping about ten feet away, and there they all waited a moment.

Slowly, the door handle turned, and just as slowly the door opened.

Terrance and Stacy wore proud smiles as they saw the little Amazon in her new dress and with her hair up. Diana drew a gasp, her eyes widening as she saw her daughter dressed formally for the first time.

Slowly, Elissa strode out of the room, nervous eyes darting from one person to the next as she emerged. The dress sparkled as she moved and rustled just a little. The skirt was all the way to the floor and nearly the same color blue as the trousers she wore as Golden Angel. White stars ringed the bell of the skirt and two lines of them ran on the outsides from her waist to the floor. A gold belt wrapped around her waist and separated the skirt from the top, which was bright red, fit her very tightly and was strapless, leaving both of her shoulders and her upper chest bare. Her Golden Angel symbol was across her chest and was the highest point on the top piece, yet low enough to show off just enough of her generous bust line. When Terrance ordered her to twirl around with a simple gesture with his index finger, she did so, belling the skirt out as she did and showing that her back was completely bare all the way to the gold belt except for a broad red strap right under her shoulder blades that held the top piece in place. Her hair was worn up with long, curly locks that ran from just behind her temples and almost all the way to her shoulders. Her eyelids were lightly painted blue, there was just the hint of blush on her cheeks and she wore an unflattering, nervous expression on her face. Her tiara was on her brow and long gold, star shaped earrings that were studded with many diamonds dangled from her ears, drawing attention to her long neck.

Her eyes darting about from one person to the next, the girl swallowed hard and asked nervously, "Well?"

Diana looked her up and down once more, nodding as she replied, "You are absolutely stunning, Little One."

A little smile curled Elissa's red lips. "Really?"

Stacy answered for her, "Oh, most definitely. You are totally hot in that gown."

Looking down at the gown she wore, Elissa took the skirt in her hands and pulled it up from the floor a few inches, then she ran one hand over her belly before looking back at them. "I sure hope I don't have to fight in this!"

"It is not to make fighting," Terrance informed, "it is to make Goddess Elissa look fabulous." He strode toward her, looking down at the gown as he performed his usual tugging and fussing over what she wore. "Yes, everyone will recognize Goddess Elissa as Golden Angel and they will marvel over her stunning presence." His eyes shifted to hers. "And Elissa will wow everyone with her beauty and light feet on the dance floor, yes?"

"I hope so," she mumbled, looking away. "I am so nervous!"

Diana laughed under her breath and shook her head, setting her hands on her hips as she said, "You'll face down Metallo and take on people who are shooting at you and you're fine. One little dance and you're a nervous wreck."

Stacy turned a smile to the Amazon Princess and informed, "I've noticed that about her. By the way, I did her hair and make-up earlier. Does she look okay?"

Approaching the little Amazon with slow steps, Diana nodded and assured, "She looks beautiful, Stacy. You did a wonderful job with her."

"I had a beautiful subject to work with," the petite fashion designer informed.

Looking around the side of the girl's neck, Diana commented, "Nice earrings."

"Thanks," Elissa said shyly as she reached up to touch one. "Daddy gave them to me."

"He sure did," Diana confirmed. "Okay, are you ready to go?"

The little Amazon grimaced and informed, "I haven't decided on shoes yet."

"Here we go," Stacy mumbled.

Terrance grasped his chin, looking down to the bottom of the skirt as he considered, then he announced, "Red Stilettos in patent leather and four inch heels." He looked to Stacy and raised an eyebrow.

"Definitely!" the short young woman exclaimed. She glanced around, finally finding a stack of boxes in a chair near the couch. Hurrying to it, she beckoned to Elissa when she got there before turning to pull the right box from the middle of the stack.

Followed by her mother and Terrance, Golden Angel paused as Stacy pushed other boxes and a slip over on the couch, then she turned and sat down when directed to.

Stacy sat on the floor in front of her and took the first red high heeled shoe from the box. They were made mostly of a few thin straps and one slightly thicker one that would buckle around the ankle. Brushing the skirt aside, she grabbed the young Amazon's ankle with hurried motions as if she could not wait to get the shoe in place.

This was something Elissa was not accustomed to and she looked up at her mother with an uncomfortable expression, and got a reassuring look back.

With both shoes in their places, Stacy sprang up and took Elissa's hands, ordering, "Come on! Let's see how they look!"

Elissa lifted her skirt and looked down at the high heeled shoes she now wore, shoes that fit her perfectly. "Wow," she mumbled. "I sure hope I can dance in these."

"You'll do fine," the short blond girl assured. Checking her watch, her eyes widened and she declared, "Wow! You've got to go!" She took the young Amazon's shoulders, raising her brow as she ordered, "And I'm going to want every detail as soon as you get back!"

Elissa nodded and assured, "No problem." She drew a breath and turned toward her waiting mother. "I might have to go throw up first."

Laughing under her breath, Diana took the girl's arm and led her toward the door, assuring, "You'll be fine, Junior. Let's go."

Outside the hotel, the doorman held the doors open for Wonder Woman and Golden Angel as they emerged. Evening had settled and darkness was kept at bay only by the artificial lights all around.

And Golden Angel was looking up at the taller Amazon,

complaining, "I am so nervous!"

"I'm guessing such jitters are to be expected," Diana said as she stared at the long black car ahead of them. "You just need to relax. Oh, and remember to eat while you're there."

Venting a sigh, the girl looked forward and grumbled, "Yes, Mother." She stopped about ten feet short of the street, her mouth falling open at the sight of the big black limousine that awaited her with the driver holding the door open. Still slack jawed, she turned wide eyes up to her mother.

Diana pushed her along, asking, "Did you really think we'd let you ride your bike to this thing?"

Elissa slid into the huge rear compartment of the car first, looking around her at all of the lights, the leather ceiling, the deep carpeted floor…

Diana pushed her the rest of the way in and sat down beside her.

Their destination was not terribly far and Elissa was quiet for most of their trip, just staring out the window at the passing scenery.

Nudging her daughter with her elbow, Diana offered her a little smile when she got her attention. "I thought you'd be anxious about getting there, Little One."

"I am," the girl confirmed as she looked back out the window. "Just nervous."

"What are you nervous about?" the Amazon Princess asked.

With a shrug, Elissa softly replied, "I don't know." Her attention snapped back to her mother and she desperately asked, "Are you sure I look okay?"

Shaking her head, Diana assured, "You are beautiful, Junior. I'll bet every girl there will wish she was you. Just hold your head up and show everyone that confidence that you show the world as Golden Angel."

Elissa nodded and her eyes strayed. "Confidence. Yeah, just show confidence." She felt the car take a couple of hard, low speed turns, then it stopped, and her anxiety seemed to double. Grabbing onto her mother's hand, she loudly announced, "Okay, I'm seriously freaking out a little!"

"You'll do fine, Junior. Just image that someone is going to shoot at you."

"Not funny, Mom." Elissa drew a hard breath as the door opened and she gave her mother one more desperate look.

"You're going to do great," the Amazon Princess assured. "You have my every confidence. Now get out there and show them what a little Amazon can do, and for Hera's sake have some fun!"

With a nod, Elissa offered, "Thanks, Mom."

Diana kissed her daughter's cheek, then motioned with her head to the waiting photographers. "Go on, Junior. Have a great time."

The gymnasium had been decorated in spectacular form. The hundreds of silver stars and crescent moons that hung from the ceiling sparkled as they moved about to the limits of the wires that held them. A huge ball made of thousands of mirrors rotated slowly right in the middle of them. Long, sparkling ribbons of tinsel were hung from seemingly everything, including the tables that were off to one side and the buffet beyond. Above the stage was an arch that bore the words that described the prom's theme, words that were in huge, glittery letters and read, *The magic of the night sky.* A band was beneath the arch, which on a second look appeared to be more of a shooting star, was playing a song with a slow rhythm to it, one ideal for slow dancing. There were many formally dressed kids about, hundreds it looked like, and as the door closed behind the little Amazon they all seemed to stop what they were doing and look her way.

Elissa's eyes darted about nervously as she felt everyone's attention on her. Finding Zack in here was her first priority, and that did not seem likely. Drawing a deep breath, she slowly strode in a few steps, waggling her fingers at a group of girls and offering an uneasy smile as she approached. She was startled as someone grasped her shoulder from behind and she spun around, smiling broadly as she looked up into Zack's eyes.

He wore a black tuxedo with tails and the look of him in it took her breath away. When he took a step back from her, she took the opportunity to look him up and down, and noticed he was doing the same.

Zack took her hand and gently raised it up to her chest level, and only when she felt something wind around her wrist did she notice the corsage he held, the same one he was slowly tying around her wrist.

Elissa swallowed hard, her full attention on what he was doing.

She found catching her breath to be something of a chore, and when the pretty flower was in its place, she finally turned her eyes up to his.

Without a word, he turned and backed toward the dance floor, pulling her with him by the hand, and she followed easily. Once there, he pulled her to him and took her little waist in his big hand, and her hand found his waist. They moved as one to the music that was playing, staring into each other's eyes. While they still had the attention of nearly everyone in the gym, neither seemed to notice anything around them as they slowly danced. Nothing else seemed to exist. Elissa forgot all about the lessons she had been given by her father and Mister Cobblepot. The movements were more instinct, automatic as she followed his.

The song ended and he turned toward the tables, once again leading her by the hand to where he was sitting.

Covered in white cloths, the long tables were clearly to accommodate eight students at a time and the table he took her to already had four there: Two boys and two girls. Centerpieces were blue and silver rockets surrounded by yellow flowers and there were two at each table.

Zack pulled a chair out for her and she daintily settled into it, brushing her skirt back as she sat down. He pushed her chair in effortlessly, then took her shoulder and asked, "Would you like some punch or something?"

She nodded and looked up at him, offering a smile as she replied, "That sounds great." Watching him stride toward the buffet, that anxiety began to return as she realized she had been left alone with four other kids she did not know, and her eyes slowly strayed to them. All of them were staring at her, and the thin girl with the blond hair who wore a very nice and somewhat revealing teal gown did not have an approving look for her.

The other girl had long, curly black hair that she wore up and a light blue gown that contrasted her very dark skin, and she rested her elbow on the table and her chin in her palm, giving Elissa a hard stare before she finally observed, "So you're Golden Angel."

Elissa only glanced at her before turning her eyes down to the table and nodding as she replied, "Yep, that's me."

"Uh, huh," the girl in blue said with a disbelieving tone. "And how are we supposed to believe you're really her? I always heard she's an Amazon and that her mother's Wonder Woman."

"All true," Elissa confirmed as she folded her hands on the table, staring down at them and feeling more and more like this was yet another place she did not belong.

Sitting right across the table from her, the boy with the girl in blue, also very dark skinned with very short, curly black hair and wearing a navy blue tuxedo, huffed a laugh and shook his head as he chided, "This ain't Golden Angel. Zack's crazy if he thinks he can pass her off as an Amazon."

The other boy, a fair skinned fellow with red hair who looked to be about as big as Zack also laughed.

Now they weren't just doubting her, they were mocking her date, and this simply did not sit well. Slowly, her eyes shifted to the dark skinned boy who sat across from her, her brow low over them as she asked, "And who exactly are *you* supposed to be?"

"Name's Todd Marshal," he replied with a raise of his chin. "I'm the Rocket's All-State Linebacker and starting power forward for the B-ball team."

She nodded in slight motions. "Uh, huh. Sure you are."

He clearly did not like that and folded his hands on the table as he leaned toward her. "You dissin' me?"

With a slight raising of her brow, she nodded, then asked, "What do you intend to do about it? I'm guessing you won't do anything because you don't want to get shown up by a girl."

Todd laughed under his breath and looked to his red haired friend. "This chick's trippin'!"

Everyone laughed, and Elissa just smiled.

Zack set her drink down in front of her and sat down beside her, looking to the other boy as he ordered, "Just cool it, Todd. Believe me, you don't want to mess with this chick."

"Come on, Zack," the girl in yellow said. "We know this ain't Golden Angel. Just give it up!"

Todd added, "Yeah. Why would she want to come to prom with you, anyway?"

Elissa looked to her date and just shrugged.

The girl in blue shook her head and asked, "How much did he pay you to come with him, Honey?"

Giving her a long stare, Elissa looked back to Zack and raised her brow. "These are friends of yours? Really?"

"Usually," he mumbled.

Rolling her eyes, Golden Angel leaned back in her chair and forced a loud breath from her, finally asking, "Okay, so aside from someone shooting at me how do I prove I am who I am?"

"You can't," Todd insisted.

"Why don't you arm wrestle her?" Zack suggested.

Elissa looked to him and hissed, "Zack! What if I hurt him?"

Todd laughed, then slammed his elbow onto the table and held his hand ready to receive hers. "Oh, it's on now! Come on! Let's see what you got!"

She turned an unsure look to Zack, then shrugged and leaned forward, planting her elbow and taking his big hand in her own small, dainty looking hand. "Just so we're clear on this," she warned, "if you get hurt it's your own problem, kay?"

"Whatever," Todd laughed.

Zack stood and grasped their clenched hands, looking to them in turn. "Ready?"

Staring at each other, they both nodded.

The girl in the teal gown looked hard at Elissa's forearm, her gauntlet, and her eyes widened as she stammered, "Um, Todd..."

Lifting his hand, Zack barked, "Go!"

Clearly, Todd meant to end this contest quickly and humiliate this girl definitively, and to that end he poured all of his strength into taking her arm over.

Golden Angel's arm moved about an inch as Todd strained against her with all his might, lowering his head as he fought to slam her hand down.

Showing no effort at all, Elissa rested her chin in her palm as she stared at him and held him in a hopeless stalemate. She just watched his struggle for a few seconds, then finally raised her chin from her hand enough to inform, "He said go."

Todd turned perplexed, fearful eyes to her.

Elissa raised her brow. "You ready to start or what?"

He poured in one more surge of power, throwing his weight into the effort, and this time her hand moved another inch or so. Finally, he grabbed on with his other hand in a last ditch effort to defeat her.

With a little smile, Golden Angel glanced at her date, and when he smiled back and nodded to her, she finally looked to her opponent and slammed her hand down along with both of Todd's, and he stumbled from his chair when she did.

Massaging his right hand, he stood fully and backed away, his wide eyes locked on her.

She still had her chin in her palm as she stared back and informed, "You have to dance with me now." A little smile touched her lips and she winked at him.

The red haired boy drawled, "Whoa!"

Zack glanced around at his friends and finally introduced, "By the way, guys, this is Golden Angel. Angel, this is Marci, Cody, Tanya, and you know Todd."

Elissa looked to them in turn and waggled her fingers at them, greeting, "Hey."

Todd sat back down, his wide eyes still on the Amazon girl as he absently said, "You really are Golden Angel." Suddenly he loudly declared, "That's wicked sweet, man!"

Everyone else stood and approached her, extending hands and trying to tell them what huge fans they were, and she did her best to accommodate everyone.

Another girl, a very thin young woman who wore thick glasses and wore a white gown that almost looked too big on her, hesitantly approached the table, hugging a notebook to her chest as she did. Her full attention was on the young Amazon and she seemed fearful, but when Zack's friends were all seated she closed the last few strides and drew a deep breath as she greeted the young heroine with an enthusiastic, "Hi!"

Elissa looked up at her and smiled, and did not have the chance to say anything before the notebook was thrust at her.

"I don't want to bug you," the thin girl assured, "I just wanted to see if you would sign my book. I got Wonder Woman to sign it a couple of years ago and a bunch of others."

Taking the notebook, Golden Angel nodded to her as she said, "I'd love to." She set the book down and opened it, asking, "Where did Wonder Woman sign it?"

"Two more pages," the girl answered enthusiastically.

Elissa turned two more and, sure enough, found her mother's

signature right in the middle of the page. Looking up to the thin girl, she started, "I don't have a…" She stopped as she saw the girl offering her a pen and she smiled as she took it. "You came prepared." Looking down to the notebook, she added, "I like that." She wrote a message, signed *Golden Angel* in as big a print as her mother had, then closed it and offered it back.

"Thank you!" the thin girl squealed as she snatched the book from Elissa's grip. Spinning around, she seemed to dance as she made her way to her own table and group of friends, most of them girls.

Zack bumped the Amazon girl with his shoulder and warned, "You'd better get ready for more of that."

She smiled and bumped him back with her shoulder, shyly saying, "Oh, it's cool. I don't mind." When the music resumed, her attention snapped toward the dance floor as kids began to head that way, and she smiled and grabbed onto his hand, springing up as she barked, "Come on!"

Everyone from the table rose and followed them to the dance floor in the center of the gym.

Time simply blurred by. Elissa found herself having the time of her life and for the first time she found herself enjoying the company of kids her own age. She danced almost nonstop, pausing between sets of music to allow her date to rest, taking some time to nibble on what the buffet offered, drink punch, and many times she would dance with other boys while Zack caught his breath, especially Todd who she insisted owed her a dance or two. Other girls who had felt threatened by her presence early in the evening found themselves embracing her and very soon new friendships were being forged. She shared her attention as generously as she could and the smile she wore did not leave her lips very often. For a few hours, nothing else in the world existed, and for the first time in her life she was simply a normal, seventeen year old girl.

Finally, they all found themselves back at the table where they laughed and talked of whatever was on their minds. Only background music played for a few minutes, this presumably to give everyone a break and many of them needed it.

While this happened, the girl in the white gown who had asked for an autograph earlier in the evening approached the table with hesitant steps and was accompanied by four other girls behind her, two of whom dealt with weight problems and all of whom seemed to have issues with self esteem. This was a group that found itself shunned by their peers, but this night they seemed eager for the attention of a young superheroine.

"Hey," the girl in white greeted.

Elissa half turned and looked up at her, then to her friends and offered them a huge smile. "Hey, Dudes! I haven't seen you out on the dance floor much tonight. What's up with that?"

One of the plump girls, with long black hair and wearing a frilly pink gown, replied, "We couldn't all get dates." She seemed a little resentful of this and it was clear in her tone and not lost on the young Amazon.

The music resumed and Golden Angel looked toward the dance floor, then she smiled broadly and sprang up, knocking her chair over as she grabbed the white clad girl's arm and looked over her shoulder to the table, announcing, "Come on! Girls only this time!" Shepherding all of them to the dance floor for another long round of dancing, she had a fresh spring in her step and this time the boys were content to just sit and watch.

Todd rested his elbow on the table and his cheek in his palm as he watched his date with Golden Angel and about thirty other girls. "Man, I tell you. She's something! Any more at home like her?"

Zack smiled and shook his head as he also watched. "She's an only child."

"That's too bad," Cody drawled.

While the music was fast and the beat was good, Elissa and the other girls stayed on the dance floor, sometimes dancing in pairs and sometimes in groups. After about ten minutes of this, and after most of the other girls present had joined them on the dance floor, Elissa and her group from the table trotted back that way as fast as their high heels would allow and hurriedly took their seats, and all of them pushed away from the table and reached down to their ankles.

Tanya threw one of her shoes onto the table and immediately reached for the other, mumbling, "Yeah, that's what I'm talkin' about."

As the other two girls rose from their chairs, Elissa set her shoes on the table and grasped Zack's arm, assuring, "I'll be back in a little bit."

He just watched as she and the other girls, now all barefoot, charged back out to the dance floor.

Todd shook his head as he watched them and said, "Boys, this night just got a whole lot more interesting."

Eventually, slower music resumed and the girls were joined out there by their dates.

Elissa held onto Zack's shoulders as his hands had her waist, and she stared up into his eyes as they slowly danced across the floor. A little smile would not leave her lips, and finally she said, "This seems kind of familiar."

"What does?" he asked, smiling back.

"Looking way up at you like this," she replied. "Those four inch heels evened us out just a little."

"I kind of like it better this way," he informed, "but you sure looked hot in those heels. Want to put them back on?"

"They kind of hurt my feet," she informed. "I don't know how women can wear them all day."

He just shrugged.

A rumbling of conversation among many people started all at once and they looked that way, toward the front door, and Elissa's heart sank.

Wonder Woman strode in with Black Canary and Fire right behind her. She stopped about ten feet in and scanned the gym, her eyes finally locking on her daughter. Seeing the disappointment on the girl's face, her lips tightened, her brow tensing as she felt it a little herself.

Golden Angel looked back up to Zack and grimly informed, "I think it's time for me to go."

Zack looked toward the door, toward Wonder Woman, then he turned his eyes back to his little date and held her a little tighter. "You know, I think they won't mind waiting until the song's finished."

"You trying to get me into trouble?" she asked with her brow high over her eyes.

He shook his head. "Just trying to hold onto you every second I can."

Elissa smiled and drew a little closer to him, sliding her hands to the backs of his shoulders.

The song finally ended and he held her hand all the way back to the table. All of his friends met them there and the girls reluctantly sat down to put their shoes back on.

Just holding hers in her lap for a moment, Elissa stared down at them and vented some frustration in a hard breath, then she looked to Zack and offered, "Thanks for a great time tonight."

Diana had approached unnoticed and took her shoulder, smiling when her daughter looked up at her. "How's the prom?"

Black Canary set her hands on her hips, adding, "And where's the little girl's room?"

The thin girl in the white dress led the way as a group of girls approached the table. "Hey Angel, we just wanted…"

All of their faces lit up and eyes widened as Wonder Woman turned to face them.

"Wow!" One of them shouted. "It's Wonder Woman!"

Grasping the thin girl's shoulder, Black Canary asked, "Do you know where the little girl's room is?"

"Black Canary!" she squealed.

Glancing at Diana, Black Canary nodded and confirmed, "Yeah. Now can you—"

"Will you sign my book?" the thin girl in white begged, clasping her hands together.

Canary growled a sigh, then conceded, "I'll sign whatever you want!" She grabbed the thin girl's arm and barked, "Little girl's room! Now!"

Folding her arms, Fire watched as her colleague was escorted across the dance floor, and she shook her head. "I told her not to drink all of that tea before we left." She saw a boy out of the corner of her eye and she turned to face him. He was of average stature and wearing a black tuxedo and white shirt, and thick rimmed glasses. His hair was slicked back and he had the olive skin of someone of Latin descent. Raising her chin to him, she asked, "You come with a date?" When he shook his head, she approached him and suggested, "How about you get me some punch then?"

He gratefully took her side and led the way to the buffet.

Wonder Woman looked down at her daughter and folded her arms. "Have you been dancing barefoot all night?"

Elissa shrugged and admitted, "About half of it." She held her shoes up and informed, "These kind of hurt my feet to dance in for long."

Raising her brow, Diana confirmed, "I hear you, Junior." She looked around her as the music resumed, and she nodded. "Looks like quite a party."

Still holding her shoes in her hand, Elissa stood and faced her mother, a begging tone in her voice as she asked, "Mom, is it okay if I stay for just one more dance?"

Wonder Woman's eyes found Cody and she patted her daughter's shoulder as she stepped around her. "Do what you want, Junior." She looked to Marci and asked, "Mind if I borrow him for a few?"

"Be my guest!" Marci offered.

When Cody stood, Diana took his arm and turned toward the dance floor, stopping as Elissa took hers.

"We aren't leaving?" the young Amazon asked.

Diana smiled at her. "I said I'd be here at ten. I didn't say anything about leaving at ten."

A broad smile overpowered Golden Angel's lips and she watched her mother stride onto the dance floor with her date's red haired friend, and she said in a low voice, "Best mom ever."

Zack stood and took her hand, pulling her out toward the dance floor as he announced, "You heard Wonder Woman. Let's get out there and dance!"

The atmosphere of the prom grew even more festive with three of the Justice League's finest present and taking turns borrowing other girl's dates. They also took time to sit and chat with students and the teachers who were chaperones. Wonder Woman even danced with the school's principle!

Eventually, time wore down and midnight approached. Weary prom goers were more content to sit and talk while others plotted what to do after leaving the prom. Still, the mood remained festive and all spirits were high. With only a half hour left, about a quarter of the kids had already departed for all night parties they would attend after.

With the evening starting to draw to a close, something was still missing and Elissa was unsure what to do about it. Another round of fast dancing was clearly not going to do it and when they retired from the dance floor this time they returned to their table, which was littered with mostly empty plates and plastic punch cups and the girls' shoes and sat down to catch their breath. Diana, Black Canary and Fire all joined them there.

Flopping down in her chair, Golden Angel still wore a smile as she looked to Tanya and declared, "Best prom ever."

"Yeah girl!" Tanya concurred.

Marci stood and said, "Bathroom."

Elissa and Tanya also sprang up and they all headed that way, and Elissa looked over her shoulder at Zack, giving him a shy, sweet little smile when she saw him.

He smiled back and waved to her, just sitting there and watching as she hooked her arms into the other girls' and strode away.

Fire folded her arms and looked down at him, bluntly asking, "So have you kissed her yet?"

Zack and his two friends all looked to her, and he asked, "Who? Oh, Elissa?" He looked back toward the bathroom and stammered, "Um... Well, no."

Raising her brow, Wonder Woman set her hands on her hips and barked, "So you haven't kissed my daughter?"

Not looking at her, he shook his head and assured, "No, Ma'am, I haven't."

Black Canary strode up behind him and slapped the back of his head with a loud pop, demanding, "What are you waiting for?"

Rubbing the back of his head, he looked back at her, then to Wonder Woman, confusion in his voice as he managed, "Huh?"

Fire explained, "She's waiting for her prom kiss."

He looked nervously up at Wonder Woman, his eyes a little wide as he started, "I'm, uh..."

"You're on your way to disappointing her," Diana scolded. Her eyes narrowed and she added, "And believe me you don't want to disappoint my daughter."

Zack exchanged looks with his friends, then stood and turned fully to Wonder Woman. "You, uh... You *want* me to kiss her?"

Black Canary stepped up to him and poked him in the chest. "Look, bonehead, every girl wants that special kiss on that special night, and believe me, if she leaves here disappointed then we're all not going to be real happy with you."

"Yeah, come on, boy," Fire insisted. "Don't let this chance slip through your fingers."

Todd informed, "I would have already. In fact, I've been kissing Tanya all night."

Half turning, Zack pointed out, "Yeah, but Tonya's your girlfriend."

Diana took his shoulder, drawing his attention back to her and she offered him just the hint of a smile. "Tonight, Golden Angel is *your* girlfriend, and yes I'm okay with you kissing her, just this once." She glanced behind him and backed up a step, mumbling, "Here she comes. Fire, Canary, let's check out what's left of that buffet before they put it all away."

Elissa, Tanya and Marci arrived at the table just as her mother and the other two Justice League heroines were departing, and they all watched as the three women strode with purpose toward the buffet.

"What was that about?" Elissa asked as she turned her attention back to Zack.

He just shrugged, then took her shoulder and said, "I'll be right back, okay?"

She watched as he strode quickly and stiffly toward the stage, leaning her head slightly as she wondered what he was up to.

Marci sat down and grabbed her shoes, grumbling, "I guess it's time to put the pain givers back on."

Tanya moaned and reached for hers. "If I didn't look so good in these I'd throw them to the curb."

Golden Angel also sat down, taking one shoe and pulling her skirt up to see her foot. "They really should outlaw these things. I mean, it's not like guys have to wear uncomfortable stuff like this."

Cody looked to Todd and barked, "We had to come here in tuxedoes to impress you guys!"

All three girls said in one voice, "Wah!"

As Elissa finished buckling her other shoe, Zack finally returned and offered her his hand. "I think we have one more dance in us, Angel."

She looked up at him and a little smile curled her mouth as she slipped her hand into his. When she stood, a slow song began to play, a perfect dance song, and she held his hand as he led her to the dance floor. Todd and Cody both took their date's hands and all of them followed.

Holding her hand in his, Zack slipped his other hand around her waist and pulled her close to him, closer than he had held her all night. As they moved slowly to the music, Elissa slipped her hand around his back, looking up into his eyes as they danced. Suddenly, the world seemed to disappear and all that was left was the two of them and the music they danced to.

He raised his hand to her face, gently brushing her cheek with the backs of his fingers as he offered, "Thanks for coming with me."

"Thanks for inviting me," she countered.

"I wish this evening could go on forever," he said in a low voice.

"Me too," she confirmed, her hand slowly sliding up his back. "Unfortunately, things are as they are and at midnight I'll turn back into a pumpkin."

He laughed and shook his head. "I wish things were different and you..." He trailed off and looked away.

"And what?" she prodded.

"If you were just a girl here at school, do you think you'd be my girlfriend?"

Elissa's lips tightened, and when he looked back down to her she nodded. "Yeah."

He smiled and his fingers brushed across her cheek again, but this time his hand opened fully and he cupped her neck right below her ear and slowly lowered his mouth to hers.

Closing her eyes, Elissa raised her chin and met his lips gently with her own.

Wonder Woman, Fire and Black Canary were all watching from the buffet tables across the room, and all three simultaneously raised a hand to their chests and loudly drawled, "Aw!"

Zack's kiss turned into more than just the meeting of his lips to hers and Elissa gratefully received the passion he offered her, raising her hand to his head and gently grasping the back of his neck as he pulled her closer to him.

The moment seemed to last hours, and still it was over much too quickly as the song ended.

He drew away slowly and met her eyes, and they both shyly smiled. Zack would not ruin this moment by speaking and this time took her under his arm instead of by the hand and the two clung to each other as they slowly strode back toward the table.

Leaning her head against his chest as she wrapped her arms around him, she drew a deep breath and confessed in a wisp of a voice, "That was nice."

"Yeah," he whispered.

Wonder Woman met them there, setting her hands on her hips as she announced, "I really hate to end this fairy tale but I'm afraid we have to go."

Still leaning on her big date, Elissa looked up to her and nodded, barely able to call on her voice as she conceded, "Okay, Mom."

Diana, Black Canary and Fire led the way, saying their farewells to those they encountered as they made for the front door, followed closely by the young Amazon and her date. Once outside, they found the limo waiting and Golden Angel's heart felt a little heavy as she saw it.

Halfway there, she stopped and turned toward him, and he took her hands. They stared into each other's eyes, savoring this last moment of their first and final date together.

"I guess we say goodbye now," he said softly.

She nodded, her eyes glossed by tears as she could only muster, "Yeah."

Zack raised a hand and brushed her cheek with his fingers once more, then he grasped the back of her neck and pulled her to him for one last kiss, one which they took the time to enjoy.

Finally, reluctantly, Elissa pulled away from him, holding onto his hand until she had backed out of reach. With one last smile at him, she slowly turned to the limousine and slipped between her mother and Black Canary.

"Angel," Zack called after her. "If you're not doing anything later tonight, there's this after-prom party at—"

"Good night, Zackary," Wonder Woman bade pleasantly but with a slight tone of warning as she slid into the car after her daughter.

Waving awkwardly, Zack said, "Okay, then. Good night."

As the door closed and the women settled in, Elissa snuggled in close to her mother and laid her head on her shoulder, closing her eyes as a sleepy little smile curled her mouth.

Sitting on the seat right across from them, Fire and Black Canary exchanged smiles and long looks before turning their attention back to the girl.

Diana slipped her arm around her daughter's shoulders and pulled her in tight, also smiling as she asked, "You had a good night, then?"

Elissa smiled a little broader and drew a deep breath before announcing, "Best night ever. It was just... just perfect."

Kissing the girl's head, Wonder Woman stroked her hair and said, "I'm glad you had fun, Junior."

Slowly, Elissa nodded.

"I guess you're okay spending the night at the mansion, aren't you?" Diana asked.

Elissa did not respond.

Fire whispered, "She's fallen asleep."

Nodding, Diana informed, "She's had a big night. I hope she'll remember this for a long, long time."

"I guarantee it," Black Canary assured in a low voice. "She looks so sweet and innocent sleeping like that. Diana, how did such a sweet girl come out of you?"

The Amazon Princess' brow lowered over her eyes as she looked to the blond woman across from her.

CHAPTER 14

It seemed that the best way to evaluate Golden Angel's abilities in combat was to have her spar in the Watchtower's holographic training facility in her crime fighting garb. The setting chosen was a rundown street in the middle of an unnamed city that was littered with a few broken down cars and trash and junk. Many of the buildings were clad in either faded red brick or gray cement and most of them had windows broken out. Her opponent this day was a fictional bad guy who was dressed in the black, loosely fitting attire of a ninja and was quick and very agile. The strength on this holo-robotic opponent had been turned up to surpass that of the little Amazon he fought and he seemed just a little quicker as he threw punches and kicks at his elusive little opponent. A black wrap covered his face and head and he wore a blacked-out visor over his eyes. His sword was still on his back and he seemed to be relying on his skill to outfight his much smaller opponent.

Standing some distance away, Batman watched without expression as his little daughter dodged away again and again, occasionally deflecting a strike on a gauntlet or rolling over her shoulder to evade a kick.

Wonder Woman stood beside him, a proud look on her face as she watched the girl, and she was shaking her head. Finally she shouted, "Angel, quit messing around and just finish him!"

Elissa smiled and finally held her ground. The ninja charged and threw a hard punch that she easily swept aside and as he tried to throw a kick she wheeled around and slammed her heel solidly into his chest.

As her opponent fell, she turned to her parents and set her hands on her hips, barking, "A ninja? Really? That's the best you could do."

Raising her brow, Diana pointed out, "And that was level nine. Dinah only spars this simulation at level seven."

"Computer," Batman summoned, "resume session at level twelve."

The ninja sprang back up with an angry yell and his small opponent casually turned to face him.

With a glance at the Dark Knight, a little smirk took the Amazon Princess' lips as she ordered, "Computer, disable safety protocol." When Batman turned his head to give her a disapproving look, she simply folded her arms and advised, "Just watch."

They did watch. The ninja's attack was far more ferocious and after a moment he reached over his shoulder and drew his sword.

And Elissa smiled ever so slightly, readying her arms to meet this new threat. She engaged again, now facing an opponent of much greater skill who was brandishing a sword. Even at this higher level she seemed to have little trouble with him. Slashes of the blade that she did not dodge she simply knocked away with her gauntlets.

Diana glanced at the Dark Knight and asked, "Do you see it?"

"Do I see what?" he countered.

"How she fights," Wonder Woman replied. "I trained that girl her whole life in Amazon movements and tactics and she still falls back on her instincts." Her eyes slid to him. "She still fights like you."

He raised his chin slightly and informed, "Well, she does come from good bloodlines."

Diana smiled and bumped him with her shoulder, and he subtly bumped her back with his.

Once more the ninja hit the ground, and this time he stayed there.

Elissa, holding the sword she had taken away from her opponent, raised her brow and asked, "Anybody else need a butt kicking?"

"That's enough for today," Batman informed. "Go get something to eat and we'll catch up to you."

With a little nod, Golden Angel complied, "Yes sir," as she tossed the sword down and strode toward the exit behind them. She paused after she passed them and turned to ask, "Can I take on one of the simulations that you guys train with after lunch?"

"We'll see," Wonder Woman assured. "Just remember that you're on duty this afternoon."

With a little frustration in her voice, Golden Angel grumbled, "I know, Mom," as she whipped back around toward the door.

Entering an elevator down the hallway, she smiled as she saw

Green Arrow already there and greeted, "Hey, GA! What's happening?"

"Well hi there, other GA," he said with a smile. "Just on my way to meet Dinah for lunch."

She leaned against the wall beside him as the door closed, folding her arms as she observed, "So you guys are like an item or something?"

Slowly nodding, he replied, "Yeah, I guess you could say that."

They arrived at the cafeteria where Elissa filled her tray as usual and then parted company with Green Arrow to sit at a table by herself and allow Green Arrow and Black Canary some alone time.

As Elissa ate her lunch, a song she liked began to play from one of the pouches around her back and she was quick to reach back and remove the small, new cell phone, sliding it open as she raised it to her ear and greeted, "Hello?" She smiled. "Oh, hey Zack. What up?" She picked at her lunch with her fork and smiled a little broader. "Oh, that sounds fun. When is it?" Shaking her head, she went on, "No, I can't tonight. I have watch in a couple of hours. No, I don't get off until in the morning." She raised her brow. "I guess we can do lunch tomorrow. Where do you want to meet? Oh, yeah! I love that place! Just remember not to tell anyone you're meeting me there. About noonish? Yeah, sounds good."

She listened to him for a moment and took the opportunity to slip a fork full of fruit pie between her lips, and when through with that she took a long drink of milk before saying, "No, it's been kind of boring the last few days. Just not much going on, I guess. Oh yeah, I'm with some of my faves tonight." Smiling again, she picked at her lunch with her fork and said, "Well, Superman's here, and Green Lantern, Green Arrow, Mom, Black Canary... Yeah, there's a bunch of us. I hope so. I think Superman and I work great together." She took another drink of milk. "I don't know. We usually go in pairs or groups. It all depends on the mission." A shadow fell over her and she looked over her shoulder to see Fire standing beside her with her lunch tray, and she motioned to the seat beside her with her head. "Hey, I got to go. Can I call you tomorrow? Sweet! Okay, well enjoy the party and try to remember those of us who couldn't come. Catch you later."

As Golden Angel slipped the phone back into its pouch, Fire sat down beside her and raised her brow, looking intently to her as she asked, "Still seeing that boy from the prom?"

Elissa shrugged and looked back to her plate. "It's not like we're dating or anything, I just like spending time with him and his friends." Her eyes slid to Fire. "We are allowed a life outside the League, aren't we?"

"Well of course," Fire confirmed. "You just got to be careful about that life."

"Got it under control," Elissa assured. "He already knows I'm Golden Angel and I meet him wearing street clothes and my glasses."

"And nobody recognizes you?"

Taking another big bite of her pie, Elissa shook her head and replied, "No, it's a pretty sound disguise. Works for Superman, doesn't it? Besides I..." She trailed off as she saw Fire shift her attention slightly behind her. With some difficulty, she swallowed what was in her mouth and turned her head the other way, looking up.

Batman stared back at her with a hard expression and his arms folded.

Smiling nervously, Golden Angel waggled her fingers and greeted in a meek voice, "Hi." When he just stared back for a few eternal seconds, she swallowed hard and fear began to break through her features.

"You're still seeing this boy?" the Dark Knight demanded.

Hesitantly, she nodded.

Batman raised his chin slightly. "And you gave him your number?"

She pivoted in her chair to face him and defended, "Not to my official phone! I'm not *that* stupid!" More long seconds of his cold stare worsened that horrible crawl in her stomach and she barked, "Really!"

"What number did you give him?" he growled.

She stared back nervously before looking away. "Um..." she stammered. "I, uh... I got another phone."

Batman set his jaw.

"It isn't traceable to me!" she assured, looking back up at him. "I mean... Okay, it was Golden Angel who got the phone but they—"

"How are you paying for this?" Batman questioned.

This time she drew a deep breath before answering. "I got this prepaid plan and I paid in cash so that nothing can be traced, and once a month they send me a bulletin letting me how much I owe and I pay for it out of my allowance." When her father held his hand out, she knew to reach behind her and take the phone from its pouch, and surrender it to him. The anxiety she felt was clear on her face as he punched controls with his thumb and looked into the data she had there.

"How many people have your number?" he demanded.

"Just some of the kids from the prom," she replied nervously.

"How many?" he growled.

"Sixteen," she replied sheepishly.

"Including this Zack you were talking to?"

She turned her eyes away and corrected, "Seventeen."

He closed the phone and shifted his attention back to her. "Do you know what your enemies would do to the contacts you have here?"

Elissa lowered her eyes, now feeling frustration boil up in her as she said, "I just want some friends to hang out with. They aren't security risks and they aren't people who pose a threat to the world."

"You hope," he added. Setting the phone down on the table beside her, he turned and swept toward the door with long strides, ordering, "Just be sure you protect the information you have, Angel, and make sure that phone does not fall into the wrong hands. And don't get too close to this Zack kid. The last thing you need is some boy distracting you."

Looking to her father as the door slid shut behind him, a rare defiance took her eyes and a childish pout curled her mouth down. With her brow still low and her gaze still locked on the door her father had disappeared through, she slowly took the phone from the table, feeling humbled and a little humiliated. Again. But this time she was not so willing to be put in her place, not even by Batman.

WW

Golden Angel found herself brooding well into the evening, but really did not care. She wandered the station for a couple of hours, went back to the commissary for a snack of fruit and orange soda, went into the control room just to see what was happening, and finally she found herself entering the room she shared with her mother where she hoped to spend the rest of her shift alone. However, when the door opened, Wonder Woman turned from the bed and faced her, and she seemed surprised to see the little Amazon.

Setting her hands on her hips, Diana greeted, "There you are, Little One. Where have you been all night?"

Elissa folded her arms and looked away, mumbling, "Nowhere."

With a raise of her brow, the Amazon Princess observed, "Someone sounds a little cranky tonight."

"You agree with him, don't you?" Elissa demanded in a low voice.

Diana sat down on the bed, crossing her legs as she asked, "About what?"

"About me having friends outside of the Justice League," the little Amazon replied in a snarl. "About me going out sometimes to have fun with kids my own age."

"I agree he has reason to be concerned," Diana replied. "He told me you have a phone to use for personal use and I really don't see anything wrong with that, but you have to be careful with it, Little One."

Through clenched teeth, Elissa closed her eyes and growled, "Would you please not call me that! And maybe you guys can trust me for once. I'm not going to go out there and do something stupid. I just want a few friends to hang out with and have fun sometimes."

Leaning her head, Diana's eyes narrowed and she reminded, "You chose this life, Junior, and yes, sometimes it can be very frustrating, especially when you want to have a social life, too. If you want to do this then you have to learn to make sacrifices. That's just how it is."

"And there it is again," the little Amazon grumbled.

Diana stood and set her hands on her hips. "And there what is?"

"The way you talk down to me," Elissa barked, turning eyes that displayed her anger toward her mother. "I'm not a little kid anymore and if I'm not going to be an equal member of the team then maybe I don't belong here!"

Her brow tensing, Diana strode toward her daughter, stopping halfway there as she snapped, "Would you mind telling me why you are behaving this way?"

"Because I'm tired of everyone treating me like I'm a little girl!" Elissa cried. "You do it, the other League members do it, the authorities do it..." She threw her arms up and yelled, "The bad guys do it! I'm doing everything that everyone asks me to do and I'm still just a little kid to everyone! What the heck am I supposed to do to get even a little bit of respect from you guys?"

The Amazon Princess snarled, "You can start by not raising your voice at me. If you want to be treated like a grown-up you might want to start acting like one."

"There you go again!" Elissa shouted as she backed away a step. Looking away, she shook her head, not able to understand why she felt so frustrated, not knowing to care. "You know," she began again, unable to purge the frustration from her voice, "Zack's been wanting me to go out with him more. I think he really likes me and I think he might just want me to be his girlfriend." Her eyes slid angrily back to her mother. "I guess you would have a problem with that too, huh?"

"Yes, I would," Diana confirmed, "and I can give you a hundred reasons why that's a really bad idea!"

"Of course you can, Mom, because I'm too young to have a boyfriend, I'm too young to have friends of my own and I'm too young to have any kind of a life that's not under someone's thumb."

"That is not what I am saying at all!" Diana barked back.

"I'll always just be a little kid to you, but I'm not. Any good mother could see that by now!"

Diana's spine went rigid and she raised her chin. Though she maintained her composure, inside she struggled hard not to lose her temper. "Little girl, I may not be perfect but I've been a damn good mother to you!"

"Sure you have," Elissa countered. "A good mother can see that her daughter is growing up and maybe trust her to make some decisions on her own!"

Grinding her teeth, Diana growled back, "Your decision making hasn't been what I would call good."

"Yeah," the Amazon girl spat back, "a lot like yours. A lot like your decision to keep me away from my own father most of my life." She wheeled around and rammed her finger into the button that would open the door, finishing as she stormed out, "No good mother would have done that."

"Elissa!" Diana shouted as the door closed. Slowly, she approached the door and ever so gently placed her hand on it. Her hands shook and she bowed her head as she fought back the need to cry.

WW

This argument with her mother only caused others from the past to surge up into Elissa's thoughts to join it. Though she felt something was amiss, she could not realize it and did not really even think about it. She was able to put on a brave face for others but she avoided the other senior members of the League and found herself spending time with younger heroes and heroines who were on watch.

Hours later found her in the cafeteria again to enjoy another sizeable meal, this time with Fire, Black Canary, and Hawkgirl. She had managed to put the argument to the back of her mind and start having fun with those she shared the table with and they found themselves telling stories and laughing with each other, and for a while Elissa forgot she was the youngest person on the station.

This came to an abrupt end as a folder full of papers and photographs hit the table beside her tray of empty dishes and a tense quiet suddenly found them all as they looked to the folder.

Looking almost fearfully to it, Elissa turned her eyes up to the dark form who had come up on them unnoticed, and her eyes widened slightly.

Batman was as expressionless as he always was and just stared back, and a few tense seconds later he said in his deep, haunting voice, "I thought you might like to know a little more about this boy you seem to like so much. You should read that before you think about wearing his letterman's jacket." Without another word he turned and strode toward the doors, his cape sweeping ominously behind him.

She watched him leave, then she turned her eyes down to the folder. With hesitant movements, she slowly opened it with one hand and read the first page, then turned it over to read some of the second. This one she brutally pushed out of the way to reveal a couple of photographs, old and new pictures of Zack. Moving these aside, she read the pages under for a few moments, and tears filled her eyes. Slowly, she shook her head, then she covered her mouth with one hand and sprang up, running out of the cafeteria as the first sobs began to force their way out.

Fire, Canary and Hawkgirl watched after her, then they turned their eyes down to the folder.

Black Canary picked up the last page Golden Angel had read, her eyes panning back and forth, and her lips slowly drew apart. Looking to the door, she shook her head and murmured, "Oh, that poor girl."

Some distance down the corridor, Elissa finally stopped and slammed her back against the wall. With her boots pressed close together and pushing her against the wall behind her she bowed her head and fought back her tears as best she could. She did not want to cry but the issue seemed to be forcing itself with more determination than she had willpower. She raised a hand to her eyes, pulling a broken breath into her and struggling not to cry, struggling to regain her composure and be the grown-up she touted herself to be.

"Hey," someone greeted.

Her attention snapped that way and fixed on Atom as he stood in front of her with an expression of concern, and she was quick to wipe a tear from her cheek when she saw him.

"You okay, kid?" he asked.

Hearing him call her "kid" grated on her nerves but she did not succumb to the animosity she felt for it this time and just nodded, assuring, "Yeah, I guess." She looked away and folded her arms over her belly. "Atom, can I ask you something?"

"Sure," he replied.

She heaved a sigh as she stared down the corridor. "What am I supposed to do if I don't feel like I can trust anyone anymore?"

He folded his arms and answered, "Well, you have an advantage on the rest of us there, Angel." When her attention slid back to him, he went on, "You have that gift of insight that you seem to be using pretty effectively. Seems like that would tell you who you can trust and who you can't."

Elissa just stared at him for a few seconds as she considered, then, "But what if I really want to trust someone? Do you think that would cloud my insight?"

"It might," was his answer. Folding his arms, he continued, "I find that once you become aware of something then it's easier to deal with."

She looked down and nodded. "You make all of this sound pretty simple."

"Things usually are," he informed. "Most of the time we overcomplicate really simple things in our own heads. I've done that plenty of times myself." Reaching to her, he grasped her shoulder and asked, "Is there something you need help with?"

Slowly, she shook her head. "I just need to fix things, and—"

"Hey," he barked. "We're a team here, a family. We don't let each other go through hard times alone."

Staring back into his eyes, Golden Angel's mouth tightened and she considered what he had told her. She drew a long breath and said, "There isn't anything anybody can do. My parents won't let me have a life, there's a boy I really like who wants me to be his girlfriend and my parents have it in for him, Red Panzer is out there somewhere and I'm pretty sure he wants to kill me… I just can't deal with all of this!"

"Your problems are the team's problems, Angel," he countered.

"You're really sweet," she said softly.

He smiled.

Elissa turned and strode down the corridor, saying, "I have a call to make."

WW

Darkness was still a couple of hours away, but the streets of downtown Gotham always grew dark much earlier than dusk. Tall buildings were like dark and forbidding canyon walls. Street lights were already beginning to come on in areas and a few restaurants were bustling with activity.

One of these clearly catered to younger people. The neon sign that hung in the window was in the shape of a guitar and had the establishment's name in the center: *Strum*. A few tables were outside but most of the activity was inside where people still in high school gathered and even college students could be found in the booths or small white and chrome tables. Many of the people patronizing the restaurant had laptops open, many others had their cell phones out and were texting. Still more had come to socialize.

One, a rather large high school student wearing a black tee shirt and blue jeans, awaited someone, a girl he really looked forward to seeing. Standing near the entrance with his hands in his pockets, his attention darted about at the activities within, and often that attention would linger on some pretty girl who would appear in his field of vision.

"Zack!" he heard over the noise and music within, and when he turned he smiled as he saw who he was awaiting.

Elissa was dressed comfortably in a pink tee shirt, short white shorts with pink stripes down the sides and lightly made white slip on shoes. Her black hair was down and flowed to her mid back and she wore an expression of distress on her young face. In public like this she always wore her glasses, but this day she did not.

She hurried to him and fell into his arms as he turned to meet her, laying her head on his chest as he embraced her.

"You okay?" he asked with concern in his voice.

"No," was her reply. "We need to talk."

He led her to a booth and they sat down across from each other, and he reached across the table to take her hands. "You sounded pretty upset on the phone."

She nodded, looking down to their joined hands. "I don't think my mom wants me to see you anymore." She drew a breath, shaking her head as she went on, "She said awful things and I think she'd do anything to keep us apart."

"So what do you want to do?" he asked with gentle words. "I mean, considering who your mom is I don't think it would be a good idea—"

"I don't care!" she barked, turning her eyes to his. "This time I'm doing what I want and I'm going to see who I want!" Her voice softened and her eyes were suddenly glossy and vulnerable. "I really like you and..."

"You want to be my girlfriend?" he asked with a little smile.

Elissa stared back into his eyes, her own widening, and she bit her lip. With heavy breaths, she smiled and nodded to him, and she gasped, "Yes!"

He pulled her toward him and they both leaned across the table, Elissa standing as they drew closer, and she leaned her head and closed her eyes as he took her lips with his.

Later, they strode down the sidewalk in a part of the city that was away from the bustling crowds. A few businesses were still open, but there were more abandoned buildings here and the area was much dirtier. Weeds grew tall outside of abandoned warehouses across the street, but two teenagers hardly noticed. He had his arm around her and she walked close to him, one arm around his back while the other wound around his arm, and she held his hand tightly.

"You still seem kind of out of it," he observed.

She sighed. "Yeah, I just hate being on the outs with my mother like that, you know? I just hate when we fight, especially about stupid stuff."

"You think she'll warm up to me?" he asked.

Elissa shrugged. "I don't know. She's being a total... Well, she's not being very reasonable right now. I think we need to just keep us a secret until she comes around."

"Okay," he conceded. "So how do I get you out of this mood and get you to smile?"

"I don't know if you can," she snarled.

"Sure I can," he countered. Unexpectedly, his arm closed around her neck and his other hand came across her body, grasping her belly and side right under her ribs.

She jumped and squealed as he tickled her mercilessly and finally she twisted to try and get away from him, screaming, "Stop it!" Very quickly she was laughing uncontrollably and struggling in his tightening grip, screaming anew as he found that her hip was even more ticklish.

A short time they wandered down a darker street. The sun had set and only a few street lamps illuminated the street they were on. His arm was around her neck and draped over her shoulder and she held onto this arm with both hands as they walked. Silence went with them for a while and they just seemed to enjoy each other's company on this slow stroll toward nowhere.

Finally turning her head to look up at him, Elissa asked, "McDade street, huh? So are we going somewhere or just going?"

His eyes slid down to her and he smiled. "We're going to meet the gang at this place where we hang out. It's an abandoned building of some kind that we just kind of took over."

Her brow tensed. "Isn't that kind of trespassing?"

With a shrug, Zack replied, "I don't know. I know the guy who owns the building and he doesn't mind us being there."

She nodded and looked ahead again. "So where is it?"

He pointed ahead of them and answered, "Right down the street. That's the entrance over there."

"And the owner won't mind us hanging out there?" she pressed.

Zack shook his head. "No, he doesn't mind. In fact, the light's on and I'll bet he's there tonight."

"Cool," she said. "So I get to meet the whole gang and the guy who owns the building you hang in."

"Yeah," he sighed.

There was a long sidewalk to the front door of this old looking warehouse, a place that looked run down and had not seen maintenance for many years. There were office areas behind boarded up windows. The doors in were steel clad double doors that were dark and rusty. Most of the paint had faded and peeled from it and it was dirty, scratched and dented. One light dimly illuminated it from one side, and this had Elissa's attention, as did the numbers painted on the building right beside the door.

"Seven two seven one," she observed. "Sounds catchy. So, you've got electricity in this place, too?"

"Yeah," he confirmed, "we got power. There's a lot of stuff in there that we need electricity for." He reached over her shoulder and knocked on the door.

She looked back at him. "So is there a secret handshake I should know?"

Zack met her eyes and smiled a strange, possessive smile, and his brow seemed low over his eyes as he replied, "No, you don't have to learn a handshake." His eyes shifted to the door as the lock was turned. "You just have to say 'hi' to the head guy."

Elissa looked back to the doors as they opened and her eyes widened as they filled with Red Panzer! She drew a loud gasp and retreated a step, running into Zack and her hands went behind her, grasping his waist. Before she realized what was happening, his arm wrapped around her body, pinning her arms to her as his other hand slammed a cloth over her face and pressed it there. She screamed behind it and as she drew a breath her lungs filled with the acrid fumes that came from it. Zack's grip on her tightened and he lifted her from the ground as she struggled hard to get away from him, whipping her head back and forth as best she could with fearful and muffled cries, but he was very strong, unnaturally strong, and she could not match his strength.

She felt the strength drain from her. Her arms were quickly fatigued and fell to her sides, legs that had been kicking violently were suddenly still and her feet dangled half a foot from the ground, her eyes rolled back and closed and with one more desperate shriek behind the chloroform soaked cloth consciousness abandoned her.

As the girl went completely limp, Zack held her tightly to him, and finally he lowered the hand he held the cloth over her face with and allowed her head to roll forward until her chin rested on her chest. Dropping the cloth as he reached down and took her behind the knees, he swept her into his arms in one effortless motion and held her small frame to him, cradled in his thick arms.

Mechanical whines and hums sounded as Red Panzer strode from the doors, his attention locked on the unconscious girl.

Zack was also staring down at her, and slowly he looked up at the mechanical Nazi, raising a brow as he smiled almost evilly. "She came here with me just like you said she would, Herr Panzer."

WW

Elissa drew a deep breath through her mouth as she slowly awoke, first aware that her throat was very dry and a little sore. Struggling back to consciousness was a bit of a chore and a soft moan escaped her as she rocked her head to the left, then the right. She became aware of a very thin pillow beneath her head and the coldness of the air around her. Forcing her eyes open, she blinked to clear her vision and tried to sit up, and a gasp shrieked into her as she realized that she was strapped down! Looking down to her body, her eyes widened as she first saw the thick black strap that was across her shoulders. She felt another around her neck. Her wrists were tightly cuffed and secured to the bed or table she lay on with thick cable. She had been undressed and a white cloth was draped across her chest, another over her hips. Another strap held her legs down above her knees and still another bound her ankles together and to the platform she lay on. Still another was tightly across her hips, right over the white cloth that covered her.

No way! she thought, pulling against the cuffs that held her wrists. When they would not yield she tried again, clenching her teeth and pulling as hard as she could to free herself, but to no avail. Feeling a sting in her left arm inside the crook of her elbow, she raised her head as high as she could, seeing that an IV was plugged into her arm beneath a piece of white tape, and a new surge of panic swept through her. Glancing around her, she saw that she was in some kind of laboratory with white cabinets and shelves along two walls and what appeared to be medical equipment distributed about. "Oh, Hera!" she breathed desperately. With her heart pounding away within her, she cried out as she threw her head back and fought with all she had to break free.

"You may as well relax," a middle aged woman with a German accent advised. "I doubt if even your mother could break out of those restraints."

Elissa ceased her struggles and looked to the left to see a tall woman approaching.

With her black hair worn in a bun behind her head, the woman looked through thin rimmed glasses at a clipboard she held. Dressed in the white coat and trousers of a doctor or scientist, this was a woman in her forties or early fifties, one who clearly took care of herself. Her thin face was attractive but betrayed her years and her eyes, so dark brown they were almost black, shifted from the clipboard to the girl who was bound to the table.

Elissa stared dumbly back at the woman as she reached her.

Raising her chin, the woman's eyes narrowed and she observed, "You seem spirited. Well, we can surely take care of that."

"Where am I?" the Amazon girl demanded in a fearful voice.

"You will be told what you need to know," the woman snapped, "when you need to know it. Ask no questions and do as you are ordered to do."

As the woman turned smartly and strode toward one of the counters that was laden with lab equipment, Elissa barked, "They're going to come looking for me, you know!" She tensed as the woman laughed.

Shaking her head, the woman in the white coat held the clipboard to her and strode back to the helpless girl, shaking her head as she informed, "They have no idea where you are, little girl. You saw to that nicely yourself. They don't know where you are and they have no way to find you."

"They'll find a way," the little Amazon assured.

The woman bent close to her, boring into her with her gaze as she countered, "You are a naïve little girl to think so, and if they come, we will be ready for them."

Elissa was unsure what to say or do and just watched the woman return to her station across the room. She found herself a captive of an enemy she feared the most and she struggled to suppress the panic that tried to well up within her. Unable to break her bonds and with no tools to help her get free, she would have to rely on her wits, and she knew that would be a grim prospect at best. Even as she struggled for something to say, she heard the hiss of a sliding door to her right and looked that way, her eyes widening as Red Panzer strode through with his hands folded behind him.

He approached the table she was strapped to and stopped a couple of feet away, staring down at her from behind the blacked-out lenses of the metallic skeleton mask that protected his face. He was silent, simply standing there motionless.

The young Amazon's heart pounded and her chest heaved as she had to force each breath into her.

His deep, synthesized voice split the silence in the room with, "Are you afraid?"

She could only nod in response, unable to force her eyes from his.

"Good," he commended. "Perhaps you are finally learning." He slowly reached toward her, and the metal contacts in his palm and fingers buzzed as electricity surged into them.

Elissa cringed and shrank away, a breath shrieking into her as his hand neared her face, and finally she turned away and begged, "Please don't!"

The buzzing stopped and his metallic fingers gently stroked her cheek. "It is best you remember your place here, little girl. You will help me bring about the downfall of your people, and eventually the world. As I told you before: You will be a part of the New Order, or you will be crushed by it." Raising his face, he looked to the woman in the white coat who had turned to face him, and he ordered, "Begin the procedure."

Elissa gasped and looked to the woman who approached with a syringe that had a very long needle. "Um..." she stammered,

"What—what are you going to do to me?" She could barely breathe as she stared up at the woman who now stood over her with the syringe, and she shook her head. "Wait! Please don't do this to me! Please don't!" She looked desperately to Red Panzer, pleading, "Don't! Please don't!"

Ignoring the girl's pleas, the woman reached for her arm, taking the IV line and shoving the needle into a catheter in the line. Slowly, the liquid from the syringe was injected into the solution that was entering Elissa's vein from the IV bag.

"What is that?" the girl cried as she watched the plunger of the syringe push the thick liquid into the line, into her body! "What are you doing to me?"

The woman looked to Red Panzer and informed, "Since she is of Amazon bloodlines the serum should work quickly and we should see results almost immediately."

"Serum?" Elissa shrieked. "What kind of serum? What is it going to do to me?"

"Lie still," the woman ordered as she injected the last of the serum.

The first of it entered her vein and there was a warm sensation that began to travel up her arm, a sensation that was almost hot and grew hotter. The girl whimpered as she felt the sensation spread through her arm, into her chest. From there it began to spread all over her. Tears escaped from her eyes and she began to shake as the sensation grew more intense, more painful. Turning desperate eyes to Red Panzer, she cried, "It hurts!"

"Rest assured," he said, "the pain will grow much worse and in a moment you will be in agony you cannot even imagine."

Horror took her eyes and she began to shake. Muscles all over her started to cramp and every nerve started to feel as if they were starting to burn.

"When we complete the process," he went on, "you will be much stronger than you are now, just as I promised a year ago. Do you remember? The promises we exchanged? Do you remember my generosity?" He bent closer to her, his skeletal faceplate stopping only inches above her face. "Your betrayal?"

The pain started to become unbearable and she groaned against it, clenching her teeth as she began to shake more violently. Sweat began to bead up on her and in seconds began to roll from her skin. She turned away from him, tightly closing her eyes as she strained to say, "I didn't want you to do this to me."

"You were lying then or now," Panzer observed, standing fully and folding his hands behind him. "Now suffer for your betrayal."

His words reverberated in every particle of her being, everything she was and every thought and feeling. All of her body was under the control of the serum and she could feel a conflict inside of her, a war being waged with each cell. Panzer had been right. The pain that suddenly surged through her was far beyond her comprehension, far beyond anything in her experience and all control she had on all levels was lost.

Elissa threw her head back, her eyes tightly closed as she screamed a primal scream, her whole body shaking and convulsing. That same primal urge fought her bonds and poured every ounce of strength into that task. Conscious thoughts were gone and there was only the pain and the battle against her restraints. At some point, she mercifully fainted.

An unknown time later, perhaps hours, perhaps only moments or seconds, her eyes opened to thin slits. Shallow breaths were slow to enter her. Her entire body was sore and drained. Vision returned grudgingly, but she could hear voices.

"I don't understand, Herr Panzer," the woman said desperately. "It acted quickly and appeared to be working. I can only assume that her system rejected it and her Amazon immune system was able to—"

"Speculate on your own time!" Panzer roared. "You told me the serum would work on her!"

"I..." the woman stammered. "It must be her immune system. If we find a way to suppress it we may just succeed with an augmented serum."

Panzer growled.

Forcing her eyes open, Elissa looked sleepily to the big mechanical Nazi. She blinked to clear her vision and as he came into focus she was sure he looked annoyed as his attention was locked on the tall woman in the white coat.

"This is still experimental," the woman explained in a shaking voice. "It was meant to be used on those of normal bloodlines and I thought the—"

"Save your explanations for another time," Panzer snapped, turning his attention down to the restrained girl. "I have other uses for her. Keep working, Doctor, and remember the penalty for failing me."

Elissa could feel the anxiety that surged up in the woman and she looked that way, seeing her staring up at Red Panzer with wide, horrified eyes.

In stiff motions, the woman turned to the workbench and assured, "I shall not fail you, Herr Panzer."

Red Panzer turned and strode toward the door, a door that wisely slid open as he approached.

Elissa watched the door close, then she looked back to the doctor and raised her brow, observing with a sleepy voice, "He sure seems mad about something."

WW

Given a long white tee shirt to cover herself, Elissa was escorted into a lower level, a brightly lit area with white painted walls and a white tile floor. It seemed even more antiseptic and sterile than the laboratory she had just left. The floor was very cold on her bare feet but she barely noticed, and she did not put up a struggle against the two black clad people who escorted her down the wide corridor, each of them holding one of her arms in a grip that was slightly less than painful.

The black body armor they wore was identical to the genetically enhanced people she had faced before, but she did not recognize either of these two. One was a man with military cut brown hair. The other was a woman with very short cut dark blond hair. They both wore shiny boots that covered their shins, belts with an array of close-in weapons like knives and short clubs, and a few black canvas pouches that no doubt held other equipment. Each clop of their boots was as one and echoed from the concrete walls all around them, easily drowning out the little Amazon's soft foot falls.

Doors lined the hallway about every twenty feet, but up ahead they were much closer together, and this is where she was taken.

Their silence was unnerving and Elissa glanced to each of them in turn, finally looking up at the big man on her left. She cleared her still dry throat and asked, "So, how is the food around here?" When she got but a sour glance in return, she nodded and looked forward again. "Yeah, I figured. I guess ordering pizza's out of the question."

The woman jerked on her arm and ordered in a harsh voice, "Quiet!"

"Ow!" Elissa complained, shooting the woman an irritated look. "Stop it or I'm telling Mister Panzer!"

A door slid open and she was shoved inside to stumble to the middle of the eight by eight foot room.

Stopping herself, she wheeled around as the woman entered behind her and stopped only a step inside.

Setting her hands on her hips, the big woman raised her chin and warned, "You are being watched. Do not try to change and do not try to escape. If you misbehave in any way you will be gassed. You will notice the vents that feed air to the room on either side."

Elissa looked, seeing two very small vents on the walls at her sides.

The woman continued, "We can flood this entire room in seconds and you will be unconscious before you hit the floor. You will remain quiet and wait for someone to come for you. If you are not then you will receive a visit you will not like. Do you understand?"

Hesitantly, the girl nodded.

Without speaking further, the woman backed from the room and the heavy metal door slid shut.

Elissa took a moment to look around her. There was one bed on a side wall, a small and simple bed that was neatly made and had a single white blanket and a flat pillow on top of it. A lavatory was right across from the door and a metal stool was perfectly centered on the far wall. The walls were white; the ceiling was white metal grate with bright light filtering through it. The floor was gray concrete and polished, very smooth, very cold.

Looking up, she saw two black, metallic domes that were about the size of tennis balls that were clearly cameras, one in the opposite corner of the other.

She drew a deep breath, folding her arms over her chest as she scanned the room once more, then she turned and stepped onto the bed, turning to pick up the pillow as she took its place. There, she sat down and pressed her back to the corner of the room, hugging the pillow to her chest as she drew her legs up. Burying her chin in the pillow, her eyes were pools of fear as she stared blankly across the room.

And waited.

WW

Despite her situation Elissa drifted off to sleep where she sat, slumping over to one side to be caught by the concrete wall. Her chin still rested in the pillow she hugged to her and her head had rocked over and gently come to rest against the wall. She still sat huddled where she was and slumbered peacefully for a time unknown. Even as a hiss sounded from the door as it slid open she did not awaken.

Someone kicked the bed and her eyes finally flashed open, blinking as they struggled for focus.

The two black clad guards were back, and the woman ordered, "Get up. Herr Panzer has summoned you."

Elissa stared back at the woman for long seconds before she slowly straightened her legs and laid the pillow back in its place. Planting her palms beside her hips, she hesitantly slid toward the edge of the bed and stood, shrinking away from the guards as they reached to her and took her arms.

Back down the corridor and to the elevator door, they stood there as they waited for the elevator car to arrive.

She looked to the man again and asked, "So, is it dinner time or what? I'm starving!"

His eyes slid to her and he remained expressionless.

With a raise of her eyebrows and a nod, Elissa looked back to the elevator doors.

The doors opened and she was escorted in and once again held between them.

"Any idea what Mister Panzer wants me for?" she asked as the elevator ascended. "I'm hoping he doesn't want to try that stuff again. That really hurt." She looked to the woman. "So, you've had it done. Did it hurt that much when—"

"Quiet!" the woman snapped through bared teeth.

Elissa wore a frown as she looked back to the doors, grumbling, "Well if you're going to be mean I'm not going to talk to you."

"Then I'm going to be mean!" the woman snarled.

Huffing a breath through her nose, the little Amazon looked up at the man who held her other arm and asked, "Is she always a total—"

"I'm mean too," he interrupted.

She looked back to the doors and mumbled under her breath, "You're also a butthead."

Elissa was taken to a rather large room, one that appeared to be an emptied gymnasium of some kind. The floor was concrete as were the walls and the high ceiling was covered with that same metal mesh that protected the many lights that illuminated the room. About thirty by thirty feet, there was another doorway across the room, one that was closed by two doors that were each about two and a half feet wide. As she was escorted in, Elissa froze as her gaze was filled with Red Panzer.

He stood in the middle of the room, staring at her through the lenses of his metal, skeletal mask. Two of his black clad minions were at his sides, two very large people, and he dwarfed them both. Slowly, his hands clenched into fists.

Though she had managed a small victory against him almost a year ago, Elissa still found herself terrified of him, found herself trembling, and her mind was a whirlwind of panic. When the guards took her toward him, she no longer walked so easily with them, drawing back as they forced her closer to the huge, mechanical Nazi.

Panzer's attention remained fixed on the terrified girl as she was forced closer to him, and he set his hands on his waist as she was stopped and held before him well within arm's reach.

Elissa could not take her eyes from his as she was held forcibly under his gaze. Each breath into her was forced and carried enormous weight. In an instant, she felt her confidence nearly gone.

Looking to the guards who held her, he motioned with his head for them to back away, and they released her and complied.

No longer restrained by the powerful guards, Elissa still found herself unable to move or even avert her gaze from her massive captor. She shrieked as he reached for her face, but still could not bring herself to retreat, not that there was anywhere to go, anyway. When he cupped her jaw in his big, metal hand, she tensed and held her breath as she expected him to shock her and she drew away ever so slightly.

He raised her face, tightening his grip on her slightly. "Just as before," he observed. "No fight in you? You aren't willing to do battle with me again?"

She shook her head in quick motions.

Panzer nodded, then released her and sidestepped around her.

Tensing up, Elissa's eyes followed him as he strode around her toward the door, but she did not move otherwise. Closing her eyes, she forced herself to purge the terror she felt from her. Wonder Woman could do it. Wonder Woman always seemed to control everything around her from within her own heart and mind. Surely Wonder Woman's daughter could do the same. Slowly drawing a breath, she forced the horrifying images of her fate from her, forced her own personality to return. What was going to happen was going to happen and it was time for her to just accept that. When she did, a strange peace washed through her, a peace that she was sure came from her heart, that most precious gift given her by her mother.

Opening her eyes again, she realized that it was time for her to go to work, time to be the heroine that was expected of her, and the young woman that these people were sure was broken. With a clear mind, she looked to the big, black clad people who had been standing at Panzer's sides. They did not follow him, and both looked to her with hard expressions.

And Elissa's eyes locked on the woman. She recognized the red hair, now in two long braids, and she recognized her face, her build, those hard eyes. Turning slightly toward the big woman, Elissa set her hands on her hips and said, "Ursula?"

The woman raised her chin slightly.

Everyone in the room turned toward her.

With a big smile, the little Amazon, strode toward Panzer's red haired minion and ultimately wrapped her arms around the woman's waist, hugging her tightly as she declared, "Wow, girl! It's been, like, forever!"

Ursula turned a rather uncomfortable look to Red Panzer.

Drawing away, Elissa looked over the big woman and nodded, her gaze fixing on her hair as she said, "Now that is a totally cute look for you! Those braids are seriously hot!"

Hesitantly, Ursula raised a hand to one of the braids that was draped over her shoulder.

Elissa folded her arms and nodded, assuring, "Yeah, that totally

works on you. You've got that whole Bohemian strong woman thing going on." She leaned her head. "I don't know if black's your color, though. If I live through the day we can try some stuff out..."
Panzer cleared his throat behind her and she turned around, seeing that the white clad woman from the laboratory had joined him. "Oh, sorry. My bad. We were just catching up." She glanced around her and asked, "So what's up in here, anyway?"

Red Panzer looked to Ursula and the other guard and motioned with his head again, and they backed away. Looking back to the girl who now seemed to bristle with confidence, he folded his arms and observed, "You seemed to have misplaced the fear you had a moment ago."

She nodded. "Yeah, Mom's always on me about losing stuff."

"I see," he said with a slight nod. Raising his chin, he ordered, "Change."

Elissa blinked, then glanced aside and asked, "Change what?"

"Into who you are," he replied.

"This is who I am," she countered.

A sigh growled out of him. "I wish to see you as Golden Angel."

"Oh!" she declared as if just realizing what he was talking about. "Yeah, I can do that." She strode back to the middle of the room, extended her arms and began to twist at the waist, then she froze, her eyes locked on Panzer. "Um, you guys mind stepping out for a minute?"

"Just change," he growled.

Grasping her hips, she barked back, "I can't with all of you watching! Turn around or something!"

"Change!" he roared.

She defiantly folded her arms and shouted back, "You can't watch me change! I mean, come on! I'm still a minor!"

Panzer turned his head to look at the doctor, then his attention returned to the girl and he loudly commanded, "You will change!"

"Yes," she complied, "I will change, but not until you perverts step outside!" She glanced around her. "The girls can stay, but you guys have to go." Looking aside, she just stood there and waited.

Red Panzer's patience seemed to be running out and he looked to the doctor.

Turning her eyes up to him, the doctor raised her brow and

suggested, "I don't know how she does this, but her modesty does seem reasonable. I am sure she will comply without further problem and we will be sure that she does."

He stared down at the white clad woman for long, horrifying seconds, then he looked to the man who stood behind the girl and beckoned to him before turning toward the door.

As they left, Elissa called after them, "I'll just be a minute, guys, okay?" When the door closed behind them, she looked to the doctor, to the blonde woman guard who remained, and finally to Ursula, smiling as she said, "You guys are totally going to love this. It's really cool!" She extended her arms and twisted at the waist, then turned hard the other way. The golden light flashed and enveloped her completely and in three turns she was dressed as Golden Angel. Stopping her spin, she set her hands on her hips and faced Ursula, that smile still curling her mouth as she asked, "So what do you think?"

The big red haired woman pursed her lips, raising her brow as she nodded.

Elissa turned and held her hands to the sides of her mouth, shouting through them loud enough to make her voice growl, "You can come back in now!" When Red Panzer and his two male guards entered, she held her head up and asked, "Okay, who wants to throw down?"

Ursula and the other woman guard took her arms, holding tightly at the elbows and wrists while Panzer and the male guards approached her. Looking her up and down, he leaned his head and ordered, "Doctor, take her belt and check her pockets."

The white clad woman strode to the restrained girl, looking down at her belt and studying it for a moment.

"It unbuckles in the back," Elissa informed.

Reaching around the little Amazon's waist, the doctor found the buckle and unfastened it, taking the belt from her, then she handed it off to Red Panzer. Pulling her front pocket open, she reached in to find what was in there, and she jumped and retreated as the girl squealed and twisted away.

"Sorry," Golden Angel offered. "I'm wicked ticklish there."

She twitched and giggled as the doctor checked her other pockets, much to the annoyance of her captors. When all was clear, the doctor turned and nodded to Panzer.

With his attention locked on his captive, Red Panzer folded his arms and ordered, "Take her to her cell."

When he turned to leave, Elissa barked, "Wait!"

He hesitated, half turning to look her way.

"Um," she started, "I haven't had dinner or anything and I'm really starving! Can you spring for a pizza or something? Oh, and some orange soda if you think about it. I think you can get a discount if you—"

"I shall arrange for something," Panzer interrupted.

"Pepperoni and sausage with extra cheese and jalapenos and mushrooms," Elissa added, "but I'm not picky. Oh, and breadsticks."

"I will see to it," he grumbled as he turned to leave. "Doctor, arrange her lunch."

"Lunch!" Golden Angel barked. "It's lunchtime?" She looked up to Ursula. "No wonder I'm so darn hungry!"

She walked down the corridor with the two women who still held her arms without resisting and was actually rather chatty.

"Oh, and you have no idea," Elissa rambled on. "Sometimes I just *think* humidity and my hair won't do a thing! And, believe me, I've thought of braids, I just haven't done it yet. I really don't think I could—"

"Do you ever shut up?" the blonde woman shouted.

"Excuse me!" Elissa barked back. "Ursula and I are talking hair, and there's nothing more important… Oh, wait. I can see you don't really care about how you look."

The big blonde woman stopped and wheeled the girl around, snarling, "Watch your mouth you little brat or I'll fill it with my knuckles!"

Ripping her arms from the women's grips, Golden Angel curled her hands into tight fists and stepped right up to the much larger woman, holding her shoulders back and her hands ready as she shouted, "You want to throw down? Let's do it right here and now!"

Ursula grabbed the little Amazon's shoulder and pulled her back, also taking the blond woman's shoulder and pushing her away a step as she maneuvered herself between them.

Thrusting a finger at the girl, the blonde woman yelled, "You just need to keep that big mouth of yours shut, little girl!"

"Get bent, you moose!" Elissa yelled back.

When the two tried to engage each other again, Ursula stepped fully between them, one hand holding Elissa and the other holding the blond woman. Looking to her colleague, Ursula motioned with her head for her to leave.

Pointing to the Amazon girl as she backed away, the blonde woman assured, "This isn't done, you sawed-off little shrimp. Just wait until I get you alone!"

"Oh, I am so scared!" Elissa chided. "You catch me alone and I'll kick your butt so hard your mother will get hemorrhoids!"

Ursula pushed Golden Angel back another step and raised her palm to the blonde woman, ordering her with a look to just depart.

Elissa watched the blonde woman wheel around and storm the other way with narrow, angry eyes. Folding her arms, she spat, "You ever run into someone you just didn't like?" She turned and strode with slow steps toward her cell. "I mean, there's just no reason to act like that. She didn't even try to join the conversation."

Ursula caught up to the girl and took her side.

Looking up to the big redhead, Golden Angel observed, "You don't talk much, do you?"

Ursula shook her head.

"Kind of keeps you out of trouble that way, huh?" the girl guessed. "I don't know how many times I've said the wrong thing at the wrong time. Sometimes I wish I didn't say so much at all." She turned her eyes forward again. "I just can't help myself, I guess. Some people are just talkative."

Ursula nodded.

Elissa looked up at her again. "You aren't, though. You're more of a good listener." She nodded. "I can respect that."

Turning her head only slightly, the big red haired woman looked down to the little Amazon girl, and only the hint of a smile touched her mouth.

They arrived at the cell and Ursula entered the code to open the door, then she extended her hand in an invitation for the girl to enter.

Striding in, Elissa mumbled, "I hope they remember my pizza." She turned and waggled her fingers at the red haired woman as the door closed, bidding, "Catch you later."

Locked in again, she crossed her arms over her chest and turned to look around her. Venting a deep breath, she glanced about and observed, "Well, I guess it's time to get back to all of this nothing to do."

She sat on the bed and pulled her boots off, allowing them to just drop to the floor before retreating to the corner of the bed where she had been before. Sitting cross-legged this time, she took the pillow and hugged it to her as she had done before, rocking her head back to let it rest against the concrete wall behind her. Her eyes slowly closed and she whispered, "Almost time."

Elissa had almost dozed off when her door opened and she looked to it, her eyes widening as she saw Zack enter with a pizza box and a bottle of orange soda. Her teeth clenched as she watched him lay the box down on the other end of the bed, then he turned and took the stool from the other end of the room, setting it close to the bed.

He sat down and put the bottle down beside him, leaning forward and resting his forearms on his thighs as he asked, "So what's up, girlfriend?"

Looking away from him, Elissa snarled, "I am not your girlfriend."

"You're already breaking up with me?" he barked. "That's not cool!"

She ground her teeth and just stared at the wall beside her.

He smiled. "So you want to make out?"

"If you touch me," she warned, "I will break both your arms."

Zack huffed a laugh. "Oh, so now you don't like me anymore? What's up with that?"

"I'll tell you what's up," she snarled. "I don't have any use for a guy who would betray me like that."

He sat up straight, holding his head up as he countered, "Who betrayed who? I believe Herr Panzer offered you a position in the New Order and you accepted and then you betrayed *him*. You gave him your word and you lied."

"I never gave him my word," she corrected, "and I never had any intention of joining him and his stupid New Order."

"You just don't get it, do you?" he barked. "Red Panzer has offered us all a chance to be free of crime and the disorganized, corrupt governments of the world, rid of hunger and unemployment and all that. Everybody will have their place."

"Yeah," Elissa laughed, finally looking at him, "as long as they're willing to give up their freedom and their happiness and cave to whatever Panzer wants them to do. Oh, and anyone who doesn't conform will be killed, won't they?"

His eyes narrowed. "Sacrifices will have to be made to bring this corrupt sewer of a world under control."

"You're really buying all of this, aren't you? Do you know how sad that is?" She shook her head and looked away from him. "And to think I used to like you."

"The Reich has given me a life and a purpose," he informed through clenched teeth. "I had nothing before. I was—"

"I read your file," Elissa interrupted. "You were a ninety pound weakling, picked on by other kids and living in foster care because your father ran off and your mother overdosed and died. At some point and seemingly overnight you put on a hundred pounds of muscle, grew about a foot taller and started playing football in high school." Her eyes slid to him. "You were also taken out of foster care and put into a so-called family who is supposed to be caring for you, but instead they poisoned your screwed-up little mind with all of that *New Order* crap and you ate it all up just like the naïve bonehead you are!"

He sprang up, glaring down at her as he yelled, "Red Panzer gave me a new life and new hope! You wouldn't know what it's like to be small and weak and picked on by everybody around you!"

She raised her brow. "Seriously?"

"How could you know?" he growled, his brow low over his eyes.

Slowly, Elissa set the pillow aside, straightened her legs and slid from the bed, and when she was standing in front of him she grabbed his shirt and yanked him toward her, glaring up at him as she shouted, "I am a five foot, five and one half inch tall, one hundred thirteen pound—*Amazon!*"

His expression was one that told her that he refused to respond to her, refused to sympathize with her, though inside she knew that he was feeling what she had said. "And still," he began with low, hard words, "you refused the gift that Herr Panzer offered you, a gift that would make you stronger than any of your kind."

"He tried to force it on me," she snapped back. "He put that stuff in me and it hurt so bad I thought I was going to die. And it didn't even work! Do I look bigger and stronger to you?"

"Then they'll make it work," he insisted.

Elissa brutally pushed him away from her. "Are you saying I'm not good enough?"

"You said yourself you are small for your kind," he pointed out. "Is that what you want to be your whole life, small and weak and inferior to all around you?"

Slowly shaking her head, she asked, "I'm not inferior to all around me, just other..." Setting her hands on her hips, she looked away and asked, "What happened to that boy I used to like? What happened to the boy who saved me on the ship a few..." Her eyes widened and she slowly turned her attention back to him, taking a step back as she breathed, "You didn't evade capture at all, did you?"

Zack looked aside and folded his arms and was clearly scrambling for something to say.

"The whole thing was a set-up," she accused. "You were after one of us and... Were you trying to get me all that time?"

"No," he confessed. "You were not the target, but you presented a unique opportunity."

"Who was the target this time?" she asked.

He turned to leave. "It isn't for you to know."

As he opened the door, she demanded, "Did you ever like me at all or was that all just a lie, too?"

Zack paused at the doorway, his eyes on the floor before him. Slowly, he looked over his shoulder with hard, cruel eyes as he informed, "What's to like about you? You're pretty, you're hot, but you're also shallow, flighty and pretty self-absorbed."

Clenching her teeth, Elissa slowly raised her chin as she stared back at him with eyes that tried hard to hide the hurt he had inflicted.

"You're all about you," he continued cruelly. "I was just something convenient for you."

"That isn't true," she strained to say through clenched teeth.

"You know it is," he confirmed. "My heart will go to a real woman who has the wisdom to give her loyalty to the Reich, not some air-headed little self righteous girl like you." He turned and strode out the door with no more regard for her than he would have for someone he did not know.

"You suck!" she screamed as the door closed. She backed away and clumsily sat down on the bed, and as she squeezed her eyes shut, she bowed her head and covered her face with both hands as the first hard sobs sent quakes through her whole body.

WW

An hour or so later found her curled up on the bed, hugging the pillow to her as she stared blankly across the sterile little room she was locked in. She had not eaten the pizza that was brought to her, even though she really needed to. Having cried all she could, she felt empty and alone inside.

The door slid open and Ursula strode in, stopping halfway into the cell as she set her hands on her hips.

Elissa's eyes slowly found her, eyes that were red and swollen from crying, eyes that were devoid of hope. She stared back at the big red haired woman, finally pushing herself up and swinging her feet to the floor. Drawing a deep breath, she asked in a defeated voice, "I guess Panzer wants me for something?"

Ursula just nodded.

Elissa turned her eyes down and nodded back, softly conceding, "Okay. I just have to get my boots on." She pulled one boot on, then picked up the other and just stared at it for a moment before looking up at the red haired woman. "Did you ever have anyone just totally break your heart?"

Her lips pursing slightly, Ursula nodded.

"It's horrible," Elissa said in a meek voice as her eyes strayed across the room. Slowly shaking her head, she whimpered, "I really thought he liked me. Even after he brought me here, I thought..." She closed her eyes, bowing her head as she forced a hard breath from her.

Ursula strode toward her and patted her shoulder in a reassuring gesture that the young Amazon could never have expected from the big woman.

Since her capture, she had been escorted to where she needed to be in the complex by two guards who held her arms securely the whole time. This time, joined by a male guard who walked on one side of the girl, nobody seemed to feel the need to hold onto her, and in fact when the man tried to take her arm, Ursula simply looked to him and shook her head.

Pausing at the elevator, Golden Angel kept her eyes down and did not speak as she waited between her much larger escorts with her hands folded before her. She was not sure what they wanted her for, but her future looked rather grim, and she knew that she had only one more card to play. She also knew that the big red haired woman who she had fought well on two other occasions was not so forceful with her anymore.

Before the elevator doors opened, she looked up to the big woman and nudged her with her elbow, nodding when she had her attention and offering, "Thanks for understanding."

Ursula's eyes slid back to the doors as they opened and she simply nodded.

They emerged from the elevator into some kind of control room that had a huge control console all along the far wall. This was a rather big room, about eighty feet wide and perhaps forty deep from the elevator to the console across from it. There were many people working in there, some in gray uniforms, some in the black body armor of Red Panzer's augmented army, while others were in white technician's garb. Most of these in white were seated at the console, but a few sat at smaller work stations off to the right, and this is where Elissa was taken.

She subtly glanced about, hoping to keep her observations unnoticed.

The male guard grabbed her arms and brutally jerked her to a stop.

Heavy boots approaching from behind made the girl's spine go rigid and she slowly raised her head, knowing who it was who neared.

Red Panzer's steps were slow and hard on the polished concrete floor. His hands were folded behind him, his attention on the young Amazon. As he reached her, he turned his attention to the white topped table that was to her left, and finally he said, "You are still useful to me, so you will not die as of yet."

"Thanks," she offered sheepishly.

The guard holding her retreated and Panzer took her arm, turning her toward the table.

Elissa looked down at it, seeing her Justice League communicator right in the middle of the table and plugged into an array of instruments and a computer.

"We have figured out how this works," he informed, "but I would like to be certain of a few things."

She nodded and complied, "Okay."

"The blue button," he said harshly.

"Emergency transport," was her reply.

"Green button," he demanded.

"A kind of mute, some kind of observation mode, I think. I've never used it."

"The two black buttons?"

"Power on and I don't know what the other one does."

Panzer nodded.

The doctor approached from the main console, her eyes full of suspicion and locked on the young Amazon as she observed with a suspicious tone, "You sure are compliant."

Golden Angel looked to her and stammered, "You, uh... You look pretty today too." Shifting her attention to Panzer, she subtly shrugged.

Panzer grasped the back of Elissa's neck and led her toward the main control panel, and she did not dare to resist him. Looking ahead of her, she saw a metal chair set up that faced the opposite wall from the huge view screen and a camera about ten feet away from it, one that had a bundle of wires that ran from it to the work station where her communicator was resting. The chair itself was metal and had no arms, but it did have thick straps dangling from the back and legs and Elissa knew that was her destination.

Taken to the chair, she was maneuvered into place before being pulled brutally into it and she sat rather hard. Two black clad guards grabbed her wrists and pulled them behind her while two women in gray uniforms began to secure the straps around her chest and legs. In a moment her legs were tightly strapped together and secured to the chair while another was tightened around her shoulders and upper chest, and another around her waist. Handcuffs were clamped around her wrists, holding her arms behind her and yet another strap held her arms tightly to the back of the chair at the elbows.

Panzer stood at the side, his arms folded as he watched his people bind the girl.

Looking up at him, Golden Angel spat, "Are you *that* afraid of me?"

"This will help make sure you cooperate," he replied. "As for you, just accept that you are my prisoner and do not try to signal your Justice League while I am addressing them."

"Signal them and tell them what?" she barked. "That you kidnapped me and whisked me away to your secret lair Hera knows where? That you're holding me captive and you intend to use me as a bargaining chip against the Justice League somehow?" She huffed a laugh and looked away from him. "Somehow, I think they'll be able to figure that out on their own. Duh!"

He looked to the man with the camera and ordered, "Make sure we are transmitting to them on my signal."

The man, who wore white laboratory attire, nodded to the mechanical Nazi and assured, "As soon as you signal I'll throw the switch and we'll be on their secure channel, direct to the Watchtower."

"Very good," Panzer commended as he turned toward the camera.

Elissa tensed as he slid his metal hand under her ponytail and grasped her neck, and she knew what was eventually coming. Struggling to defeat her fear, she forced herself to look into the camera, and as the light went on her eyes shifted to Panzer and she defiantly grumbled, "Butthead."

CHAPTER 15

Diana combed a hand through her hair, her eyes on the floor before her as she strode down a corridor of the watchtower with Black Canary on her right, Batman on her left. Distress was in her eyes, an anxiousness she almost never felt, almost never displayed, but this day it was all too apparent.

"Look," Black Canary insisted, "you've got to remember that she's a teenager and there's a lot suddenly going on with her."

Batman added, "A lot going on like a sudden surge of hormones that she doesn't know what to do with."

"Exactly," Canary assured. "I know you're used to bubbly little Golden Angel, but try to realize that she's a teenage girl, an *Amazon* teenage girl. That means that she's a hormone infused emotional ticking time bomb and half the time she's going to go off and not even realize it."

With a slight nod, Diana softly agreed, "I suppose so."

J'onn's voice blared over the station intercom, "Batman, Wonder Woman to the control room immediately!"

They looked to each other, then ran toward the control room.

With Black Canary on their heels as they charged from the elevator, they ran toward the crowd that had gathered around the main viewer and easily pushed through.

Diana slammed her hand down onto the console, her wide eyes locked on the image of her daughter strapped to a metal chair as her old enemy had a grip on her neck. Breaths entered the Amazon Princess reluctantly and she managed, "Great Hera!"

Batman looked on seemingly without expression, but his spine was rigid, his hands clenched into tight fists.

Martian Manhunter looked to them, a certain strain in his voice as he said, "I'll play back the message from the beginning."

The image flickered and in a moment it started over.

"Heroes of the old order," Red Panzer's synthesized voice greeted.

"You know who I am, and I know who all of you are. As you can see, I now control one of you. Today, her life is in your hands. I am sure, Fräulein Wonder Woman that you will not want to see your daughter harmed, so I think it is best that you convince your colleagues to cooperate and meet mein demands."

"How did he get his hands on her?" Diana shouted.

Panzer continued, "If you wish to see the girl alive und unharmed, you will abandon your Watchtower. You will land your Javelin trans-atmospheric aircraft equally in North Korea, Iran, and Sudan. My troops and I will transport aboard the station to take possession of it."

Batman's eyes were fixed on his daughter, and narrowed.

"The girl will accompany us," the Nazi madman went on, "and you will have the station cleared before we arrive. If any one of you remains, they will be killed and she will be made to suffer." He looked down to the restrained Amazon girl, and his grip tightened around her neck. An audible buzzing rattled the console speakers and the girl threw her head back and screamed as her captor sent shots of electricity through her, directly into her spine.

Diana covered her mouth and backed away, slowly shaking her head as she witnessed the torture of her little girl.

It lasted only a couple of seconds and Panzer turned his attention back to the onlookers, warning, "You have one hour."

The screen went blank.

"J'onn," Batman summoned as he reached to his belt to remove a pen and pad, "play back the whole message, video only."

Turning away, Diana found herself shaking, her wide eyes unable to focus as she babbled, "I can't watch that again. I… I can't. What is she doing there?" Finally, she shouted, "What is she doing there?"

Superman grasped her arms, calling, "Diana! Snap out of it! We have to think clearly."

"He has my daughter!" she yelled back, tears filling her eyes.

"We'll get her back," Superman assured.

"How?" she demanded. "He could be anywhere with her. Anywhere!"

"We can track the signal," Superman insisted, turning his eyes to J'onn.

Martian Manhunter looked to the Man of Steel and slowly shook his head. "The signal was encrypted and sent out to relay stations all over the continent. We have no way to isolate where it came from in an hour if at all."

Diana clenched her teeth, pulling away from Superman as she backed up into the console. "He must have planned this. He must have planned to get her somehow."

Sitting at the console and watching the screen as he intermittently scribbled on the pad, Batman assured, "He did, and she planned to let him."

Wheeling around, Wonder Woman looked to him and barked, "She *planned* to get herself captured? That's insane!"

"J'onn," Batman said. "Play it back again."

Firestorm raised his chin as he watched the screen. "Come on, Bats. The kid isn't *that* crazy."

"You should know by now that she is," Batman confirmed, "and she's about as reckless as they come."

Slowly shaking her head as she watched the viewer, Diana breathed, "What was she thinking?"

"Calm down, Princess," Batman ordered. "Our little girl knows exactly what she's doing."

"How can you say that?" Wonder Woman shouted. "Look at her!"

"Yes," he confirmed, "look at her. She's signaling us right now."

Everyone looked closer, but none seemed to see it.

None but Captain Atom, who stepped forward and mumbled, "She's blinking in Morse Code."

"She has Atom with her," Batman assured, "she's sent the address and a timeframe." He stood and tore a page from the pad, turning to the Martian Manhunter. "Here's where we need to go. They have an underground complex beneath an abandoned warehouse in North Gotham." He turned and faced Wonder Woman, asking, "You in?"

"Of course," she snarled, her eyes darting to the monitor.

"Anyone else?" the Dark Knight asked, his eyes sweeping the crowd of Justice League heroes.

Everyone stepped forward.

CHAPTER 16

Returned to her cell, Golden Angel would be closely watched this time. Having kicked her boots off again, she sat cross legged on her bed and munched on some of the cold pizza and drank her orange soda right out of the bottle, handing it off to the big red haired woman who was guarding her. Ursula was sharing the pizza, sitting in the chair that was moved closer to the bed. She seemed to listen to the girl who chatted away, keeping her eyes on her and closely monitoring her movements for anything aggressive or suspicious, and yet she was remarkably at ease, more so than she had ever been with an old rival so close.

Taking another big bite out of her slice of pizza, Elissa shook her head and rambled on, "Oh, it was totally awesome. I'd never done anything like that before and it was so much fun! Of course, then I find out he's the one who is going to narc me over and turn me into your boss, but it was still… I don't know…" She looked up toward the ceiling and breathed, "Magical."

Ursula actually smiled and nodded in subtle motions.

Folding her hands in her lap, Elissa looked to her watchful guard and hesitantly asked, "So, um, I don't want to pry or anything, but…" She shifted and sat up a little straighter. "Okay, just glare at me or something if I'm out of line, but why don't you ever talk? I mean…" She retreated to the wall behind her as the door slid open and Panzer strode in with long, heavy steps.

"Out!" he ordered, stopping in the middle of the room.

Ursula shot a fearful look to her captive, then stood and turned to the door, hurrying out.

Elissa's wide, horrified eyes were locked on the huge, mechanical Nazi as he stared at her from behind the lenses of his metallic, skeleton mask. She slowly lowered her hands to the bed, planting her palms beside her as her fear grew second by second.

"What have you done?" he demanded.

"What..." she stammered, "what do you mean?"

"You know what I mean!" he roared. "How did you sabotage the system?" When she had no answer and could only stare at him with those wide, confusion laced eyes, he stepped toward her, raising a hand that arched with electric current from palm to fingertips. "Tell me what you did!"

She shrieked and retreated to the corner, cowering there with her gaze locked on his hand, his instrument of pain. "I... I didn't do anything! I've been locked up in here the whole time!"

He moved in closer to her, bringing his open hand close to her face as he demanded, "Do not lie to me! What did you do to the system?"

"I didn't do anything, I swear!" She was shaking, shrieking with every breath she took as she struggled to retreat further into the corner. "You have to believe me! I've been locked in here ever since you got me!"

"Then how did you do it?" he shouted.

Finally looking to his face, she desperately cried, "I didn't do anything! You guys have been watching me every minute so when could I have?"

His hand lanced toward her, taking her by the throat. He pulled her from the bed, standing fully as he held her close to him by the neck and he watched her struggle in his grip, watched her try to pry his fingers from her, watched fearful tears well up in her eyes. With an irritated growl, he threw her from him and she slammed into the corner of the wall where she had been cringing a moment before, and she crumpled back down to the bed.

Holding her throat, she slowly pushed herself up and looked up at him with those defeated eyes.

"Know this," he warned. "Mein armor has been enhanced. I now have more than twice the strength that you remember and mein armor cannot be breached. I am quicker and much more heavily armed than you remember and you can do nothing that I have not already anticipated. If you expect to do battle with me again then believe me you will not do so well as our last encounter." He bent closer to her. "And I *will* certainly kill you, most unpleasantly."

She retreated from him again, backing into the corner as she gently grasped her throat, nodding as she confirmed in the fearful voice of a little girl, "I understand. I'll be good."

Elissa could only quietly watch as he turned and strode from the room. She slowly drew her legs to her, wrapping her arms around them and resting her chin on her knees as she kept her gaze fixed on the door for some time even after she knew he was not coming back.

There she sat to await the inevitable.

And the inevitable came with a mechanical hiss as the door opened—and Atom strode into the cell!

Elissa sprang forward, sitting on the edge of the bed as she reached for her boots, complaining, "About time you got here!"

"I've been busy," he assured. "I managed to knock out most of their security systems so we can move freely without being detected. Did your message get through?"

With her second boot halfway on, she froze and looked up at him. "Uh, I was kind of hoping you would know."

"I haven't heard anything," he reported. "If we're going to make our move then we need to make it now, or at least get the heck out of here and wait for reinforcements."

Golden Angel sprang up and nudged him back a step. "First things first." Extending her arms, she twisted one way, then spun the other, was enveloped in a flash of golden light and three spins later her attire was complete again, including the blue cape given to her by the Nordic Champion. Checking her belt to make sure everything was in place, she looked to Atom and nodded, saying, "Okay, let's do this."

Their first priority was just getting back to the surface unnoticed, and this was where Atom's special abilities were to come in handy. Too small to be detected, he held Golden Angel close to him as he flew through air shafts through the complex to find one that would lead to the surface. During this search they would pause many times to overhear what was being said between Red Panzer's people. Most were near panic as the sabotage that Atom had inflicted to the main control console was seemingly spreading. Power systems especially were affected and lights flickered on and off in places, and at one point, the whole ventilation system simply stopped working, this according to Atom's master plan.

They emerged through a small air shaft in the middle of an abandoned concrete warehouse where they landed and he restored them to normal size.

Looking around them, they were quick to notice that darkness had settled and the inside of this warehouse had little light to aid them.

"Great," Atom grumbled. "You got a flashlight in that belt?"

Elissa shook her head and assured, "Don't need one."

A mechanical bang sounded from behind them and lights flared to life, saturating the entire warehouse in a bright light that illuminated everything. A few stacks of pallets were distributed about, empty crates and piles of trash. An old forklift was about fifty feet away, missing a front wheel and rusty from neglect. Another stack of crates, one looking as if it had been more recently put there, was to their right, and beyond it was the office area that had both windows broken out and the door leaning against the wall from the doorway.

Looking to Atom, Golden Angel set her hands on her hips and asked, "So, is this enough light for you?"

"It'll do," he replied, his eyes sweeping the area. "Something tells me we aren't alone in here."

Elissa's gaze darted about as black clad, armed people began to emerge from shadows and from behind stacks of crates and pallets, and she countered, "Ya think?" Watching at least two dozen of Red Panzer's soldiers emerge from their hiding places, many of them genetically augmented, Golden Angel slowly assumed her battle stance and readied her arms, her attention darting from one to the next as compact machine guns were trained on her and Atom, and she mumbled, "We are in some major serious doo-doo here."

"Tell me you are as good as your mother at deflecting bullets," Atom urged.

"Let's do some math," she suggested. "A couple of dozen of them, one of me with two arms and they all have machine guns. You have a back-up plan?"

"Making it up as I go," he informed grimly.

Elissa glanced about again, and without warning she stepped away from Atom and announced, "Okay, that's it! Drop your weapons, you are all under arrest!"

There was the simultaneous sound of machine gun bolts being pulled back and most of the gunmen took a more accurate aim.

Swallowing hard, she stepped back to Atom and mumbled, "Well *my* idea sure didn't work."

A pop and breaking glass briefly preceded a light going out, then another, and another, all in a row to their right. As they turned that way, some kind of impact was heard, a muffled grunt and someone hitting the floor. A weapon hit the concrete with metal and plastic clacks.

Golden Angel peered into the darkness as another gunman disappeared behind a stack of pallets.

Two more lights were knocked out on the other side of the warehouse and the sounds of a brief struggle followed.

Panzer's soldiers grew restless as they looked around them, only a few keeping their weapons trained on Golden Angel and Atom. A red blur whooshed by and two more found themselves disarmed, then knocked cold a second later.

Glancing about, Atom informed in a low voice, "It looks like your message was received loud and clear, Kiddo."

Something crashed through the roof and Superman slammed onto the floor in front of them a second later, then Wonder Woman behind them. Firestorm landed to the left, Green Lantern to the right.

Machine guns blared to life and Wonder Woman called, "Junior!"

Elissa wheeled around, taking her mother's side as the two of them deflected bullet after bullet. More bullets ricocheted off of Superman, still more off of a glowing green wall from Green Lantern's ring. Firestorm swept his hand and the incoming rounds simply popped into puffs of smoke halfway to him, then flames exploded from the floor in front of him, lancing outward toward the gunmen in front of him, all of whom ran for cover.

Atom slammed his fist into his palm and shouted, "Let's get some!"

The small circle exploded in all directions and Panzer's men found themselves in a disorganized retreat. More justice league heroes burst in through doors and windows, and many more were already there.

Kneeling behind a stack of crates, Green Arrow took careful aim and loosed an arrow with a bulbous tip, one that streaked by and slammed into one of the gunmen who was taking aim at Wonder Woman from behind. The impact was enough to knock the man from his feet and cause him to lose his grip on his weapon and small weighted cord lanced out to entangle him.

This would be a one sided battle and many of Red Panzer's troops fled, some running from the building to be captured by police and others disappearing into the many hidden tunnel openings that would take them into the complex below.

With this part over, Golden Angel was quick to find her mother and ran the short distance to her, calling, "Mom!"

Diana swung around and grasped the girl's outstretched arms, and Elissa grasped her mother's.

Her brow held high, Elissa's eyes were pools of distress, of emotional turmoil as she tightly gripped her mother's gauntlets, and with tears in her eyes she started, "Mom..."

"Later," Wonder Woman ordered with an authoritative tone. "I don't think we're done here yet. How many more are there?"

Looking over her shoulder, Golden Angel called, "Atom!" Her attention turned back to her mother and she reported, "I don't know, but he has more augments, many more. Mom, Zack is one of them!" She slowly shook her head, almost sobbing as she admitted, "You were so right. Everything you said, everything you and Daddy tried to warn me about."

"I said later," Diana barked. "Focus, Little One. We need you with a clear mind right now and I need to know all that you do about the complex below."

Elissa shamefully lowered her eyes and admitted, "I was locked up most of the time and I didn't get to look around much. There are three levels..." Her eyes darted back to Wonder Woman. "He said his armor is much stronger than he had before, that he is much stronger and has better weapons and that he's ready for anything we can throw at him."

Diana's eyes narrowed and she demanded, "Red Panzer?"

With a nod, Golden Angel confirmed, "Yes. He warned me not to challenge him again." She drew a breath that entered her reluctantly. "We have to get out of here! Mom, he almost killed you and—"

"Use your gift," Diana ordered.

"My gift of protection," Elissa breathed. "I can only protect three people at any given time."

"That will be plenty," Atom assured as he reached them. "Diana, you and Superman for sure."

Without hesitating, Elissa reached up and grasped her mother's neck, looking into her eyes as she said, "Diana, Princess of the Amazons, until the sun rises anew, Red Panzer can bring you no harm."

Slowly, a smile curled Wonder Woman's mouth and she gently grasped her daughter's gauntlets. "Just like last time. I can feel your protection." She looked past the girl and called, "Superman! Get over here!"

He hovered over to them and gently set down beside Elissa, and she turned to him even before his feet settled to the ground, grasping his neck as she had Wonder Woman's as she said, "Superman, until the sun rises anew, Red Panzer can bring you no harm."

As she finished, the large stack of crates across the room began to tremble and the two halves of the stack slowly began to move apart.

Everyone stopped what they were doing and turned to see what was happening.

Slowly, from between the parting stacks of crates, two huge figures rose from the floor.

Stepping forward first, Metallo wore the same black trousers and boots as the other soldiers, but no shirt. Some additional armor was apparent in form fitting plates over his chest and belly and a green glow came from a circular opening in his chest and his eyes. His head seemed better protected as well and seemed to have additional sensors around what appeared to be a helmet that covered most of his head, and yet it was clearly a part of him. His arms were thicker, more mechanical in appearance and closed hatches in his forearms were obviously hiding something.

Bane strode forward and took his side. Somehow, he looked even bigger! He wore similar trousers to Panzer's soldiers, but only a black utility vest covered his chest. Form fitting plate armor covered his outer arms, chest, belly and back. He also wore a snug helmet, and the leather mask he usually wore was replaced by metal, though the same design was painted on it. Around his waist was a belt that had many items suspended from it, most notably what appeared to be a huge gun of some kind.

"Ah, crud," Elissa mumbled as she backed away a step. Slowly shaking her head, she breathed, "I should have waited."

"For what?" Wonder Woman questioned.

"You aren't protected against those two," the girl replied, "and I can only offer protection against one enemy at a time. Mom, I'm sorry!"

"We'll work with it!" Diana assured. "We managed before." Her attention darted to her daughter and she demanded, "How long until sunup?"

Elissa shrugged. "I don't even know what time it is."

"You're our edge," Wonder Woman informed. "Find someone and protect them against one of those two and be ready at dawn to do it all over again."

Golden Angel glanced around and asked, "Who?"

Metallo began to slowly advance, Bane with him.

"Use your best judgment, Junior," Diana ordered.

Her eyes sliding to her mother, Elissa stammered, "Uh, you sure that's a good idea?"

Diana looked back to her and smiled confidently. "You have my trust to make the right choice, Golden Angel."

Elissa's chest heaved up as she stared back into her mother's eyes, then she took the Amazon Princess' shoulder and nodded before turning to go about her task.

But who?

She ran for a way, toward Green Lantern who stood on the other side of the warehouse, then she stopped and turned toward the two advancing bad guys, raising her head as she realized the platform had descended and Red Panzer's augmented soldiers began to climb out and charge toward the Justice League heroes. "Well crud," she mumbled, realizing that many of the heroes who were present did not know what they were facing. Her gaze shifted to Metallo as he raised his arm and she gasped loudly as two barrels rose from his forearm. "Oh, no," she breathed as she realized he was not firing just any bullets. Spinning around, she ran back toward Wonder Woman as Superman took her side and she screamed, "Mom!"

Metallo fired this built-in machine gun and Wonder Woman's arms swept up to deflect his rounds, but Superman had heard Golden Angel's warning in the tone of her voice and he darted in front of the Amazon, taking the armor piercing rounds square on his chest and belly.

Raising his other arm, Metallo warned, "I am ready for you as well, Superman." A single barrel emerged from his forearm and he fired only once.

And Elissa ran by and took the round on her gauntlet in a cascade of white and green sparks, stumbling and rolling over her shoulder and back to her feet. "Lantern!" she screamed as she turned to face the two advancing bad guys.

As Metallo raised his arms to fire again, Green Lantern responded with a glowing emerald wall between him and his team mates, and the rounds fired from his guns slammed into it and all stuck. While he was concentrating on this, one of Red Panzer's augments charged from behind and slammed a fist into the back of Lantern's head, knocking him out cold, and the emerald wall disappeared in that instant.

"Totally not good," Golden Angel mumbled. Not willing to hesitate more than that second, she charged and leaped into the air, spinning around to slam her boot solidly into the side of Metallo's head and knock him off balance. Coming down, she sprang into Bane, slamming her shoulder into his gut with all her might and managed to knock him off of his feet. Again she was quick to roll to her feet and turn to face the black clad augment who charged her, and she wheeled fully and slammed her foot solidly into his chest.

Bane got to his feet much faster than one would think he could, and he turned to take the little Amazon from behind, only to be intercepted by a blue and red streak that slammed into him and knocked him across the warehouse.

As Superman landed, Metallo turned and raised his arm, taking aim at the Man of Steel at close range as he announced, "It looks like we end this feud now, Superman."

Wonder Woman grabbed Metallo's arm and easily thwarted his aim into the ground in front of him, then she spun with him and slammed him back-first into the ground, burying his back about a foot deep into the concrete. He rolled to all fours to spring back up but she was upon him quickly again, slamming her fist into his back to take him back down.

Superman set himself as Bane charged him again, and his eyes widened slightly as he saw the slight green glow coming from one pocket of his vest, and he could feel the effects of the kryptonite as the big mercenary neared. Backing away, he realized that both Metallo and Bane were ready for him.

And so did a little Amazon.

Grabbing the augment she fought by the arm when he punched at her, she wheeled herself around with a loud yell, throwing the big man at Bane's feet, and when Bane stumbled she half spun and slammed her boot solidly into his gut as he went down. As he crashed to the ground, she leaped on his back and tried to tear the vest from him, but he reacted quickly and rolled to his side to get at her.

Holding Metallo by the ankle, Wonder Woman spun around and spun the mechanical bad guy with her, slamming him hard into the concrete again and this time he crashed all the way through it, into the packed ground beneath it. Turning quickly, she saw her daughter tossed to the ground and charged the big mercenary as he got up.

Bane turned quickly as the Amazon Princess was nearly upon him, dropped to one knee and punched straight forward, slamming his fist hard into Wonder Woman's belly.

She was doubled over and knocked backward by the blow delivered by an enemy who was suddenly much stronger than he had been and as she rolled to the floor some distance away he stood and turned on Superman.

Flash streaked by, tearing the small piece of kryptonite from Bane's vest pocket as he passed, and he offered, "Thanks," as he sped away.

Raising his head, Bane backed away a step as he patted his vest where the kryptonite once was, and he realized that he now faced the Man of Steel without the weapon he needed most.

Metallo pushed himself out of the crater Wonder Woman had slammed him into and turned his head as she sluggishly got back to her feet. Looking to Bane as he less than confidently squared off against Superman, he raised his arm from the broken concrete and took careful aim with the weapon that protruded just behind his wrist.

Elissa had been jumped by the same augment she had fought before and managed to deliver a kick to send him stumbling backward, and too late did she see the metallic enemy taking aim from just behind the Man of Steel, and too late she shouted,

"Superman!"

Metallo fired a single shot and the kryptonite-tipped bullet crashed easily into his shoulder and he yelled as he was half turned and reached for his stricken shoulder. Bane delivered a crushing punch that spun Superman around where he collapsed and came to rest face down on the concrete.

Drawing a gasp as she watched the Man of Steel fall, Wonder Woman fought off the shock she felt and turned quickly on Metallo as he rose fully from the shattered concrete and turned on her—and he raised his other arm to take aim at her with the weapon that raised from that arm, and as he trained it on her, he said with a voice laced with humor, "I have something specifically for you, Wonder Woman. Deflect this if you can."

Before he could fire, a bat-arang with a blinking red light wedged itself between the weapon's barrel and Metallo's arm and an instant later it exploded and the cybernetic villain yelled as he stumbled backward, sparks and smoke trailing from his arm. An arrow slammed into his head and exploded and he stumbled and fell this time.

Batman took Golden Angel's side, looked to Green Arrow who took cover behind a stack of pallets and nodded to him, and Green Arrow nodded back.

Pushing Batman brutally aside by the arm, Elissa crouched as she wheeled around, springing up into the belly of the augment who nearly had Batman from behind. Grabbing onto him, she shouted a mighty battle cry as she drove forward and down, slamming the big man back-first onto the concrete floor with everything she had. She rolled and leaped from him and spun around, nodding to her father as she informed, "I got your back, Batman."

"Chip off the old block," he said with a little smile. Spinning around, he saw Metallo locked in combat with Wonder Woman—and Bane lumbering toward him! Narrow eyed, he took his battle stance and prepared to meet the big mercenary who would be upon him in seconds.

Elissa grabbed onto his shoulders from behind and quickly barked, "Batman! Until the sun rises anew Bane can bring you no harm!"

Bane reached them and tried to throw a punch at Batman, and he hesitated. He found himself unable to act against the Dark Knight, and this clearly confused him.

Batman reached behind him and took the little Amazon's arm, then darted aside with her as Metallo slammed into Bane's back and knocked them both to the floor.

Very quickly, Metallo sprang up, turning to face the Amazon Princess, but Bane took his shoulder and half turned him.

"No," the big mercenary ordered. "Take Batman. I'll handle the woman."

Seeing them trade opponents is not what Elissa had expected and she took her father's side, assuming her battle stance as she mumbled, "Ah, seriously?"

"Go take care of Superman," the Dark Knight ordered. "I've got this."

"Are you sure?" she questioned, shooting him a concerned glance.

He reached behind him, under his cape and barked, "Go!"

She backed away and watched her father hurl an exploding bat-arang into Metallo's chest, and when it exploded and the cyborg stumbled backward, she darted around him and sprinted the short distance to where Superman lay. Dropping to her knees, she slid the last few feet to him and laid her hands on his back, then she quickly turned him over and looked over the wound that glowed a strange green. Clenching her teeth, she called upon her healing gift and her hands were illuminated in a gentle golden light. She could sense that the bullet had disintegrated inside of his shoulder and that the kryptonite fragments within were slowly killing him. As she had done before, she closed her eyes and pressed her hand over the wound. That green glow emanated from between her fingers as she drew out the kryptonite, and when she felt it was all out of him she concentrated on healing the wound itself. Even with the kryptonite now out of him, he was still very weak. She drew a long breath, opening her eyes as she looked down at him, then she looked down to her hand where the tiny piece of kryptonite had reformed into a single crystal. Half turning she threw it from her, then looked up to see Firestorm streaking in to attack Metallo from behind. Even with Superman down, the Justice League was slowly turning the tide.

Elissa looked the other way, seeing that Bane had Wonder Woman in a bear hug from behind and had her lifted from the ground as he tried to crush the life from her. With her teeth bared and her arms pinned to her, Diana struggled to free herself but seemed unable to match the huge man's strength. Elissa had experienced his strength when she had faced him before, but she also knew that her mother had defeated him before. Something had changed, and she knew that Panzer was at the heart of it.

Her eyes locked on her target, Golden Angel stood and reached behind her, to one of the pouches on her belt. As Wonder Woman continued to struggle to free herself, the small Amazon half turned, then she hurled the little metallic orb as hard as she could right at his head. Right before it hit, Wonder Woman wrenched her shoulder and slammed her head into his face as hard as she could and in doing so moved her forehead right into the orb's path, and Golden Angel cringed as it hit the middle of her mother's tiara and exploded with a loud bang and a blinding white light. This stunned both the Amazon Princess and the big mercenary she fought and Bane staggered back a step as they both tried to clear their wits.

Still looking a little dazed, Diana shot a glare at her daughter and shouted, "Junior!"

Her teeth clenching, Elissa grimaced and offered, "Sorry."

Another flash-bang slammed into the side of Bane's head, this one thrown by the Dark Knight, and his grip on Wonder Woman loosened enough for her to break free. As soon as she had solid footing she wheeled around and drove her heel solidly into Bane's belly, doubling him over, then she spun fully and slammed her other boot into the side of his head, sending him to the floor. She knew he was not down for good but still sprinted to her daughter, looking down at the Man of Steel as she demanded, "Is he going to be okay?"

Elissa's eyes shifted to Bane as he slowly got to his feet and she reported, "He needs sunlight to recover fully." Her head whipped around and she saw Metallo in a futile effort to catch Batman, and quickly he changed targets as Firestorm flew in on him from the side. A breath shrieked into her as Metallo raised his other arm and shot a yellow foam at Firestorm at close range before darting aside, and firestorm slammed into the ground and rolled to a smoking stop, seemingly unconscious. "They're ready for us," she declared desperately. Looking down to Superman, she knelt down beside him and reached to his belt, taking his communicator. She laid it on his chest and pushed the blue button, then she sprang up and backed away.

Superman was enveloped in a shimmering light, and in seconds he was gone.

Diana took the girl's shoulder, nodding to her as she offered, "Well done, Junior, but we still have an uphill—"

"Mom look out!" Golden Angel shouted.

Wonder Woman spun around and planted her boot solidly into Bane's jaw, and as he staggered backward she ordered, "Don't take any unnecessary risks! We'll need you come sunup. See if you can keep some of those augments busy."

"Or inside the complex," Elissa suggested. Grabbing her mother's hands, she said, "Leave that part to me. Can you guys hold your own up here?"

"We'll be fine, Junior," Wonder Woman assured, "but I do not want you going down there alone."

"Most of the bad guys are already up here," the little Amazon informed, "and you guys will have your hands full here on the surface. And I really want to do some damage to the lab equipment he's making these augments with."

Looking over her shoulder to check Bane as he got to his feet, Wonder Woman met her daughter's eyes and repeated, "No unnecessary risks. If you see Red Panzer or a number of augments you can't take I want you to get out of there, understood?"

"Understood, Mom," the girl confirmed. With that she pulled away and wheeled half around, running toward the elevator that would take her below, the same one Bane and Metallo had emerged from. When she arrived, she found the platform already lowering and was quick to jump on it, reaching to her belt with both hands as she crouched down to meet the next wave of augments. As the platform descended and she could see five black clad figures standing right in front of her, she threw three golf ball sized white orbs as hard as she could at their feet with her right hand as her left raised a mask to cover her mouth and nose.

The orbs exploded with loud pops and a white cloud quickly rose to envelope the augments who were waiting for the platform to take them to the surface. As Golden Angel backed away, she found herself cornered in a shaft that the platform settled itself into, one just big enough to allow it to lower into. The augments in front of her coughed and tried to wave the gas away, and one charged through the haze of gas and attacked her.

Easily sidestepping, she kicked him in the shin to trip him and sent him head first into the wall behind her. The other four hit the floor in seconds.

Still holding the mask to her face, Golden Angel strode confidently through the cloud of anesthetic gas and down the corridor, and when she was clear of the gas she removed the mask and put it back in its place on her belt. She looked back at the unconscious augments and smiled as she waggled her fingers at them.

Red Panzer's people had been unaware, but as they had escorted her through the maze that was this underground complex, she made mental notes of features unique to certain areas, especially numbers beside doorways that all looked alike They were also unaware that she could read German and this made navigating almost easy to her. Right now, she knew she had to find her way to the elevator.

The elevator doors slid open and she stepped fearlessly into the corridor. Three of Red Panzer's white clad scientists hurried from a door to her left and froze as they saw her—and she saw them. In seconds the last of them hit the floor and when Golden Angel was sure they were unconscious she strode on.

Reaching the door that would take her through some kind of workshop and to the laboratory she sought, she stopped in front of it, then looked to the keypad to the right, grumbling as she realized she would not be able to open it. The walk back to the three unconscious scientists was short but aggravating and she hurriedly rummaged through pockets until she found the access card she sought. Back at the laboratory, she slid the card through the slot and the door responded with a hiss as it finally slid out of her way.

She strode confidently through the workshop, which was about forty feet long, less than twenty wide and was lined with four metal topped work benches on each side. They were all clear of tools and projects and most of the tools were neatly put away in boxes or other holders on shelves beneath. None of this interested her. The door directly in front of her did.

As she arrived, she swiped the card as she had done before, but this time an annoying tone sounded and the words ZUGANG VERWEIGERT appeared in red on the small readout, and this meant access denied.

"Un-freaking believable!" she shouted as she wheeled around to go back to the scientists she had knocked out.

Golden Angel arrived at the three scientists to find one of them, the only woman of the three, had roused and was trying to quietly wake another until she found the young heroine bearing down on her.

Elissa folded her arms as she stopped only a foot away to loom over the cowering scientist, her eyes narrow and laced with spiteful recognition.

The doctor raised a trembling hand as if to shield herself from the girl's wrath.

Grinding her teeth, Golden Angel finally reached down and grabbed the woman's lab coat, hoisting her easily to her feet. She strode forward, driving the woman back and into the wall. Though the doctor was a little taller, she seemed to know that this little Amazon was not to be trifled with.

"Here's the deal," Elissa snarled. "You're going to get me into the lab and tell me everything I want to know. You don't and you're going to be on the receiving end of a serious butt-kicking." Still holding the doctor's lab coat, she turned and forced her along.

When the laboratory door opened, Golden Angel threw the woman about ten feet inside and watched her crash to the floor as she strode in after her. Pointing down at her, the young Amazon ordered, "Don't move!" in her most intimidating voice, then she looked to the table she had been strapped down to, a table that was bolted to the floor. Her eyes shifted to the doctor and she informed, "If you don't want to end up strapped to that thing like I was you'll do exactly what I tell you, got it?"

The doctor had pushed herself up on her palms and frantically nodded.

Elissa took a moment to scan the laboratory, then she strode to the station where the Doctor had spent the most time working and picked up a note pad. She thumbed through a few pages, read, and thumbed through a few more.

"It is written in German," the woman informed in a shaky voice, "and I will not translate it for you!"

"Kein problem," the young Amazon informed in perfect German, "Ich kann Geldstrafe des Deutschen gerade lesen." She turned the page and smiled. "It's one of four languages I know pretty well."

Fear coursed along every nerve of the Doctor as she watched the Amazon girl read.

Golden Angel suddenly wheeled toward her and shouted, "What DNA tests?"

The Doctor looked away.

Clenching her teeth, Elissa threw the book onto the bench and stormed to the woman, grabbing her by the lab coat again and hoisting her from the floor, this time high enough to leave her feet dangling. "Answer me! What did you do?"

Her jaw trembling, the Doctor did not seem to be able to answer.

Golden Angel's eyes narrowed and she snarled, "I'm going to set fire to this lab and blow it up. If you want to be strapped to that table you had me strapped down to when that happens—"

"All right!" the Doctor conceded. "It was DNA testing..."

Elissa raised her chin, fearfully asking, "On who?"

"You," was the Doctor's reply.

Setting the woman down, Golden Angel's grip tightened on her lab coat as she jerked her toward herself. "What for? What kind of test was it?"

Her mouth trembling, the woman sheepishly replied, "Paternity."

Elissa's eyes widened, her lips parting in fear as she stared back at the woman. Her brow lowered over her eyes as she demanded, "Where are the results?"

"Herr Panzer has them," the Doctor replied shakily. "He matched them to a world wide database and has sold the results already."

Looking away, Golden Angel mumbled, "Not good." She looked back to the woman and snapped, "Here's the deal. You have thirty seconds before I blow this place up and destroy everything inside if it, and if *any* of my information gets out then believe me I will hunt you down and beat you against the wall like a rug! Got it?"

The woman frantically nodded, and when the girl released her she turned and fled.

Turning to the work benches, Elissa set her hands on her hips and scanned them for anything useful, asking herself aloud, "Now what in here burns really good?" Shaking her head, she removed one of her last two exploding batarangs from her belt and spat, "Oh, the heck with it!"

In a moment the laboratory was a flaming disaster and Golden Angel backed out of the room and allowed the door to slide shut in front of her. Looking to her right, she saw the control panel that would open it and she kicked it as hard as she could, allowing the circuits within to pop and sizzle as the whole system shorted out. Nobody would be able to get in there to salvage anything before the fire consumed it all. At least *that* lab would not produce any more augments and the blood they took from her would be destroyed once and for all. Still, there was the issue of the blood that had already been tested, but that would have to wait for another time. Now it was time to go.

She backed away a few more steps, watching through the little window as flames consumed more and more of Red Panzer's precious equipment, supplies and research. The ventilation system was doing a nice job of keeping the flames hot and she smiled as she slowly turned, her eyes sweeping the workshop she had retreated into. Taking the last exploding batarang from her belt, she turned toward the door and froze as her eyes filled with Red Panzer.

He stood in the doorway, the only other way out, and his full attention was on her. The control panel near the door beeped twice and the solid door closed behind him—and the mechanism loudly clattered as it locked. The panel beeped twice more and they were both sealed inside.

"It is blast proof," he informed coldly. "I doubt that even your mother could force her way through it." He raised his head slightly. "You have become quite an annoyance, little girl, and I shall do what I should have done when you were first brought here."

Elissa mumbled, "Ah crud," as she backed away from him. Her grip tightened on the explosive batarang she still held and her finger found the small button that would arm it. When he strode toward her, she yelled as she hurled it at him with all her might, sending it thirty feet across the room to impact his chest dead center. The explosion sent a shockwave back that made her ears pop and she shielded her eyes as it blew her back a step.

The blast only caused Panzer to lurch backward slightly, but he kept advancing on her.

"Such spirit to be wasted on one so foolish," he said in a mocking tone. "How will you meet your end, little girl?"

"I'm kind of hoping to put it off for a few centuries," she replied as she backed away. Stopping as she felt the heat coming through the door of the lab, she glanced over her shoulder, then looked around her in quick motions. The room was plenty long, but only about twenty feet wide and the walls had work benches coming out about four feet, cutting down maneuvering room. At this point, she only wanted to stall, and she prayed that help would find her in time.

"Let me make it quick," he suggested.

Setting her hands on her hips, she barked back, "Now where's the fun in that? Maybe I want you to work for it." She gasped as that big gun emerged from his left arm, her eyes locked on it as she raised her hands before her. "Hang on a minute! Is this really how you want to…"

He took aim at her with it.

"I guess it is," she mumbled, her gaze locked on the muzzle. She raised her eyes to his face and played the last card she had. "Well go ahead and shoot me, then you can go back and tell all of your people that you had to shoot me because you knew I'd kick your butt if you fought me fairly." He actually seemed to consider what she said, and her hand moved swiftly, taking the grapple from her belt and aiming it carefully to one side of him.

Before he could react she had fired it and the cord fed out perfectly, then slacked as the hook buried itself in the far wall. With a push of the button, the grapple pulled her brutally forward and she leaned back against it, sliding on her heels around him. Quickly nearing the far wall, she leaped up and kicked as hard as she could, slamming both boots into the middle of the door to knock it from its track, and she hit it with a very solid clunk.

Falling to her side on the floor, she was quick to roll over, lunge to her feet and face Panzer, who was turning toward her, then she looked over her shoulder and announced, "You sure are right about that door. It didn't budge!" She backed up against it as he advanced and sweetly asked, "So, um, how do you open it?"

"It will open once you are dead," he growled. "Too many times have you interfered with mein plans, but after today you will interfere no more." As he reached her, his gun retreated back into his arm and he threw a hard punch at her.

Golden Angel darted aside barely in time and the solid blast proof door shuddered under the impact, and the steel succumbed to the metal fist of the mechanical Nazi. Staying low, she tried to get behind him as he turned, tried to use her superior speed and agility to some kind of advantage, but despite his extra bulk he was even faster than the last time they had met and spun around to strike at her again as she dodged away from him. Backing up quickly as he swung his arm at her again, her back slammed into one of the work benches and as his other arm came at her she threw herself aside, rolling over her shoulder as his fist crashed through the metal bench right where she had been.

He spun around and struck again and she caught his fist on her gauntlets and stumbled away. Panzer advanced, reaching to the work bench he had just smashed and tearing it from its holdings against the wall and floor. He threw it hard seemingly right at her head and she predictably ducked under it, and this was exactly what he wanted. As the bench crashed onto the other side of the room she sprang up and tried to retreat from him, raising her arm when he swung at her again, but this time he grabbed her wrist, her gauntlet and loosed a surge of electricity into her.

Screaming, Golden Angel's entire body convulsed, and a second later she was swung around and hurled against the unforgiving concrete wall. She collapsed limply and fell face down to the workbench beneath where she hit the wall, lying motionless for long seconds as her enemy turned and slowly approached her. With a little moan, she pulled her arms to her and pushed herself up, raising her head to get her wits back to her, but she did not recover in time. Panzer was upon her and slammed his open hand down onto her back, and she screamed again as he pushed her to the metal work bench and shocked her again.

As the girl struggled to breathe, he took her by the ankle and spun around, hurling her across the room where she crashed back first into the benches on the other side, and the one she hit most directly collapsed toward the wall as she struck it.

Elissa found herself lying twisted on the floor, once again trying to regain her wits, but this time she forced them back to her, forced herself up and standing before he could reach her again. She stumbled toward the sealed door, reaching to her utility belt as she heard him closing on her, and as he reached for her she wheeled to the left, swinging that arm to send a flash-bang directly at his face.

It struck and exploded and his advance halted. He turned his face away and raised his hand as if to ward off another and Golden Angel struck as quickly as she could, ramming her shoulder into his belly and driving him from his feet and hard to his back on the solid concrete floor.

Not waiting for him to recover and get his hands on her again, she sprang off of him, leaping away and catching herself on her palms, springing off of her hands and somersaulting quickly to her feet, and she wheeled around as soon as her boots found the floor.

Instead of rising from the floor, Panzer directed his arm at her and deployed his gun again, sweeping from one side to the other as he opened fire.

Elissa leapt up onto the benches on one side, crouching there as he fired blindly across the room. The rounds he fired tore through the concrete wall and the door to the burning lab and the young Amazon knew that these were the bullets that would pass right through her gauntlets. She braced herself as he sat up and half turned, and when he directed his gun at her she jumped from the bench, narrowly avoiding his next salvo. Her boots hit the floor and she bounded twice to the other side, hurling herself up onto the benches on the other side where she pushed off of the wall and rolled back onto the floor, staying a split second ahead of Panzer's arch of fire.

He stopped firing long enough to turn fully and stand, and this time he raised his other arm. A much larger barrel, about an inch and a half in diameter, slid from his outer arm and he directed it toward the elusive girl, firing just as she moved.

She barely got out of the way in time and the round struck the edge of the work bench behind her, and this one exploded. The blast threw her across the room and she slammed head-on into the tool laden shelves on a bench across the room and the shelves collapsed under her and tools retreated in every direction scattering across the floor. Bleeding and stunned, she whimpered as she struggled to push herself back up. Panic struck as she heard those heavy boots approaching again and she staggered back to her feet, turning on him just as his hand slammed into her throat and closed around her neck. She grabbed onto his wrist with both hands, her eyes wide as she looked up into his skeleton like mask, as he picked her up and wheeled around with her.

Panzer turned sharply, spinning all the way around as he raised her up, then he slammed her down hard onto the metal top work bench, so hard her back and head caved in the metal where she hit, and on impact the girl went limp. Still holding her throat, the maniacal Nazi stared down at his helpless, unconscious adversary for long seconds. Her eyes were closed, her lips ajar and her arms fell to her sides, and she breathed in the slow, rhythmic breaths of sleep.

Slowly, he withdrew his hand and allowed her head to roll away from him.

"Almost too easy," he growled as he held his right arm over her. In a shriek of metal the blade hidden there lanced forth, stopping with a horrible clink. He held his hand in a fist as he just stared down at her.

The ceiling trembled from the battle that raged above and in his secret compound.

"No," he said as if to correct himself. He took her arms and raised them over her head, crossing her wrists as he held them to the table with his left hand. "You will see this coming." Lowering his right hand to her belly, he placed his palm and fingers against her bare skin there and shot in a brief surge of electric shock. Her body convulsed and she cried out as she was awakened by the pain, blinking rapidly to bring the world around her into focus.

Consciousness finally returned to her, as did the realization of her predicament. With a couple of hard jerks she tried to free her hands, then she froze as she looked up into his face. Her eyes darted to the scimitar-like blade he held over her and she tensed more as he slowly directed the tip of it toward her belly, and she whimpered and tried to shrink away as he pushed the point of it against her skin.

"You will know the price of defying me," he informed with an authoritative tone. The lenses slid away from his eyes, retreating to the sides of that metal mask, and the blue of his eyes was of no comfort as they narrowed. "Look into mein eyes as I slowly bring the pain of death."

"Later," she corrected. Drawing her knees to her chest, she curled her body over and sent the heel of one foot solidly into his chin, snapping his head back and forcing him to lurch backward slightly. This loosened the grip he had on her wrists just enough and she jerked her hands free of him, rolling backward ending up on her feet. As he tried to recover and swung the blade at her she leapt aside, somersaulting backward to the floor to end up on her feet again. This time she stumbled, still feeling stunned from her impact with the work bench and she staggered away from him as quickly as she could as he turned and advanced on her again.

His machine guns emerged and he raised his arm before him, and this time he was far too close for her to easily dodge away.

As he fired, Elissa swung around in what she knew was a futile attempt to elude him. She felt the bullets slam into her back. It was like being punched by someone with sharp knuckles and she staggered forward and fell to her knees, catching herself on her hands.

The guns stopped.

She looked over her shoulder to see him just standing there, and he seemed confused. Looking down to her back, she was surprised to see no holes in the mantle she wore, no impact points.

Panzer trained his weapon on her and fired again and the Amazon ally coated projectiles struck the mantle as before. Ripples of blue light were sent out from the impact points and the bullets lazily bounced harmlessly away.

Silence gripped the room again and the two just stared at each other.

"Huh," Golden Angel finally said. "Who knew?"

Clearly angered by this new development, Red Panzer strode toward her, and this time she was too slow to elude him. He grabbed onto her arm, then wheeled around and threw her toward the other end of the room, watching as she bounced off of the wall on one side, spun around and awkwardly hit one work bench, then another before careening into the wall beside the door. As she struggled to stand and get her wits back about her, he raised his other arm, taking aim with the grenade gun, and he fired one shot.

Elissa instinctively swept her arm to deflect it and it exploded, slamming her back into the wall again. This time she crumpled to the floor. Shrapnel had been repelled by her Kevlar clothing, but it had also found her where she was not protected. Pushing herself back up, she bled badly from one shoulder, two deep wounds to her belly, and a long cut across her cheek, another over her eye. Her ears rang and she could not get her wits about her. Covering her wounded belly with one hand, she slowly staggered back up, her eyes unable to focus as she looked to the advancing Nazi madman.

Panzer took her by the throat and picked her up, once again slamming her down onto the work bench. Already dazed and wounded, she simply did not have anything left to fight back. His mechanical hand squeezed around her throat and he pushed her down hard against the bench top.

She desperately grabbed onto his hand with both of hers, finally alert enough to defend herself, but it was too late.

"Look into mein eyes," he ordered. "I will be the last thing you see as you die."

The door exploded into the room, taking much of the wall with it and Panzer half turned that way.

"Demon!" Beowulf shouted as he charged into the room. Much of his body was encased in a gold colored, form fitting armor. His gauntlets were also gold in color and each brandished two blades that swept back from the outsides. A new mantle swept behind him, a white one with elaborate gold embroidery along the edges and what appeared to be a golden Nordic helmet covered his head from the top to the base of his thick neck all the way around and was etched in ornate Nordic symbols.

Not intimidated by his larger, mechanical foe, the Nordic warrior stormed right to him, and as the big Nazi turned fully to receive him, Beowulf struck with a mighty yell, slamming his fist solidly into his enemy's metal face.

Red Panzer's head snapped around and he staggered backward, recovering an instant before the Nordic Champion's other fist rammed hard into the center of his chest plate. This blow knocked him from the floor sent him hurling through the room back first to crash through the heavy door to the burning lab with an ominous bang and flames exploded from the doorway.

No longer interested in his fallen foe, Beowulf turned his

attention to the little Amazon girl who still lay on the broken workbench and stared up at him from her back. He quickly took his helmet off and tossed it onto the bench beside her, then he took her hand and informed in a slight voice, "I am here now, Schatzi. Safety has found you."

Elissa could only nod as she stared into those dark blue eyes of his.

He raised a hand to the headpiece he still wore, touching a pink gem that was near his temple as he pulled his other hand from hers and laid it gently on her bleeding belly. A pink light sprayed from the gem, then from the hand he touched her with, and quickly it spread all over her, enveloping her in a pink glow.

Drawing a deep breath, the little Amazon girl felt the light as a sweeping warmth that blanketed her completely. She felt it penetrate her many wounds and soothe the pain from them, felt it seep into every part of her and all of the aches and soreness fled from her battered little body. Strength poured back into her and awareness and in seconds he took his fingers from the stone he touched and the warm light faded, but not its effects.

With a nod, he assured, "Your wounds have been attended to, Princess." He tapped the pink stone and explained, "It is from the amulet of Eir, our Goddess of Healing, and she assured me that it would one day..." He raised his head slightly. "That it would one day protect my heart."

Elissa smiled and took his hand with both of hers. "It worked nicely, Handsome." She sat up, still staring into his eyes as she informed, "Did you know your mantle will deflect bullets?"

"It is meant as a protector," he informed. "As you see, it keeps more than a night chill away."

She nodded. "Thank you, Beowulf. You've saved my life twice now."

Hearing a crash from the burning lab, she hopped down from the bench and turned at the waist, clinging to the Nordic champion as she saw the huge form that strode from the fire. "Ah, crud. We need to..." She trailed off as Beowulf grasped her shoulder and she watched as he took his helmet and turned fully to the nightmare that approached them.

Taking a few steps forward, Beowulf slid his helmet back onto his head and assumed his battle stance as he shouted, "I am ready for you, demon!"

Red Panzer strode from the inferno and directed the large barrel at his enemy's chest, assuring, "And I am ready for you." He fired a grenade with a true aim and watched as it slammed into the Nordic warrior's chest.

Elissa backed up into the bench as she watched her champion slam onto the concrete floor on his back. Drawing a loud gasp, she saw Panzer direct both arms, both guns on the big Norseman and she cried, "No!" as he opened fire.

The burst Red Panzer fired into his downed enemy seemed to last forever as kryptonite tipped and the armor piercing Amazon alloy sheathed rounds hammered away at their target. Seconds and a few hundred rounds later it was over and the big Nazi slowly lowered his arms and smoking guns, staring down at his victim as the smoke cleared.

Slowly shaking her head, Elissa whimpered, "No," as she also looked through the clearing smoke.

Beowulf sat up and sprang to his feet with a speed that did not appear to belong to someone his size. He seemed unscathed but for blackened impact points all over his armor and he stood there for long seconds with his brow low, his teeth bared and his hands clenched into tight fists.

Panzer took a step back.

With heavy, long strides, Beowulf strode forward and shouted, "Put away your toys and fight me with honor!"

The guns retreated and that blade lanced forth from Red Panzer's arm and was taken by a hum and crackle as arcs of electricity spat from it. Beowulf reached to his side, to his belt to retrieve a small hammer, one that looked like it would easily fit into one's pocket. The dark wooden handle was very short and completely engulfed by the big Norseman's hand and the hammer head was a slightly tapered rectangular piece of gray iron, one with the edges evenly rounded off. There was nothing special about it. It was just a little hammer.

Seeing it, Elissa raised a hand to her head and mumbled, "Aw, man!"

Shaking his head, Panzer pointed to the hammer and scoffed, "You mean to fight with that little thing?"

"I mean to kill you with it," Beowulf growled back. Suddenly he held the small hammer above his head and shouted, "Mjölnir, awaken!"

Lightning spat from every part of the room with ear shattering cracks that made the young Amazon ball herself up and cover her ears. The small hammer burst into a blinding spectacle of lightning and fire and in seconds a boom sounded as a shockwave exploded from it.

Beowulf slowly lowered his arm. The once small hammer was enormous with a long handle that was encased in bronze that was riveted in what appeared to be gold. Now the size of the Norseman's combined fists and deeply etched with ancient Nordic symbols, the hammer head seemed to glow and occasionally would spit a small burst of lightning with a sharp crack. A chain hung from the other side of the handle, gold in color and about a foot long and ending in a solid bronze ball about half the size of a man's fist.

Red Panzer took a step back, his attention on the hammer as he lowered his arms. Looking to the big Norseman, he demanded, "Tell me who you are!"

His eyes narrowing, the Nordic warrior replied in a deep, menacing voice, "I am Beowulf, Champion of the Norseman."

"I am Red Panzer," the mechanical Nazi countered, "and I too am a champion of the Norsemen."

"You are not!" Golden Angel barked. Looking to Beowulf, she reported, "He's a Nazi butcher and a murderer and he's trying to take over the world!"

Beowulf glanced at her, and slowly raised his chin. "Nazi. A follower of Hitler, the Führer."

"Yes," Panzer confirmed as he took a step forward. "It was the will of the Führer that we rule this world, that we bring back the ancient ways of our people. With the new Reich we can do so."

"I know of the Nazis," the big Nordic Champion said with a soft, sympathetic voice. "The Nazis promised a world free of corruption, promised to bring back the honor of the ancients."

Slowly, Golden Angel shook her head.

"The Reich was meant to bring our people from despair," Beowulf went on.

Elissa shouted, "The Nazis also butchered millions of innocent people and started a horrible war!"

Beowulf just glanced back at her.

Holding his hand out, Red Panzer offered, "Join me, Champion of the Norsemen, and together we will usher in a new age and build a new world, a Nordic world, a German world!"

The big Norseman looked down to Panzer's metal hand.

"Beowulf, please," Golden Angel pled as she slid down off of the work bench. She took his arm and he simply pulled away.

"Mind your place, Amazon," Beowulf growled. He transferred his war hammer from his right hand to his left, then he took Panzer's hand in a powerful grip.

Elissa's mouth hung open as she slowly shook her head and backed away.

"Let us bring order to the world," Red Panzer said.

"Yes," Beowulf agreed, "bring order to the world." His grip on Panzer's hand tightened and he jerked the mechanical Nazi toward him, glaring up at him as he roared, "A world without your kind!" He brought the hammer straight up, slamming it into the bottom of Panzer's chin.

Red Panzer's head snapped back and before he could recover, the hammer drove home right in the middle of his face.

Beowulf half turned and delivered a solid kick that knocked the huge, mechanically encased man toward the burning lab and hard to his back. As his enemy struggled to get back to his feet, the Nordic Champion took the hammer by the end of its handle and bade, "Come and fight me!" He allowed the Nazi to stand, keeping his eyes trained on that metal, skeleton mask as he poised himself for battle.

"You will die like the rest," Panzer growled as he advanced.

"Perhaps someday," Beowulf said with a smile, "but not today."

With the smoke from the burning laboratory starting to burn her eyes, Golden Angel backed away as she watched the two engage.

With a swing of his arm, Red Panzer brought the blade hard against his enemy, and Beowulf met it with his hammer. When the two weapons met they did so with a brilliant flash and spitting, crackling lightning. This continued for a moment as each struck and the other parried. The much larger Red Panzer advanced, and his foe slowly retreated. As Panzer brought the blade down yet again and it was blocked with the hammer yet again, the mechanical Nazi quickly adjusted and grabbed onto Beowulf's arm, and he unleashed the full power of the shocking contacts in his hand. Beowulf yelled as the electricity surged through him, throwing his head back and closing his eyes as Panzer drove him backward.

In seconds the Nordic Champion looked to his foe with eyes that glowed blue and he clenched his bared teeth as he shouted, "Lightning is among the elements I control!" He knocked Panzer's arm away, breaking his grip with the electrified hand and he swung hard with his war hammer, connecting with the Nazi's head again.

Panzer slashed and his blade glanced off of the Norseman's chest plate in a cascade of sparks.

With another mighty yell, Beowulf brought the hammer down again, only to have it blocked by Panzer's blade, but this time his fist torpedoed right into the Nazi's chest, knocking him backward through the air and toward the burning lab again. He dropped the hammer only to catch it by the bronze ball at the end of the chain. Swinging his forearm around, he swung the hammer in a circle, his eyes on an enemy who struggled to regain control of his wits. Faster and faster the hammer spun from the chain until it cut the air with a sharp whine and was but a blur. The glow from the hammer head grew brighter and brighter to form a pale blue ring of light.

Red Panzer prepared himself to meet his foe once more, and he shouted, "It is our destiny to rule the world together, son of the Norsemen!"

Beowulf shook his head and countered, "You and your kind are a disgrace to our people! It is *my* destiny to put you down!" With a mighty yell he swung his weapon once very wide, then loosed it toward his foe in a brilliant display of pale blue lightning.

Mjölnir struck Red Panzer square in the chest and the explosion of fire and lightning blasted him backward into the burning lab. There was a crash from within there and flames rolled out along the ceiling as smoke trailing debris fled from the room.

Turning toward the young Amazon, Beowulf enveloped her in his arms and mantle and pulled her to him, shielding her from the explosion from the lab that tore into the work room and shattered work benches and scattered tools, debris and burning embers in every direction. When it subsided, he looked over his shoulder to the inferno behind him and raised his open hand, ordering, "Mjölnir, return."

The hammer flew head first from the burning lab and quarter turned to slam itself handle first into the Norseman's palm.

Elissa coughed into her fist, then pushed away to arm's length and looked up to the Nordic Champion as he looked down to her. "How did you know to come for me?" she asked.

He smiled and tapped the blue stone he had pressed into her tiara, the stone that had taken the place of the star there. "The shard of the Eye of Odin. I could sense you were in peril."

She raised her brow. "And you couldn't come five minutes sooner?"

"Got here as soon as I could," he laughed. Looking down to his belt, he slid the hammer into its ring there and ushered her along, ordering, "Let us get you out of here."

Golden Angel took his hand and turned fully, agreeing, "Totally! We need to get topside and give the Justice League a hand. The bad guys are way stronger than they were and..." She looked over her shoulder at him as they entered the main corridor, and she offered him a little smile. "You ready to go kick some butt, Champion of the Norsemen?"

With a smile back, he assured, "I am at your side, Amazon Princess."

They arrived at the surface to see that Metallo and Bane and more than a dozen augments had most of the Justice League either down or retreating.

Battered and bleeding, Green Lantern landed beside them and stumbled, falling to all fours, and Golden Angel rushed to his aid, kneeling beside him as she laid her hand on his back.

He looked over his shoulder at her and shook his head. "They have countermeasures to everything we can throw at them, even my ring." He motioned to the side of the warehouse. "Firestorm's over there. They have some kind of radiation absorbing foam that took him down, him and Captain Atom. Flash is down, Arrow and Martian Manhunter are down and we don't dare bring Superman back in with them firing kryptonite tipped bullets." He pushed himself up and stood, stumbling aside and was steadied when Beowulf took his arm. Looking down to the little Amazon, he grimly reported, "Kiddo, Wonder Woman's down."

Elissa gasped and took a step back, her wide eyes locked on Lantern's. Quickly regaining her wits, she demanded, "Where?"

He motioned to the other side of the warehouse. "Over there. Batman's pulled her to cover but it's only a matter of time before the…" He looked to the right and set himself, taking a step back.

An augment, a really large, square jawed man who was dressed in the same black commando gear as the rest, charged toward them with two slightly smaller ones behind him.

Green Lantern retreated and shouted, "My ring's drained!"

"We got this!" Golden Angel insisted as she turned fully to meet them.

The largest of them and one at his side turned on Beowulf as the other attacked Golden Angel.

With a single swing of his fist, the Nordic Champion knocked the largest of them out cold, then the same fist swung around and slammed into the other's head, taking him down as well.

Elissa sidestepped and kicked her opponent hard in the belly, wheeled completely around and slammed her boot hard into the side of his head. He went down, but rolled to his feet to face her again, and Beowulf dispatched him with a single blow from the back of his fist. She looked up to him and smiled, holding her fist to him, and he seemed to know to bump it with his own. Glancing at Lantern, she grasped the Nordic Champion's hands and said, "I need to get to my Mom." She looked over her shoulder to Bane and Metallo, who still advanced toward a group of elusive Justice League.

"Leave them to me," he ordered. "You two find Princess Diana."

Green Lantern grabbed onto the Norseman's thick arm and shouted, "They've taken down the best of us! You can't take them alone!"

Beowulf smiled and patted Lantern's shoulder. "I've taken demons and giants many times, my friend, and I shall defeat them, too." He motioned across the warehouse. "Go now. See that she arrives safely to attend Princess Diana." His predator's gaze shifted to the two super villains and he strode that way.

As Green Lantern raised his hand to protest, Elissa simply grasped his arm and assured, "Don't worry about him. He just kicked the crap out of Red Panzer. Now come on and show me where Mom is!"

Their attention was on the Norseman as he advanced toward his next battle.

Stopping only twenty or so feet away, he shouted, "You there!" When they turned to him, he smiled and took the hammer from his belt, swinging it in a circle by the chain as he asked, "Which of you falls first?"

Metallo raised his arm and the smoking barrel of his gun with it. He fired a short burst that slammed into the Norseman's chest—and bounced off in green flashes.

His eyes shifting to the metal mercenary, Beowulf shifted his stance, then he yelled and hurled the hammer in a streak of blue light, sending it with a sharp aim right into the kryptonite chamber of Metallo's chest. In a bright flash and explosion of lightning and fire, a boom shook the warehouse as the hammer drove Metallo from his feet and backward into a stack of pallets that exploded into thousands of fleeing parts as he hit them.

Bane also watched, half turning as he watched his partner dispatched with a single blow.

When the smoke and airborne debris cleared, Metallo lay sprawled on his back and not moving with the handle of the hammer protruding from his chest. Smoke still rose from him and an occasional spark of electricity spat from around it.

Looking back to the big Norseman, Bane knew he had a size advantage, but he seemed to be laced with doubt.

"Put away your weapons," Beowulf ordered as he strode forward, "and face me as a man."

Bane threw his weapons from him and clenched his hands into tight fists as he also advanced.

Elissa wheeled around a stack of pallets and froze, drawing a loud gasp as she saw her wounded mother, held by her father. Behind them, pallets and shattered wooden debris burned and poured more smoke into the already hazy air.

Batman sat back on his calves and had pulled Wonder Woman half into his lap. He cradled her head gently in one hand and looked back to his daughter with sullen eyes. Diana was burnt and bruised all over. A deep gash was cut diagonally across her thigh, another across her belly, still another across her lower forehead and the bridge of her nose. Blood streamed from the corner of her mouth.

Golden Angel rushed to her, slamming down on her knees as she breathed, "No!" Looking to her father, her eyes were wide and fearful and she slowly shook her head.

"She tried to take Bane and Metallo by herself," he reported. "They're both twice as strong as they used to be and we knew this, and still she thought she could take them both. I told her..."

"I know," Elissa assured, looking down at her battered mother. "She listens about as well as... Well, I do." Slowly, the girl placed her hands on the fallen Amazon Princess, one on her belly and one on her wounded thigh. Closing her eyes, she bowed her head and the golden light began to spray from between her fingers. Soon, this light erupted into a warm golden fire that enveloped Wonder Woman completely. Many colors of light sprayed from Diana's wounds and they began to close and mend.

In a moment, the golden light faded and Elissa whimpered as she rocked forward, barely catching herself before she fell. Blinking her eyes back open, she looked to her still sleeping mother, to her father, and nodded to him. "She'll be okay, but she has to awaken on her own. It will take some time."

"Then we need to keep the augments off of her," Batman informed.

"All over it," she assured.

Green Lantern looked down to his ring and reported, "I need to get this recharged."

"Go on," Batman ordered, "and get back here as quick as you can. We'll hold out."

Lantern nodded back, then took his communicator and worked the controls. Light shimmered around him and in a few seconds he was gone.

With her solemn eyes on her father's, Golden Angel asked, "What now, Batman?"

He looked behind her, to two augments who had seen them and were approaching. Turning his eyes back to the girl, he informed in his deep, monotone voice, "We go to work, and hit them head-on."

Elissa smiled.

Batman gently lowered the slumbering Amazon Princess to the ground, then he stood and took Golden Angel's side.

She set her hands on her hips and watched them near from about forty feet away, then she looked up at the Dark Knight and informed, "I'll take the big one on the right."

"Go for it, Angel," he replied.

They charged out to meet the augments, Batman reaching to his belt and Golden Angel running ahead of him.

Bane and Beowulf were content to settle things with their fists and as they fought a savage fight many of the augments stopped their pursuit of the battered Justice League and turned to watch the battle. Many of the Justice League also stopped to witness this fight of titans.

Both were very skilled, very experienced. Bane enjoyed a size advantage, but quickly learned that strength favored his slightly smaller foe. Throwing a hard right at the Norseman, he was prepared to have it blocked and half turned to kick his opponent in the belly, and finally connected. Beowulf staggered back a few steps, smiling as he set himself to receive the big mercenary again, and beckoned him on. Bane struck relentlessly and Beowulf knocked away punch after punch, but as of yet had not made much effort to strike back, only throwing token punches from time to time to keep his opponent off guard.

Near Wonder Woman, Golden Angel spun around and slammed her boot solidly into the side of her opponent's head, sending him to the concrete floor with a dull thump. Looking quickly to her father, she smiled as she saw his opponent had his back to her, and she ran the twenty feet or so that way, leaping into the air and raising her arm to bring her gauntlet down hard onto the back of his head. When the augment staggered forward, Batman slammed a hard uppercut into his chin to finish him off, then he stepped aside to let the black clad henchman fall.

Golden Angel and Batman looked to each other, then to the battle that raged in the center of the warehouse, one that Beowulf finally seemed to start taking seriously.

Bane's frustration seemed to be mounting and he finally retreated a step to get his bearings and catch his breath.

Rather than pursue, Beowulf set his fists on his hips, a smile on his face as he shook his head and observed, "You look like you need to catch your wind, my friend. I'll give you a moment."

The Norseman was mocking him and Bane knew it. Growling, he clenched his hands into tight fists again and charged forward, this time lowering his shoulder. Beowulf reacted quickly and also lowered his shoulder, and the two met head-on in a loud clack of armor. Bane's next realization was slamming back first to the concrete. Beowulf stood over him, shaking his head as he set his fists on his hips again. Bane raised his head and looked up at him, then slowly his head settled back to the floor and rocked to one side, his eyes closing despite his best efforts to keep them open.

Elissa threw her fist up and screamed, "Yeah!" as she saw Bane leveled and now unconscious. "That's what I'm talkin' about!" Powerful arms wrapped around her and pinned her arms to her sides and before she realized she was lifted from the floor. Squeezed so hard she could barely breathe, she struggled with all she had to free herself, but to no avail.

Batman tried to intervene but was attacked from behind as well and a well placed fist to the back of his head almost rendered him unconscious. He staggered and fell to his knees, catching himself on his palms as he fought to remain conscious.

The augment holding Golden Angel looked down to Batman, to his colleague, then to her as he smiled and informed, "Next time you should finish your opponent before you turn your back on him."

Elissa fought wildly as he squeezed her even harder and she cried out desperately as she fought to at least free her arms.

"Hey," the augment holding her said to the other. "Come over here and chloroform this little brat. I think Red Panzer wants her alive."

The other augment slammed face first onto the ground. Elissa's struggling ceased and she and her assailant looked down to the unconscious augment. Still tightly holding the girl, the augment looked over his shoulder, then slowly he set her down.

Golden Angel broke free of him and darted away a couple of steps before turning on him, but he was turning his back to her, and facing Wonder Woman!

Her hands set on her hips, Diana raised her brow and suggested, "You can give up quietly or Golden Angel and I can have some fun with you. Your call." When he hesitantly raised his palms to her and backed away a step, she smiled and nodded to him, commending, "That's better."

Golden Angel leapt up and slammed her gauntlet into the back of his head anyway, and this time he was unconscious before he hit the ground.

Looking to her mother, Elissa set her hands on her hips and nodded to her, and Diana smiled and nodded back.

As her mother approached, Golden Angel looked away and down as she recalled something, and she mumbled, "Ah, crud."

Wonder Woman half turned her head and asked, "What is it?"

Looking up to the Amazon Princess, Elissa fought panic as she informed, "One of the lab people down there said they ran DNA tests on me to… Mom, they know who my father is! She said Panzer sold the information to the highest bidder!"

Beowulf had reached them by that time, followed by a few battered members of the Justice League, and he informed, "We will stop them, then."

"It isn't that simple," Diana informed as she stared down at her daughter. "That information could have been transmitted or emailed anywhere by now."

Rubbing the back of his head, Batman got to his feet and corrected, "I don't think so. Transactions of that nature usually take place on paper. The buyer will want something tangible. I'm fine, by the way."

Diana looked to him and said, "Good to know. We have to find those results and destroy them."

"I already blew up the lab," Elissa informed.

"The results most likely were not in there," Batman said. "With the complex under attack—"

"Car door!" Golden Angel shouted. She spun around, to an open door and pointed that way. "That was closed a minute ago!"

"Good eye, Angel," Batman commended as he looked that way.

A hum from the middle of the room drew their attention and they looked behind them.

"Great Hera!" Diana exclaimed as Red Panzer rose from the floor on the elevator platform. With him were four more armored augments, all armed with long barreled weapons.

Beowulf turned and took Golden Angel's shoulder, his brow low over his eyes as he ordered, "Go to the outside and attend to that,

Schatzi. He is mine to do battle with."

Grasping his hand, Elissa ordered, "You just be careful, okay?"

He smiled an amused smile and nodded to her, then he turned to Wonder Woman and nodded to her before striding fearlessly toward his next bout with Red Panzer.

Batman raised his chin, his eyes on the departing Norseman as he asked, "You aren't going to give him a hand?"

Golden Angel took his shoulder and smiled as she informed, "Seriously, he won't need it." Wheeling around, she looked to the open door on the other side of the warehouse and the obstacle course of pallets and crates between her and it and she barked, "Come on!" Before her parents could respond she darted that way, wheeling around a tall stack of pallets, hurdling over a large crate...

As her feet contacted the floor on the other side of it, the floor dropped from beneath her and she barked a scream as she dropped nearly fifteen feet into the complex below. She landed in a crouch, lowering one hand to the floor for balance as her cape settled perfectly behind her. Looking around her, she recognized the big training area she had been taken to before. It was not empty this time and as she looked around she saw two bodies lying near the wall to her right. A loud gasp surged into her as she sprang up and ran to them.

Crouching down beside Black Canary first, she reached to her throat to check for a pulse, then she looked her over for injuries. Canary was out, lying on her back with her hands bound behind her, her ankles bound together. Looking to the left Elissa saw Fire lying on her side with her hands also bound behind her and lumps of some kind of yellow foam all over her.

"Our latest little fly," a man observed from behind her.

Golden Angel sprang up and swung around to find herself facing three augments, one a large man, one a large woman with short brown hair and the third...

A little snarl took Elissa's mouth and her eyes narrowed as her gaze found Zack standing between them, dressed in the black commando gear and body armor the others were. He stared back at her with a look of disdain and hard eyes that told her she was nothing more to him than just another target. Screaming from the back of her mind was the reality that she was barely a match for one augment, and now she faced three. She could not hear that, could not respond to it. All that mattered were the laments of her broken heart, and the boy who had caused her that pain was now in her sights.

The two adult augments strode toward her.

Golden Angel responded too quickly for them to react, her hands darting across her belly to her utility belt, into two pouches there and hurling two small white balls at the faces of the two augments in a blur.

The small orbs each hit their intended targets and exploded into a white gas. Coughing and backing away, they raised their hands to their faces and seconds later collapsed as the anesthetic gas dissipated.

Zack watched the two larger augments fall, then he turned a challenging glare on the girl as he growled, "Don't expect that to work on me, little girl."

Reaching behind her, Elissa unbuckled her utility belt and pulled it from her waist, tossing it behind her to where Black Canary rested. Her hand found the chain that held her cape together and unfastened it, and she pulled it from her and folded it over her arm, her eyes on him the whole time as she half turned and tossed it onto Canary.

"Not going to try to gas me, too?" Zack spat.

Slowly shaking her head, Elissa informed, "Oh no, Butthead. You aren't getting off that easy." She began to approach him with slow steps, cracking her knuckles as she neared him. "I'm kicking your butt old school."

"You only think you are," he snarled as he set himself to receive her. "I'm going to show you what happens to people who betray Herr Panzer. Bring it on!"

Even as he assumed his battle stance, Golden Angel strode right up to him and her fist was a blur as it jabbed up toward his face and slammed into his nose hard enough to snap his head back. As he staggered backward and reached for his face, her other fist connected with his jaw in a brutal uppercut and his head snapped back again and he staggered further. She wheeled around and slammed her boot into his belly and this time he was taken from his feet and slammed into the wall about seven feet from where he was kicked.

Elissa stopped her pursuit and watched him crumple to the floor, and she folded her arms as she watched him push himself back up. "By the way," she informed coldly, "I'm dumping you."

He glared at her as he slowly stood and wiped some of the blood from his lip that had oozed from his nose.

She strode toward him again, this time throwing a hard right cross, but this time he was ready and blocked her strike, and he connected with his own, slamming his fist hard into her bare belly. The wind exploded from her and she doubled over and stumbled back a few steps, not recovering in time to avoid his other fist before it slammed into her eye. She spun around and fell, lying sprawled on the floor for long seconds as she seemed to try and get her wits about her. When he approached and reached for her, though, she wheeled over, grabbed his wrist and drew one leg to her right before ramming her heel into his belly. Spinning around, she sent her other foot at him but he recovered in time to block her kick with his arm.

Zack turned out to be better trained than Elissa had thought and this match turned into a pitched battle of strike and parry. Much more agile, she danced about and avoided most of his strikes rather than blocking them. Pound for pound she was a little stronger, but he was much larger and this more than offset that advantage. Quickness and agility became her weapons and she backed out of range each time he tried to strike, only to dart in again to strike back. Skill favored neither as each played to their strengths, but Golden Angel had been trained by masters of many disciplines, and the teachings of one of them were what she called upon now.

Feeling himself beginning to tire, Zack knew this fight had to end, so after throwing a jab that she quickly avoided, he lowered his shoulder and charged her and she did not respond in time to avoid him. He grabbed her around the waist as he rammed his shoulder into her belly and easily picked her up and ran her into the far wall as hard as he could.

Elissa cried out as the air exploded from her and before she could get her wits about her again he turned and threw her toward the center of the room. She had the presence of mind to twist herself and throw her shoulder down, rolling awkwardly to come to rest on her back. As quickly as she could, she turned over and pushed herself up, but he was already upon her and wrapped an arm around her neck. Before the crook of his arm could close around her throat, she got a hand under his elbow and pushed up enough to bring it close to her mouth.

Zack shouted in pain as she bit his arm and he threw her away from him. She spun around and lunged, slamming her fist solidly into his belly, then brought the other up under his chin. Stunned, he staggered backward and she struck at his face and body many more times, baring her teeth as she did. He finally blocked her fist and struck back, punching her hard in the eye and snapping her head around. This time she stumbled backward and he pursued, connecting with her face two more times and her belly once. Finally, when he jabbed at her face again, she arched her back and turned and his fist barely missed her. Sweeping her left arm, she knocked his arm around and half turned him and her other fist slammed into his side right below his ribs. This clearly hurt him and he staggered away from her, just the right distance for her to throw a kick that connected with his belly and doubled him over. With blood streaming from her mouth and nose and a cut above her left eye, she yelled in Amazon fashion and lunged at him, swinging as hard as she could.

When her fist contacted the side of his head, he was spun all the way around and staggered. He clearly did not have his wits about him when he turned back to her, also bleeding from the nose and one corner of his mouth and he did not seem to know to raise his arms to protect himself. She swung many more times, knocking his head back and forth until he fell straight back, falling flat on his back to the floor with a loud thud.

Golden Angel held her fists ready, breathing in hard, loud breaths as she watched him lie there, and finally she shouted, "Get up!"

"Don't think he's going to," a familiar woman's voice behind her guessed.

Swinging around, the wide eyed young heroine assumed her battle stance and was ready for another fight, but she relaxed and slowly lowered her arms as her eyes met her mother's

Wonder Woman was standing in the open doorway with her arms folded and raised her brow as she asked, "Do you feel better now?"

Elissa half turned and looked down at her battered and unconscious ex-boyfriend, and she nodded. "Actually, I do." She looked back to her mother and raised her head, close to catching her breath as she asked, "Do you think he knows it's over between us?"

"I'm sure he does," Wonder Woman assured. She approached the girl, her eyes also on the unconscious augment as she observed, "Looks like you had some rage in there to deal with."

Turning her eyes down, the young Amazon nodded and confessed, "Yeah. It was building up even before he... Mom, I don't know what my problem was. You didn't do anything but I was so angry and you didn't deserve what I said to you. You really didn't. Mom, I'm so sorry."

Diana reached to the girl and pulled her to her, wrapping her arms around her daughter as she soothed, "Shh. It's okay, Little One." She vented a breath through her nose and corrected, "Sorry. I suppose I shouldn't call you that anymore."

Elissa slipped her arms around her mother and assured, "It's okay, Mom. I want to be your Little One as long as I can. I really didn't mean any of that. You're a great mother and I didn't have the right to say any of that to you. I don't know what was wrong with me and I'm sorry!"

As her daughter hugged her tightly and nuzzled against her chest, Wonder Woman smiled and laid her cheek on top of the girl's head, closing her eyes as she just savored this one tender moment amidst all of this chaos.

The mechanical hiss of the door sliding shut drew their attention and Diana turned, her eyes widening as they filled with a burnt and battered Red Panzer.

Golden Angel clung to her mother as she mumbled, "Ah, crud."

"Very convenient to find you both here," the mechanical Nazi drawled as he slowly raised his arm—and the big machine gun mounted to it. "You have managed to disrupt my operation here, but I will surely feel compensated by killing you both right now."

"Hey!" Black Canary called, drawing everyone's attention. She had clearly only revived a moment ago and had struggled to sit up. With her hands still bound behind her back, she snarled as she informed, "You aren't killing anybody on my watch, buddy!"

Wonder Woman ordered, "Cover your ears," and she and Golden Angel both did.

Black Canary's mouth gaped open and she bared her teeth as a loud, high pitched shriek exploded from her.

The shockwave slammed into Red Panzer and drove him into the blast proof door behind him and much of the door buckled under the impact. He raised his hands to the sides of his head and shuddered under the sonic onslaught.

As soon as it ended, Wonder Woman pushed her daughter toward Black Canary and ordered, "Free her!" as she charged the stunned Nazi.

Before Red Panzer could get his bearings the Amazon Princess yelled a mighty battle cry and rammed her shoulder right into the middle of him, driving him back against the heavy door and almost through it. As he bounced back, she grabbed onto the gun mounted in his arm and spun around, wrenching the weapon from its place there as she hurled him toward the concrete wall behind her and almost through it. Even as he tried to raise his other arm and deploy his other weapon she was already upon him, knocking his gun aside and slammed her fist hard into his chin, snapping his head back.

As Wonder Woman battled her old nemesis, Golden Angel crouched down beside Black Canary and reached for her bound hands. They met each other's eyes and Golden Angel smiled, declaring, "Girl power! Totally!"

Black Canary looked to the other side of the room, then clumsily scrambled halfway to her feet and pushed Golden Angel aside, barely in time to avoid Wonder Woman who slammed into the wall back-first with a loud grunt. The two watched the Amazon Princess crumple to the floor and Canary shifted her narrow eyes to the advancing mechanical madman.

"You learn slowly, Fräulein Wonder Woman," he chided.

Black Canary stood and shot back, "So do you, Panzer!" Her mouth swung open and she sent a short but powerful burst at him.

The shrieking shockwave slammed into him as before and sent him backward into the concrete wall, and cracks in the pattern of a spider web reached out in all directions from behind him as he struck.

Golden Angel sprang into action quickly, charging him before he could get his bearings. Even as he pushed off of the damaged wall she leapt into the air and torpedoed into him feet first, slamming him back into the wall where he had hit seconds before and this time dust and small chunks of concrete fell from the wall. She hit the floor on her side and rolled quickly back to her feet as he pushed off of the wall again, her eyes widening as that blade slid from his right forearm again. As he advanced on her, he swung the blade at her and she deflected it on her gauntlet, then again, and again, backing away from him the whole time.

The far door opened and five more augments, four of them huge men, rushed into the room, angling toward Black Canary and Wonder Woman, who was struggling to recover her wits and stand. Canary knew she was outmatched but attacked them anyway, quickly finding herself surrounded and overwhelmed. The large woman and one man grabbed her arms and forced them behind her and the man clamped a hand around her throat.

As Wonder Woman stood, the other three attacked her, two of them taking her arms—and greatly underestimating her strength! As they tried to force her arms behind her, she took a step back to brace herself, then she leaned forward slightly and forced her arms forward and together, ramming the augments' heads together and knocking them out cold. She thrust her arms out and back, throwing them from her, then she turned on the two who held Black Canary, starting toward them only to stop as her eyes found her daughter backing away from the huge mechanical Nazi as he struck at her over and over.

"Go!" Black Canary shouted as best she could through the man's strangling grip. "I've got this!"

With a nod, Wonder Woman charged to assist her daughter, and when almost there Red Panzer wheeled around and struck with the blade, and she barely blocked it in time with her gauntlet. His other hand seized her arm and she screamed as he jolted her with a lethal electric shock.

Watching her mother convulse from the shock, Golden Angel attacked, and Red Panzer was ready for her, spinning back and slamming Wonder Woman into her. She fell to the floor with her barely conscious mother on top of her and was quick to push the Amazon Princess from her, rising up to her knees as she faced their enemy again. When she saw Panzer raise his arm and direct the huge maw of the grenade launcher at her, she held her arms ready and grumbled, "Ah, man!"

He fired and she crossed her arms in front of her and took the round on her gauntlets. It exploded and blew her across the room where she slammed back first into the wall next to the door. Her next realization was lying on her side on the cold floor with her back and shoulder leaning against the wall behind her. Her ears were ringing and she drew her legs to her, struggling to clear her mind as she knew that he would send another grenade at her at any second. Looking to Panzer through the clearing smoke, she slowly raised her head and pushed herself up as she saw him already taking aim at her.

"No," he said with an almost patronizing tone. Slowly lowering his arm, he took aim at Wonder Woman, who was fighting to reclaim full consciousness and was just pushing herself up on all fours. "You will watch your mother die first, then I will attend to you."

Sluggishly getting to her feet, Elissa fell backward and against the wall, yelling to her enemy, "This is between you and me, Fritz! Leave her out of this!"

He leaned his head as he took careful aim at Wonder Woman. "She was a part of this long before you were born, little girl, and now she will die for opposing me."

The trap door on the ceiling that Golden Angel had fallen through crashed inward and Superman hit the ground hard right behind Red Panzer, and when the mechanical Nazi turned, the Man of Steel punched him hard in the chest.

Golden Angel dropped to the floor, barely avoiding a collision as Red Panzer flew backward and this time through the wall behind her. She looked over her shoulder and into the hole created by her enemy, smiling as the dust began to settle and little bits of concrete still fell from the top of the hole he made going through the wall. Pushing herself up, she stood and looked to her mother as Superman helped her to her feet.

Wonder Woman raised a hand to her head and nodded, her eyes still closed as she assured, "I'm okay."

With a big smile, Elissa met Superman's gaze and said, "Glad you're feeling better, big guy."

Still steadying Wonder Woman, he smiled back and nodded to her. "Wanted to thank you in person." He looked to the augments who still held Black Canary and asked, "Are you guys going to let go of her or do I have to come over there?"

The augments released her and raised their hands before them as they backed away.

Superman nodded to them and complimented, "Good call."

Released by her adversaries, Black Canary hurried to the still unconscious Fire and knelt down beside her.

A metal hand wrapped around Golden Angel's throat and she shrieked as she was picked up and slammed into Red Panzer's battered chest. She grabbed onto his arm with both hands, her wide, fearful eyes locked on Superman.

He strode through the hole in the wall and pressed the tip of the blade from his right arm to the girl's side, and she shrank away from it as much as she could.

Superman set himself for battle again, glaring at the mechanical Nazi as he ordered, "Let her go, Panzer!"

"I have heard you use a power of protection on others," Red Panzer informed, "and now you will use it on me."

Looking up at him, Golden Angel's lips slid away from her teeth as she hissed, "I won't! You'll just kill me anyway."

"I will do no such thing," he assured. "Use your protection and make me invulnerable to Superman, and I will let you go."

Her eyes slid to the Man of Steel and her expression was one of terror and doubt.

His hands clenched into tight fists, he clenched his jaw and nodded to her, ordering, "Go ahead, Angel."

She hesitated, but finally closed her eyes, bowing her head as she softly said, "Red Panzer, until the sun rises anew, Superman can bring you no harm."

Still a little dazed but standing steadily on her own, Wonder Woman stared at her daughter with fear and disbelief in her eyes and slowly she shook her head.

Superman's brow lowered over his eyes and he harshly informed, "You got what you want, Panzer, now let her go."

Red Panzer's attention turned to the Man of Steel—and he laughed. "And what if I refuse, Superman? What do you intend to do about it?"

Looking back and up at him, Golden Angel barked, "If your word's no good then maybe you shouldn't lead the New Order. Maybe—"

"Quiet, child," Red Panzer ordered, his attention still on Superman. "Of course I'll release her." He brutally threw her across the room and she controlled her impact with the wall as best she could, still crumpling to the ground after.

Wonder Woman rushed to her as Superman and Red Panzer squared off.

Panzer turned his left hand and grenade launcher almost all the way over and a series of mechanical sounds came from his arm, then he trained the grenade launcher on Superman. "I still have one kryptonite round here for you, Superman, but perhaps I'll see just how much punishment you can withstand before I use it."

Diana pulled her stunned daughter to her feet, looking toward the Nazi and drawing a gasp as a damaged but battle ready Metallo strode through the door behind Panzer, his full attention on the Man of Steel.

Elissa looked toward them, her eyes narrowing as she mumbled, "Time to win that acting award." She tore away from her mother's grip and ran to Superman, wrapping her arms around him as she loudly begged, "No, please! Don't do this, Mister Panzer. Please don't!" She wept and buried her face in Superman's chest, shaking her head as she cried, "Please don't hurt Superman, please!"

Metallo and Red Panzer exchanged looks.

With tears streaming from her eyes, Elissa looked up to the Man of Steel and whispered, "The sun's up, isn't it?" When he nodded, she glanced around as her mind scrambled. Two enemies deadly to him and she could protect him only from one.

Metallo raised his weapon as well and asked, "Do we kill the girl, too?"

Red Panzer looked to Wonder Woman and demanded, "Surrender to me and she will be spared, otherwise our kryptonite rounds will fire right through her and kill them both."

Diana's attention turned to her daughter. She knew she dare not, but her love for her daughter would be her undoing. Closing her eyes, she bowed her head and slowly nodded.

Elissa looked over her shoulder to Panzer, to Metallo, and her eyes widened as inspiration struck her like lightning! Looking back up to Superman and meeting his eyes she whispered, "Superman, until the sun rises anew, kryptonite can bring you no harm." She was not sure it would even work until she saw his expression change, his lips part and his brow lift ever so slightly.

Motioning to Wonder Woman with his head, Superman ordered, "Go on over there with Wonder Woman, Angel. It'll be okay." His subtle wink confirmed what she needed to know.

Still, she clung to him and would not leave until her mother approached and took her by the arm.

Desperately, Elissa looked to Red Panzer and shook her head, pleading, "Mister Panzer, you can't! Please!"

Red Panzer and Metallo both raised their weapons and Panzer growled, "His fate is sealed, child."

Both fired.

The grenade exploded squarely on Superman's chest in a green cloud and the kryptonite tipped rounds also found their mark, striking him through the smoke from the exploding grenade.

A deathly silence followed.

As the smoke cleared, Metallo and Red Panzer slowly lowered their arms and weapons.

Superman folded his arms and stared back. There was a confident little smile on his mouth, almost cocky. With the kryptonite no longer a threat, the projectiles simply became weapons that were useless against him.

In a quick motion, Red Panzer looked to Golden Angel and loudly demanded, "What have you done?" He reloaded his grenade launcher, directed toward her, and fired.

In a blur, Superman was suddenly between the weapon and the Amazons and the grenade exploded on his chest.

"You still can bring me no harm!" the mechanical Nazi insisted, "and you still have us both to deal with."

War hammer in hand, Beowulf dropped through the trap door and slammed onto the floor, landing in a crouch and steadying himself on the fingertips of his free hand. Slowly, he stood, his eyes locked on Red Panzer and his brow low over them.

"He can bring you no harm," the big Norseman shouted, "but I surely can!"

Golden Angel took her mother's arm and half turned her, assuring, "They've got this, but I think Black Canary could use a hand."

Superman charged Metallo, Beowulf charged Red Panzer, and the two Amazons jumped into the middle of the augments. With kryptonite no longer a factor, Metallo found himself outmatched by Superman. Red Panzer found himself retreating from the onslaught of the Nordic Warrior and his enchanted war hammer, and the augments stood no chance against Wonder Woman, and they fared even worse with Golden Angel and Black Canary in the mix. With a loud yell, Beowulf slammed Mjölnir into Red Panzer's chest with all his strength and drove the mechanical Nazi hard through the concrete wall. Metallo swung and Superman caught his upper arm, lifted him from the ground and slammed his fist into the cyborg's chest and knocked him through the same wall, creating a huge hole beside the one Panzer had disappeared through.

Beowulf looked to Superman and nodded to him, commending, "Well done."

"Back at you," the Man of Steel countered.

They turned and looked to the battle that raged behind them, catching it as Wonder Woman bounced the largest of the augments off of the wall and then turned to the man her daughter fought. Black Canary was hopelessly outmatched but occupied one while Wonder Woman and Golden Angel dispatched the rest. Skill and speed were her allies and she backed away, dodged and parried as her opponent attacked relentlessly, and while his attention was focused on her, Superman took him from behind and hurled him across the room, slamming him into the far wall.

The fight was brutally short and when all of the bad guys seemed to be down, Superman looked to the holes created by Metallo and Panzer and advised, "We'd better see to those two."

Beowulf nodded to him again and they both went after Panzer first, only to emerge from the hole seconds later without him.

"Where did he go?" the Norseman asked, his perplexed eyes on Superman.

"What?" Elissa barked loudly. "He's gone again? Come on!"

Superman went after Metallo, shaking his head as he looked through the hole. "Metallo's gone, too. Looks like they've retreated."

Wonder Woman set her hands on her hips, her brow low over her eyes as she informed, "We go after them this time. This has to end and end today."

"Agreed," Superman said.

A thump in the distance sent tremors through the floor and dust and bits of debris fell from the ceiling.

Black Canary glanced about and nervously asked, "What was that?"

All of their communicators blared to life with Green Arrow's voice warning, "They've set the whole complex to self-destruct! Everybody out! Now!"

"We need to get everyone out of here!" Wonder Woman shouted as a nearby explosion rocked the room they were in.

Their escape was quickly made and friend and foe alike were evacuated from the warehouse. Superman emerged with the last of the unconscious augments seconds before the entire floor of the warehouse exploded and the building crumbled into the collapsing tunnels and rooms below. The ground shook as a huge shroud of dust rose over it, and in one last act of defiance a massive explosion tore through the rubble and sent concrete and metal debris everywhere. Green Lantern confined much of the explosion with a dome of light from his ring, minimizing the damage to surrounding structures and ensuring no one else would be injured.

In the early morning light, a crowd of Justice League, police and firefighters watched the dust settle.

Elissa stood between her parents and in front of the big Norseman as she stared into the debris with blank eyes.

"Well," Green Arrow observed as he slipped his arm around Black Canary. "We stopped them."

"But we didn't catch them," Golden Angel pointed out. "All of this and he still got away."

Batman added, "With Bane and Metallo. That's going to be a problem later, I think."

Lowering her eyes, Elissa meekly asked, "How many of our guys were hurt?"

"Nine," Green Arrow replied. "Atom and Flash took the worst of it."

Elissa closed her eyes.

"They're aboard the Watchtower already," Arrow went on. "J'onn had them transported directly to the infirmary."

Nodding, Golden Angel turned and looked up at the Nordic Warrior. "Thank you for coming to save me and thanks for helping us."

A smile curled his lips and he brushed her cheek with his fingers. "It was my honor, Schatzi. I will again, Odin willing."

"Will you stay for a while?" she pled.

Hesitantly, he shook his head. "I wish I could, Amazon Princess, but I have much to answer for and Odin will have many questions."

Elissa's mouth tightened and she replied with a reluctant nod.

"Perhaps I come back soon," he suggested, "assuming the Gods are not too angry with me."

"Yeah," she whispered to him with a strained smile.

Superman approached the Nordic Warrior and extended his hand. "Well thanks for your help, Beowulf. I'm pretty sure that if you want to do this full time you'll have a place waiting for you in the Justice League."

Shaking Superman's hand, Beowulf nodded to him and said, "It was truly an honor to fight among you. Odin willing, perhaps someday I join your Justice League." He glanced about, smiling as he informed, "For now, I have many quests awaiting me." He looked down to Golden Angel and took her hands. "Farewell, little Amazon Princess. I go with you in my heart."

She smiled. "I'll catch ya later, B-wulf. Don't be a stranger, kay?"

He bent to her and she rose up on her toes to share a kiss with him.

As he backed away from the little Amazon, Beowulf looked around to those who watched him, raising his hand as he bade, "Farewell to you all, and know it is an honor to fight with you." With that, he bowed to Wonder Woman, then turned and strode to the street as his ship settled down on a cushion of glowing blue mist.

They all watched as his ship lifted from the ground and streaked high over the city to disappear into the rising sun.

Black Canary playfully punched Golden Angel in the arm and observed, "You sure know how to pick'em, don't you?"

"Yeah," Elissa confirmed dreamily. She looked up at her mother and solemnly informed, "We need to get to the Watchtower. I seem to have some work to do."

"First things first," Batman informed, turning his attention to Wonder Woman. "We need to find who he sold those genetics test results on Golden Angel to."

She looked back at him and took the lasso from her belt. "I think before Red Panzer's people go off to jail it's time to ask a few questions."

CHAPTER 17

Penguin slowly closed the door to his lavishly decorated office at the rear of the Iceberg Lounge. The antique, hardwood desk was dark and huge and had a high backed leather chair behind it that was black with a white center on the back. A few trinkets were on the desk, all figurines of penguins and other birds, along with a few stacks of papers, an ornate antique lamp and a granite pen holder with two pens in it. Bookshelves were on the left and right walls, all burdened with different volumes of books. Behind the desk was a glass display case that was filled with expensive looking items, jewel adorned items. In front of the desk were two expensive leather chairs, angled to face the chair behind the desk.

Hobbling to the desk, Penguin grasped the edge of it with his free hand and leaned heavily on it, staring blankly down at the desk for long seconds before he set the large white envelope on it in front of him, and then that held his attention.

Something shuffled behind him in the corner of the room to one side of the door.

Penguin half turned his head, not really looking at who lurked in the corner of the room. He did not have to. "At some point," he finally said, "you'll learn that you can just come in the front door."

"I think we both prefer it this way," Batman countered as he advanced a few steps.

Nodding, Penguin looked back to the envelope on the desk and agreed, "I suppose so." He drew a breath deep into him before he spoke again. "Do you remember when I said she is a remarkable young woman?"

"I remember," Batman assured.

"Does she know who her father is?" Penguin asked.

"Yes," the Dark Knight replied.

Cobblepot took the envelope from his desk and turned, daring to walk right up to the dark form who loomed over him. As he offered Batman the envelope, he informed, "It is unopened and contains tempting possibilities for those of ill intent. It cost me a fortune, but I think it was money well invested."

Batman slowly took the envelope and his hand retreated with it behind his cape. "I'll see to it you're compensated."

"Don't bother," Penguin said as he turned toward his desk. "You told me once that she seeks the best in people, often to her detriment. That is a fine quality, one I hope she will never lose." He leaned on his desk again, staring down at it for a moment before he spoke again. "Perhaps the next time you see her you will tell her that my dance floor has been a lonely place since our evening of dancing and kippers. I wish for her to know that she will always be welcome here, and she will always find safety here." He half turned his head again. "And, of course, she is welcome to use the front door should she choose to visit again."

"I'll pass that on," Batman assured.

Penguin nodded and looked back to his desk. "I will charge you with guarding that secret as if it is your own. For all of her strength and fine qualities, she is a girl who still needs the protection of others."

"For once," the Dark Knight said, "we agree."

CHAPTER 18

A day passed. Injuries were attended to and life in the Justice League appeared to be returning to normal. The search for Red Panzer, Bane and Metallo turned out to be fruitless. They had all just disappeared, as had many of the captured augments who, for reasons unknown, were released from the specially designed cell block they were held in. Red Panzer's reach still got to places they all knew it should not have, but now the Justice League was watching for him and preparations were made for their next encounter with him. This had been a wake-up call. The League had nearly been sorely defeated, but for one hero who had come to the aid of a little Amazon girl.

Golden Angel herself had been very quiet since the battle. She had been instrumental in healing injuries and stayed aboard the watchtower to help attend to things, but the bubbly girl everyone had become accustomed to was not to be found.

A meeting was called and the senior members of the Justice League assembled in the conference room. Why the meeting was called was a mystery, but the feel was not good.

All eyes went to the door as it slid open and everyone fell quiet as Golden Angel hesitantly entered the conference room.

She would not look at any of them and her eyes were on the Justice League communicator that she held tenderly in her hands. Her expression was blank and her steps small, slow and apprehensive.

The senior Justice League members quietly watched her approach the table, and watched a moment more as she stopped at the table beside Superman, her eyes on the communicator still.

Elissa drew a breath, then gingerly laid the communicator on the table, staring at it in silence for a moment before she finally raised her eyes, finding first her mother, then her father. In a meek voice, she finally said, "You were right." She turned her eyes down again.

"I'm not ready for this. I thought I was and I thought I was doing okay, but..." She loosed a hard breath. "I almost got people killed. I didn't listen when I should have, when everyone tried to warn me about... about Zack. I didn't want to believe you."

"But you had to know," Batman pointed out.

She nodded in slight motions, confirming, "I had to know, and I got in way over my head again."

Black Canary folded her hands on the table and leaned forward. "Angel, you also really compromised Panzer's plans and his installation in Gotham is destroyed."

"We weren't ready to take him on," Elissa pointed out.

"But now we know his strengths," Wonder Woman informed. "The next time we meet we'll know what to expect."

"What I did was still really irresponsible," Angel said softly. "I should have involved the team, but I wanted to do it myself, find out for myself. I guess I'm just not mature enough to do this yet. I thought I was, but this kind of proves that I'm still just a kid. I don't belong here"

"I don't agree," Superman countered. "I'd say just that realization and the fact you came to all of us with this shows how mature you are."

She looked down at the communicator again and nodded, softly offering, "Thanks." Her eyes glossed and she turned away, striding with quick steps toward the door, and she paused to say, "Thank you for giving me a chance," before she left the room.

WW

An hour later found Elissa in her mother's quarters, stuffing the clothing she had brought into her duffel bag and trying to straighten up before her mother arrived.

It was not to be.

She heard the door slide open and shut and she hesitated, then resumed her labors and stuffed in the last shirt she had to pack.

"Where are you off to?" Diana asked.

"Home," the girl answered as she closed the bag. "This was all a huge mistake. I should never have left home to begin with. You were right. You were always right." She turned and sat down on the bed, but would not look at her mother. "I need to learn patience and train as hard as I can." She shrugged. "Who knows? Maybe I'll mature up and even grow an inch or two in the next few years."

Diana folded her arms and looked to the floor.

"I don't want you to worry about me anymore," Elissa said softly, looking down to her hands, clasped in her lap. "At least if I'm safe on Themyscira you won't have to worry, and we can see each other whenever you have time, just like before."

Slowly, the Amazon Princess shook her head, and she could only say, "No."

Elissa looked to her mother, and Diana looked back at her.

"You aren't going back to Themyscira," Diana informed. "You aren't going to just run and hide."

Tears filled the little Amazon's eyes and she cried, "I failed, Mom! I failed!"

That authoritative look returned to Diana and she nodded, confirming, "Yes, Little One, you failed. You don't listen, you can't seem to work with a team and you still bite off more than you can chew." She set her hands on her hips. "You came here to be a hero, to find the hero inside of yourself and by Zeus that is what you are going to do! You will *not* go running home to hide in disgrace and failure!"

"He's going to find me!" Elissa cried. "Mom, he's going to come back stronger than ever and he's going to find me and he's going to kill me next time!"

Diana raised her chin, her eyes narrowing slightly as she asked, "Panzer?"

The girl shamefully turned her eyes down and bowed her head, and she nodded and admitted in a tiny voice, "Mom, I'm so scared."

Diana felt for her, but still she pushed pity aside. Lowering her hands to her sides she shouted, "So that's why you want to run and hide! *That's* why!" She strode to the girl and grabbed her arms, jerking her up from the bed and holding her firmly before her. "I did not raise a coward and you will not hide from him! By Hera, don't you think everyone here has enemies?"

"They aren't like Panzer," Elissa whimpered.

Framing her daughter's face with her hands, the Amazon Princess turned the girl's attention to her and agreed, "No, Little One, they aren't like Panzer. Many of them are much, much worse. But you don't see anyone out there hiding from them, do you? Your father does not run and hide from Bane, Superman does not hide from Metallo, Green Lantern doesn't—"

"But mom!" Elissa cried, "look how strong they all are!"

Diana grasped the girl's hair and countered, "Look how strong you are. You are so close, Elissa, so close."

"To what?"

A little smile finally touched Wonder Woman's lips. "To finally being one with Golden Angel."

Elissa slowly shook her head. "Golden Angel isn't strong enough, Mom."

"She is as strong as she needs to be," the Amazon Princess pointed out, "and more than cunning enough to outwit any foe. She has proven that many times."

"I still have nightmares," the girl admitted in a whisper.

Diana combed her fingers through her daughter's hair. "And those nightmares will follow you if you run from them. Face them, Little One. That is the only way you can ever make them go away."

Elissa turned her eyes down and nodded. Drawing a breath, she shook her head and confessed, "This is turning out to be a whole lot harder than I thought it would be."

"All the more reason for you to stick it out," Diana said as she turned toward the door. "You aren't running home, Junior, and you aren't going to hide from Panzer or those you've promised to protect here."

"But I can't do this anymore," the girl whined.

Diana paused at the door and half turned to look back at her daughter. "I raised a daughter who knows never to give up, especially when she is battling for justice. You made a lot of promises here, Elissa, and it's time you learned to take responsibility for those promises and those you made them to, and you'll learn nothing hiding under your bed back home. No, you aren't ready for the Justice League and you aren't ready for the Titans, but Patriarch's World is not yet ready to give you up." She turned and opened the door, ordering, "Follow me."

They returned to the conference room where the senior members awaited them, and she got hard, authoritative looks from all of them. Drawing her shoulders up as she approached the table, Elissa folded her arms over her belly and could not seem to look at anyone for long, and as her mother strode around to her waiting chair, Golden Angel stopped well short of the table and turned her eyes down.

"We had a long talk," Superman started, "and we've come to a decision. I'm afraid you can't just quit." A little smile curled his mouth and he finished, "You know too much."

She glanced at him and assured in a mumble, "I won't tell anybody."

"You aren't getting the point," Batman informed.

Elissa looked across the room and said as bravely as she could, "I just can't do this anymore."

"Angel," Wonder Woman said gently, "we've all talked it over and we've all realized that it was not fair of us to ask you to do this full time. You put in more hours than a lot of seasoned people here and I think that is the part you just weren't ready for." When her daughter finally looked to her, she raised a brow and pointed out, "I think what you really want is a life of your own, not as Golden Angel but as a teenage girl. Am I right?"

Elissa looked away from her and considered, then she shrugged and admitted, "I guess so."

"We're ready to facilitate that, kiddo," Green Lantern informed. "We want you to have that life but we also want you to stay on with the League."

Black Canary smiled. "We've grown kind of fond of you and we all agree we'd like to keep you around. You bring things to the team that only you can and I can't imagine this place with you gone permanently."

"What about the Titans?" Golden Angel asked.

Batman replied, "We're certain that you still can't take orders from your peers, so that's on hold until you learn to. I've spoken to Red Robin already and he wants you to know there is a place on his team for you whenever you feel ready."

Raising her brow, Elissa looked to him and mumbled, "He said that?"

"Further," Batman went on, "I believe you have a city you vowed to protect, and you've been gone for some time."

She looked down again. "They'd rather have Wonder Woman."

"No," Diana laughed, "they wouldn't. I've already spoken to the mayor and police chief and they were both ecstatic about the prospect of you returning. You're still a sworn in police deputy in that city and they've been hoping you would remain so."

The little Amazon turned her eyes to her mother, and a little more confidence was there.

"And we want you to stay in the Justice League, Junior," the Amazon Princess said straightly, "and we're not willing to take no for an answer. You won't have to be on watch as long or as often as you have been and we talked about calling you in when we most need you, that way you'll have the life you deserve."

"And a new identity," Batman added. When his daughter's attention snapped to him, he raised his chin and asked, "Are you up to a new challenge?"

Depression was yielding quickly to elation and Elissa's face lit up with anticipation as she replied, "The daughter of Batman is always ready for a challenge."

"Good," he commended. "We're going to go over your new life later, but I'll give you the highlights now. You are not Elissa Prince anymore. Your name is Elissa Madding."

Golden Angel raised her brow and breathed, "Madding?"

"You live with your older sister, Stacy," the Dark Knight continued, "and you have since your mother passed away and your father disappeared."

Elissa smiled. "Stacy's my big sister now?"

Diana replied, "Yes she is, and she is in charge when you are not Golden Angel." Her eyes narrowed and she snarled, "Understand?"

Quickly nodding, the girl complied, "Yes ma'am. Stacy's in charge."

"Remember that," Wonder Woman warned. "She has your father and I on speed dial and if you get out of line—"

"I won't!" Elissa assured as she raised her hands before her. "This is so cool! Stacy's going to be my big sister and I have a secret identity!"

"That you will protect at all times," Superman ordered.

Batman added, "We don't want to have to do this more than once, so get it right the first time. You are a fourteen year old high school freshman transferring from Central Gotham High School and you'll start attending classes next semester."

"Aw, come on!" she cried, setting her hands on her hips. "I have

to go back to school? That's totally..." She trailed off when
Superman loudly cleared his throat and gave her a very disapproving
look. Turning her eyes down, she folded her arms and mumbled,
"Fine."

J'onn folded his hands on the table and gave her a hard stare,
saying with an almost humor laced tone, "That seems like it will be
your biggest challenge."

Black Canary stood and walked around the table, taking the
communicator from the table near Superman. As she strode by, she
tossed the communicator to Golden Angel and informed, "Welcome
back. You have the watch tonight. I'm going home." She took her
own communicator from her belt and called as she left, "Black
Canary to Green Arrow..."

All of the Justice League stood and made their way to the door.

When Superman patted her shoulder as he walked by, she threw
her arms around his waist and stopped him, hugging him tightly.
With a little smile, he slipped an arm around her and hugged her
back.

Everyone patted her back or shoulder and or hugged her as they
walked past. Even the seemingly emotionless Martian Manhunter
paused and looked down at her, roughing her hair before continuing
on his way.

The last two to leave were Wonder Woman and Batman, who
stopped and stared down at her, Wonder Woman with her hands on
her hips and Batman with his arms folded.

Elissa looked to them in turn, folding her hands behind her as she
offered, "Thanks, guys. You're the best."

Wonder Woman sighed, "We know, Junior, we know. By the
way, we're both leaving, too." She patted the girl's head as she
walked by. "Have fun tonight and don't take any unnecessary risks."

Watching as the two strode for the door, she asked, "So where are
you going?"

"Your dad's private island in the Bahamas," Diana replied. "We
decided we deserve some time off."

Throwing her hands out, the little Amazon cried, "And you can't
wait until your kid can come?"

"No," they answered together as the door slid shut behind them.

"That's totally bogus!" she shouted, setting her hands on her hips.

The door opened again and Batman stepped back in. "Once you and Stacy get settled into your new apartment I'll need you back at the mansion, first thing next week."

She raised her brow and asked, "A little father daughter time?"

"No," he replied as he turned to leave. "I think it's time you met your brother."

"Yes sir," Elissa complied, and as the door slid shut behind Batman her eyes widened, her mouth dropped open and she barked, "Wait! What? I have a brother?"

Made in the USA
Middletown, DE
15 August 2020

15525701R00225